The Friendly World Virus

Frank N. Anderson

Published by Frank N. Anderson, 2024.

This is a work of fiction. Similarities to real people, places, or events are entirely coincidental.

THE FRIENDLY WORLD VIRUS

First edition. July 12, 2024.

ISBN: 978-1777031640

Written by Frank N. Anderson.

July 2024

Cindy,

Enjoy the journey
with Livie + friends
as they seek out
a better world.

Frank

THE FRIENDLY WORLD VIRUS

CHARACTERS IN THE BOOK:

- The initial "tribe": Livie, Hannah, Finn, Preet, Bo, and Saba.
- Livie Romée-Padalino. Twenty-eight years old and works as a private investigator. Lives in a condo in Washington, DC, not far from the Washington Monument.
- Hannah. Livie's best friend. Twenty-eight years old and works as a social worker.
- Finn. Longtime friend of Livie and Hannah's. Works at Georgetown University as their main computer tech.
- Preet. Friend of Livie and Hannah's. Owns a yoga studio.
- Bo. Preet's boyfriend.
- Saba. A friend of Preet's. Works as a lobbyist for alternative energy companies.
- Milhous Aldrich Brant. Presidential candidate in the 2032 USA election.
- Abby Finkler. Presidential candidate in the 2032 USA election.

- Fairleigh. A computer tech who is part of the Friendly World Network. Becomes a friend to Livie and Hannah.
- Rafael (Raf). Twenty-six years old. Neighbor of Livie's from Israel.
- Draw Nedwons. A tech nerd with extremely high intelligence. Livie's former client.
- Annie. Client of Hannah's and mother of three kids.
- Hugo Wainwright. Friend of Livie's who takes Annie in.
- Thomas Brackett. *Washington Post* columnist.
- Abelina Balogun. *Washington Post* columnist.
- Twiggy. Livie's childhood friend who died when she was young.
- Larry Dubash. Owner of the private investigative firm Livie works for.
- Maggie Romée. Livie's mom.
- Theo. Friend of Livie's mom.
- Dr. Grant Solbey. A musician and professor who is part of the Friendly World Network.
- Ervin Anvari. An Iranian who is part of group who hires Livie as an investigator.
- Jing. Part of the group that hires Livie as an investigator.

Chapter 1

The Virus Strikes

The ghost of the internet would loom over her life and determine if she was to be a villain or a hero.

November 4, 2032

Having put out the last of the snacks, Livie looks out the window of her thirteenth- floor Belmont Street condo. Her eyes roam across the view—which her realtor described as "stunning"—promising that in daylight, she would be able to see the White House and the Washington Monument. The thought draws Livie's eyes up to the realtor's gift—a sheer, magnifying blind that, when pulled down, enlarges the view from the window. She pushes her slight, five-foot-one frame up to grab the blind but then let's go of it, as if it would be too much bother to pull it down.

Livie tucks a few loose stands of her blond hair behind her ear. She diverts her gaze from the rolled-up blind and squints in the direction of the White House. She wonders who might occupy that bastion of power when *this night* was over—as if a revelation of the evening's outcome would suddenly appear.

Her gaze drops to the vehicles below. The driverless vehicle lane moves smoothly as vehicles—with solar-panel roofs—travel at the same speed, like a line of wagons on a train track.

Livie can't see the faces of those who remain unmoving in the parking lot of the other lanes, but she can feel their sad, tired expressions. The sound of their windshield wipers plays in her head, swiping from side to side like a metronome racing time. Would the gloom brought by the rain and wind prove to be a harbinger of the night's conclusion? The cold drizzle outside seems to fall in defense of her mood.

She inhales deeply and pushes the air out of her lungs, hoping that the restlessness she feels will exit with it. Is anxiety about the future her natural state?

The sound of the doorbell abruptly plugs the spiral of her negative thoughts.

"Hannah has arrived," drones the doorbell's facial recognition device, announcing the first of Livie's friends.

Relief floods her emotions upon hearing Hannah's name. If she could pick who would arrive first, Hannah would be her first choice. Every time.

Livie makes her way to the door as she calls out the unique word to unlock it for her friend. “Unzip!”

She thinks back to the time Hannah lifted her spirits as Livie was leaving law school behind. Hannah's words replay in her head, an infusion of oxygen for her soul.

"Livie, you are holding things down too tight. It's as if you have taken your emotions, your determination, your tenacity, your skills, your wit and sharp analytical abilities and pressed them all down. You zip it up tight. Unzip it, Livie. Let them out. You're an amazing person, and you are keeping it all zipped down. Unzip it, Livie!"

Livie smiles at her friend as the door swings open.

Hannah is carrying a pair of shoes and a brown bag. She reaches out with her free arm to hug Livie, pulling her close against her taller and larger frame.

"So, looks like I'm first to arrive. Can I help with anything? I brought vodka and juice."

Livie takes the drinks Hannah holds out for her, and they make their way to the kitchen.

"So, what's with the shoes?" Livie asks as they start putting out plates and glasses.

"Those, my dearest friend, are for you. I saw them on sale, and they have these cute little zippers on the back."

Hannah holds up the baby-blue heels, rotating them to show Livie the zippers at the back.

"Aren't they just perfect for you?"

Their friendship has always included a little gift-giving here and there. Livie imagines Hannah in a store seeing the shoes and thinking of her, as she has often felt the same pleasure wash over her at seeing something she'd buy for her friend. She walks over to look more closely at the shoes.

"Hannah, you know me better than anyone. These *are* perfect for me."

Their hug lingers as Livie whispers a thank you in Hannah's ear before heading back to the kitchen.

"You get your hair done? I love the shades of blond in the brown."

Hannah sways her head from side to side, showing off the highlights in her long, rich-brown hair.

"You look beautiful my friend, and I'm so glad you arrived first! Gives us some time—just the two of us."

"Me too Liv. You seem a bit tense and tired though. Did you not sleep well?"

Livie shrugs. "I don't know why, but I'm a bit wound up about what might happen tonight. Do you really think Brant could become president?"

"Of course, Brant could win. We had Trump, after all. Brant has already told everyone he has won, see?"

Hannah holds up her phone, directing Livie's eyes to the screen. Brant created a program that allows him to broadcast messages to all cell phones in the country. Such a message would interrupt whatever else the person was doing on their phone. To everyone. Simultaneously.

After threats of lawsuits, Brant created an application form that allowed people to opt out of receiving the messages. He brags that only fifteen percent have opted out.

Livie looks at Hannah's phone and rolls her eyes as she reads the message. She wishes her friend would join her in opting out.

Brant's message is in a handwritten font. The black script pops out on the bright turquoise background.

Vote and we win. It's that simple. You vote. We win. Make America Dominate Again.

Milhous Aldrich Brant

"Why are you still getting those?" Livie's voice has a sharp edge to it that she can't keep under wraps. "You know it just encourages him and his brand of politics. You have essentially signed up to be part of his campaign team. He crows about *all* these supporters he has that get his messages...and. that. includes. you...Hannah."

Hannah touches her friend's shoulder to soften the mood that has creeped into the room.

"I always admire your passion, Livie. But...I think you're making a bigger deal about this than it is. I just like to be kept informed of what he is up to, that's all."

Livie moves a couple of steps away, as her fury over the message has yet to run its course.

"There are many other ways to stay informed. What a great message it would be to Brant if a large number of people—on. this. day.—were to opt out of his messages."

"Liv, we've talked about this many times. Can we just move on and talk about something else?"

"He thrives on making his messages controversial with a hint of excitement. He makes them just alluring enough to keep people on the hook, not wanting to risk missing out on something by opting out. But you won't miss anything. His messages lack any real substance!"

"Okay, you got the last word," Hannah said with a sigh. "Can you fold up that soapbox now? What about the rest of the night? Is Preet bringing her hot boyfriend Bo?"

Livie catches Hannah's eye in her peripheral vision as she breathes out of her nose.

"Oh come on! You have to admit, he *is* pretty hot."

Livie looks at Hannah, mustering a stern expression as she admires her friend's ability to drag Livie's thoughts to another subject. In an instant, the conviction in her voice is replaced by a playful tone.

"Does Preet know you have the hots for her boyfriend?"

"Livie, you have to admit, he is some serious eye candy."

"Sure, but he has quite the find in Preet. She's intelligent, classy, athletic—and a smart businessperson."

"Smart businessperson? She works as a yoga instructor, doesn't she?"

"That's right, but she pretty much runs that studio. I've told her she should open her own."

"Finn has arrived," intoned the doorbell.

Livie wishes she was quicker to wipe the frown from her face at the mention of Finn's name.

"Oh, don't be too enthusiastic, Liv. You had to know that I was going to invite him. Besides, he will bring some good debate to the conversation tonight."

They met Finn at university. Initially Livie found him to be friendly and always helpful with his skills in fixing her computer or phone. His tall, slender, six-foot-three frame and unusually long eyelashes for a guy made him naturally attractive, and it was easy to see what Hannah saw in him. Later though, his overuse of polysyllabic words and hard-bitten opinions made him seem arrogant and insecure to Livie. He always needed to let others know he was the smartest one in the room. Hannah saw him through an entirely different lens. She would insist he join them at gatherings, emphasizing his clever intellect, studious look, and deep, sexy voice. Livie knew the two of them would eventually date, just like she knew they would break up. After their breakup, Livie thought Finn would just be a footnote in their friendship, but Hannah continued to invite him to parties or gatherings with other friends. Hannah seemed to go through periods where she'd get sucked into Finn's orbit, like some planet.

Livie is thinking back to the time when she begrudged the space Finn took in Hannah's life, when Hannah's voice breaks through her fog of memories.

"Well, if you're just going to stand there, I'll let him in. Unzip!"

Hannah gets up and moves to the door to greet Finn with a hug as he enters.

"Greetings, fellow humanoids, beings of superior intelligence and friends of mine."

As if to break up their lingering hug at the door, Livie jumps in with her own greeting.

"Hey Finn. Is that how you greet people at work in the morning?"

Hannah gives Livie a "really?" look from behind Finn's slender frame—beseeching Livie to be nice.

"At my work? I don't think so. Too many people who skipped the line when they were handing out intelligence."

"But you work at Georgetown. Isn't it a bastion for intelligent humanoids?"

Livie can see Hannah's lips mouth "pleeeeze", and before Finn can respond, she reaches out and touches his forearm as a signal to her friend.

"I'm just giving you a hard time Finn. I'm glad you could make it tonight."

"Thanks Livie. It's okay, really. Actually, my new position at the uni only reinforces that intelligence doesn't always flow out of that place. I've warned them for the last couple of years that their system was vulnerable to an attack, and that's exactly what happened, just as I predicted. Now I've been asked to lead a team to clean it up and fix it for them."

"You have a new job? When did that happen?" Hannah asks, leaning closer to Finn.

Livie closes her eyes to prevent the eyeroll she feels coming on.

"It's more of a two-year project. Their system was hacked—by some Russians, I believe. They lost access to most of it. I saved them from having to pay Bitcoin to the terroristic hacker and regained access. Now I'm leading a team to rebuild the system and improve the uni's online presence—which was rather primitive until they gave me authority to overhaul it. The parsimonious university has discovered it will cost them more if they don't invest in this."

"I thought you were considering leaving the university, Finn?"

Livie's voice spikes at the word "thought", giving her question a heckling tone.

"The uni's not my long-term plan, but I can really put my signature on their electronic database, so it's good for now. Maybe tonight's outcome will bring opportunities."

"Really? How so?"

"Well, I'm not a Brant fan, but he does accentuate the use of technology, unlike what we've seen with the present administration."

"So...you want to see Brant win tonight?"

"No, don't read me wrong on that. I think much of what he plans will be rather pernicious. Most of what he says includes a penumbra of vagueness and error. But, I do think he will win. His message today, like it or not, will inspire a lot of people, and his sycophants will be..."

Livie locks eyes with Hannah as she pleads with her friend to change the subject. Hannah gets the message and interrupts Finn mid-sentence.

"Livie, it's almost seven. Perhaps we should get the TV ready? You think Preet and Bo will be here soon?"

Livie moves towards the kitchen—her exit from the living room mirroring her exit from the conversation with Finn.

"We can watch from the kitchen, as we have the food out here. I thought the others would be here by now. I forgot to mention, Preet said she was also bringing a friend who she met at yoga."

Livie moves the lightweight forty-six-inch TV, which is on a telescoping shelf, out from the kitchen counter. She adjusts the TV to just the right angle, turns it on, and puts the sound on mute. Finn's baritone voice fills the space again.

"You know Livie, I could easily set up small projectors in this place. Then you could cast the display onto any wall, blind or...any surface, really. You would be able to adjust the size of the picture if you like and could show it on something like that smart cappuccino machine you have. You could tell it to make you a drink while watching the screen on its surface! I could even have it create a white background to project on, so the display won't be distorted by the sheen of the stainless steel."

"Thanks Finn. That sounds fascinating but unnecessary to me. I think using technology to that extent is keeping too many people on the couch, living numbing, sedentary lifestyles."

Hannah moves forward, putting herself between her two friends to free them from an escalating discourse.

"So, you said Preet is bringing a friend tonight. Do we know who she is?"

"I don't. I think she said her name is Saba. Preet says she's friendly and will fit in well with our group. I don't know anything else about her."

Finn nods towards the TV.

"Looks like some early results are in that have Brant in the lead."

Finn's words draw their attention to the bright light of the TV and a graphic that shows Brant with early leads in Vermont and Kentucky.

"Well, I think we can all exhale now; nothing too surprising there. It could be the states out west that determine who wins tonight, and those results are still hours away."

"I wouldn't be too sanguine about that, Livie. Brant could win enough votes in the eastern states to be declared the winner long before that. Vermont should go Democrat, and he's leading there."

Livie's thoughts are boiling like a pot of water on a stove as Finn speaks, but before the words can make their way out of her open mouth, the voice from her doorbell interjects.

"Unknown has arrived."

"Who could be that be?"

"I could fix that for you so that your software can recognize anyone, even strangers, unless they were truly off the grid."

Livie simply ignores Finn's suggestion as she picks up her phone and clicks on the app to check who is at the door. The app shows a captivating, dark-skinned woman with a wide, inviting smile. She has near perfect white teeth, framed by full brown lips that rest below well-defined cheekbones. Her black hair is done up in a casual bun, and her thin, arched eyebrows give way to deep-brown eyes that sparkle with confidence.

"Oh, that must be Preet's friend. Unzip."

Saba enters the room with the confidence of someone who is accustomed to a warm reception from a crowd of people.

"Hi everyone! One of you must be Livie?"

Livie is already moving towards the door and reaching out her hand to welcome the stranger, but Saba responds by opening her arms for a hug as if they are old friends.

"We don't need to be so formal. I'm Preet's friend, and she told me this would be a friendly crowd to spend the evening with?"

Livie accepts her hug, noting that Saba's heels masks that they are close to the same height.

Hannah introduces herself and Finn at the same time, annoying Livie by creating the perception that they may be a couple. Finn tells Saba how he met Hannah and Livie when they were at university together. He uses this to springboard the conversation to his work and his expertise in technology. Saba only acknowledges Finn by stating that the world seems to be getting lost in technology before she quizzes Hannah and Livie about their occupations and lives. As Saba seems to choreograph the conversation, Livie watches Finn—he seems lost, like a cork floating at sea.

Finally, Finn finds his voice and squeezes it into the banter.

"So, what about you Saba? What do you do for a living?"

The light from the TV pours into the room, and Saba's next words serve up another discussion about the election.

"I work for a consortium of alternative energy companies."

A long pause hangs in the air as the three of them provide a symphony of silence, waiting for Saba to elaborate.

"I can see you are all curious as to what exactly I do for those companies, and let me say, it's not nearly as exciting as it may sound. I work for them as a government lobbyist."

The silence following Saba's response crashes loudly into the room, until Hannah slices through it.

"Sooo, Saba...um, you know we are a fairly opinionated bunch, and a lot might be voiced tonight about various politicians."

"Oh, of course, and I hope to join in on that for sure."

"Sooo...if a name or two of people you know were to come up, it wouldn't be awkward?"

"Oh, now I see what has taken all the air out of this room. You don't need to worry about me. Sure, I have connections in the White House, and I certainly could tell some stories. Shrewd but heartless men and women of various sins populate that place. They are not generally friends of mine. It's my job to get to know them and understand what makes them tick, but I keep that separate from my personal life."

Finn, seeing his opportunity to latch onto the conversation, jumps in before Saba's pause can become another sentence.

"So, what do you think of Brant's message today then?"

"I don't know, what was M.A. Brant's message?"

Finn either doesn't pick up on the sarcasm in her voice or chooses to ignore it as he pulls out his phone to show her the message.

"I don't need to see it, Finn. I don't get his messages. If he has something of value to say, I have friends on the hill who will tell me about it. You're the first to mention it to me."

Finn takes that as an invitation to share Brant's message, his voice exuding the giddiness of someone sharing a surprise.

Vote and we win. It's that simple. You vote. We win Make America Dominate Again.

"Well, I can see why none of my contacts bothered to share that with me," Saba responds acerbically. "Just more bravado from an old white guy who wants to take us back in time. Make America dominate again. What does that mean, exactly? I can tell you that for Brant, it includes revitalizing the fossil fuel industry and building more war machines while taking taxes from the working class and handing it to corporations."

Saba suddenly stops herself, realizing that the passion in her voice may have startled the people she has just met.

"Oh, sorry if I got carried away there, Finn. Are you a Brant supporter?"

"Huh? Oh no, no...certainly not. His support of the big corporations alone..."

Hannah reaches out and puts her hand on Finn's shoulder as a sign of support and rescue.

"Finn is like us Saba. We're all anti-Brant tonight."

Livie has been watching the interaction unfold like an enjoyable play. She is about to insert her part when the doorbell chimes.

"Preet has arrived."

Hannah quickly moves to the door as Livie shouts "unzip". Preet walks in with open arms and embraces Hannah. Bo is behind her carrying a tray of food that Livie moves to take from his hands.

"Here, I'll take that Bo. I'll add it to our other options for tonight."

Preet catches Livie's eye and launches one arm out for a hug, which Livie returns before walking back to the kitchen with the plate of food.

"I see you've met my friend Saba. Sorry we're late."

"Yes Preet, we've all met. They've already grilled me about my politics."

Saba's laugh that follows appears forced, but her wide, open-mouthed smile projects the intended lightheartedness of her response. The earlier tension and hushed tones soon disappear, and the room fills with voices as the friends mingle and catch up on their lives. Preet is taking in the chatter as she holds back her news, waiting to be asked. Livie picks up on the anticipation in her friend's posture.

"So Preet, what about you? Anything new in your life?"

"Yeah, actually. A big change is coming to our lives."

The voices in the room instantly fall silent. It's like a spotlight has fallen on Preet as all eyes are drawn to her and she puts a hand on her stomach.

"Are you preg...?"

"Hannah! No!" Preet reaches for Bo's hand. "Not that it would be a bad thing, though. I'm...well..." Her voice starts to crescendo with excitement. "I'm opening my own yoga studio!"

Preet's news brings smiles, laughter, and pleasure to the faces of the others as the atmosphere turns festive.

"Where and when?" Hannah squeals, matching the excitement of Preet's announcement.

"Well, right now the space is a campaign office for the election."

"For a Republican or Democrat?"

"Saba, I'm pretty sure Preet is joking with that one, right Preet?"

Preet looks to Bo, who steps in to answer Livie.

"Actually, there is a campaign office next door to where Preet's studio will be. The place used to be a sewing machine supply store, and I'm going to be working on the renovations for the next month to turn it into a yoga studio, including venting that will allow for hot yoga."

Livie is captivated as Bo describes the renovations he will be doing to the studio, and she hears Hannah's voice in her head saying how hot he is. His wavy, strawberry-blond hair hangs low on his forehead, occasionally drooping over his eyes enticingly. While his physique is kept under wraps in a winter sweater, Livie can visualize his flat abs that explode into a chiseled chest, seemingly held up by the bulge of his biceps stretching the fibers of his sweater. Saba's voice breaks through her trance.

"Where's this studio located?"

"Well, it's actually just on the edge of Foggy Bottom."

"Nice and trendy. I know a lot of politicians who hang out there."

"And it's close to GW," Finn adds.

"That's right Finn. You work at George Washington?" Preet asks.

"No, wrong uni. I'm at Georgetown, which is more like a city in itself. But George Washington is centrally located in the city. So, it's a great spot for your new studio."

"Thanks. I'm excited about the location. So, even though it's not close to your university, do you think you could give me some advice on setting up an online presence?"

Finn takes the question as an invitation to sit on the throne of his intellect as his baritone voice once again fills the room. In an ostentatious display of his knowledge of the subject, Finn expands in detail on various social media options and how to target specific audiences. After he uses several acronyms that only those in the marketing industry would know the meaning of, Saba interjects.

"So Finn, I'm sure Preet is glad she will have your expertise to help with the promotion of her business, but your passion for this use of technology seems kind of...Brant-like?"

Livie's eyes scan the faces of her friends in the hope that Saba's question hasn't intensified the tension in the room. Hannah picks up on her concern and loops her arm through Finn's as she jumps in to answer Saba's teasing accusation.

"Now Saba, you're not trying to cause some conflict, are you? We all know Finn can't stand Brant. He may share his passion for utilizing technology to build our communities, but like the rest of us, he hopes tonight will bring an end to Brant's political career."

Preet looks at Hannah with grateful eyes as she lets out the remaining air from the tension balloon in the room.

"And...with that, it's after seven now, so how about we see how this election night is unfolding?"

They all collectively turn towards the TV as Livie turns on the volume to the news that Brant's opponent for president, Abby Finkler, has captured Vermont and is leading in Kentucky.

Finn's voice takes on a sudden falsetto pitch.

"Wow, if she takes Kentucky, Brant's demise could actually come tonight from this *election*."

The spike in Finn's tone at the word *election* almost goes unnoticed, except for Preet's question.

"Finn, you said *election* like you expect his demise, even if he *is* elected?"

Finn averts his eyes from Preet and stares at the light coming from the TV, which provides the room with an immediate distraction.

"Didn't mean that, really..."

Finn clears his throat as the others wait for him to continue.

"Some of his ideas are bound to create a lot of strife. He could be in for a rocky road if he wins, don't you all think?"

"His security will be intense, if that's what you mean?"

"You'd know better than I would, Saba, but I'm not saying someone might take him out, just that someone may try to sabotage some of his plans; slow him down maybe."

"Oh, I don't know about that. He's not trying to build a wall across the country that he needs billions for. Most of his changes will be technological and social. They'll infringe on rights that I think will make us all feel less secure, while he surrounds himself with security night and day."

"I could not agree more Saba. I like some of the technological advances, but instead of using them for the betterment of mankind, I'm afraid Brant will use them to coil the tentacles of big business' infringement on our lives."

Saba turns her head and looks at Finn with admiration. Finn continues to fulminate against government infringing on their freedoms, and Saba stares at him like he is some new discovery. The two, who at first seemed hardly fated for friendship, make a connection that would ultimately change the future.

"Well, you two can stop talking like that, because he's not going to win. Look—Finkler is ahead in Delaware and Maryland," Livie says.

"She should be ahead on those two."

"Sorry Livie, but Finn is right about that. And it looks like Kentucky is going to Brant after all."

"Come on Hannah, you are supposed to encourage me here! Tell me Brant isn't going to win."

Preet moves to hug Livie from behind.

"It's okay Livie, you will still be able to get your cup of joe with your Green Planet Coffee app tomorrow."

Thinking of the simple pleasure of her favorite coffee in the morning, Livie smiles at Preet as she voices a thought they have shared many times before.

"For sure—can't let the simple pleasures in life become mundane or lost to the stresses of life."

Bo adds his voice to the scene, announcing what they are all watching on the screen.

"Well, lots of predictability coming at us now. West Virginia and Georgia to Brant. Virginia looks close. Doesn't Finkler need Virginia though?"

"She sure does. Come on Abby, you can still win this!!"

Saba's cheer for Finkler pulls an invisible string that moves them all closer together, as if the solidarity of their resolve in front of the screen will affect the outcome.

The group gasps and groans as the results roll in like a thick black cloud. As Brant takes Michigan, Nevada, Minnesota, and Utah, Hannah starts a cheer for Florida.

"Come on Florida, you can still keep this guy out of the White House!"

"Yes, come on Florida for Finkler!"

"Florida we need you!"

"Come on Florida!"

As their cheers echo through the apartment, Florida falls for Brant, as does North Carolina and Pennsylvania. As it appears Ohio is about to be declared as Brant's, Saba announces the winner before the networks can.

"Friends, Brant will be disastrous for our country and our world, but not all will see it that way. He will drive further division in our cities, I'm afraid. There's so much poverty and hopelessness out there these days, as many can't make ends meet and dreams of home ownership are lost for most. Yet sadly, many will see his election as hope for change."

"Well, he won't fix the housing market that has screwed everyone who's not wealthy, that's for sure. I hope this doesn't make it that much harder to open my little yoga studio."

"I don't think it will Preet, but I'm afraid Brant will start a war of some sort. When people feel the hopelessness that Saba mentions, oddly, the prospect of war can be seen as an avenue of relief."

As Livie listens to Finn's projection of the potential for war, she feels suddenly numb and detached from the conversation. The voices around her take on a muffled quality. Can she continue to live in this city with Brant as president? The question and its ramifications ring loudly in her head, drowning out the others' chitchat. She drops into a kitchen stool like a wilted flower.

The broadcast of Finkler's concession speech, followed by Brant's voice claiming his victory, play in the background while the chatter amongst the friends slowly dissipates. Preet yawns and looks over at Livie.

"Livie, can I give you a hand cleaning up? We should get going, but I don't want to leave you with a mess."

Preet's words spur everyone into action. Leftovers are packed into the fridge, and dishes are washed and put away. The sudden surge of activity has tapped the last of Livie's energy. She says goodbye to her friends and makes her way to her bedroom.

With her friends now all gone, she hears only the harsh silence of her empty apartment and the voice in her head. *Has this really happened? Is Brant now our president?* With vigor, Livie rips back the blankets on her bed, deposits her body on the warmth of the top sheet, and pulls the blankets over her. She wishes she could just hibernate to avoid what may be coming to their world.

She doesn't toss or turn; she just lies there, waiting for sleep to take her. Just as her body welcomes sleep's embrace, the silence is broken by the sound of a crash. Then another. Then another.

Livie opens her eyes as the sounds of a succession of vehicle crashes ring in her ears. She bolts upright, tosses the blankets aside, and rushes over to the window.

The harsh sounds of metal crashing into metal has subsided, and Livie's jaw drops as she sees the pileup of driverless vehicles below. The carnage stretches the entire block.

"What the..." Livie is now wide awake, adrenaline coursing through her like a jolt of caffeine. She reaches for her phone to search for information on the scene below.

But instead of her usual home screen, she sees an unusual, florescent pink background with black block letters that read:

BROUGHT TO YOU BY:
THE FRIENDLY WORLD VIRUS
WELCOME TO THE INTERNETLESS WORLD

A WORLD WITHOUT:

- CYBERCRIME
- IDENTITY THEFT
- CYBER BULLYING

A WORLD WHERE THE RIGHT SIDE WINS

A WORLD WITHOUT THE INTERNET

A FRIENDLIER WORLD

THIS MESSAGE IS PROVIDED BY:
THE FRIENDLY WORLD NETWORK

Chapter 2

News at Green Planet

Livie tugs the door open to step into the sounds and smells of Green Planet Coffee, reflecting that the very act of reaching for the door signals a departure from her normal routine. She would usually be here at 6:30 a.m. and be greeted by someone opening the door as they exit the busy coffee shop.

This morning her routine is broken. It's the day after. The day after a night of sleepless wonder. After she received that message from "The Friendly World Network," her phone was abuzz with calls and messages. The first one was a frantic call from her mom, who she hadn't heard from in months. While speaking to her mom, Hannah called her—just as her mom's voice grew shrill with anxiety. As she heard the click of the voice message Hannah had left, it was her dad's number that popped up on the screen.

What followed was a night of calls and missed calls. Frantic, scared voices. Every time Livie tried to log onto the internet, she saw the same luminous message about the Friendly World Virus. When she finally went to bed, she spent a tortuous few hours falling in and out of sleep as the night crawled by.

Just when a couple of hours of steady sleep had saved her, the alarm on her phone went off, followed by a call from her boss, Larry. He told her not to bother coming into work—"until the internet comes back on." This made her angry, and she wanted to tell him that he'd hardly have a business if it wasn't for her. She hung up him, wondering if her career was even relevant without the internet, as her body, moist from sweat, clung to her bed.

"Larry Dubash, you were always an unreliable dumbass," she whispered to herself.

Now here she is at 11:08 a.m., opening the door to Green Planet. The sixty-three seats are largely empty, except for a group that has congregated close to the fireplace and a smattering of others spread throughout the coffee shop.

The familiar has become strange. Livie doesn't recognize anyone as she scans the bodies occupying the seats and absorbs the muted stares of those looking her way. Suddenly, she feels like a non-union extra with no lines in her own life. She doesn't even recognize the barista who is waiting to greet her.

The comforting scent of caffeine seeps into her pores as she approaches the counter.

"Good morning, and welcome to Green Planet. Just before you order, you should know that we can only accept cash today."

"Oh, really? Ummm...not sure if I..."

Livie reaches for her overstuffed purse as her voice trails off. She stopped using cash for anything over a year ago. She receives and exchanges most of her currency by text messages. But she digs her hand into her purse anyway, hoping the barista would sympathize and grant her a coffee for her efforts. She releases her empty hand from her purse, looks up with her best sad puppy eyes, and stares at the barista, letting the silence fall between them. She needs coffee. Coffee...that simple, mundane pleasure that her body is crying out for as a lifeline to normalcy.

Livie doesn't realize she is acting out a scene the barista has already witnessed many times that morning.

"I was hoping you'd have some cash," the barista said. "Not many have had money this morning, and those who didn't all left in search of an ATM. I'm not sure how many of those are open or even have *any* cash, but maybe the bank down the street will?"

"I just need some coff..."

Before Livie could finish her sentence, a woman appears beside her, bringing motion to the stillness as she holds out a ten-dollar bill.

"Here, let me get your coffee for you. You look like you could use some."

"Thanks. You've no idea how much I appreciate this."

"No problem. My name is Fairleigh."

Livie introduces herself and collects her coffee, sipping gratefully as she follows Fairleigh to an area with two comfy chairs and a small table. Fairleigh gives off an aroma of earthiness. Her brown hair is straight with a middle parting and two pigtails that rest on her shoulders, framing a long, thin neck. The crinkles around her eyes authenticate her smile and give the slightly huggable appearance of an affable goat. With her brown thermos and beige sweater draped over a chestnut-colored shirt, Livie wonders if the woman's favorite color is dirt. Fairleigh deposits herself into one of the comfy chairs as she picks up a book from the table.

"This is my regular coffee shop. I don't think I've seen you here before?" Livie ventures.

"You probably haven't. I usually brew mine at home but stop here later in the day. You're probably used to coming here earlier in the morning?"

"It's that obvious? I'm used to recognizing everyone here in the morning. I don't even know the barista."

"The barista is Angela, and I think she was the only one they could get to work. The others are out trying to sort out their lives. A lot of people have had their routines disrupted with the events of last night."

"Ya, I suppose you're right. What about you and your routine? You usually come here to read?"

"I do sometimes. I decided with all the chaos out there today, I would take the opportunity to relax. Take time for myself, you know. I can go into work later."

Livie notes that Fairleigh's strong posture and relaxed look is in contrast with the tetchy expressions on the faces of everyone else she has seen since the internet broke down. Her voice is warm, inviting, and calm. Livie studies Fairleigh as she lounges in her seat and opens her book to read.

"Whatcha reading?"

Fairleigh closes the book on her thumb, revealing the cover and title: *Momentum's Force*.

"It's a fictional novel about the story of a family that faces significant changes and discoveries. It's about how those shape their lives. The premise behind the title is that all of life and the decisions we make have a momentum to them—for good or bad. It was written several years ago by a little-known author, Andres Ballsuch."

"Hmmm...sounds interesting. I don't see others reading today. They're talking about what happened last night and what's going to happen now with the internet down. You don't seem concerned?"

"Concerned? Oh, no. I think it's better, actually. Certainly far more relaxing. No need to worry about the email I might have missed or what someone might be saying about me on social media. I haven't had to make a million different decisions before my morning coffee because I haven't been bombarded by information, emails, and demands as I usually am. It's, like, suddenly a more polite world. I can just quietly sit here and read my book."

"Just looking at the faces of the others here, it seems most are pretty unhappy or anxious about everything."

Fairleigh glances up and scans the room with a curious look on her face.

"I suppose you're right, though I also see people actually talking to each other instead of looking at their phones all the time. Except for the odd text, I guess."

Fairleigh's words prompt Livie to look at her own phone to see several texts demanding to be opened—the latest from Hannah. The first words of the long text read, "WTF. What is with people?! We need to talk..."

Livie looks up at Fairleigh, who has gone back to reading—her composed, restful expression conflicting with the current of text messages Livie has received. Wanting to continue the conversation but not intrude on her reading, Livie tilts her head to the side and speaks as if she is just spewing her thoughts aloud.

"It's like we have all been pushed into a small, tight world of our own. So many are acting like trapped birds, fluttering and panicking to get away."

"That's quite the observation. I think others could find safety, simplicity, and more meaningful relationships in that world. The anxiety and panic you are seeing are likely just people adjusting to change."

"Adjusting to change? I don't imagine the internet will be down that long."

Fairleigh appears to have swallowed something as Livie spoke. Her expression becomes stern, like a teacher ready to deliver a lecture to a misbehaving student.

"Don't be counting on that. I think it's best to enjoy the change; embrace it as a better, saner life."

Feeling scolded, Livie's anxiety erupts to the surface.

"How can you say that?! I came in here for coffee and all they will take is cash. I haven't had any cash on me for at least two years. Is every place going to want cash now? I pay all my bills online, and my mortgage. My heat won't come on without the internet. My job requires the internet. My life requires it. I might lose my job. Maybe my condo. How am I supposed to adjust to that?" Livie gets up to leave. "I need to find a bank to get the cash required in this new world."

Fairleigh stands up too and reaches for Livie's arm.

"Hey, sorry Livie. I didn't mean to upset you. Let me give you some cash. You may not easily find a bank without a long lineup and available funds."

Livie looks at the twenty-dollar bill that hangs in the air between Fairleigh's fingers. Just twelve hours ago, she would have dismissed it as an unnecessary annoyance, but now, it may represent all the purchasing power she will have for a while. Still, her sense of self-reliance, built with tears and heartache over the years, asserts itself with a sharp intake of breath before she spits out her response.

"I don't take money from anyone; I can look after myself. Thank you, though."

"Livie, of course you can. Please, let me lend you the cash. Just until you can access your money. I'll give you my phone number and you can pay me back."

Fairleigh's warm and inviting smile has returned as she reaches out and puts the twenty in Livie's hand. Livie doesn't resist as her fingers clutch the bill.

"If you want to give me your number, I can send you a text, and then you'll have mine," Fairleigh says.

"No."

Livie looks at Fairleigh, realizing her abrupt response has startled them both.

"It's just...it's just that I already have a lot of unread text messages waiting for me, and I don't want to look at them right now. Could you just write your number down on a napkin for me?"

As Fairleigh reaches for a napkin on the table and sits down to write out her number, Livie drops her body back into the comfy chair next to her.

"I don't know where I was going anyway. I'm not sure I want to go back to my place yet, and my boss phoned me this morning to tell me not to come into work."

"It's the loss of the internet that kept you from working today?"

Livie gives Fairleigh her best wide-eyed "really?" look, reserved for those that point out the obvious.

"Oh hey...look, I didn't mean for that to sound so...so snooty. Many people can't work today with the sudden loss of the internet. So, you're in good company there. I really just meant to ask what you do for work."

"Snooty, eh?" Livie pauses for a moment, tasting the word as she considers how to respond.

"I don't think that was snooty, actually. I work as a private investigator, and my specialty is family and corporate investigations. While I can think of many aspects of the job that don't require the internet, I can't imagine doing the job without it. The research we do, the legal applications and the surveillance requires it for sure. Then there is the correspondence we have with clients—which of course is email or text or some instant messaging. I don't know how we would provide our services without the internet, not to mention advertising. Maybe people won't even need us without the internet." Livie pauses in reflection and then adds, "I worked so hard to get to where I am. I was so proud to call myself Livie Romée-Padalino, private investigator."

"Livie, the private investigator profession has been around a lot longer than the internet. The job may be different in some respects for sure, but I'm sure most of your skills would easily transfer to a non-internet world. Take me, for example. I work as a computer programmer, so the internet is woven into most of the work I do. But there's a lot of work a computer programmer can do without the internet."

"A non-internet world? Do you really think this isn't just temporary?"

"I'm just trying to analyze how this could have happened. It clearly would have taken a lot of planning and strategizing to shut down the entire internet, worldwide. I'm sure those behind it would have also made plans to counteract any efforts to bring the internet back."

Livie hangs onto Fairleigh's every word as she tries to track what she is saying, while her mind, on a tight rope, races with what all this would mean for her.

"At my work, everything we do could simply collapse without the internet. We gather information on people and corporations online. We can find their emails, their family history, dates of birth, pictures, credit reports, property they own, net worth. We can find all that online—on the internet. Just recently, I helped a family locate a long-lost loved one who was in another country. I spent days researching on the internet and looking at pictures on various social media accounts. I couldn't have done that without the internet. Our whole client base, information on them, and all the ongoing investigations are all stored online, in the cloud. Oh wait...do you...you think the cloud is lost too now? Has all that information just disappeared?"

"No. Certainly not. Well...it shouldn't be, anyway. The cloud isn't some mist of data floating above us. It's just large computers that store the information, which can be accessed remotely. People could access the cloud right now without the internet by going to where the data is stored. I can actually remember when my parents used to have discs that they stored their information on before the cloud existed. That technology is still there to transfer the data to, if necessary. So, it shouldn't be lost. Not yet, at least."

"Not yet?"

"Well...the people behind this internet shutdown didn't say anything about deleting the information stored on central computers."

"Okay, hold that thought. I need to refill my coffee."

After retrieving a fresh cup of brew, Livie places it on the table beside Fairleigh's thermos and sinks back into the comfy chair as if it is her own.

"So if the information in the cloud is safe, how do we access it?"

"Shouldn't be too difficult, actually. It would be through the companies that own the central computers that hold the information, like Apple, Amazon, Google, Apeteq, and Cylance. Governments generally have their own servers. I'm sure it's just going to take time for the various companies and individuals to retrieve the information."

As Fairleigh explains the nuances of how the central computers work, Livie's curiosity drops into the wide void of everything she does not know. The conversation takes on a rhythm, from a quickstep as they reflect on everything the internet provides, to a slow waltz lamenting all that would be lost without the internet and what would replace it.

Livie wonders how she would stay connected to some of her friends that she met online and who live in other states and countries. Friendships that were fashioned through blog discussions, chats, common interests, pictures swapped, and confidences shared. Even her close friends in Washington she keeps in contact with online.

Fairleigh listens intently as Livie speaks, her passion rising and falling like a tide coming in.

"Friendships are important to all of us, Livie. Not all the methods of communication we use are lost because there's no internet. Many of the technological advances that have brought us these modes of communication will still be available. You can still use your cell phone to call and to text from anywhere. Without the internet, you won't have the data capacity to send pictures or videos, but," Fairleigh points to Livie's cell phone for emphasis, "the high-end camera you have in that little device still has all its capacities."

Livie reaches for her phone and opens the picture app. She immediately sees the photos from the previous night; photos of her and Hannah, Finn, Bo, Preet, and Saba.

"Yep, as you can see, those pictures stored on your phone are all still there, and I'm sure your device still has plenty of capacity for a lot more."

As if to put those words to the test, Livie clicks on the camera app, holds up her phone, and takes a picture of Fairleigh. Almost immediately, the pixels form together and the image pops up on her screen: the woman with the brown pigtails and warm, closed-mouth smile sitting with her earth-toned thermos in front of her.

"Okay, I'll let you keep that one. I'm usually a bit sensitive about people taking my picture, but it doesn't matter as much now, I suppose. Pictures are such an important part of our lives, aren't they?"

Fairleigh notes Livie's slight nod as she continues to scan through the pictures on her phone.

"They tell a story of our lives. As I watch you scanning through your pictures, it reminds me of a time recently when I was with a friend. She was showing me pictures from a trip she took and others that were just from her day—all on her phone. She told me stories as we looked at them, laughed, and even cried a bit. You can't get all that from a picture sent with a text message. I think much of our communication today misses many parts of what real discussions are: tone, facial expressions, laughter that you can feel and not just hear, body language you don't have to just imagine or make up, pauses and differences in pace. Conversations that take in all those senses add meaning and dimension to a conversation; to a relationship, really."

"I get that...I do. But...I kind of like being able to control what I'm going to say before I send a text or an instant message to someone. Real-time discussions can be frustrating and...kind of frightening at times."

Fairleigh purses her lips as she holds in the surprise she feels at Livie's response and waits for her throat to unconstrict before responding.

"Hey, I know there are concerns about what's lost without the internet...but the internet being shut down is not like a Luddite thing."

"A Luddite thing?"

Fairleigh explains that the term "Luddite" is often associated with people who are opposed to technological advances in society. The term originated with nineteenth-century English textile workers who destroyed machinery, including automated textile equipment like weavers because they feared that automation would replace their labor and put a lot of them out of work.

"A world without the internet still possesses much of the technological advances we've made and could potentially make a lot of jobs much more interesting and diverse. The internet has given us a wealth of information at our fingertips with the press of a few buttons. However, there have been some real human costs associated with that. You said you work as a private investigator. I imagine you've often relied on facial recognition software to identify someone?"

"Ah, yeah...like every day. Like that time I mentioned, when we located a lost loved one for someone. And sometimes in cases of corporate fraud, a company will send us a video or pictures that we can use to identify someone using facial recognition. The pictures can be only partial or even a bit fuzzy. We have a program that will fill in the gaps."

"Really? Do you even leave the office in a case like that?"

"Oh yeah, we insist on meeting with the client in person to go over what we have gathered in the file."

"The file? Like a digital file?"

"Of course."

"Well, I'm sure that a lot of the technology, like the ability to zoom into an image and store it, will still be available without the internet. The facial recognition wouldn't be, nor perhaps details about an individual that you gathered from online sources and added to the digital file. *That* doesn't mean the work of a private investigator isn't needed in society. It is. You may find that *without* the internet, there will be more need for your kind of work because people won't be able to do their own investigations so easily. You may find that without the internet, your *own* analytical and creative abilities will be utilized more. The work could actually be more interesting, as many people have found the internet dumbs down the work they do, and their own skills are not utilized as much."

"I'm not so sure about that. I don't think you understand how complex these things are and what is only possible through the internet."

"Look Livie, I may be a bit older than you. I can still remember my parents' CDs and even cassette tapes, but like you, I'm generally a digital native. I was just entering grade school when the internet arrived in force, so I grew up in a digital world, just like you. I'm just saying that a lot of the technological advances we have made can be extracted from their reliance on the internet and be used without it."

"Okay, can you give me an example?"

"Sure. GPS."

"GPS works without the internet?"

"GPS has been around longer than the internet. Its source is satellites, not central computers."

"So that means my running app will still work. The GPS in my vehicle..."

Livie pauses briefly as her mind races with thoughts of all the uses of GPS. Then, like a jolt of energy that courses through her and propels itself out in excitement, she rapidly starts listing them.

"So I'll still be able to find my car if I forget where I parked it. The anti-theft device on it will still work. I can still locate myself on a hike, play Pokémon GO, and go geocaching. Airplanes can still fly. Search and rescue can still use it. I know a friend who uses GPS to track her cat, and a colleague uses it to know the whereabouts of her toddler. I have GPS on my luggage. What about the drones used for surveillance...I think they use it for farming and ships? Oh, there must be a million other GPS applications..."

Livie pauses to replenish her lungs, and Fairleigh uses the opportunity to vault into Livie's monologue.

"Livie...slow down a little. Yes, all those are likely true but not quite as simple as you presently use them." Fairleigh hesitates and raises her palm for a pause as she formulates in her mind how to best articulate her explanation.

"GPS uses satellites that are positioned above the earth to give you a location on the earth. GPS, or the Global Positioning System, was actually developed by the US military many decades before either of us were born. But it didn't have much practical use for regular folks like us because the military jammed the signals so that you couldn't get an accurate reading. They didn't want it being used in military action against them. When that was finally lifted—in the 1990s after the Cold War with the Russians ended—it was made available for civilian use. However, a GPS reading can tell you where you are on the earth's globe, but you need that position to be on a map to complete the picture for you. That's where the internet usually comes in. However, you can use a preloaded map with a GPS to show where you are, even without internet."

Livie looks up at Fairleigh, thinking deeply. Fairleigh allows the moment of reflection to hang, patiently waiting on her new friend.

"Wait...so is that why the driverless cars crashed? 'Cause they lost their maps without the internet?"

"The driverless cars crashed?"

"Last night. That's how I woke up to find out about the internet. I heard the cars crash. Aren't they run off GPS?"

"Ah yes, of course. Those cars are also synced with a sequence of precisely timed traffic lights. The traffic lights were clearly compromised, and I suspect that once one vehicle crashed, it caused a knock-on effect. It probably didn't help that none of the driverless cars have a steering wheel in them. Those poor passengers were left helpless without the ability to just take over and steer themselves out of trouble."

"Okay, makes sense now."

"Did you see this morning that none of the traffic lights were working properly?"

"No, I didn't notice. I walked, I don't live too far away."

"I walked as well, but I saw some vehicles at malfunctioning traffic lights. Things were going more slowly than usual; the lights were being treated as four-way stops, and each person had to take their turn. No one rushed the light, and there were probably fewer accidents."

"It all sounds so chaotic."

"It does right now. But those driverless cars can still operate without the internet, as can the traffic lights. As the various technological advances are untangled from the internet, it will unzip all the potential we possess. I'm sure there are people working on making that happen already."

"Did you say unzip?"

"Um...yeah...why?"

"Oh...nothing...just made me think of someone."

The pattern of their conversation, with Livie's inquisitive questions and Fairleigh's conviction and confident responses, crackles between them on various topics. Livie expresses anxiety about losing things like home and ride-sharing, money management and banking apps, online head-to-head games, music sharing, instant news reporting, online shopping and education, listening to podcasts, and particularly social media.

Fairleigh gives calm, detailed, and practical responses to each of Livie's questions. Livie listens, her expression wavering from an inquisitive glint in her eye to a skeptical crunch of her lips. Fairleigh details how the technology that enables head-to-head games and music sharing would work in a non-internet world. "The graphics and level of sophistication in those games are all still there, and people can play them against each other, wirelessly, when they are in close proximity. The technology that allows a thousand songs or all those games to be stored on a small memory stick is not lost. Podcasts, music, games, etc. can all be recorded and stored on small devices and shared as such. Banking may change, but it will probably be a whole lot safer as a result."

Fairleigh states her opinions as facts as she expands on the pitfalls the internet has brought to society. The loss of privacy with the ubiquitous use of cameras and facial-recognition technology, which she refers to as surveillance capitalism; the pervasiveness of advertisers in their lives who can access data from their phones for targeted ads; the use of artificial intelligence to dumb down many occupations that used to provide great satisfaction and better incomes; being constantly bombarded with information and endless options to choose from; and how citizens are generally seen as consumers to be manipulated.

“I for one am glad to see the curtain drop on the parasite that is social media,” Fairleigh continues. “It's digital colonialism! Its main purpose, and in fact reason for being, is to collect as much data from everyone as possible, store it, and organize it to sell it.” She fixes her green eyes on Livie.

With her emotions roaming just under the surface, Livie tries to visualize this "power over our lives and the joy that will rise out of it" that Fairleigh spoke of.

When Fairleigh indicates a need to use the washroom, Livie looks at her watch and realizes that, while it felt like her life was frozen in time, she has actually been in the coffee shop for over four hours. She says she should get going and says goodbye to her new friend as a thought pops into her head.

"Just thinking that I have grown up with the knowledge that everything lives on the internet forever, and now— if you are right—that 'forever' may have ended."

Fairleigh acknowledges her insight with a nod and a smile that slowly stretches out to her cheeks. As Farleigh reaches out her hand to Livie, she knocks her thermos over.

Livie instinctively reacts to catch it. She misses, but bends over to pick it up off the floor.

"Oh, thanks. I'm pretty sure it's empty."

Livie confirms that the thermos is empty as she hands it back to her new friend, noticing the initials "FWN" engraved on the lid.

"I'm so glad we met, Livie. Maybe I'll see you here again?"

"Yes, I think you will. Anyway, I must say that I still hope the internet comes back on soon."

With that, Livie leaves the coffee shop for what seems like a long walk back to her place, which is just three blocks away.

As she turns the corner to the last block before her apartment, the muddle of thoughts swirling in her head are crowded out by the dominant feeling of mental fatigue.

"Livie! Wait up!"

"Oh, hi Raf."

Rafael lives in the building next to Livie's. On more than a few occasions when she was out, he seemed to appear suddenly to chat with her. Hannah called him "beautiful" the first time she met him.

His wavy, stark-black hair, bedroom eyes with long eyelashes, and olive skin certainly garnered more than a passing look. At twenty-six, Raf is only two years her junior, but Livie thinks he acts more like a teenager than an adult.

"I've had a long day Raf, I just want to get back to my place and relax."

"Long day, you say? Probably true for most. I felt confused and lost most of the day. Couldn't go to work, none of my apps work, and I actually got *really* lost a few times. You know, I didn't realize that I don't actually know the names of most of the streets around here. Of course, my map app wouldn't work."

Livie picks up her pace as Raf talks faster in response.

"So, did you get any cash today? I went to five banks and stood in a super long lineup for a while, but then because it wasn't my bank and I didn't have my account information, they couldn't help me. So I'm shit out of luck! Who carries cash with them anymore?"

Livie was glad that Raf just kept talking instead of waiting for her to respond.

"Anyway, thank gawd the internet's coming back on in a few days."

Raf's words stop Livie in her tracks. She almost loses her balance as her momentum is forced to an abrupt stop, and she reaches for Raf's arm.

"What did you say? The internet's coming back on?"

"Ya, I heard Brant on the radio. He said they have a team of tech experts that are hunting down the terrorist that infected the internet, and that they will have it back on and running in seventy-two hours."

"Brant said that, did he?"

"Well yeah, he did."

"Well *that* certainly makes it so then. If Brant said it, I guess we can trust it to be true."

Livie starts walking again, hoping the sarcasm in her voice has registered with him.

"So...you sound skeptical, then?"

This time she stops to face Raf directly.

"Raf, Brant makes up lots of things. You said he called them terrorists? Did he offer any evidence to support that?"

"I dunno. I didn't hear it. He said they could be Russians. But, hey, don't you want the internet back, Livie?"

Livie starts walking again and catches Raf's question over her shoulder.

"Of course I do, Raf. I'm just not sure I'd rely on Brant's words. Maybe whoever shut down the internet did it because of him."

"Oh, I hadn't thought of that. Anyway, I also heard that the *Washington Post* is starting up their printing presses again, and for the first time in years they are going to print an actual newspaper tomorrow."

Livie arrives at the walkway to her building, located just before Raf's, and she stops to thank him for the information. While she didn't invite his company on the way home, as she planned to use it to process what she had learnt from Fairleigh, she had to admit, he at least made her want to check on the news of the day.

"Well thanks for the chat Raf. See you soon."

"For sure. Maybe I'll catch you sometime tomorrow?"

"Do any of us know what tomorrow will bring?"

"That's true. Say, I want you to know that I may have a lead on someone to get cash from tomorrow, if you need a hand with that?"

Livie isn't sure what to believe at this point and is just anxious to get into her place.

"That's good to hear Raf, let me know if that turns out to be real."

With that she says goodbye, and they go their separate ways.

Livie enters her building and takes the elevator to the thirteenth floor. As the elevator doors open, she glimpses someone with long, dirty blond hair standing outside her door just down the hall. The image injects her with a sense of relief. Though feeling exhausted, she really dreaded coming back to an empty apartment. Loneliness is a silent, cruel judge that doesn't always rule in her favor. While any number of her friends would have filled the void, joy momentarily leaps into her being knowing it is Hannah—the one person she can talk to and who can help make sense of what is happening around them.

Hannah must sense her presence, as she turns around as soon as the elevator doors open.

Livie runs to her friend, her voice echoing in the hallway.

"Hannah, what happened to you!?"

Even as Livie rushes to greet her friend, she can see the puffed-out lip, an eye that looks like it's starting to go black at the edges, her right arm limp at her side, and her torn blouse.

"Sorry...I didn't mean to startle you. I just haven't been home yet to clean up—I came straight here. You haven't been answering my texts."

Hannah tells her she was texting to ask for Livie's help; maybe get her some clothes to bring to her work. Livie is wrenched with the feeling that she let her friend down as Hannah explains what happened.

Hannah tells her about single moms, seniors, mental-health patients, and homeless people who were at her door seeking help.

"These people, Livie, don't have extras at home for emergencies like most of us. Their needs are basic: simple food to fill their stomachs, basic toiletries, and cash. We insisted that they all have a bank account, and now none of them can access their money. They showed up anxious, scared, and angry."

"So...you went to work today?"

"Livie, of course I did. People's needs don't just stop because someone shut off the internet. We have to improvise and get creative in times like these...I can't just abandon people who rely on me like that."

Livie's energy is awakened as she listens to her friend's stories, cleaning her up using her first aid kit and a washcloth. Hannah is alive with details of how she came to look so physically beaten.

"We only had so much food at the office, and I needed to get cash. So I raced out of the office with a government check in hand. Livie, I thought I'd get to the first bank, express that my need was urgent, and there wouldn't be a problem. But...like wow...some people have lost their minds! The first bank had a lineup out the door, and no one would let me through. Same thing happened at the second and third banks, which were even more hostile. I tried to get through and just got yelled at, kicked, and pushed for my efforts. Finally, I had enough when I got to the fourth bank. I wasn't leaving without cashing that check."

Hannah's speech accelerates as she tells Livie how she charged into the crowd yelling that it was an emergency. While some pushed her forward, others kicked and ripped her clothes. With a sense of pride, she tells Livie that she was punched just before reaching the teller, but others cheered as she planted her feet at the front of the line and held out the check to be cashed.

Livie ran the scene through her head like a movie. Her friend in a superhero cape, leaving the bank to a round of cheers before running back to the office with the cash in hand for those in need.

"You're a hero, Hannah."

"Oh, stop. It wasn't that big of a deal. I'm being too braggadocious about it. But enough about me, what excitement did you experience on this crazy day?"

Chapter 3

Hopes & Heartaches from Day 2

"Nothing in this world stays the same, no matter what you do."

Livie always enjoys trading banter with Hannah when she makes absolute statements.

"Nothing?"

"Oh come on girl. You know I love you, and that's never gonna change. You know what I mean. Life is constantly throwing different things at us. We have to adjust and make up new ways to clean up the shit around us."

"The shit around us?"

"Okay, the thorny roses too. We shouldn't just roll with the punches life sends us, but punch back some!"

Hannah balls up her hands and punches the air as if her point deserves more than the words can contain.

"Your passion is inspirational, Hannah."

"My passion? You mean for my work? Like most passions, it's a love-hate relationship."

Ah, her work. The discussion comes around full circle. Hannah's work was the topic that dominated the couple of hours after Livie found Hannah at her door. Hannah was full of stories of her clients, "people with real needs." She told Livie they were short-staffed and that she could get Livie on a short-term contract to help. "Just while you are waiting for your boss to need you again," she said. For Livie, Hannah's work brought up memories of when she was thrust into foster care as a child. That was why she hadn't joined Hannah in pursuing a career in social work.

When Livie just stared in response, Hannah paused before filling her friend's intentional silence.

"Oh, I know that look. Livie, your childhood isn't going to creep up and smother you because you put in a few shifts. Plus, I'll be there working with you. It'll be fun." When Livie's expression still didn't change, Hannah gave in. "Okay, I'll change the subject. How about we talk about your day?"

So they chatted about Livie's day. Her lack of cash at Green Planet and being rescued by a stranger named Fairleigh. She told Hannah, in more detail than she intended to, about the substance of her conversation with Fairleigh. She was still pondering much of what Fairleigh had said and was planning to take more time to process it all before sharing it with someone else. But it just spillled out of her—first in a slow trickle, then in a steady stream of details. She conveyed the static, the connection she had occasionally felt between her and Fairleigh, but she didn't realize that she was also expressing admiration—until Hannah offered an observation.

"Sounds like you made a new friend who's quite grounded and a wealth of information."

"Well, I think Fairleigh is wrong about the internet remaining off," Livie countered quickly.

"Nothing in this world stays the same, no matter what you do."

From there, the segue back to Hannah's work and her proposal took just a few simple moves on the chessboard of their conversation.

"But the love-hate of the work is what makes it so dynamic and engaging, Livie. I just want you to give it a try. Right now, there's this unique opportunity, and we could really use you. Please."

She emphasizes her final sentence with a squeeze to Livie's shoulders and an expression of hope.

Livie turns from her as her voice rises and fills the air.

"Shit! Shit! Shit Hannah! How do you do this to me? Get me into things. Okaaaay! Enough already! I'll do it. I'll try it for one day. One. day. only...then we'll see."

Hannah raises her hands and puts her entire body into an excited applause.

Livie smiles and shakes her head at her friend.

"Alright then, but I have one condition. You have to stay here with me tonight. Then we can go in together tomorrow."

"Sounds great. Shall we stop at Green Planet on our way? Maybe see if we can catch Fairleigh there?"

~~~~~~

Livie and Hannah arrive at Green Planet with a curious desire to people-watch on this second day of the non-internet world. The sounds of chatter spill out into the street as they open the door to the nearly full café. Hannah immediately points to the lineup at the till and the large sign, in bold block letters, that now hangs above the barista: "No Debit. No Credit. No App. No Whining."

"It appears a lot of people have managed to find some cash."

"No kidding. That seemed like such a major hurdle just yesterday. This place was practically empty when I was here then."

"You see her anywhere?"

The moment they walked in, Livie scanned the crowd for the earth-toned woman with the green eyes and pigtails.

"Nope...not yet, anyway. I see some empty chairs over there," Livie points to come seats close to where she and Fairleigh had sat, "shall I grab them while you get our coffee?"

Hannah's smile is all the response Livie needs as she quickly moves to claim the seats. Livie sits down, looks up, and relaxes her shoulders at the sight of a familiar face.

"Livie, so good to see you here. Were you here yesterday?"

"Yeah, I was...but much later in the morning than usual."
~~~~~~

Livie knows Heather only from Green Planet. Part of her morning routine is a brief chat with her "coffee friend." The scrambled condition of her brain the last two days has crowded out some of her routines, including looking for Heather when she arrived at Green Planet.

"Well, I was here at our usual time, you know, six-thirtyish. But wow, the place was almost empty. They only took cash of course, and I had none, so I didn't stay long."

"But you have cash today?"

"Oh yeah, and thank gaaawd...a friend of mine scored a fair bit, so I was able to borrow some." Heather scans the room as she pauses. "Chatting with a few others here, the stories all sound similar. The few who have been able to get cash are lending some of it to their friends."

Hannah arrives with their coffees, and Heather rushes a goodbye with the same mouthful she uses to say hello to Hannah.

"Friend of yours?" Hannah asks as Heather hurries from the coffee shop.

"Yeah, you could say that. I only ever see her here with my morning coffee, though."

Livie shares with Hannah what Heather told her about the flow of cash in the café.

"Hmmm...that's sort of heartwarming to hear, actually. I was wondering how all these people had cash because my experience at the banks yesterday was that it was a hot commodity. Amazing how quickly some have adjusted."

"I'll say; just listen to the buzz of chatter in this place. That certainly wasn't the case yesterday."

"Well this isn't my usual coffee shop, but I think I see a difference. Look at that group over there, Livie."

Hannah nods her head in the direction of a group of five well-dressed individuals that look around the same age as them.

Everyone in the group is sitting forward in their seats, their bodies leaning into the conversation. The light in the room scatters their shadows over the table, giving the impression of a group huddled close around a campfire.

"Looks like a deep, engaging conversation."

Livie thinks of the contrast to the hushed stares and vanished chitchat from the previous day.

"Yeah, I see that. I know those people from this place. Usually they sit together, but you'd see them all on their phones while they drink their coffee in silence."

Hannah quizzes Livie about several other people in the café that are sitting in pairs or groups, and they make similar observations.

"I guess a lot of the chatter is about what this world is like without the internet."

"That and what's going to happen next."

"What do think is going to happen next?"

Livie squints past Hannah's shoulder, as if gazing into the distance will provide an answer.

"I wish I knew. I don't believe Brant when he says the internet's coming back on, but I hope he's right."

"You aren't pinning your hopes on that are you?"

"What do you mean?"

"I think some people are already starting to adjust to this change, while others are probably frozen and hoping it will just pass. But what happens if it doesn't? I don't want to lose three days waiting for that."

Livie drops her eyes back down to meet her friend's gaze as she ponders the words.

"But what if it just comes back on and then you've made a bunch of unnecessary changes?"

Hannah quickly scans the faces of many in the café, wondering if they are all having the same discussion as she thinks of the immediate impact the situation has had on their lives.

"So, the *Washington Post* apparently is—or has—produced an actual hard-copy newspaper today. We should get one."

"Why? Wouldn't it just be yesterday's news?"

"I suppose. Livie, do you have your book club tonight?"

"No...well, usually yes, it would be tonight, but we meet online. We obviously can't do that tonight."

"Maybe you could invite the book club members over to your place?"

"Hannah, I don't know these people that well. I think that'd be awkward."

"Okay, so how about we get together tonight at your place and invite Preet and Bo...and Saba..."

"Were you not going to add Finn to that list?"

"Well...sounds like you just did."

Livie deliberately prevents her eyelashes from blinking so as not to interrupt the stare she shoots at her friend.

"Oh come on Livie. You know I'm just going to invite him anyway."

Hannah quickly taps a group text into her phone to invite everyone and breaks Livie's silence with, "Shall we say 6:30 tonight?"

"Sure."

"There, it's done. We should make sure to pick up some wine after work."

"Look at you, my cash-wielding friend."

"Well it doesn't look like I'm the only one. Look at the guy over there, handing out cash to the people around him."

Livie follows Hannah's gaze to a group in the far corner of the café.

"Strange that I don't recognize that guy...the one with the cash. I don't know everyone's names obviously, but all the faces in here are usually familiar to me."

Hannah takes in Livie's distant, quizzical gaze.

"Speaking of the familiar, have you chatted with your mom or dad since..."

"Yes."

"That was an abrupt response. Didn't go well?"

"No...I mean, it was okay. It's just that my mom only calls when something dramatic is happening, as if we have nothing else to talk about...and my father...well, my father only calls when he feels he has an obligation to do so. My birthday comes once a year, as does Christmas, so I guess it's a bonus, this little *extra* call from him. If only that damn internet would shut down more often..."

Hannah reaches out and gives her friend a one-armed hug as she watches her face for any tears.

Livie looks away as thoughts of her parents threaten to drag her under.

"What about someone from your uncle's family?"

Livie lets out a muffled chuckle as she pushes back any thoughts that might hinge her to her family.

"They are sour that he left me money for the condo. I think my membership in that family has been revoked."

"I just thought maybe..."

Hannah reads the stop sign on Livie's face and pushes herself up from the chair.

"Let's get out of here. Won't hurt if we get to the office a little early."

~~~~~~

As they approach Hannah's office, the scene immediately crawls up Livie's spine and transports her back to her childhood. Three
~~~~~~

preschool children are blocking the door to the office as they cling to a disheveled-looking woman whose frightened expression would cause many to look the other way. Not so with Hannah, who greets her like a favorite cousin in need. Hannah hugs the woman and reaches out to embrace the children—her expression radiating sympathy.

"Oh Annie. Whatever's happened, we will help. Let me get the door and get you inside."

As they enter the office, Hannah whispers to Livie that Annie is usually without food and funds and often has bruises that she tries to conceal with clothing and her posture. Once inside, Hannah ushers everyone into a room that is painted in soft, milky pastels—pink, green, and lavender. It has a couch, two recliners, and a table, as well as a box of toys in the corner.

Hannah shows the children the toys, and they quietly leave their mother's side. The transition is so natural, Livie can hear the silent sounds of the trust Hannah has established with them.

Livie sits quietly as she listens to Annie telling her story to Hannah. Annie is clearly comfortable in the familiar room.

The intensity of the abuse Hannah mentioned is evident with Annie's shakes as she tells them what happened. The dam she constructed to hold back the tears comes down as she tells them the threats her husband made if she didn't return later with some cash. He is known as a petty thief, but cash has become scarce on the streets. Each part of Annie's story comes with a plea of fear in her eyes and a defense for her husband's actions. It isn't his fault. He's under a lot of pressure. She can do more to make it easier for him. He's had a hard life. He's a good father and husband who just loses control sometimes.

Hannah listens to it all, offers comfort, and tells Annie it is not her fault. She can help her leave and find her a better place. As Hannah pulls out a notebook and suggests they work on a plan together, the door opens to the wide eyes of a woman who focuses on Hannah.

"I'm so sorry to interrupt. Hannah, we have an emergency and really need your help."

The woman's eyes fall on Livie as she is finishing her sentence.

Hannah looks at Livie and mouths "you got this" before turning back to Annie.

"Annie, I need to go. I'll come back, I promise."

Hannah pauses as she lowers her eyes to meet Annie's. Annie catches the warmth in Hannah's gaze and lowers her head as she nods in acceptance of Hannah's departure.

"Livie's here, and she's a very close friend of mine and works here too. She's going to help you."

The click of the door closing behind Hannah disturbs the silence between the two remaining women, but it doesn't break through Annie's bowed head or defeated posture.

Livie's moist eyes drink in the bruised character of the woman sitting in front of her as she constructs what to say in her head.

"Annie, your life's going to get better, and I can help you get there."

Livie hopes the words will penetrate with sympathy and a feeling of hope as Annie's shoulders heave with a muffled sob.

Livie lowers her eyes to try and catch Annie's as she articulates what she has constructed in her head.

"Look Annie, I know I don't completely understand your situation and the pain it must bring you. You've just met me, and maybe you're scared. I was in a situation many years ago where I was scared. Scared of what might happen. Scared of the future. Feeling the only option was to go back to the situation I was in."

When Annie's eyes remain downcast without any response, Livie fills the silence again.

"Trust is something a person has to establish, I know. It can be such a fragile thing. It's not really fair that I'm asking you to trust me...you just met me. But please Annie. Let me help you."

Annie raises her eyes, which are swollen and damp, and rakes them over Livie once before settling her gaze on her children.

"You have beautiful kids, Annie, and I know you want a good life for them. I've got some ideas to help, and you don't have to do anything you don't want to."

"What ideas?"

Annie's voice is so soft, Livie wants to be sure she heard her right.

"My ideas?"

"You said you have some ideas."

Livie moves towards Annie so that they are now just a couple of feet apart. She wants to move even closer but is afraid that the invasion of her personal space may startle Annie to retreat. Give her some hope for a better life, Livie tells herself.

"I know what I'm going to suggest will be hard, but I think you shouldn't go back to him. I can find some other housing for you and your children."

"He won't..."

Livie reaches out and gently places her hand on Annie's.

"He can't stop you Annie, and we can help to make sure he doesn't try."

"How you gonna do that?" Annie's voice is stiff.

"We could phone the police, and they could arrest him."

Livie says this with her usual blunt edge that she wishes she knew how to soften—but Annie responds with hope in her eyes, even as she stares into the empty space above where her children are playing.

"You really think they'd arrest him?"

"It's not my decision Annie, but I'll do whatever I can to help you in making that happen and then get a restraining order against him so he can't contact you."

She speaks with definitive certainty, keeping her own doubt at bay.

Annie's gaze falls on her children again.

"He's their father."

Livie moves to catch Annie's gaze and then joins her in observing her children play. Telling herself she needs to take the risk to keep the momentum of the conversation going, she is propelled by something her uncle once told her.

"Annie, of course he is...but it's not a healthy situation for your kids. They're like a bumblebee in a jar. Their lives are restricted by what they see and what they're experiencing. It's not just restricting them but could suffocate them too—just like the bee in the jar. They need someone to take the lid off." Livie pauses as she catches the corner of Annie's eye. She speaks slowly and deliberately. "You're that someone, Annie. You're strong. You came in here. You came here for help and that shows how strong you are...Let's do this together. For them. For you."

"Okay..." Annie's voice seems to restrict as she swallows and then pushes out the words. "But then where do I go after that?"

Livie can see from her expression that she has unlocked some secret password at just the right time that broke through Annie's fear and tapped into her resolve.

"I have a friend with a big house and lots of room for your kids...I think he'll let you stay there."

Annie turns her head and looks directly at Livie with moist eyes. Her expression, full of meaning, has lost the despair she came in with, but still holds a sense of disbelief. She is used to outcomes that just frog march her back to the life she dreads each day.

"How about I call him and see?" Livie prods.

Annie nods her head in agreement as a smile starts to form around the edges of her eyes. Livie steps out of the room to make a call.

Livie phones Hugo Wainwright. Hugo was a client of hers who lost his wife and two children in a car accident. It left him with a big empty house where he felt alone and lost. The devastating loss of his family led him to hire an investigator to find his living sister as he sought to fill the hole that was blasted into his life and emotions. Lodged in Livie's memory is the day she was able to reunite him with his sister and her son. She brought them to his big house, and she witnessed this big burly guy pour his emotions and heart into the sister he had not seen since he was a child. Hugo has kept in contact with her since, thanking her many times for making his life "more whole again." She knows that he still lives in the house by himself, and he has told her that he would like to put it to use to help others someday. *Maybe that day could be today*, Livie thinks as she hears his voice on the other end.

"Hi Livie. Always pleasant to hear from you. How are you with this no internet?"

Livie doesn't waste time in cutting to the purpose of her call and does her best to explain Annie's situation to him. Hugo agrees to take in Annie and her kids as he expresses his indebtedness to Livie. But his tone of voice is too carefully composed to convince Livie. She suggests he meet them first to try it out temporarily.

"Sure...though I doubt I'd turn them away once I meet them. If you think this'll be a good place for them, I'm happy to offer it...at least temporarily. I'm not much of a cook though; they'll have to figure that out themselves."

With the housing in place, Livie turns to head back into the room when she sees Hannah coming towards her.

"Livie! What's happening?"

"I was just making a phone call to arrange some housing for Annie and the children."

"Oh...okaaay. So, Annie has agreed to leave her husband?"

"I think so...but I told her we would call the police to get her husband arrested."

"Really?! Wow...you got further with her than I have."

"Are you coming back to help then?"

"I'm still dealing with another emergency and was really just coming back to see how things are going...but I should come help you with calling the police on her husband."

When the two of them return to the pastel-colored room, Annie is on her feet and restless. She speaks fast, telling them that she wants to leave and "go home." Hannah has seen this before and allows the disappointment on her face to show, which Annie picks up on.

Hannah's expression freezes Annie, allowing Livie to fill the gap with her news about the housing and that Hannah is there to assist with the call to the police. Livie's assertive approach, stating things as if they have already been decided, melts Annie back onto the couch.

Hannah takes the lead in phoning the police, who arrive to interview Annie before proceeding to arrest her husband for abuse. Hannah, seeing how Annie has learnt to trust Livie, leaves to attend to her other matter as the police arrive. Livie supports Annie throughout the police interview, offering words of reassurance and a comforting touch as needed. After the police leave, Livie takes Annie and her three children to meet Hugo at his house. Hugo is his usual warm, sociable self, expressing excitement to see them and creating an inviting atmosphere. Livie watches Annie as she gradually lets down her guard and begins to feel at ease.

While Hugo shows them the house and the rooms they can stay in, the police phone to confirm that Annie's husband has been arrested. Annie's shoulders visibly drop at the news as the stress drains from her face.

After Livie assists Annie in retrieving some belongings from her place, she goes grocery shopping with her and gets her settled back at Hugo's. She leaves Annie her cell number should she need anything, and then heads back to Hannah's office. As Livie parks, she sees that the building is dark, except for a solitary light coming from a corner inside Hannah's office.

Livie sends a text to Hannah and watches for her shadow inside. Hannah responds that she will be out in a few minutes. Livie pockets her phone and leans back in the comfort of the vehicle seat. She closes her eyes and fills her cheeks with air before letting it out with a deep push. The exhaustion from the day has hit her, bringing with it a breeze of contentment that seeps into her pores. Knowing Annie is safe at Hugo's calms her spirit, and the feeling of having made a difference has her hoping the day was as important to Annie as it was to her.

When Hannah raps on the window, Livie reaches over to unlock the door, keeping her eyes closed. Hannah jumps into the passenger seat.

"You look like you've had quite the day?"

Livie simply nods as a smile crawls across her face.

"Well, you'll have to tell me all about it, but we need to get going. It's almost six. Remember Preet and the others are coming over to your place tonight?"

While driving, Livie fills Hannah in on the details of her day with Annie. Hannah is astonished at the developments and tells Livie about the tortuous efforts she made previously to get Annie to leave her husband and have him charged. Livie can feel the heat from her own glow as Hannah praises her for getting Annie to a much better place. Careful not to throw a damper on things, Hannah expresses some concern with housing Annie and her children with a stranger.

"Hugo's not a stranger, Hannah. Not to me anyway. Trust me, he's solid, and Annie's happy."

"Okay...but it's not an approved place for her. Did you explore something with her extended family, perhaps?"

"She can't go to her family. She no longer has membership there."

Hannah has heard this tone from Livie before. It's a tone that states the conversation on the subject is over—for now at least. Hannah lets the silence hang for a few more seconds before she shares the details of her day. Her time was largely spent dealing with an eighteen-year-old in foster care who barricaded herself in a room as she spewed violent threats to the family she was living with. "That was the emergency I had to leave for," Hannah explains.

Livie glances at her out of the corner of her eye as she maintains a steady speed on the freeway.

"Well, I'm glad you're dealing with that one and not me. Say, is that a newspaper sticking out of your bag?"

"Ah yes. I almost forgot about it. I scooped it up from the coffee room before leaving. It's the *Washington Post*. I haven't seen an actual printed newspaper like this in years. It could be a real memento in the future. I was thinking it'll be good fodder for the discussion tonight with everyone. Would you like me to read you the headline?" Hannah pauses for effect.

"What!? Was that a question?! Of course, read it!"

Hannah puts on her best radio voice, articulating each word like its own statement.

"Flights grounded. Borders and markets closed. Banks crippled. Chaos everywhere."

"Oh geez, they couldn't sound just a tad more hopeful?"

"Well, the first sentence under the headline reads, 'How long is this going to last? Will the internet be back tomorrow?'"

"That must be referring to Brant's statement."

"For sure, but I also picked up something else in the coffee room today."

Hannah pulls out a sheet of bright-colored paper covered in handwritten bold block writing.

"What's that?"

"One of the staff brought a few copies of these in. She said she got them from a local coffee shop. It's about a rally planned in front of the Washington Monument tomorrow. 'Keep it turned off,' it says. The rally is to tell government to stop trying to get the internet back—that the world is a better place without it."

Livie parks the car as Hannah reads the last part on the colored paper.

"What?! A rally to keep the internet off? Who would organize such a thing?"

"It doesn't say. It just says the rally will start at the Washington Monument at 4 p.m. tomorrow night."

"Well, whoever put that out clearly hasn't read the *Washington Post*."

"Perhaps. So, what do you think? Want to go?"

"What?! To the rally!?"

Chapter 4

Whose Side Are You On?

Livie looks out into the dark sky—the clouds brooding over the city as they threaten to release their pent-up loads. She registers her friends' voices as a hum in the background while her mind pinwheels through the activities of the day and the uncertainty of the future. The image of the joyous surprise on Annie's face when Livie left them at Hugo's is swirled into a cocktail of images from her day, along with confusion over what to expect next in her life.

As a lightning strike over the Washington Monument illuminates a section of the city, Livie feels the touch of Hannah's hand on her arm.

"Hey, you gonna join our tribe?"

"Our tribe?"

"Yeah, we should have a name, don't you think? You, me, Finn, Peet, Bo, and Saba. Our tribe."

Livie snorts a laugh.

"Yeah...you know how to reel me in, Hannah. Of course I'll join *our tribe,*" Livie looks back out the window, "I'm just watching the storm that's brewing."

Hannah lifts her head to join Livie in taking in the view outside the window.

"It certainly looks to be quite the show. Actually, we're waiting for Saba to arrive, and then Finn's going to read to us from the *Washington Post*."

For Livie, the novelty of an actual printed newspaper has been lost to the events of the day; events that rain down into her being and puncture her ability to concentrate.

"Okay...I'm coming over to join the tribe."

As Livie turns, she hears Preet's excited voice crack.

"Saba's here."

Livie catches Saba's eye and quickly looks away, shamed by the confidence in the other woman's gaze.

"Saba, you've made it!"

"Of course, Hannah. I wouldn't miss this. Can't wait to hear about everyone's day without the internet."

Finn looks up from the *Washington Post* newspaper that he has spread over the island in the kitchen, and his quizzical stare latches onto Hannah, looking for instructions.

"Well Finn is anxious to read excerpts from the *Post*, but maybe tell us about your day first?"

"Oh...okay. Well, most of my day was spent trying to hunt down information on what the government is going to do with the borders and travel. You probably know they have pretty much frozen all that. With no ability to scan passports, they don't want anyone leaving or coming into the country. Especially coming in."

Saba pauses, feeling as if the room is moving while everyone looks at her. Preet cuts through the silence.

"So, what did you find out then?"

"Nothing. Not really, anyway. I think...do you mind if I sit? It's been a long day, and I haven't eaten since this morning."

Livie finds a strange satisfaction rushing over her at Saba's sudden show of vulnerability, and she springs forward to grab one of the kitchen chairs.

As Saba sits, sipping water between nibbles of cheese, the details of her day spill from her as if a valve has been released.

Her day began with a call from one of the companies she represents. They were wondering if the grounding of air travel was just what the world needed for the environment and if something could be done to keep it that way. Another company phoned, desperate to travel and looking to get a special pass from the government to fly. The competing interests of her various clients marooned her passion for the work.

Livie takes in each of Saba's expressions, grinding them through her mind, assessing her level of trust in their new friend. The rejections Livie has experienced in her life have made her guarded, hesitant to trust too freely, and something about Saba sits in the pit of her stomach like an indigestible substance.

Finn starts reading the headlines from the *Washington Post* out loud. His voice crescendos each time he moves to a different headline, projecting a growing excitement, or alarm.

"No cash, no buy."

"Travel frozen, visitors stranded!"

"Stock market halted!!"

"Stampede at the banks brings ambulances!!!"

Hannah walks up behind Finn and rests her hand on his right shoulder. Her fingers crawl over the bone to the crevice close to his neck and dig in, applying pressure to stop his momentum.

"Finn, I think we can all imagine the headlines based on the obstacles we all faced today. Is there an interesting article you could read to us?"

Finn starts flipping through the pages, slightly pausing at each before he stops at the editorial page. Hannah lifts her hand off his shoulder and points to a headline that catches her eye.

"There's one! 'Keep it off or turn it back on.' Looks like a good debate. Read that one to us, Finn."

"Okay, well, it looks like an editorial that presents a deliberation on the issues, with opposing views of for and against the internet's existence."

Saba looks at Finn as he chooses his words, wondering if he wishes he wrote one side or the other of the debate.

Finn pauses and looks up at everyone for a brief moment, like a storyteller building the suspense. He clears his throat, preparing his sonorous voice to fill the room, looks back down, and starts reading.

> *"If we were to take a public poll and ask if people would like to see the internet come back on or not, the results would be overwhelming. It IS the topic of discussion wherever people congregate. It is at the top of everyone's minds. Often it is framed as a question. When is the internet coming back on? It's not a debate in most circles. People want the internet back. They want their life with the internet back.*
>
> *But this is only the second day without the internet. Will those discussions change as people experience a new normalcy of life without the internet? Many reading this have only known a world with the internet, where so many things are a simple click away. But throughout most of history, the internet did not exist, and many societies functioned quite well without it. Maybe even better, some might argue. Not convinced? Below, from two of our writers, we offer you the debate. Internet or no internet? First up is Thomas Brackett, who articulates the popular reasons for returning to an internet world, with thoughts you may not have contemplated. After Brackett, we give you Abelina Balogun and her ardent style presenting the opposing views."*

Finn looks up and pauses, as if measuring the level of the suspense crackling in the room. Saba looks into his eyes, trying to read them, surmising that Finn is a maven of information and has likely already read the arguments on the pages he holds. Will the inflections in his voice give away which side he is on?

The silence in the room waits for Finn to continue as he clears his throat, looks down, and fills the room with his baritone voice again.

"Why we need the internet back
Thomas Brackett

Who turned out the lights?

We had a world with brightness and clarity. A world that was alive with a buzz of activity, a connectedness that brought families and friends together and expanded across the globe.

We had commerce that allowed previous enemies to trade with each other and brought goods from around the world to our own doorstep. We had a world with medical advancements that enabled access to the same medical care and often the same doctor, whether in Bangladesh or New York. We had a world that was principally peaceful compared to other eras, largely due to the worldwide communication and trade network that the internet provided. We had a world where cultural differences could be recognized and even celebrated without the deep racism and discrimination we saw in past generations. The internet, with easier access to world travel, broke down walls of prejudice and gave everyone a window into lives and cultures significantly different than their own. It has deepened our understanding of one another, even in a world of diverse views, outlooks, goals, cultures, and experiences.

The internet enabled us to produce things with precision and at a speed that would have blown the minds of our ancestors. A world—our world—that enabled each of us to explore our own creativity and individuality in likeminded groups and allowed us to grow our wealth as individuals, as a nation and as a race. A place where we could realize our true potential. The world truly was at our feet.

Then the lights were turned off and it all stopped. Our world fell apart and abruptly became a confusing and terrifying place to live. Where there was order, we now have disorder. The worst parts of human behavior, so bent by our culture and the environment in which we live, have surfaced. You know this to be true because if you haven't experienced it yourself already, you have seen the pictures and heard the stories of stampedes—every person for themselves—that have been the scene at every bank. Like walking by a street with a series of broken windows, this is an environment that invites disorder, looting, and violence. It has brought an unnerving distrust of every stranger on the street. Kindness and common courtesy are disappearing from our communities.

Perhaps, like so many, you are scouring your fridge, freezer, and cupboards to see how long you can survive with what you have—if you can't buy any food for a while. You don't have any cash and haven't carried cash for a long time, but suddenly it has become the only currency in the internetless world we have been plunged into.

The darkness has taken much from all of us. The headlines of this newspaper tell the stories. Airplanes are grounded. Borders are closed. Your bank and credit cards are useless.

The stock market has shut down, robbing many of the necessary access to their money. The friends you only knew online have suddenly disappeared from your circle, as if they all just vanished, leaving you with no evidence of their existence in your life.

What else have you lost in less than forty-eight hours? Answer this question out loud. I can almost hear each of you, screaming or weeping as you list off all the things that have disappeared to be replaced by an empty void.

As the images of those things are rollercoasting through your mind and taking your emotions for a ride, your private information is being exploited. Yes, you read that right. All those things that you have stored 'in the cloud,' much of which you can't access now, are in the hands of those who did this. Your pictures. Your videos. Your text messages. Your emails. The record of your online habits. Your passwords. Your bank account. Your credit cards. Your friends' contact information. Your life.

We can't simply rebuild our world without the internet. That would cost lives. Estimates are already rolling in—a third of humanity will be wiped out as food production and economies screech to a halt. Then there is the devasting effect this has had on our mental health. This is worse than the global pandemic of 2020 and 2021.

When the internet was suddenly turned off the night of our election, it was alarming. It was rude. Annoying. Shocking. Disturbing. The fear is settling in. That fear is robbing us every hour that this goes on. It's dominating our minds, taking our sleep with it, and depositing many into a state of depression.

The loss of the internet has deeply disrupted our lives on a personal level, but the most devastating is the impact on our communities, our nations, and our world. The shutting down of the internet is an act of war. We haven't had another world war, in large part due to the interconnectedness of our world—which the internet has provided. We had truly reached a stage of a global ecology, a global economy, and global scientific advancement that has benefited us all. The global sharing of information has meant that a war couldn't bring the victors the economic prosperity or political power that it could have done in the past. The data-driven information economy is something we all share. Well, something we all shared until it was taken from us by those who shut down the internet and stole it. They call themselves 'The Friendly World Network,' and like many propaganda machines we have seen in the past, they are quite the opposite of what they call themselves. They are power-hungry warmongers.

We need to find the robbers, the culprits, the warmongers that turned the lights out and put them back on. Bring us back the light!

Why we can live without the internet
Abelina Balogun

Let's all take a breath. Breathe. Inhale. Exhale. Feel the life-giving oxygen in the air expand your lungs and then release again.

When something devastating happens in our lives, it helps if we can stop and take time to breathe. To relax, take stock of where we are at, and reflect on what is truly valuable and important to us. It's a time when we reach out to those we love and trust. The folks who help us sort through our feelings, make sense of the chaos around us, and join us in imaging our lives past the wreckage that threatens to submerge us into a life of despair.

In the calmness of taking those breaths, I can see clearly what my life was like <u>with</u> the internet. How suffocating, mentally exhausting, and all-consuming it all was. Sure, I could have just turned it off. If only it didn't have those addictive properties of always offering more, the fear of missing something, and the demands of our culture that simply wouldn't permit us to 'go off the grid.' At least not for very long.

The internet cluttered our lives with: information overload, stored pictures, data on our lives that could fill several libraries, and an abundance of online 'friends' that are far too numerous to truly maintain what we know friendship should be. A person or people that we can be genuine with, are loyal to and appreciative of. A person that we want to be more of a giver towards than a taker. Often those are things like: a simple smile, a hug, a kind word, a listening ear, a shared meal, or a shoulder to cry on. Someone we love, someone we can be honest and real with. Someone we have shared experiences with. How many of our online 'friends' fit any of those characteristics? The internet promised connectiveness, but more often delivered a prison of loneliness instead.

We can do better. We can have a better world. A better life for all of us. As with other life-changing events that have happened to us, the life waiting for us beyond the wreckage of the internet is greener, happier, and more fulfilling.

Perhaps you are thinking, 'okay, maybe a lot of that's true, but I still just want to get the internet back and my life with it.'"

Saba studies Finn as he reads and sees the small veins pulsing in the side of his neck. His tone is precise, and he is speaking with purpose. *This isn't a reading,* she thinks. *This is a speech.*

"I completely agree with that sentiment. I have found myself screaming for the internet to come back on too.

But when I calmly analyze why I feel that way, it's primarily because of the sudden jolt of shock the loss has brought. What if it hadn't been so sudden and we knew it was coming and could plan for it?

Usually, it's the small, slow, incremental things that change our lives more than some major events. If you decide you want to run a marathon and are not a runner, you have to first learn to run a mile, then two, then three, and build up to the 26.2 miles. Each step feels like an accomplishment along the way, giving you encouragement and momentum to go further the next time.

The internet suddenly shutting down has not given us the joy and the accomplishment we would have experienced had we incrementally weaned ourselves off it to declutter our lives.

In 1871, the City of Chicago comprised sixty-five thousand buildings. It had glorious courthouses, churches, opera houses, emporiums, hotels, houses, and businesses. Many of those proud structures had historical significance, including the courthouse, where Abraham Lincoln's body lay in state. It was a glorious city 'of everlasting pine, shingles, shams, and veneers,' with most of its structures, like the roads around them, made of wood. Then the great fire of October 8, 1871 rolled torridly throughout the city, and in just over twenty-four hours left it in ashes. Imagine being there and watching the place where you lived and grew up, where your memories and experiences reside, all go up in smoke. Literally. One newspaper at the time described it as 'The Greatest Calamity of the Age.'

What came out of those ashes in Chicago was a massive rebuild—a coming together of people and a sense of community like they had never experienced. Within six weeks, the city boasted two hundred new buildings of brick and stone. That was just the beginning of what is now one of the most beautiful, cherished cities in America. The great fire of 1871 was the catalyst for that.

I am sure that, as the residents of Chicago looked at their burnt city, they stood in shock and bewilderment and maybe despair—like many of us feel today with the loss of the internet. But once the people accepted their fate, it became the catalyst for something far better than what they had lost.

We have not moved on yet and are stuck because too many of us have not accepted the loss of the internet. We need to do that. Then we can get on with the job of building the new and better world without the internet. Many of us are caught up in fear right now. Fear that has crowded out our thoughts and left many with just a dull rhythm of getting through the day. We have forgotten the force of the resilience of the human spirit. We need to see past our fear and give courage some space. Courage—the opposite of fear—will loosen the grip of dread in our lives and bring hope.

After reading this, I don't expect the scales to suddenly fall from your eyes and for you to convert to a non-internet-world champion.

Let's all breathe and get some perspective here. We have been presented with a great opportunity to remake our world, our society, and our lives. We can choose the path of a better life with real connectivity with those we care about and a saner, friendlier place to live, work, and play. A place where rank, status, and wealth hold less sway. The loss of the internet has levelled the playing field and given us a chance at a better life. Like the folks in Chicago in 1871, we will survive, move on, and create something better."

As he finishes the last line, Finn lets his voice trail off—following it with a pause that allows the echo of the words to hang in the air. Livie, staring at him like an eagle looking down at its prey, prematurely interrupts the silence.

"Well sorry you couldn't have read that last one with more enthusiasm, Finn."

Saba's shoulders, as if suddenly pricked, stiffen at Livie's sarcastic remark.

She looks at Finn as the ripples of Livie's words wash across his face, the smug smirk draining from him, leaving a vulnerable child in its wake.

Saba glances briefly at Livie, then moves to Finn's right with four deliberate steps, her heels striking the floor. She leans down and whispers in his ear, "That's exactly how I would read it."

Saba pauses briefly, as if there is more to come. She swings her head around to face him; their noses almost touch, and his lips part as if waiting to feel her wet lips against his.

She winks at him, moves her face to his other ear, and tickles it with her breath as she speaks.

"I think fate may yet bring you to your destiny."

Silence enters the room, pirouetting among them in waves, its awkwardness hovering. Each of the tribe's minds are churning with which side they are on. Livie feels the reproach of the silence and looks at Hannah, her eyes pleading. The silence takes another dance around the room, making its presence known.

Hannah finally dismisses it.

"So...what time is the rally tomorrow?"

Chapter 5

Storm's Brewing

Livie pulls the zipper up on the back of the baby-blue shoe, stands up straight, and takes in her own reflection in the mirror. Twisting her body sideways, her eyes follow the path from the end of her pastel-pink skirt, down her legs, and to the heels that infuse her with a wave of confidence. Her thoughts jump to Hannah. She can already hear her excited voice when she sees Livie wearing the shoes at the rally.

Livie wonders if her bond with Hannah will grip as tightly after the rally, or even at the start of it when Hannah sees her on the opposing side. Or perhaps there is a middle ground she can navigate in the debate?

The sudden, sharp *rrring* from her cell phone interrupts her thoughts. She reserves the distinctive analogue ringing sound for one person. Her mother. Its sound captures her thoughts and takes her back to the many condescending and critical words that kept her company for so many nights. She allows the five rings to play their chorus before her voicemail picks it up.

Eager to regain control of her thoughts, she picks up the phone and taps the button to speed dial.

Just hearing Hannah's voice brings her warmth and comfort.

'Hey, I was just thinking of you."

"Really? Anything I should know?"

"Just that I'm glad you're my friend."

"Thanks Hannah. I can't imagine how I'd survive without you as a friend."

"The feeling is mutual, Livie. I'm a little worried about you after last night though, are you okay?"

Livie's phone lights up with a notice of another call trying to break in. Her mom again. *Fitting*, she thinks. "You okay?" she can now hear in unison from Hannah and her mom. Two voices. The same question. Two different meanings. One supportive; the other needy.

"Livie? You there?"

"Yes...yes. Sorry, another call was coming in."

"Oh, I can go. We can chat at the rally."

"No. I mean, please don't. It's just my mom calling."

"Oh. Have you heard from her since...?"

"No...well, yes, the next morning. I was just a sounding board for her rant about how scared she was. I don't know why she's calling me now. She probably needs me for something."

"Livie, just take her call. You know she'll keep calling anyway, and then it will be on your mind. Take the call and call me back after it. We'll get to chat before the rally."

"I know you're right, but I..."

"I'm hanging up now. Take the call and then phone me back, okay?"

"Okay."

Livie stares at her phone as Hannah's voice suddenly disappears. Her phone is ringing, but she just stares and listens to it with some amusement. Her mom's timing is so often disruptive. She wants to listen to her mom's voice message before phoning her back, so she allows it to ring until it stops. When the phone goes suddenly quiet, she gives it a few seconds before hitting the voicemail on her phone.

"Hi sweetie. It's Mom of course. You okay? The disease that has hit the internet has left me feeling marooned somewhere by myself. Parts of it I like, but right now I'm feeling I hate it. But hey, I have an idea that I think would be good for both of us, and I want to tell you about a change I have made. Give me a call back. Soon please."

Livie listens to the voice message again, tracking the inflections in her mother's voice in search of a hint of what she might have in mind. "Soon please," with a hint of a whine at the end of please means she's anxious about something. "A change" she has made hardly registers—Livie has heard that before.

Livie stares into the room for answers, and almost like an echo, silence returns. Whatever her mom wants to talk about, it is certain to be something that leads to a familiar destination. A demand for some daughter and mother time alone.

Livie has regretted each time she has given in to these requests. Requests that come packaged as an inherent obligation because she is her mother's daughter. The daughter she feels abandoned her when "she needed her most." That guilt card has been used so many times, Livie hardly recognizes it anymore. She just accepts it for what it is. Hannah will remind her that she was just sixteen when she left her mom's—thus "abandoning" her. Hannah will emphasize the fact that this was after her mom had "rescued" her from foster care a year prior. Foster care she was forced into because of her mom's behavior and inability to manage. It doesn't matter. She is still her mother, and that somehow comes with obligations Livie can't shake. It's like a piece of clothing that has been sewn into her skin. But this time, she tells herself, she will shed it. She has her own issues to sort through, and her mom will have to figure her issues out herself.

With aggression, she pulls up her mom's name on her phone and hits the dial button.

"Oh Liv, I'm so glad you called. I was just about to try again. This is such a dreadful time, with so much uncertainty. I feel as if I have lost so much over the last few days. I can't contact many of my friends. So many of them I only have contact with through the internet, and now it feels like they are lost forever. But I have some good things happening too I want to tell you about, and now I have you! I'm so thankful for that. You okay?"

"I'm doing okay, Mom. I have friends who are not just online."

Livie didn't intend the dig at her mom, but she has long tired of her mom not taking responsibility for her own life. The remark just seeped out of the pool of resentment within her.

"You've always been gifted with the ability to make friends better than me, Liv. I'm happy for you. I've gotten better at that though; I have to tell you. Did you get the message I left?"

Livie knows this is her mother's way of hoping that Livie will initiate the discussion about them getting together. She's determined not to take the bait.

"No, I thought I'd just call you back instead."

"Oh, okay sweetie. Well, I have a request to make of you."

A request? That's not the language Livie was expecting. She was braced for a more definitive statement of what they were going to do and when.

"Okay...what is it, Mom?"

"Well, you remember that place we camped on Deerfield Lake by Charleston years ago?"

"Of course I do, Mom."

Her mom is referring to the place of some of Livie's dearest childhood memories. While most of her childhood memories haunt her dreams or throw up roadblocks preventing any advancement of her self-confidence, Deerfield Lake stands out, mostly, as a warm blanket of memories that she can run to for comfort. The reason was her childhood friend, Twiggy, who she called Twinkie. She went along on a few of their trips, some even while Livie was still in foster care. Twinkie's presence made the place come alive for her. She remembers her friend and the bond they made there to be friends forever.

Her last experience at Deerfield, when she was sixteen, she'd like to erase from her memory; so, When she reminisces about her times at Deerfield, she thinks only of the good times. She thinks of her and Twinkie. Memories of those times flood her with such emotional intensity that it's like it happened just a weekend ago. Twinkie's sudden passing five years after their last visit to the lake gave those memories a peaceful place for Livie to escape to.

The mention of Deerfield softens Livie as she listens to her mom's request that they go back there together. Perhaps returning there could calm the restlessness she feels?

"We can stay at the cabin at Deerfield Lake. It's a place where I've recovered some peace and silence in my life, and we could plan for a few days? Together...at the cabin and lake, I mean. Would you be interested in doing that?"

Livie lets the ensuing silence linger as she processes the invitation. Is this a real request or some duty she has to fulfill? Could she actually say no, or would that just bring out the well-worn guilt card? As Livie mulls over these matters in her head, her mom jumps in to fill the silence.

"I understand if you don't want to, Liv. I'm sure you're already consumed with other things. Sorting out this non-internet life...and maybe the memories of Twiggy are too much?"

"Oh Mom, no...that wouldn't be a reason for not going. I just have a lot else going on right now. Can't wrap my brain around going away somewhere at this point."

"Okay, I understand sweetie. I'll leave the offer open though. Let me know if you change your mind."

"Thanks Mom. I should go, I have plans to get together with Hannah."

"Okay, I won't keep you dear. Love you. Bye."

As soon as her mom hangs up, Livie looks at her phone as if it offers a pathway between the mother she knows and the one whose number just disappeared from the screen.

No demands. No authoritative tone in her mom's voice. When she didn't just agree, there was no guilt card played.

Livie takes a couple of healthy gulps of air, filling her lungs and cheeks. The liberation she expects to fill her is somehow tethered to the need to be wanted and connected to her mom.

Livie picks up her phone and sends a text.

"A cabin at Deerfield for a couple of days sounds wonderful. I'm just too busy with lots going on right now, maybe we can plan another time? Love you."

Livie looks at the message again. She deletes the "Love you" and replaces it with "Thanks for the idea, Mom, hopefully we can make it work sometime," then hits send. Unable to escape the thoughts swirling in her mind, she sends a second text, this one to Hannah.

"Hey, let's just chat at the rally, okay? I have a few things to do beforehand. I hope you don't get angry at the sign I am bringing."

She stares at the screen again, deletes the last sentence, and hits send.

She is fearful that if she talks to Hannah now, she will answer many questions that are not asked, and her responses may be different tomorrow. The cloak of vulnerability that she often donned in the past still lurks in the shadows.

She decides to combat the feelings by mustering her courage and channeling her energy into making a sign for the rally.

Chapter 6

A Rally in Support of an Internetless World

Four Months later, March 2033, St. Paddy's Day.

Since the last rally they attended nearly four months ago, Livie's relationship with Hannah has been defined by a series of disputes. Some petty, some that she maintained were important principles she couldn't back down from. "Values before tribe," she told herself. It's how she governed her life. It just never applied to Hannah before. They often had heated debates about ideas and opinions, but they always shared the same core values—or so it seemed.

It all started at that rally four months earlier when they were clearly on opposite sides of the internet debate. Livie knew going to that rally that they would have differing views—it was obvious from the signs they both made, never mind the debates between them. But their friends were also divided. Finn and Preet, like Livie, had signs in support of bringing back the internet, though Finn didn't seem to display his with the enthusiasm she expected. Saba and Hannah had signs in support of keeping the internet off, and Bo, though declaring he was on the fence, had a sign that seemed to support the internetless world. In fact, Livie laughed at Bo's cheeky sign, even though she disagreed with its premise. Thinking about it now, she still finds it funny: "I never had any online friends. But I'm friendly." *So much like Bo,* she thinks. Anti-establishment and non-conformist in a non-advertised way. At the time, the debates between Hannah and Livie were still lighthearted and often laced with playful mockery of each other's views.

When their "tribe" left for the rally that day, they were all laughing at each other's signs. They may have had various views in their little group, but they were all still friends and still referred to themselves as a tribe. After the rally, Bo and Preet were still together, and Finn and Saba had actually, and somewhat startlingly, become very close friends. But a divide started to form between Livie and Hannah—born from hurtful comments—which became more of a chasm in the months following the rally.

They had a terse exchange at the rally. Livie called Hannah naïve, and Hannah called Livie stubborn and closed-minded. No one ever called Livie closed-minded before. She always prided herself on being open to new ideas and accepting people as they are. She was the one who could accuse someone of being closed-minded, like her mother for example, but not her. Hannah, of all people, knew this. Livie responded quickly, calling the loss of the internet "a cruel joke." To her, a world without the internet wasn't some new idea. This was an effort to go back to the Dark Ages, and she told Hannah that. The argument soon turned into a shouting match. Before they departed that day, Hannah turned and took a picture of Livie's sign, as if she needed the pic as a peg to hang the memory of the day on. When Livie shouted her accusatory question of what Hannah needed the picture for, Hannah's response came in a lecturing, condescending tone Livie had never been on the receiving end of before. "You will need this to remind yourself of your thoughtless view one day," came her sharp answer. Those words remained etched somewhere in Livie's brain, surfacing at times to fuel her anger about what happened at the rally.

Despite all that, Livie phoned Hannah the day after the rally. The conversation started out friendly, but it quickly turned nasty when Livie told Hannah that she couldn't help out at her work anymore. Hannah's response, "That's your loss Livie, I was just trying to help you out," shocked Livie into silence before she simply hung up. No goodbye. Livie reached out to Annie though, as she felt some responsibility towards her to make sure things were going well at Hugo's. She and Annie had several pleasant conversations and even met up one time. She felt a connection with Annie. Then, less than a month after the abrupt ending of their phone call, Hannah called her. When Livie saw her number on the call display, she was hopeful. Maybe Hannah would apologize, and they would have a good cry together and get over the rift between them.

But Hannah's voice and the purpose of her call still rings in Livie's ears whenever she thinks about it. After they exchanged pleasant greetings, Hannah's voice turned stern and hard.

"Livie, you're not to contact Annie anymore. You met her as a client and you as the social worker. It's not appropriate, and if you continue, we will issue a cease-and-desist order against you."

Livie asked if that was what Annie wanted, and Hannah simply said, "It doesn't matter," before hanging up. Livie has avoided Annie since, even though Annie phoned her a few times.

When Hannah contacted her a week earlier to ask if she wanted to get together again and suggested meeting up for the rally at the Washington Monument on St. Paddy's Day, Livie initially declined. She was still working out what she wanted to do with her life if the internet didn't come back on and didn't need to add more conflict to the mix. But Hannah's voice sounded sincere and friendly, and there didn't seem to be a catch. Livie knew she could really use the friendship she used to have with Hannah in her life, so she phoned her back. They talked about going to the rally, and Livie asked if Hannah was going to be carrying a sign in support of keeping the internet off. Hannah responded with, "You know the answer to that Livie, but it doesn't mean we can't be friends again."

So that was it. Livie committed to meeting Hannah at the rally. When she later read that the rally was partly due to Brant's recent announcement that the government was working with others around the world and that they were "very close to restoring the internet," she decided she would want to go even if she wasn't meeting up with Hannah. Livie still has a deep disdain for Brant, but she wants the internet back. Desperately so. She hasn't been working, other than that day with Hannah. Living off the government's "bridge money for those unemployed due to the loss of the internet" is not her style or what she wanted for her life. After watching her mom too willingly accept government handouts, she promised she would never do that. She justifies breaking her promise due to the catastrophic event of the loss of the internet, but she has had enough. So she is going to the rally now, regardless. She even made a new sign for it too.

Now the day has arrived, and she is at the rally. It feels like early spring out. Birds are chirping, and buds are starting to show on the trees. The air is cool and crisp, but things are warming up from the mid-morning sun. Spring's newness has brought a renewed hope for a better world. For Livie, maybe that means she and Hannah can patch up their relationship.

Holding her latte from Green Planet, Livie stands across the street from Monument Park, in the spot where she and Hannah have agreed to meet. She feels a shiver of nerves as she watches a swarm of people passing by—her eyes on the hunt for the familiar smiling face of Hannah. Her sign is rolled up in her handbag. She can feel the buzz around her as she sees many people with signs professing opposing views of what the world needs and should look like.

One holds up a sign above the crowd as some broad proclamation—the writing in bright, bold, pink colors: "No Internet, No peace."

As if to crowd that out, another sign, clearly being carried on a stick, pops up above that sign with its message: "Keep the intrusion of the internet off!"

A cacophony of voices debating the issues is rising in the streets as Livie looks at her watch, wondering where Hannah is. They were supposed to meet here twenty minutes ago. Could something have happened to her? Did she change her mind and is now going to just stand Livie up? She looks at her watch again and sees that another five minutes have passed. Looking around, she sees something she didn't expect. Many people are gathering in large groups with anti-internet signs, and there are a lot of hugging and smiles going around. They are a bigger group than she expected, and they don't seem to carry the anger she was bracing herself for. Could it be the same with Hannah? But then, where is she?

Livie is getting ready to leave, planning to make her way to the rally alone in the hope of finding Hannah there somehow (something that seems as likely as convincing everyone in the crowd to agree on the internet issue). She lets out a sigh, making her shoulders rise and then sink, as she decides to leave anyway. She sees the crowd heading towards the park, visualizes her path, and steps forward, when she feels cold hands wrapped around her eyes from behind. "Guess who?"

Livie turns around, relief and excitement flooding through her. "Hannah!" They hold each other in an extended hug, hanging on as if this may be the last time for such an embrace.

"So, did you bring a sign?"

"Of course!" Livie motions to the rolled-up piece of poster paper in her handbag. Hannah pulls out her sign and unfurls it with her hands. Though it is too large for her to hold both ends to stretch it out entirely, she does it with flair as if making a grand announcement.

The sign's florescent pink background makes the bold black letters jump off the page at you.

FREEDOM = NO INTERNET

Livie reacts like the letters leaped out and struck her on the arm. Her shoulders stiffen, and she takes a sudden step back. Taking a beat to tell herself to not start a row, she keeps her tone inquisitive.

"Wow, that's pretty bold. Do you think that's true, Hannah? How is it that we have *more* freedom now that the internet is down?"

Hannah bristles at the negative response and answers in a terse, lecturing tone.

"It's not *just* down, Livie. It's off. And yes, I do." Livie takes a step back and looks right into Hannah's eyes, searching for the friendly softness she was hoping for.

"Hey, I was just asking a question. I thought we were going to try to be friendly about this?"

Hannah reaches out and touches her arm.

"You're right Livie, I should try and answer your question. For me...I'm...well, you know what? I think if you listen to some of the speeches today, they will answer that question better than I can."

"Okay...so you know something about the speeches planned for this rally? Hannah, are you involved..."

"No! I mean, I'm not involved in anything, I'm just here to support the cause."

"The cause?" Livie asks the question with a challenging edge to her tone.

"That's probably the wrong word. I just mean the efforts to keep the internet off."

Amidst the noise from the crowds of people around them, silence descends between them as if the next words spoken would determine if they walk together or apart. Neither of them seems willing to puncture the silence for fear of what may come out.

A shout in the crowd disrupts their silent standoff.

"Hannah!!"

Hannah turns her head towards the voice, which is still coming from a distance. Livie doesn't move.

"Who's that?" she asks, her tone even and stoic.

"Oh, just a friend. Sally."

"You made plans to meet someone else here as well?"

"No, not a plan Livie. I only made specific plans with you."

"*Specific* plans?"

The two friends who just hugged as if they haven't seen each other for years now stare at one another like inconvenient acquaintances. Hannah turns her head to see how close the approaching person is, then turns to Livie.

"Say, can I see your sign?"

"You sure you don't want to just wait until we get to the rally? Keep the suspense alive for you?"

"Oh come on Livie, I showed you mine. I think it would be fair that you at least reciprocate that, if nothing else."

Livie looks down at her handbag, purposely avoiding Hannah's eyes as she pulls out the sign.

"Of course, and we agreed not to let this stop us from being friends, right?" Live hands her sign to Hannah.

Hannah holds it up in front of her and snorts in disdain as she reads it out loud.

"Bring the Internet back. Bring us back our liberty."

Hannah looks up at Livie and hands the sign back to her. "Hey, I'm sorry I reacted that way. I want us to be friends. I guess, for me, it's just that I have never felt as much liberty as I have since the internet went down."

Livie sees that Hannah isn't going to put the debate aside for this, so why should she? She smiles and responds.

"I didn't realize liberty could be..." Livie is abruptly interrupted by the sudden appearance of Sally, who barges between them and hugs Hannah.

"Sally, this is my friend Livie."

Sally, a little out of breath, introduces herself to Livie and then turns to Hannah to see her sign, which they hold up together. Livie sees that the sign appears to have been made to be held by two people. In fact, it seems to be too much for one person, and clearly Hannah couldn't have expected Livie to hold that sign with her. Livie thinks perhaps she should just leave, when Sally turns to her.

"How about you Livie? Do you have a sign?"

"I do. But I'd prefer to wait until the rally starts to reveal it."

"Well then, shall we get a place close to the stage?"

Hannah shoots a quick look at Livie and responds before Livie can.

"Actually Sally, Livie and I were going..."

"Hannah, it's okay," Livie cuts in. "Don't worry about me. You and Sally should just carry on. I want to get some more coffee anyway. Maybe I'll see you back here later."

Livie doesn't wait for a response as she turns—as if heading back to Green Planet. Hannah and Sally head in the opposite direction towards the Washington Monument, where a stage is set up and people are clearly getting ready for the speeches.

After a few seconds, Livie turns around and follows at a short distance behind the other two women. Something pulls at her to find out what Hannah's involvement will be at the rally.

Hannah and Sally abruptly stop at the edge of the intersection between a circular walkway and the path to the Washington Monument. It is clearly a deliberate action and a specific place. Livie hesitates and stops about twenty feet behind them, half expecting Hannah to turn around and accuse Livie of following them.

Hannah and Sally stand there chatting. Livie can overhear parts of their conversation, but not much. At one point she hears Hannah mention her name and tell Sally, "She isn't one of us." Livie can hear sadness in her voice as she says it. Livie looks up at the stage, as she assumes Hannah is waiting for the right moment to pull out her sign, when she hears an oddly familiar voice that she can't quite place coming from the side.

Livie almost gives herself away when she shrieks, "Shit!' She covers her mouth, glad they didn't hear her, and doesn't turn to look at the person arriving for fear of being noticed. But the voice, which Livie can't quite place, seems vaguely familiar.

"Hannah! I'm so glad I found you. I thought I might not be able to in this crowd. What a gathering."

Hannah kneels down and greets the three children that are close to the side of the woman who has just arrived.

Livie takes a long, hard look at the woman and realizes with bewilderment who it is. A more confident and assured person than the one she met in Hannah's office less than four months ago, before Hannah told her not to contact her again.

Livie stands in stunned silence as she watches Annie. It is like she is witnessing a magical transformation. The disheveled, scared-looking woman who looked like she might jump or bolt if you talked to her has been replaced by this strong woman looking Hannah in the eyes, smiling with her head held high. Livie didn't recognize Annie's voice right away, as the woman now spoke with certainty and confidence instead of mumbling down to her feet. Livie heard from Hugo that Annie was doing much better and had made some big changes in her life, but seeing her like this, in front of her, was still startling.

Livie stands and watches the scene, now filled with pride. She knows she made a difference in Annie's life that day. Seeing how quickly and profoundly it has impacted Annie, she's captivated in wonderment.

Livie steps forward, deciding she's going to swallow her pride, say hi to Annie, and at least be civil towards Hannah. As she moves within several feet of them, she hopes to catch Annie's eye. She sees Annie reach down, almost looking her way, but the moment is lost, as Annie doesn't see her. Almost at the same time, Hannah starts to unroll her sign and hands the other end to Annie. Livie freezes in her tracks. She watches as Annie turns towards the stage and joins Hannah in holding the sign up over their heads, both their backs squarely to Livie. She hears Hannah's voice.

"Hey, just so you're not surprised, there's a possibility that you may see Livie here."

"Really? I'd love to see her again! I bet she would be proud of the changes in me."

"Sorry Annie. I'm not sure about that. Livie is on the other side of this. She wants the internet back and is quite angry at anyone who opposes that. She'd likely say something nasty to you if she saw you holding this sign with me."

Livie stands frozen, like her feet are stuck in cement. The anger boils up inside of her, and she wants to spill it all out over Hannah. She'd be justified to, she tells herself. It was Hannah who showed hostility and anger towards her for her sign. How dare she. Turning Annie against her is really low.

~~~~~~

Hannah is disappointed in herself for participating in another hostile exchange with Livie. She thought she had her emotions under control coming here and planned for a friendly exchange. She knew Livie wouldn't share her views, but somehow, she thought she would come with a more open mind. She's angry at herself as she reflects on how she responded to Livie after she saw her negative body language towards her sign. She shouldn't have lashed out. Oh, how she wishes she could redo that response. Then it didn't help when Sally showed up unexpectedly, at the worst time. Livie must have assumed she was set up.

Hannah looks over at Annie, and it only adds to her regret. She wanted to surprise Livie with Annie joining them. She thought it
~~~~~~

would help the mood. Instead she allowed her temper to spill over, so she turned Annie against Livie. What a mess this is.

Holding her sign high, Hannah looks towards the Monument, hoping it can distract her enough to keep the tears inside. Since she received that package in the mail, she has been on edge and uncertain of herself. How did they—whoever they are—get all that personal information about her? How do they know about her covert actions at work? At least, that is how she sees the things she did—covert actions for the better good. Every time she would slip into the electronic files she didn't have official access to, she saw herself as a modern-day Robin Hood. Helping the disadvantaged, those who can't help themselves, and bringing some justice to the system. But she knows her employer will see it as illegal activity and can't help but wonder how her friends would see it.

Then there are the pictures of her that were included in the package. "Oh gawd," she whispers as she looks squarely at the Monument and tastes the salt from the tears making their way down her cheeks. Her mind goes to the note included at the top of the package. If she wanted to keep this stuff secret, she needed to help keep the internet off.

~~~~~~

Livie stands stewing while she hears Annie and Hannah shout their support for keeping the internet off. Judging by the noise around her, those for no internet have come out in greater numbers. Livie steps back to put more people between her, Hannah, Sally, and Annie and her children. She reaches down, unrolls her sign, and holds it up as the first speaker comes up to the portable mike.

He looks like he is in his mid to late forties. His round glasses give him the look of an older, wise professor. But his voice, unlike his physical appearance, is full of energy, and its baritone pitch seems to
~~~~~~

part the trees in the park to reach people as far as several blocks away. It temporarily silences the crowd.

"What a great crowd we have out here today! Good afternoon everyone! My name is Dr. Grant Solbey. I'm a local musician and educator who's here as the first speaker to tell you why we need to keep the internet off."

The crowd responds with loud cheers, until the internet supporters find their voice and attempt to drown out the cheers with boos. Livie is booing with all that her voice will allow, but she can hardly hear herself among the opposing chants to keep the internet off.

Dr. Solbey cuts his arms through the air to silence the crowd as he continues.

"Okay, maybe not all of you agree with me, but I know many of you have come out here to tell the government to stop any efforts to bring the internet back. I mean that with great sincerity and urgency. Our freedom depends on it. We need to keep it off!"

As if rehearsed and on cue, the majority of the crowd take up a chant.

"Keep it off! Keep it off! Keep it off!"

Those cheering "Leave it on!" are out of sync and clearly outnumbered. Livie is stunned. She expected to be in the majority with her sign. Maybe this is "the cause" that Hannah let slip earlier. The crowd starts to quiet down as the speaker carries on.

"This monument here was resurrected almost two hundred years ago. It has stood the test of time. But it *does not* have a history to celebrate. You see, it was built by slaves in the 1800s. We should remember that.

"Long before this monument was erected by slaves, thousands of years ago actually, humans invented agriculture—a new technology at the time that seemed to change the world. But in reality, it enriched just a tiny elite while enslaving the majority of humans.

Most people found themselves working from sunrise to sunset plucking weeds, carrying water buckets, and harvesting corn under the blazing sun. It took society a couple hundred years and several generations to escape that kind of slavery. But of course real slavery didn't go away, as illustrated by this monument we stand in front of today.

"Of course, we did eventually abolish slavery in the latter half of the 1900s. Then, when the internet came, it was like the dawning of a new age of freedom—like the world had never seen before. It promised, and initially delivered, some freedoms we couldn't have imagined. It was open source. It allowed anyone to explore life, explore other countries and personalities from their own living rooms or bedrooms. It allowed a person the freedom to create another life for themselves online. It allowed the originality of expression to explode. It truly was something made of, by, and for the people. Ah...trust me, it was like the dawn of a golden age when that happened." Dr. Solbey pauses for effect as he looks out at the crowd before continuing.

"But then it evolved into something far worse and sinister than those farms of thousands of years ago that trapped people into lives of slavery—owned and operated by the wealthy elite. It has been the platform for bullies and profiteers who only care about money. Hate speech has become only a few clicks away, pushed to the top of social media feeds by algorithms. Tapping into the negative bias that digital platforms use to make money; garnering higher and higher profits the more badly people behave." The doctor pauses again as the crowd hangs on to his words.

"But there is something even more sinister afoot than that. You see, in recent years the internet has been used to enslave the majority of humans, while the elite lived in freedom and luxury. Now the internet is the tool that could have given those same arrogant elites even more dangerous potential. It gave them access to biotechnology that they could use to give their bodies superhuman powers and longer life. If successful with those advancements, they will ensure that they and their families will be a new class of humans that everyone else has to serve. Don't kid yourself friends, those same elite are behind the efforts to bring the internet back. But shutting down the internet has stopped the momentum of the super elite in their tracks! Now we have to keep it off."

Like a choir waiting for the chorus, the crows picks up the cue.

"Keep it off! Keep it off! Keep it off!"

Dr. Solbey steps away from the mike as the crowd continues to cheer, and then, seemingly appearing out of the ground, a slender woman Livie recognizes walks up to the mike. Livie stares intently towards Hannah and sees that Sally is now holding her sign with her. As Livie's mind registers what is happening, she hears Annie's soft voice floating above the crowd.

"Hello everyone, my name's Annie."

The crowd responds in unison. "Hello Annie!"

Annie keeps her head down as she prepares to read from a piece of paper.

Livie's stare at the back of Hannah's head intensifies, as if she might bore a hole through her if she keeps her focus. How dare Hannah tell her not to contact Annie—then she goes and puts her up to this! The rant playing in her head is no longer disappointment with her friend—her *former* friend, she tells herself—but disgust. Annie's voice plays in the background of her thoughts towards Hannah.

"I'm standing here today because I'm a single mother who used to be in a terrible relationship, and since the internet went off, I feel safer and more whole. My former husband can't stalk me like he could before. I don't have fights with my kids about the time they are spending online or using up my data. My life's more peaceful. I think it's a much better world for my three children to grow up in. Please keep it off."

The crowd breaks into another chant to keep it off, and Livie looks up to see Annie holding the piece of paper she was reading from with a smile on her face. The crowd switches to cheering her name.

"Annie! Annie! Annie!"

Annie seems to stand taller as she looks up with new confidence. When she speaks again, her voice exudes fresh passion.

"I believe with the internet, it was always too easy to forget the people around us. People even right in front of us." Annie holds out her right hand, palm up. "There are people here I would call friends and many more that could be friends. Yet, with the internet, people would fire at one another from a distance, through social media and other online forums—from the safety of whatever hole they were sitting in, usually alone. We let fear, ignorance, suspicion, and generalizations be our guide. It really was like a jungle out there. Here, we come together as a community. As friends or soon-to-be friends. With a deeper understanding for each other. That is the world I want to live in."

Livie finds herself suddenly fixated on Annie. *Who is this person?* She wonders. A far cry from the timid, scared individual she helped that day.

Annie leaves the mike as another speaker steps up, and Livie sees Hannah run to her with her three children in tow. She watches them embrace in a long hug and decides she can't take it anymore. Frozen for a moment, Livie decides to confront Hannah and starts walking towards her. But as she moves through the crowd, Annie's words ring in her ears, and she stops. She doesn't want Annie to see her confronting Hannah. It's Hannah she wants to focus on, alone. She will ask to speak to her privately.

She starts moving towards the women again. She is almost close enough to be certain Hannah will hear her and prepares to shout her name when she hears her own behind her.

"Livie! What a pleasant surprise seeing you here." The familiar, soft voice stops her in her tracks. Livie catches Hannah spotting her as she turns to face the timely interrupter, still clutching her rolled-up sign.

"Raf, I...I'm a bit surprised to see you in this crowd."

"Oh, I'm just taking it in, not really participating. You have a sign though." Raf motions to the rolled-up poster under Livie's arm.

"This, oh nothing really...just if I decided to do something."

"Well, it's great seeing you." Raf looks over Livie's shoulder before looking back at her with a smile. "Looks like someone is coming over to see you. Someone you might want to avoid?"

Livie turns around and sees Hannah. Their eyes lock briefly. Livie scrunches her eyebrows down and gives a very slight shake of her head.

"You're right, Raf. I should go."

"Okay! Hope to catch you again sometime. I want to share an actual letter I received with you." Sensing that the timing isn't right, Raf starts to walk away. "But at another time."

Livie watches him walk away for a few seconds, the image of his beautiful face still in her head. She allows herself to pause at the sight of his slender build, broad shoulders, and defined calves. Taking a breath, she turns abruptly and abandons her observation perch, suddenly eager to leave as quickly as possible and avoid any potential interactions with Hannah or Annie.

Walking at a brisk pace, Livie can hear the next speaker talking about biotechnology and the wealthy making the world inhospitable for the rest of us as she ruminates about what she saw with Hannah and Annie. She is chewing on her thoughts like hard candy when she spots an unwelcome sight coming towards her.

Her shoulders sag as she sees who it is. He's in a green shirt with a bowler hat that somehow doesn't look out of place among the St. Paddy's attire worn by most of the crowd. She recognizes him right away. If it wasn't the bowler hat, the unkempt beard and baggy pants, the slouched duck walk of his frame making its way across the field left no doubt in her mind. She can feel his piercing stare even at a distance. She will never forget Draw Nedwons, if not for the unusual name (*Who names their kid Draw?* She often asks herself), then for his nerdy personality, high intelligence, and distinctive attire. A tech geek who often told her how to do her job when he was a client of hers. He often took up copious amounts of her time, boring her with information that was never relevant to the case. He was what they would call a frequent-flyer customer. Asking to "engage their services" several times, usually with some new "suspicious activity" he wanted investigated, much of which he would claim support some research he was supposedly doing. He took up more than one of her afternoons explaining various conspiracy theories to her.

Livie keeps up her pace, and he responds by jogging towards her until he is beside her. She stops to greet him.

"Livie! I've been looking for you. I thought I might find you here." He looks relieved.

"Draw, I don't work for the agency anymore. I was let go when the internet went down."

Draw pauses and scans her body, his face like a flat iron, expressionless.

"It doesn't matter. You look like the same person to me. I need your help. You can hunt down things and get the information I need."

"Information you need? Draw, I'm not working as an investigator right now. Have you tried Larry?"

Livie gives herself a short mental lecture for mentioning her former boss who let her go so quickly after the internet went down, then quickly adds, "If not Larry, there are other people in the business who may be able to help you."

"Larry's a coward. You have the courage, the chutzpah for what I need."

"The chutzpah, eh?" Livie has heard this word and others like it from him before. He picks a favorite and just keeps repeating it. She wishes she had the confidence he thinks she does.

Draw scans their surroundings, looking to see if anyone is listening.

"Can we walk and talk? I have to tell you something highly confidential that could get me killed if the wrong people heard me say it."

Livie nods and starts walking as Draw remains close by her side. His voice is quiet and just above a whisper; she has to strain her ears to hear him.

"Livie, we can fix this thing. I'm in possession of the intricate password for an algorithm that could be the key to opening other algorithms and unlocking the whole thing. I hacked it Livie, but we need to know where the central computers are."

Feeling uncomfortable with how close Draw is to her, Livie stops and takes a step back.

"Draw, I have no idea what you are talking about."

Draw looks around, surveying everyone within easy reach of them. His expression is one of fear and paranoia. He leans in closer to Livie and whispers.

"Can we go somewhere quiet where no one can hear or record us?"

Livie sees the desperation on Draw's face, and it makes her want to just get this over with as quickly as possible. She has a lot on her mind already and doesn't need this intrusion. Whatever Draw is talking about, she knows it will sap a lot of time and energy if she allows it to.

"There's a big white mulberry tree at the edge of this park," Livie points in the direction of the tree and then loops her arm to point to something past it, "just beyond it is Green Planet. How about we get a coffee and go there? I don't have much time though, Draw."

Draw nods. "I don't drink that stuff, but you can get a coffee."

Livie nods her agreement. "Let's just meet under the tree then."

As Draw makes his way to the mulberry tree, Livie heads off to seek the comfort of a cup of coffee, thinking perhaps wine would be a better option. While getting her coffee, Livie's thoughts are bouncing between Hannah, Annie, and how she might keep things short with Draw. She really just wants to get home and sort out what she wants to do about Hannah, her mom…her life.

Draw is waiting at the edge of the mulberry tree, which is just beginning to flaunt its fragrant white flowers—the early signs of spring. He is standing by himself and keeping his distance from where others are congregating. He's sweating and looks anxious. Seeing Livie make her way towards him with her coffee in hand, he pulls out a handkerchief and mops his face. Livie witnesses this, noticing the growing despair on his face, but she decides to ignore it.

"Okay Draw. So, what is it that you need to tell me?" She speaks more loudly than she intended to, and the sound suddenly seems amplified.

Draw moves closer to her. She strains to hear his muffled voice in the slight breeze that is swaying the early spring buds of the tree.

"They left an opening, Livie. On purpose, I have reason to believe. Maybe they have a double agent in their own ranks? It's through an algorithm that's protected by what should be an uncrackable code, but I got the code. An old professor friend of mine has the historical information on this, and I was able to crack the code with his help. I'm certain of it. But I don't know where the mainframe computers are or if there is another algorithm or more to be unlocked. I need you to help with this."

Livie looks down at her coffee cup, as if the caffeine might unscramble what she just heard.

"Look Draw, I don't think I can help you. I have other plans, and whatever this is, it sounds like it'd take a lot of my time. Besides, I'm going away."

"Going away? Where?"

"Deerfield Lake. It's a small, isolated place, and I'm going to spend time with my mom."

"Where's that?"

"Why does that matter?"

"It's just...maybe you can help from there. Get started on things."

Livie looks at Draw and regrets that she said anything. When her mom recently asked her again to join her at Deerfield, she was non-committal. Now she is using that in a vain attempt to escape having to help Draw.

"Why does it matter? I can't help you, Draw. Honestly, I don't even know what it is you are talking about with algorithms and some old professor."

Livie makes a show of turning away to make it clear that she is about to leave and exit the conversation, but Draw reaches out and grabs her arm. Startled, she gives him her best stern bitch look, which he either ignores or misses entirely as he moves in close to whisper into her ear. His intense eyes are wide with sincerity.

"Livie, I can bring the internet back. But I need you to help me do it."

Livie stops, steps back, and studies his face. He stares into her eyes with growing intensity, and she knows that, regardless of whatever real facts there are, he sincerely believes in what he just told her.

"That's quite the revelation, Draw. But how am I supposed to help?"

"Can't you see that? You're the investigator. You can find out stuff, get people to talk and tell you their secrets. I can't do that. I'm scared shitless of it. But you have the skills, smarts, and chutzpah for this. Besides, I don't have anyone else I could trust with this."

"I don't have time for this Draw, and I wouldn't know where to begin anyway."

"You would need to infiltrate their inner circle; get inside. Get their intel. Make friends with the enemy. The stuff I've seen you do for me before."

"The inside? The enemy? Who are you talking about, Draw?"

Draw leans close to her ear again. His voice is louder and clearer now, as if what he says will only be said once and can't be missed.

"The Friendly World Network. The anti-interneters."

His words ring in her ears. The enemy. She looks past Draw and towards the Monument, where she imagines Hannah is standing. As angry as she is with her friend, she doesn't need another thing to widen the growing chasm between them.

She turns to Draw and takes a long blink to soften his piercing stare.

"You have the wrong person for this Draw. I just can't do that right now."

Livie turns and walks away before the conversation can gain any further momentum.

Chapter 7
The Network Meets

March 2033, the night before the St. Paddy's Day rally

Jody feels a sense of belonging as she walks into the building, which is half full. *Or maybe half empty,* she thinks. Like with her biological family, she feels an attachment to this crowd—the shared experiences, goals, and objectives—although it is made up of disparate individuals. People she couldn't easily shake from her life, even if she wanted to. As with her real family, it's here where she can use her real name instead of the pseudonym and, by extension, the character, that is part of the oath to the network.

The large, windowless, barn-like building is just picking up the hum of chitchat as people stake their claims to a seat. The seats closest to the back fill up first; just like when she attended church as a child. At the front is the podium and the ten chairs for the leaders. The same leaders that were chosen from the original chat group a few years previously during the genesis of the Network.

The leaders of the Network represent a rainbow of characters hailing from a scattering of places around the globe. An Aussie, an American, a Mumbaikar (who likes to tell everyone she is from the "Manchester of India"), an American native, a Brit, a Swede, a Norwegian, a Canadian, a Frenchwoman, and a Mexican. Except for the American native, they are all present at the front, despite the ongoing travel restrictions. This in itself is a testament to the carefully crafted and relentless planning the leaders put in before the internet went dark.

Though they have communicated through cryptic texts and codified letters (that included various instructions), this is the first time the FWN has met like this since the internet went off. The last time they met was just before the election. Now, the air is abuzz with anticipation. It feels surreal that this is actually going to happen. They patch in the other members of the Network from around the globe using speakerphones, as video calls are not possible without the internet.

Dr. Grant Solbey, with his casual fatherly look, is at the podium. He welcomes everyone and asks the crowd to be quiet as the buzz of whispers continue. Solbey slices his hands through the air, a visual sign to cut the noise, and the hum of the crowd dies down enough for him to speak.

"Thank you for your cooperation, everyone. I believe you are all anxious to hear from our leaders. First, I welcome Casey Aguilar to the podium."

Casey strides up to the podium with an assured confidence, sharply dressed in a tan-colored shirt.

"Greetings everyone, and welcome..."

As the noise slowly lets out the last of its air, Casey repeats his welcome and launches into his carefully crafted speech, which he delivers like a sermon to a crowd of followers.

"When I was a small child, my parents showed me an old movie called ET.

"The movie features a small alien creature, known as ET, which stands for extraterrestrial. While there are real humans in the film, there is also this cartoonish character with a scrawny neck, pointed ears, long, bony fingers and bulging eyes, known as ET. I remember, even as a little kid, when the ET character first came on the scene, I turned to my parents and said, 'This is just fiction.'

"Since then, I have seen a lot of fiction in my life. We are witnessing it in waves from politicians and business leaders today.

"It is just fiction when they say the loss of the internet means the economy will crash. The great god of the economy that they all worship will adjust and grow with new businesses not based on the internet. The reality, the facts, not the fiction, is that businesses are more likely to be closer to where people live and work without the internet.

"It is just fiction when they say this will set technology back—what did he say? Thirty years?"

The crowd groans, and shouts of "bullshit!" become a chant that fills the air as Casey pauses and allows the energy to spread through the room.

"It's fiction, folks. All of the technology is still there and available offline. The unleashing of the creative minds of the people will make it even better! People will recapture the time lost to the shiny thrum of likes, tagged photos, mindless posts, tweets, and tiny emojis—the many things that people are addicted to. Things that we have been told are necessary simply because they exist and everyone is doing it!

"We have stopped a significant technological advancement in its tracks. The biotechnology that was set to enable the wealthy elite to become superhuman. The pain we have saved the world from with that alone makes this all worth it. But there is still much more fiction they are pushing.

"It is just fiction when they say the loss of social media will destroy relationships. Are relationships that need social media to keep them alive really worth it? Social media, with its use of backronyms and advertising tactics that exploit human psychology to reduce our choices is not a friendly outlet. They deliberately trick, confuse, and pull users in. Friends, we know they use that technology to manipulate the human brain to interfere with the free choice of the people using their programs.

"Social media has existed for the sole purpose of gathering people's private information, storing it, and categorizing it. To do what with it?!"

"Sell it!" the crowd shouts, clearly familiar with this argument, which is written on the pamphlets they all received when they entered.

"It's fiction, friends, that we are better off with social media! We, my friends, have made social media extinct!

"It will take time for people to get over the addictive loss of it, but in that move alone, we have made this a friendlier world!

"It is just fiction when they call us terrorists. We are liberating the world. Wrestling back the people's free will from the advertisers and business elites. We are setting the stage for a saner! More inclusive! Mentally safe! And friendlier world!

"It is just fiction that the internet has made our world safer. On the contrary, it has made it exponentially more dangerous. Countries can attack one another and kill—murder—people on a large scale with a sophistication that could not have been imagined even a few generations ago. We are changing that, friends. We are making it a safer and friendlier world.

"And...and friends..."

The crowd is drowning Casey out with hoots and hollers as he pauses and then continues.

"It was just fiction when they said the internet would be back on after three days! The internet didn't come back on then, and. it. is. not, coming back on now!

"If the internet is ever to come back on," Casey pauses and stares out at the crowd as his words echo around the room, "if it comes back on, it will be how and when *we*! When *we* decide!"

As Casey shouts "we decide," on cue, the strumming buildup of "Eye of the Tiger" begins to play throughout the hall.

The pounding of the drums that follows descends on the crowd, sending them into a fist-pumping dance. They sing the first lyrics in unison, "Rising up, back on the street!" but are then cut off as the music stops abruptly. The crowd moans a predicable protest that Casey silences with a wave of his hands.

"Friends, you will have plenty of time to party tonight! You deserve to party because, against great odds, we did it! We shut it down, and we are keeping it down!"

At his words, the crowd breaks out into a familiar chant from meetings they had before.

"Shut it down! Shut it down! Shut it down!"

Casey silences them again, holding up his arms.

"For many years, many of you have been at war against the internet. You've written your governments. You created songs against the Net. You wrote books about the trappings of the Net. You garnered followers through your blogs and you held many meetings, educating the masses about the perils of the internet. Did it feel like it was a lonely war at times?"

The crowd nods its agreement as shouts of "Yes!" are heard throughout the hall.

"Well, that lonely war on the internet is over! We have won!"

The crowd buzzes with chatter as Casey steps down from the podium and Nita Kotak makes her way up to take his place.

When she arrives at the podium, Nita steps up onto a platform to raise her up to the level of the mike. She pauses, her eyes scanning the crowd, as the hum of the chatter continues.

Nita starts to speak, and as she utters her first words, the chatter ceases, giving way to an air of expectation as the crowd is uniformly fixated on the podium. All eyes are on one of their most revered leaders. Nita's reputation as the principal strategist who mapped out the plans that brought down the internet has bought her a wealth of loyalty from the crowd. She knows it and plans to draw from it now to focus the crowd's attention to carry out her visionary plan.

"Mumbai, I was told. I was told this over and over again when I was growing up. Mumbai is a place where strangers are connected and legends are born." She pauses, scans the silent crowd, and then smiles. "But it's here, in this group, with people from around the world, that I have seen strangers bond and become friends, united by *our* cause. People that share *our* values. This is where legends are being made."

"Nita! Nita! Nita! Nita"

The crowd chants in admiration, and Nita moves her head back from the mike to allow the chant to fill the room.

"Nita! Nita! Nita!"

She moves closer to the mike again, and the crowd grows silent.

"Friends, thank you for your admiration; it humbles me. It makes me wish you could have met my grandmother. Her name was Mishka Madan. She was one of those Mumbai legends. When there were a series of terrorist attacks in Mumbai in 2008, her courageous actions saved many—all who were strangers to her, and many of them foreigners. She put her life on the line for strangers and became a legend." Nita pauses as she holds her emotions back from hijacking her speech. The crowd remains silent, recognizing that she needs a moment. Then she continues, her voice gaining strength and momentum with each word.

"I look out at this crowd and I see...and I see so many people who are becoming legends. People who have made it possible for us to execute our historical plan that shut down the internet."

"Shut it down! Shut it down!"

Nita smiles and then moves closer still to the mike, silencing the crowd again.

"I love the energy in this room! You are sending waves of excitement through me about what we have planned next. Because friends, shutting down the internet was critical to our plans, but now we have to move quickly to continue our campaign to win the hearts of the majority—so that our movement will grow. We have a plan that will bring many together to demand that any efforts to bring the internet back be stopped. Our vision for a friendlier world, without the poison of the internet, is just beginning in its implementation. We need all of you now to commit your efforts towards our cause as we lay out for you the next stages of our plan."

A buzz starts up in the crowd as they see Forrest Momoa making his way to the podium.

"Ah, you can see Forrest coming up here, I see."

Forrest, a Native American from Hawaii, has been in hiding since before the internet shutdown after his risk-taking made him a target for the counterterrorism arm of the FBI. His sudden and unexpected presence sent an electric current of excitement through the crowd.

"Yes, it is Forrest, coming at us like he just descended from the rafters. You didn't expect to see him here, I know, but Forrest is no longer in hiding, and he will tell you more about that as he further sets the stage for you as to what to expect next."

Nita steps aside, making room for Forrest to address the crowd from the podium.

"My name is Keanu Ikaika. You know me as someone else, but that name is on an FBI list that I can't seem to shake."

"Hi Keanu!" the crowd shouts in unison. They've done this before.

"I actually, for a moment, considered changing my last name to Snowden! But the idea is to make me less of a government target, not the opposite!" Forrest pauses briefly to allow the crowd to chuckle. "Speaking of Ed Snowden, I want to share with you something he said many years ago now. After he became an enemy of the US government for exposing the surveillance capitalism they engage in, he stated this:

> 'I don't want to live in a world where everything I say, everything I do, everyone I talk to, every expression of creativity and love or friendship is recorded.'

"When Edward Snowden said those words, the tentacles of surveillance—by government and the private sector—were just warming up. Our world would become a place where every keystroke, every purchase, and anywhere you walk outside your house are recorded. Oh, did I say outside your house? Of course, we know that all your appliances—think TVs, computers, and phones—record everything inside your house. Those recordings are sent to large companies, and in many cases governments, to analyze, catalogue, sell, and market. Think you are in the shower and free from surveillance capitalism? Nope. That is recorded too, including how long that shower takes you. Everything is recorded. Everything!"

Forrest allows several seconds of silence to fill the room before he continues.

"As a result of all that, our world has been a vicious, dangerous, and decidedly unfriendly place to live. Trying to change that by calling it out, like Snowden did and like many of you have done with books, articles, and media events—has not worked. All of that did very little to stem the tide of surveillance capitalism and the use of it to control the citizenry. The only answer was to shut the system down. That is what we have done!"

"Shut it down! Shut it down! Shut it down!" The crowd's familiar chant fills the hall.

"Friends, we could not have done that without you. But our job is far from finished. See, my name is now Keanu Ikaika. It is a Hawaiian name, and in Hawaii, Ikaika means strong, powerful, and determined." Forrest nods his head with a smirk. "Yeah, I think I can be that."

The crowd laughs.

"But what makes us all strong, powerful, and determined is what we can do together. Together, we shut down the internet! Together, we have to not only keep it shut down, but convince the majority of the populace that our world is a better and friendlier place without the internet as it was constructed."

Forrest takes a step back as the crowd now chants, "Keanu! Keanu! Keanu!"

He leans forward again and raises his voice to be heard over the crowd.

"Thank you. Thank you, my friends. Thank you very much. Now, before I leave you, I'm going to introduce the person who will give you the details of *our* plan that all of *you* are going to be a part of executing."

Forrest's words cause the crowd to go quiet. All eyes are now on the tall woman in heels making her way to the podium, her long, straight black hair glimmering in the light as she releases her wide, captivating smile.

"Friends, as you can see, here comes Genevieve Gabriella Sauveterre."

As if on cue, the crowd starts its cheer as soon as her name is announced.

"GG!" "GG!" "GG!"

Genevieve stands straight at the podium. Her long neck and wide smile snags the attention of everyone in the room.

"Bonjour."

"Bonjour!" the crowd echoes.

"Ça fait longtemps dis donc. Well, maybe it just feels like it has been a long time since we were all together, as so much has happened since then. Since we last met, we completed the execution of our plans, including ensuring all of you had enough cash in *your* currency to function not just the day after, but for at least a year or more." Genevieve pauses to allow the buzz of the crowd to rise before continuing. "But yes, let's talk about that day after—the day we were waiting for so long. You all had your training and detailed plans, written in the GG code, to infiltrate society and assuage the anxiety you would face."

Jody looks around the room at Genevieve's words. She sees many reflectively clutching their devices, which hold their fake identities and instructions written in a code that Genevieve says she created.

"Yes, protect those devices. They are your passports to the new world we are continuing to create. You know, we pulled off the internet shutdown with great precision—hours after the US election, when most will have already gone to bed. I mention this because I believe it is important that we all remember how much we have accomplished already as we move forward. We have much to do to prepare for this exciting new world we are creating. I know we will have times of discouragement and maybe even setbacks. But we are all agents for the change that our societies, our countries, and our world desperately need. We will be successful, my friends."

Genevieve motions for others to begin distributing material to everyone in the crowd. There are pamphlets with talking points, cartoons, posters, buttons, flags, poetry, and even lyrics. She details the plans for rallies that will include all those materials with musicians at each to lead crowds in anti-internet songs. Her voice rises with excitement as she tells them about the launch of their own newspapers in every major city in the world. Each newspaper will be called the city's name with "life".

"So what you will read in newspapers like *Paris Life, Mumbai Life, Sydney Life, New York Life, Beijing Life,* etc., will be stories on how life has improved in the internetless world. Stories on how communities are coming together and supporting one another.

Cartoons, poetry, spaces for debate, and letters to the editor will all be part of our newspapers, bringing real news to people's doorsteps. And we will allow a voice for the pro-interneters in our newspapers, so they won't look one-sided. But our side will be the most persuasive."

She tells them that these newspapers will be available for free at first and will be released starting the next day. Strategically, they wanted to see other major papers get their print versions out first so they don't give the impression of purely being propaganda for their cause. She states that they deliberately delayed putting these in place for several months as people "adjusted" to the world without the internet. Now, as more people are coming to accept this as the way the world is going to be, more are embracing it, and it's time to move on to more aggressive action.

"But make no mistake about it, my friends, this is going to be a war for the hearts and minds of people in every country. We carry the truth—that the world is a better, safer, and friendlier place without the internet. A truth we need people to hear about and see to believe. We are the pro-friendly movement. We will overcome and drown out those that want to go back to the hostile, unfriendly world of the internet."

Genevieve then assures the crowd that the spies they have groomed for decades, modelled after the Russian system from the 1970s and eighties, remain secure and are "doing their work" within governments and major corporations around the world. Those spies, she says, will give them all the intel they need to remain several steps ahead of any plans or developments to try and bring the internet back. Glee jumps into her voice as she announces the plans for upcoming rallies around the world on St. Paddy's Day.

"These rallies are where we are going to demonstrate that we are not only on the winning side of this war, but on the right and moral side. At previous rallies we allowed disparate voices to be heard—even encouraged, as some were grieving the loss of the internet and voicing their anger as part of that grieving processes. But now, we will dominate the rallies. We will demonstrate that the tide has changed. The new world is upon us. Those that don't embrace it will be left behind and in the dark."

Tossed into the informative stew of her speech, Genevieve advises the crowd that they have deployed other methods to "encourage" people to join the cause. This includes "reminders" of the kind of embarrassing information that would be available if the internet was to come back on —information, including pictures where applicable, mailed directly to individuals.

"Governments can expect to see more of their secrets revealed!" she finishes.

Genevieve leaves the stage to more chants of "GG!" "GG!" "GG!" as Casey comes forward, signaling that final instructions will be given before they disperse.

Casey keeps his final remarks brief, telling everyone to pick up some swag with the FWN logo on it, make sure they attend the next rally closest to where they live on St. Paddy's Day, and to follow the coded instructions sent to them on their devices.

Jody hears someone near the front ask, "Why would we have stuff with FWN on it if we are trying to stay covert?"

As if overhearing the conversation, Casey tells the crowd:

"Up until now, we've largely kept the FWN logo in the background, hidden in the weeds, if you like. Now, as the tide is changing, we want you to flash the logo wherever you go. We want it to become commonplace, even trendy. We want more to join us in making this world a friendlier place. If you are asked where you got something with an FWN logo on it, simply say that you found it somewhere—just like many others will."

Jody knows that Casey also believes the swag and logo make them all more committed to the cause. “It makes the Friendly World Network the home in our hearts,” as he has often said.

As Jody shuffles through the exit doors with the rest of the crowd, her FWN swag tucked into her oversized purse, she looks down at the stack of cartoons she was handed. The one on top shows a man kneeling in front of the internet, his head cracked open and his brains on a platter in his hands that he serves up to the internet. Jody flips the page over to look at the next cartoon, which shows two people talking. One says to the other, “Of course I believe in Bigfoot. I’m friends with him on Facebook.” The caption below reads, “It is time to get back to a real world with real friends. A friendly world without the internet."

Jody continues to flip through the various cartoons. As she finally reaches the top of the funnel of people at the exit, the last cartoon she sees shows a person in hell. The devil, with a sly grin, looks at them and says, “Your social media company brought many to me, why would you think you’d escape?”

Remnants of that image float in front of her eyes as the light of the sun’s rays casts shadows in front of her. She can still see the image of the grinning devil in front of her as she whispers to herself, “I hope we are creating something friendlier.”

Jody is several blocks away from the rally when she hears her alter-ego name called.

"Fairleigh!"

She turns to see Livie's friend from the coffee shop. Livie was the first person Jody interacted with at Green Planet "the day after," and she had another "encounter" with her at the coffee shop a few days later. Livie paid back the twenty dollars Jody had given her, and while Livie was rather feisty about her desire for the internet to return, she was also inquisitive with her questions.

"Won't this set the medical community back with the loss of technology and people's medical records?"

"How will people access their online investments?"

"What about those who have only ever worked for an online company?"

Their discussion, debate, and joint examination of the situation and its various impacts was lively and invigorating. Every time Jody went back to Green Planet after that, she looked for Livie, hoping to see her again. Then one day, this friend of Livie's spotted her and somehow knew her name—from the description Livie had given her, no doubt. Her friend didn't take the same challenging, yet open-minded approach. She seemed more willing to treat Jody, or Fairleigh, as the "sage on the stage" in terms of keeping the internet off. While encouraging and good for her ego, it has begun to wear on Jody.

Pretending not to see who called out to her, she turns back around, questions circling in her head. This must be a coincidence, right? There is no way Livie's friend could have known that the FWN was just meeting close by? While her pace is brisk in hopes of escaping a conversation, she hears her name again, this time much louder and closer.

"Fairleigh!"

She closes her eyes for a couple of seconds, pastes on her best warm smile, and turns around.

"Hannah, how are you?"

Chapter 8
Deerfield Lake

Two months later, June 2033

Livie pulls up to the gravel spot beside the cabin overlooking Deerfield Lake. She parks but keeps the engine running.

She looks towards the cabin. It looks different than she remembered, with a deck off the front that welcomes the view of the lake. An electric cord snakes along the side of the deck and disappears to the back—where she assumes it is likely plugged into her mom's car. She closes her eyes, thankful that her mom hasn't come walking out of the cabin towards her. At least not yet. The thought of escape washes through her, even as she reaches to turn the vehicle off. She still has time. Time to back out and drive away. Time to go back to her life without the intrusion of her mom in it. Time to run away, just like she did when she was sixteen.

After somehow surviving a childhood squandered in various foster homes, where she spent many of her days fearful and dejected, she was suddenly "claimed" by her natural family—the very people, led by her mom, who had rejected and deserted her as a child. She was just turning fifteen when her mom showed up with an empty suitcase for her to pack her life in. She had no choice but to go live with the deserter. A year passed by. Livie endured, with growing hate, through her mom's lifestyle, her depressed, angry moods, and her lack of engagement in her life. It made Livie feel as abandoned as a kid left on a roadside waiting for someone—or something—to deliver her to the world of her fantasies. A world where she was loved and valued. A world where she had the skills and smarts she was certain she just wasn't lucky enough to be born with.

Yet somehow, her mom had not parceled her up and shipped her away somewhere. So, a week after her sixteenth birthday, Livie fled. In the years that followed, her mom would pop in and out of her life, always as the same needy and often enraged person Livie had always known. Yet Livie managed to make a life for herself that in many ways was the opposite of her mom's. She discovered things she was good at; she could feel her confidence grow as if it was something new inside her. She made a life for herself with friends that loved and appreciated her. She developed a career that she enjoyed and was good at. She found her voice and could hold her own in conversations and debates.

Now here she was. Back at Deerfield Lake. Back in the past for a weekend away with her mom. Why? Why did she agree to this? Yes, she had some fond memories of the place, but those memories didn't clear the dark clouds hovering over whom she would be spending the weekend with. When the rage she felt for her mom eventually passed, it was replaced by a seemingly bottomless sorrow for her mom and the life she lived. Was it pity then that brought her here?

Sitting still in the warmth of her vehicle, the rain dancing on the windshield, Livie feels her anxious and on-edge emotions slowly pulse within her, bringing moisture to her eyes. She reaches into the glovebox to pull out some tissues as she looks into the mirror with blurred vision and sees her puffy eyes. "Get your emotions in check, Liv," she whispers to herself. The stillness in her car is soothing, as is the patter of rain outside. Livie's breathing has returned to its normal, relaxed rhythm when it is suddenly unhinged by the rapping sound of knuckles on glass.

Livie takes a deep breath to push away the fear that courses through her body at the sudden noise. She looks out the window, using her eyes to indicate to her mom that she is coming out.

As Livie opens the door, her mom presents her with a large umbrella.

"It's okay Mom, I can manage on my own."

"It's pouring out Livie, you should join me under the umbrella."

Livie nods her acceptance of the offer, reaches over, and grabs her water bottle. She takes a moment to enjoy its company in her hand. The scene on the bottle is of another lake—Green Lake. A place that her heart can quickly take her to for warmth and comfort. A place of delight and joy where she and Hannah became like sisters. The sister Livie never had. Hannah gave her the bottle as a Christmas gift. It's a prized possession and a comfort to her in times of uncertainty.

As Livie steps out of the vehicle with her water bottle in hand, her mom is still there with her big umbrella and Livie's suitcase that she fished out of the back seat.

"Thanks Mom, I can get that."

Livie's mom pulls the suitcase closer to herself in response.

"I've got it. Let's just get into the cabin and out this rain."

As they approach the cabin, Livie steps onto the covered deck that she doesn't recall. It smells of fresh wood. She quickly scans the deck as they enter the house. *Must be newly constructed,* she surmises.

Her mom carries the suitcase into the house and up to the loft, where a tidy bed and dresser awaits. Livie, close behind her mom, deposits the water bottle on the dresser.

"You didn't need to carry that all the way up here for me, Mom."

"It's fine, sweetie. I'm still very capable, and I want you to feel comfortable here."

Livie looks at her mom, searching her face, her eyes, her mouth. Expecting to see those eyebrows curled down towards her eyes, squinting as if sizing her up, deep creases forming around her mouth. Instead, she sees a warm and inviting smile. Livie reaches out and gives her mom a lingering hug.

"Thanks Mom. Can I get a few minutes to myself to unpack a few things?"

Her mom slowly blinks as she nods in agreement, turns around, and heads down the stairs. Livie, hearing her mom's footsteps hit the wooden floor downstairs, collapses on the bed. She stretches her arms and legs out, as if hoping to find the end of restlessness.

Several minutes pass as Livie lies motionless on the bed. Then she hears her mom's voice from below.

"Tea is on, and I've made us some biscuits."

Livie gets up, brushes her hair in the mirror that is attached to the dresser, and makes her way down the stairs, ensuring that her feet hit the creaks in the floorboards so as to announce her presence.

"Not sure if you're hungry? I just made some biscuits to tide us over until dinner, unless you missed lunch?"

Livie looks at her mom, wondering if biscuits and lunch would be the extent of their conversations all weekend—which is what she hopes for.

"The biscuits and tea are great, Mom. Thanks for going to the trouble."

Several minutes slug by as they sit in silence, sipping tea and munching on the buttery soft bread. They should have a lot to talk about. They haven't seen each other in months, and so much has happened. The rain pattering on the roof fills the silence.

"Did you get everything you needed out of your car?"

"Yes. I did. Thanks."

Livie's mom looks at the ceiling.

"Sounds like the rain is starting to abate."

"Sounds like it. I checked the forecast before I drove up, and it looks like the rain will be with us most of the weekend."

"Well then, how about we take the opportunity now to go for a bit of a walk out by the lake?"

Livie squeezes out a smile as she responds.

"For sure."

The rain has turned to a light drizzle as they walk down the path towards the lake.

"The reflection of the trees on the water is beautiful. I look forward to what it will look like in the fall. I love this place with its beauty and peace. This time of year, especially."

"It's beautiful, Mom. Why especially this time of year though?"

"I dunno. The birds and animals are out more. It has me thinking of some of the wonderful memories here. Like you remember the time we were here when you were fifteen? Your Uncle Dean was here too. It was magical."

"Magical? Mom, that was one of the worst times of my life. It's a memory I'd rather forget."

Her mom reaches over and puts her arm around Livie's shoulders.

"Oh, come on Livie. I can remember you having a good time, like when we were in the cabin, and you made those cookies..."

Livie pushes herself away a few feet and stands defensively, widening her eyes in a fiery stare directed at her mom.

"It was a terrible time for me, Mom. Why would you think it was so great?"

"I don't know...I remember it as a time in between times of chaos. It was a peaceful time for me."

"Okay. For you it was good then, but you *do* remember that I ran away shortly after that, right?"

"Yeah, why *did* you do that to me? Run away like that?"

"Do that to *you?* Are you kidding me? Mom, if I stayed...it was like going to the funeral of all my hopes and dreams every day. A life of emptiness and depression. No...no...I couldn't stay."

"So, you think that's what my life was...just emptiness and depression?"

Livie steps further away from her mom and looks out to the water. She takes a deep breath and a moment of silence while her mind churns with how to respond. She closes her eyes as she feels her mom's gaze still fixed on her.

"I don't think you appreciate, Livie, what I was going through."

Livie turns her head and looks at her mom. She sees the familiar transformation. The eyebrows curled, the squint in her eyes and creases in her mouth. Her mom's bitch look, which Livie vividly remembers from her youth, has finally surfaced.

Livie turns and starts to walk in the opposite direction.

"I'm leaving. I don't know what I was thinking coming here in the first place."

Her mom flails her arm towards her in a failed attempt to touch her.

"Oh come on Livie. I'm sorry...don't just leave. I need you in my life...give me a chance...please Livie."

Livie can hear her mom pleading as she picks up her pace to get to her car. The unctuous whine in her mom's voice just adds fuel to the flames of anger burning inside her.

"You'll survive without me, Mom. Enjoy your time at the lake," she replies sourly.

Livie reaches her car and manages to get in and start it before her mom is able to catch up. Fittingly, the rain has picked up again. As she pulls away, Livie sees the slouched, blurred figure of her mom through the rain on her windshield.

As Livie turns onto the main road, with the windshield wipers now aggressively trying to keep up with the water splashing down, she looks up at the ominous black clouds that are carrying the rain, again thinking how fitting this is—the weather matching her brooding mood. It's like she is sixteen again, running from her mom's chaotic life. But this time she is not a scared teenager running into an unknown darkness. She's an adult with her own life now, and she has her own car she can escape with.

Her foot presses down hard on the pedal as her anger fuels her aggression and desire to speed away as fast as she can.

Her mind races as the car's tires cut through the puddles that have formed on the road, sending water to both sides of the car in waves. How could she have let her mom lure her to this place again? The good memories she had of Deerfield Lake were consumed once again by the painful ones and her mom's needy, self-centered life. *That is what it is,* she concludes in her mind. Her mom filters all the good out of her life when given the opportunity. *Not anymore,* Livie resolves. She has gotten into a pattern of avoiding petty disputes and the brooding moods of her mother. Maybe she should just avoid her altogether. She could be stubborn too.

Livie accelerates again as her new resolve to push her mom out of her life forms in her mind. She glances into the rearview mirror and sees her own hardened features. Her eyebrows pointed down, her closed mouth narrowing her cheeks, and her determined stare.

She stares at her reflection for a moment as the car's front left tire hits a water-filled pothole and thrusts the vehicle to the right, towards the edge of the road. Startled, Livie jerks the steering wheel to the left to correct. The vehicle's momentum causes it to spin as the right side lifts off the ground. Livie panics and releases her hands from the steering wheel, hoping the car will spin out and come to rest. But the vehicle has too much momentum. It continues to spin, sending a wave of fear through her body. The rain has flooded the vehicle's windows, and Livie's mind, now operating in slow motion, takes in the scene, imagining the vehicle submerged under water with her in it.

As the car spins, she closes her eyes to shut out the terrifying images hurling at her.

With her eyes closed, she can feel the vehicle's momentum losing steam and hopes it stops before going into the ditch or hitting something. The vehicle is nearing the end of its built-up momentum, then tilts slightly to the left. Livie opens her eyes as she senses the right tires might start to lift. She quickly unbuckles her seatbelt and leans her body as far to the right as she can.

She lies across the seat as the vehicle settles, trying to regulate her breathing, frightened to move and cause the vehicle to tumble into what she assumes is the ditch. She has survived the vehicle spinning out of control. She can feel some aches and fatigue in her body from being tossed around. But can she get herself safely out of her car? She closes her eyes again, telling herself to remain calm and think of what to do before making any abrupt moves. Livie has learnt that she makes better decisions in times of stress if she takes the time to think and monitor her self-talk.

The vehicle isn't moving and seems steady. She decides to try and sit up, when she hears the rapping of knuckles on the passenger-side window just above her head. She doesn't move as she opens her eyes and tries to focus on the image above her. It appears a man is standing in the rain by her window. Livie moves her right leg forward as she goes to sit up but suddenly freezes at the sound of knuckles rapidly rapping on the window again. The man is shaking his head, and she thinks from reading his lips that he is telling her not to move. He then holds up his palm like a stop sign, confirming that she should hold still. He then leaves her line of sight.

Livie wants to close her eyes again so that she can push the rising anxiety and fear deep back into her being. But her eyes remain fixed on the window in hopes that the stranger will return.

As she lies there, the seconds pass like her breathing—heavy and slow. Her mind has put everything into slow motion again, and she feels the weight of it as a few minutes pass in what seems like hours. She blinks slowly, hoping that when her eyes open, she will see the stranger at her window again. A stranger that would give her hope. Hope for survival. Hope for a future.

Suddenly the back of the car drops to the left. "Oh God!" Livie screams into the void. She hears a loud clunk at the front of her car, which lifts slightly and then thuds back down. Livie starts to cry. Why did she leave the lake in such a hurry in this storm? She was safe there. She can't control the tears or the heaving of her body as the car jerks again—further down, but also forward.

Everything is suddenly quiet, except for the pounding of the rain on the vehicle. The rain sounds are amplified as she lies across the seat. Livie decides to act. She moves her legs forward and the back of the car drops again, leaving her cowering and shaking in the fetal position. She reaches her hand up to the door handle when the car jerks forward again, tossing her into the passenger seat as her hands reach to hold onto the seat's edges. She banishes all thoughts of making another move. The car jerks yet again, and she screams, "Oh God no!!" She can feel the vehicle moving forward and thinks the back lifted up, at least a bit. Things are quiet again. She tightens her grip and pushes her body inward as tight as she can, waiting for what may come next.

Her stomach as taut as a bowstring, all Livie hears now are her heart pounding like a hammer and the sound of the relentless rain. Then the rapping on the window fills her ears. Her whole body feels the relief of seeing the stranger at the window again. This time he is motioning for her to unlock the door—"slowly", his lips pronounce distinctively, his hands up as a warning sign. Livie reaches out with her left hand to unlock the door and hears the "click" of its action as the back of the vehicle drops in response. She lets out a scream of "noooo!!" as the stranger quickly opens the door and grabs her hands to pull her out. Her mind processes the image of the vehicle rolling over into the ditch with her in it, but she finds her legs to push forward to exit the car—the grip of the stranger pulling her forward.

The car doesn't fall, and Livie sees that it is now facing the opposite direction she was travelling in. As she stands in the rain, under an umbrella in the arms of the stranger, she starts to cry. She sees her car teetering on gravel that is clearly unstable, its back tire resting just on the soft edge, partly over. She doesn't need to get any closer to see that below the car is not the ditch she imagined in her mind, but a steep drop-off.

"You okay?"

Through her sobs, Livie simply nods her head in response as she buries her face into the stranger's chest.

"I'm glad I got you out. My name is Theo. How about we get out of this rain and to the warmth of my vehicle?'

Livie nods again and follows him closely under the umbrella to his vehicle, which she is surprised to see is a car just a little bigger than hers. She was expecting a truck that would match the size of the stranger who just saved her. She doesn't know what brought it to her mind, but Livie looks at Theo and sees him as a Viking. His curly strawberry blond hair, handlebar mustache, and broad shoulders that sit atop a frame that is easily close to six and a half feet, make her think of him mounting a large horse instead of crawling into a small car. Even his name, Theo, seems to fit the Viking image now in her head.

They step over a rope that was clearly used to pull her car forward, and her gaze follows the rope up to Theo's vehicle to see the end lying loose on the ground. Just above that, she sees a bumper sticker that reads: "Bring the internet back."

She stops as she surveys the scene and finds her voice.

"The rope isn't attached...did it come off your vehicle?"

"No, I pulled it off before I came to help you. I was worried that if I didn't, your car might go over and drag mine with it...I was also afraid it might break when I was pulling you from the edge."

Livie feels the weight of her anxiety fall when she sits in the passenger seat of Theo's car and feels the warmth envelop her body.

"I'm sorry. My name is Livie."

"I'd say nice to meet you, but the circumstances..."

"Oh Theo, I'm very glad to meet you. I think you saved my life."

Livie looks out the window towards her car, the view blurred by the rain.

"Do you think my car will fall over the edge?"

"I'm not sure. This storm is making the edge unstable. It could. I'm pretty sure it would have gone over if I hadn't pulled it like I did. I tried lifting it up myself to see if I could get it back on stable ground, but that seemed too dangerous and difficult."

Livie remembers the front of the vehicle lifting up and the thud when it landed as she imagines her new Viking friend trying to raise it.

"So what actually happened, Theo? I was lying on the seat, not sure what was going on."

Theo explains how he stopped when he saw her spinning out of control. He thought she might go over the edge when the vehicle stopped with the left back tire over the edge and the front left tire just on it. He quickly got out and ran to her to see if he could do something. He knew he couldn't push the car back on the road and that it could go over if he didn't do something. He keeps rope in his car and so decided to try and pull her to safety. When he was pulling her car forward though, he sensed his rope was about to break. That is why he stopped and got out to get her out of the car.

Livie relives the experience as she listens, though now with the knowledge of the cliff below her car and Theo risking his own safety for her. She can't stem the tide of the raw emotion she feels, and the tears come streaming back.

"I'm sorry, I didn't mean to...you okay?"

"It's...it's fine Theo. Thank you...gawd, I'm such a mess."

They sit in silence as the windshield wipers clear the rain, which is slowing down. Watching the wipers, Livie feels the gloom and the chill she felt when she was lying in her vehicle. A chill that is now being wiped away by a warm stillness. Livie is thankful for the few moments of silence as she processes her thoughts and considers what to do next. The storm in her heart towards her mom has eased. Now thoughts of returning to Deerfield, which seems likely, brings her a sense of refuge, but also apprehension as to what will happen next. She looks at Theo and wonders if there is another option other than going back to the cabin.

"I guess it's too risky to try and get anything out of my car?"

"I wouldn't recommend it. The rain is subsiding, but it wouldn't be worth the risk. I would suggest we phone a tow truck and hopefully get your car to safety without it going over the edge. Is there something important in the vehicle?"

"Just my suitcase and water bottle...oh wait."

Livie closes her eyes as she imagines the water bottle and sees herself putting it on the dresser back at the cabin. She sighs and lets out a little chuckle, thinking of the irony of it all. She would have had to go back to the cabin anyway.

"Actually, I just realized they're not in my car, cause I left them at the cabin."

"The cabin?"

"Oh sorry Theo. Yes, at a cabin on Deerfield Lake."

"Should I take you back there?"

"I suppose...that makes sense...I'm sure my mom will be happy to see me."

"Your mom? That wouldn't be Maggie Romée, would it?"

Livie is surprised to hear her mom's last name pronounced with the correct French accent.

"You know my mom."

"Ah yes...very pleasant woman. You must be her daughter? I wondered when you mentioned a cabin at Deerfield. You look like her. I know she was really looking forward to you coming this weekend."

"That's me. So how do you know her?"

"How about I tell you as we drive back to her cabin?"

"Yes, please."

"Perhaps you want to phone for a tow truck to see if they can rescue your car? I know the owner of one in town, if you like?"

Livie is thankful that Theo is thinking ahead and more clearly than she is. She asks him to phone the tow truck for her, which he does.

As they drive towards the cabin, Theo sheds the quiet man of few words that she met at the scene of her accident as he offers up why he is in the area. He built a log home just above Deerfield Lake a few years ago. He accentuates the details of its features with hand gestures, lively facial expressions, and a voice that crescendos when he describes the parts that he is clearly most proud of. She hears about a chandelier built from an elk's antlers, a spiraling wood staircase, a kitchen with marble counter tops and wood highlights. Theo seasons his speech with the odd swearword and humorous anecdote.

It's all entertaining to listen to and gives Livie time to relax her body, wrench her thoughts away from her accident, and contemplate what she will say to her mom when they get to Deerfield. But what she really wants to know, she asks in an emollient tone.

"You are quite the storyteller, Theo, and your place sounds wonderful. How'd you meet my mom, then?"

"Ah, I was getting to that. You see, after I finished my place, I was looking for jobs to do in the area, and your mom had just bought the cabin on Deerfield..."

"Wait...bought the cabin? I don't think my mom owns it, Theo. We've rented it at various times over the years."

"Well, you can ask her, but I'm pretty sure she bought it. I remember when the for-sale sign went up and I contemplated trying to buy it myself. I met your mom shortly after she purchased it and asked if she wanted any work done on it."

"Okay...so you built the deck?"

"Ah, you noticed. Pleased to hear that. It's quite nice, wouldn't you say?"

"It's wonderful. When was that?"

"Oh about three months ago, just as spring was hitting."

While the news that her mom purchased the cabin sits like a weight in the pit of Livie's stomach, Theo speaks of her mom as a close friend that he admires. He speaks of her as a person with a positive outlook on life, a warm, friendly disposition, and a caring heart. Livie wonders if there is another Maggie Romée that lives on Deerfield Lake.

Livie is churning over what question to ask next when she sees the road to the cabin ahead and points it out to Theo. He answers with a simple nod. As they turn onto the dirt road, Theo easily skirts the first pothole they come to, and she wonders how frequently he has driven this way as she looks up to see the cabin. Her mom is walking off the deck towards them.

The rain is fairly light now, and Livie doesn't feel an immediate need to escape. As they park, she sees her mom approaching with the large umbrella, which she thinks serves as an invitation for affectionate intimacy. She exits the vehicle, hugs her mom, and then steps back, out of the range of her umbrella. Her mom looks at her as she steps away and appears to be ready with a response when Theo, oblivious to any awkwardness, jumps in to fill the pause.

"Well Maggie, look what I found on the road? Livie here got her vehicle stuck. I was able to help her out and bring her back here."

"Really? I'm anxious to hear what happened, but Theo, where's your truck?"

"Ah, yes, I guess you're not used to seeing me pull up in a car. The truck is in the shop. Sure would have helped if I had it today."

Livie watches them converse as Theo tells the story of how he saw her car spin out and then rescued her. She sees her mom's expression of concern as she takes in the brief description of the event. The alarm is apparent on her mom's face, but for Livie it is fractured into dark colors, seen through the prism of a hurtful past. Her mom catches Livie's silent, irascible posture and turns back towards Theo.

"Well, why are we all standing out here talking about this? Let's go inside."

"I really should get going Maggie, and I don't want to intrude on your time with your daughter."

Livie's mom reaches out and affectionally touches Theo on the elbow.

"Don't be silly. You're always welcome here, Theo. Why don't you come in for some tea at least?"

Livie looks at Theo and hopes he catches the plea in her eyes to stay as she finally adds her voice to the conversation.

"I'd like you to stay, at least until we hear from the tow truck company to see if they managed to rescue my car."

Theo takes hold of her mom's umbrella and holds it as they walk to the cabin, while Livie allows the rainfall to sprinkle on her to display her independence.

Livie falls into step behind them. Inside the cabin, she immediately heads upstairs as she states the desire to change into fresh clothes. Each step on the stairs feels heavy—the day's events have built up and released a fatigue she now feels coursing through her body.

The voices of Theo and her mom fade to a murmur as Livie sheds her wet clothes, places her phone beside the water bottle on the dresser, and drops her body onto the bed.

Chapter 9
Finn

Finn pulls the steering wheel hard for the left-hand turn, thankful that he decided years ago to learn how to drive and not rely on driverless cars like many of his friends. Ironic really, that a tech nerd like him would trust technology the least.

That's part of his skeptical nature. Always questioning things. He can still hear his mom's voice from when he was growing up and when he'd question the authenticity or reliability of things. "Finn, sometimes you just have to trust. You are going to hijack all the enjoyment you can get out of life if you are skeptical of everything. Besides, not everyone appreciates a skeptic." He'd respond that he wasn't censorious or querulous in his approach, more just inquisitory, and that made him likeable. She'd respond with "don't be so persnickety." It was the kind of discourse he had with her frequently enough that he wondered if she was legitimately worried whether he'd be able to manage in life. But then, when he went off to university and graduated summa cum laude, she gave a speech at his graduation about how he would always question everything and then he'd "feel the fear and do it anyway." He has replayed that comment in his head many times since. He sees himself as a man of action. Someone who gets things done and doesn't just contemplate them, believing that if he jumps the net will appear, as will the worthwhile experience.

Maybe it was that approach to life that landed him in a relationship with Saba. While they verbally sparred when they met, he immediately admired her independent spirit and free-thinking ways. When he described her to his cousin Agrafena, he characterized her as "enormously attractive, with sex appeal that commands attention." Agrafena responded, "Seems you are smitten."

But now he and Saba have run into a barrier, and he isn't sure if it is something that they will overcome together, or if it will pull them apart. He knows that while he could just go on pretending and thus remove the barrier, he has to be true to himself. He is on the fence on the internet debate. He's also concerned about who is really behind the scenes of it all. He tried to explain to Saba that the hubristic beliefs of those involved in keeping the internet off are disturbingly similar to what has been seen from some of history's most awful dictators. People who had an agenda to bring their own version of a new world order.

But regardless of his points, Saba remains a steadfast, adamant champion for the non-interneters. Can they remain lovers, or even friends, if he stays on the fence? What will happen if he joins the other side?

He posed these questions to Agrafena to get her input, knowing that she had always been honest and direct with him. She said that she thinks Saba is like a lot of Agrafena's Russian family members. They see things in black and white, and if they can't pull you to their side, they are just as likely to set you adrift.

In fairness to Saba, until the recent rally, she rightfully assumed that he was on the same side as she was. When they attended that first rally with their friends, they had only known each other for less than a week and were hardly even friends yet. While he made a sign supporting the internet coming back on, he clearly wasn't too committed to that. Later they attended several rallies together as a couple—a couple in support of keeping the internet off. Saba was a speaker at a couple of those rallies, and Finn was right there beside her. Then came this latest rally, and the tide seemed to have changed. The anti-interneters were carrying the momentum and were clearly going to dominate the rally. He had his sign ready, and Saba had hers.

Then he phoned her the night before the rally and said he wasn't going.

When he made that call, the package he had received in the mail was on his kitchen table. He wasn't really surprised that someone could gather all that information, backed up with pictures, claims of audio files, emails, credit card statements, and online posts, including things he posted under various pseudonyms. He always told himself that those were his "digital pen names," so he was more enraged to see they had been hacked than he was disturbed.

He was embarrassed by some of it, especially some of his secretive sexual exploits that were clearly not so secretive, as well as evidence that he sometimes blew his salary on booze, gambling, and other equally disposable placebos. But he was not in shock, as others might be, that someone could gather that kind of material on him. He is a tech nerd himself who could easily hack such things. In fact, at first he thought it was rather audacious for the Friendly World Network, whoever they were, to send him this stuff. Then he started to wonder why they were sending this kind of package to people—maybe to everyone? That thought made him swear out loud. It made him want to fight back against such an invasion of one's privacy.

After the steam of his fury subsided, he told himself that it really made no difference in his life and how he would approach things. His conflicting views of a world with or without the internet were swirling within him long before that package arrived. He just felt it was time that Saba knew about his conflicting feelings about it all. At times, he found life more sensible, and yes happier without the internet. Other times, he longed for the internet days.

When the internet first went down, he immediately thought of the loss of data and information that the university kept on its mainframe computer. Had that been lost too? That night, while it was still dark out, he made his way to the campus where they kept their mainframe computers. To his relief, he discovered that most of the data was still there. Some was lost "to the cloud" that he no longer had access to, but most of it was safe, and he took measures to ensure it remained so. He even unhooked all the internet cables and connections, just in case. While they weren't working anyway, he sought to remove any possibility of the data being lost. He has since heard many stories of organizations losing everything, or almost everything.

As a result of that fateful night, Finn was able to continue working at the university and has in fact become that much more valuable to them. Without the internet, his work is no longer constantly interrupted by emails or unnecessary virtual meetings. Nor has he been working late into the night, as the world no longer operated like everything was open twenty-four seven. It has made him thankful for the loss of the internet.

But at times, he misses being able to play online games with friends or creating programs for the university that can be easily shared. He misses being able to check on his banking through a simple app on his phone or ordering his coffee before he arrives to simply pick it up.

The debate—whether they are better off with or without the internet—thunders within him every day. When he talks to his colleagues or other friends, or even strangers he meets at the bank or grocery store (which now stocks less variety than before), he hears many say the same thing. They feel the same conflict raging within their own heads. Agrafena is an exception to this. While she holds no ill will towards those that enjoy life without the internet, she wants it back. But he thinks she is overly influenced by her "black and white" Russian father in the matter. While he has learnt a lot about Russia and come to appreciate the culture through Agrafena, he thinks they often overlook the aporetic conflict between what they are told by their "motherland" and what should be their own logical thinking.

Even as Finn finishes that thought, he can hear Agrafena telling him that's "how an American would think, with their own arrogance on display." Agrafena has always provided a counterbalance to some of his thoughts. Still, he feels a lot of conflict on this issue.

It all came to a head the night before the St Patty's Day rally, when he told Saba he was going to bail on the rally. He considered telling her he was not feeling well or coming up with some other excuse, but he couldn't bring himself to articulate it for fear of sounding weak and clumsy. He has never been comfortable lying or faking things. But he didn't give her the real reason either. He just told her that he didn't feel like going. When she pressed him, he told her that he just wasn't up to it this time.

Did Saba surmise that he wasn't as big of a supporter of the non-interneters as he had been showing? Did she suspect the truth all along? Could they have a relationship going forward? Was Agrafena right, that it's a black and white issue for Saba?

The questions are beating a drum in his head as he parks in front of her condo building. He decides he's going to tell her about the package he received. It would demonstrate that his internal conflict is genuine and that he can be vulnerable with her. He mentally rehearses what he is going to say one last time before walking to her door.

The poetry of the conversations in their relationship usually starts with an opening stanza from Saba. Finn is determined to make this conversation different, and as soon as Saba opens the door, he launches into his rehearsed speech.

"Sweetheart, I'm sorry I didn't come to the rally, and it's not that I don't support you. I'm just a little conflicted about this whole thing and want to tell you some things..." Saba cuts him off, taking charge of the rhythm of the dialogue.

"Finn, as arresting as it was for me to hear that you were not coming to the rally at the last minute, I was not as surprised as you might think. I know these are confusing times for everyone, and you are an emotional person. So, it doesn't surprise me that you have conflicting emotions about this. It's okay that you do. Really. I'm fortunate because I don't. I can see clearly what a non-internet world will be like long-term, and I know without a doubt that we will be happier in it. You and I, together. In a friendlier, more peaceful world. I'm asking you to trust me in this. You've supported me throughout, and all I want from you is that continued support. If you don't want to hold up a sign or shout out your support right now, I can live with that. But I need you by my side."

It is clear that Saba has prepared this speech as well, but it doesn't affect the passion with which she delivers it. Her outlook is "black and white," just as Agrafena predicted. Finn also sees the emotion in Saba as she speaks, and the sexy "I got this" attitude that drew him to her in the first place. She caps her statement with that wide, inviting smile and perfect white teeth that raises his heart rate, every time. She isn't angry, which is what he feared. He isn't sure he can follow through with what she is asking of him, but he knows that his feelings for her can make him believe he can. The thread of his reasoning now hangs thin, weak, and vulnerable. He is cautious, deliberate, and slow in his response.

"I can be by your side, Saba. I want to be. Desperately so. But a non-internet world feels antediluvian to me sometimes. What if I can't get to where I fully believe such a world is better?" He wants her to see that while he can be reliable, there is a lot more in the drawer than the masks he wears.

Saba kisses him passionately before whispering in his ear.

"You will, darling. I'm confident of that. You don't need to rush it; let it come naturally. I think you just need to stop thinking of every apocryphal outcome and go with the flow of the changes we are seeing."

Finn wants to debate the apocryphal outcome statement, but he doesn't allow his mouth to even open to words he'd swallow anyway. With that, Saba's words ends the debate, at least for now. They decide to go out for walk together and get something to eat. Saba goes to her bedroom to get ready while Finn waits in her living room.

He scans the familiar pictures in her place, including a stunning painting of the Tidal Basin, the cherry blossoms in full bloom. His eyes move around the room and stop on a magazine with the title: *A New Democracy*. Saba works in political circles, so the magazine doesn't surprise him. What catches his eye is the name and address at the bottom left corner of the magazine. It's Saba's address, but not her name. The name above the address is Chandni Varma.

The name has his mind spinning, searching for where he heard it before. He knows he has. He is momentarily frozen thinking about it. His eyes fall on the magazine again to get a closer look, hoping it will come to him, and he sees the numbers 322 on a piece of paper that is peeking out from the magazine. He reaches for it when he hears Saba coming out of the bedroom, then instinctively retracts his hand and straightens up.

"Sweetie, I just realized that before I cut you off earlier, you said there were some things you wanted to tell me. What are those?"

"Oh, nothing really. Just that it feels strange getting things in the actual mail these days. I was so used to everything being online."

"That's true for all of us. I kind of enjoy opening the physical mail. Did you get anything in particular in the mail?"

"Not really. Just some bills and a letter from my mom."

"A letter from your mom? That's nice. Why don't you tell me about it on our walk?"

Chapter 10

Maggie's Surprise

The knock on the door and her mom's voice intrude into the strings of a dream Livie is grasping to hold on to as her mind searches for the reality of her surroundings. She opens her eyes and responds through the fog of her thoughts.

"I'll be down in a minute, Mom."

"Okay sweetie. Theo has news on your car."

News on her car. Livie chews on the words and quietly repeats them to herself. Images of her car, teetering over the edge of the road where she left it, flash before her. She opens her mouth, but then stops herself from asking if the news is good or bad.

She pushes herself up from the bed and sits on the edge. Searching for the time, she glances over at the dresser and fixes her eyes on the water bottle. Her thoughts detour to Hannah. The one person she could always rely on over the last several years. Her confidante, friend, and so often the one who would inspire her. The person who was there for her when she was in need of emotional support and love. The person who made her major life challenges seem manageable. The person who would pull the sword out of the stone.

But Hannah isn't here, and she left their last exchange in anger. Livie replays the warp and woof of that last conversation in her mind. It just serves to fuel her anger. They haven't talked since, and it has become a passive aggressive game of who will phone whom first. The tar pits of Livie's anger have kept her silent.

Livie gets up and picks up her phone from the desk, somehow imagining there would be a missed call from Hannah. All she sees is the time: 4:28 p.m. She must have slept for over an hour.

She suddenly feels a shiver and reaches down to her suitcase for clothes, only to discover it's empty. Her confusion at the image lingers for a few seconds before she opens the top drawer on the dresser to see her clothes neatly folded inside. Her mom must have emptied her suitcase, as if she knew she would be back. As if she knew she would stay. It's enough to make Livie storm off again, except the events of the day has smothered the burn within her to just escape. She looks at herself in the mirror and sees a scared, pale child, which sends a sudden explosion of fear through her. She leans forward, grabbing the edge of the desk for support, then closes her eyes and takes deep breaths. She is deliberate in changing her self-talk to get herself together and go find out if she still has a functioning vehicle.

Shaking off her groggy dolor, Livie steps into the bathroom and splashes color into her face before heading down the stairs, where she can hear Theo and her mom talking. Theo's voice, which could command a room full of people, echoes into the stairway as she descends the final steps.

"It's like the whole world has been turned upside down. Like rivers have changed their course, and stars are showing up in unexpected places in the sky. Maybe the sun will start rising in the north, as all certainty in this world seems lost. It feels like we have entered a dark time in history."

"Wow, that sounds dramatic. Whatcha two talking about?"

"Oh, hi sweetheart. Hope you had a good nap? Theo was just on a bit of a rant about the loss of the internet."

"Oh, okay. I don't like it either, but rivers changing course?"

"I think our friend Theo here is preparing for his speech at the next rally about bringing the internet back."

Livie looks over at Theo, who is leaning forward in his chair as if it might catapult him out.

"I want to ask if you've been to a rally already, but what I really want to know is what's happening with my car?"

Theo stands up, as if his sudden energy can't be contained in the chair, and he walks towards the sink with his coffee mug. He fills Livie in on the status of her vehicle.

The towing company managed to pull the car from the edge of the cliff, but there is some damage to the front wheel well, so it isn't drivable. He had them tow it to a shop to get it fixed, and it should be ready for her in two or three days.

"Two or three days?" Livie repeats as a rhetorical question. Knowing her fate is sealed, she looks over at her mom, and with a curve of a smile gives voice to her acceptance.

"Well, it's a good thing I have a warm bed and place to stay here then."

Theo then tells her about the next rally.

"It's taking place in three days as a response to all the organized rallies put on by those communistic non-interneters. You could join me if you're still here then?" he asks Livie. "You too Maggie," he adds as he reaches for his jacket and bids them farewell.

As the door clicks shut with Theo's exit, silence settles in the cabin—as if staring at the two women to see who will make the first move. The cool, humid air that slipped in through the door has already evaporated from the room when Livie's mom moves towards the kitchen. She stops abruptly and turns to face her daughter. Her voice is soft and more inquisitive in tone than the piteous whine Livie was expecting.

"Livie, can we just hit reset on this?"

"There is no reset in life, Maggie."

Livie's use of her mom's name is a deliberate move she planned after discovering her mom had emptied her suitcase into the dresser. It was a declaration of independence and pushback.

Maggie doesn't move as she clearly swallows the words she was going to respond with, takes a deep breath, and closes her eyes. Her expression remains carefully neutral. The silence circles the room again before Maggie lets out a heavy breath. She keeps her eyes shut while she responds.

"Okay…I'm not asking you to reset everything in our relationship, Livie. I know I can't just wipe out the past and that I've done things that have hurt you deeply."

Maggie opens her eyes and looks at Livie. Livie looks down and keeps the emotionless mask steady on her face, as she knows her mom has more to say.

"I'm not going to ask you to even talk about any of that if you don't want to. I just want to hit a reset on our few days here at the cabin."

Livie lifts her head and projects a blank stare as she looks past her mom. She isn't going to show any acceptance of this easily. Her mom is going to have to do more to earn it, and Livie expects to be let down, as she has been in the past. For now, she will use silence as a response in an attempt to show disinterest.

Maggie moves a few steps closer to her daughter.

"I've spent a lot of time in this cabin over the last several months, and it has given me time to reflect and think about what I want for the rest of my life. I have a lot of things in my past I'm not proud of and wish I could do over. But I can't live in the past anymore and let my life be governed by regret. I need to move forward with what I have. I can make new friends, but I also don't want to lose some of the relationships I have. Even those I know I have hurt, like you, Livie. I'm not asking you to just ignore that past, but I am hoping we can have a fresh start. At least during our time here, if that's all you can give me."

Livie looks into Maggie's eyes as she falters, now just a few feet away. She studies her mom's face, seeing if she can sift out any manipulation in the sincerity of the words. In truth, she knows that they both have shown their share of resentment. For Livie, it came from her allowing her mom to take advantage of her for too long. For her mom, she believes it has been due to her petulant refusal to take responsibility for her own life and grow up.

"Well, you shouldn't have taken my clothes out of my suitcase and put them in the drawers." Livie's voice hardens as she continues, "You shouldn't have touched my suitcase at all, actually."

Maggie moves towards her, and Livie stiffens her arms at her side, expecting an embrace. Maggie surprises her by walking past her towards the door, where she lifts a set of keys from a hook.

"You're right, Livie. I should not have done that. It was a stupid, desperate move to try and get you to stay when I knew you'd come back for your stuff. I don't have a right to expect that of you. You can gather your belongings and I can drive you away from here, if you want."

Livie looks at the keys in Maggie's hand and sees the potential freedom they could bring. But where to?

"You know I don't have anywhere to go. I have to wait here for my car to be fixed."

Maggie walks towards her with the keys in hand.

"I don't want you to feel trapped. I'll leave then, if you want. You can be here by yourself."

"You'd do that?"

Maggie twirls the keys in her hand.

"If that is what you prefer, yes. I'll just go pack up a few things."

Maggie walks over to her bedroom as Livie stands in stunned silence. She expected her mom to return her hot words with her own heat. She played it out in her mind and wondered if the result would be one of them leaving somehow. Perhaps that is what she wished for? But her mom just flipped the script.

Livie walks over to the entrance of Maggie's bedroom and watches her packing clothes into a suitcase.

"Where will you go?"

"I have friends nearby. I'll phone one of them as soon as I'm packed up. I'll be fine...and out of your hair as soon as I can. The fridge and cupboards are stocked with food, so please help yourself to whatever you want."

"So, you're not just going back home to Boston?"

Maggie stops her packing and turns towards Livie.

"I don't live there anymore. I haven't for months. This is my home now."

Maggie turns back to her packing and Livie's resolve begins to crack as the news shudders her bones. She quietly scolds herself for not knowing about the big change in her mom's life.

"I didn't know..."

"Of course you didn't Livie. Don't blame yourself for that, I didn't tell you. I wanted to sort out things in my life first."

"But now you're going to leave your home, so I can stay here by myself?"

"I'll be fine, Livie. Perhaps you will find the quiet time here by yourself as valuable as I have."

"I don't want to be pushing you out of your house...unless you want to leave?"

Maggie zips up the suitcase and turns back towards Livie.

"Of course I don't want to leave. What I want, Livie..." Maggie takes a breath as if swallowing something, then begins again. "You're my daughter, and what I want is for the two of us to have some time together here. Like I said, a fresh start for us...but I also don't want you to feel forced into something, and I don't want to spend three days sparring with you and exchanging barbs. I have a clearer picture than ever before of what I want for the rest of my life. I don't want to live with spite and sadness anymore, and I'm getting better at accepting things I can't change. I went through times when bitterness and regret claimed me every day, and I'm determined to shed that part of me. So…if you prefer to have time to yourself, I'm happy to give that to you. I know I haven't been very good at giving you things you deserve and should expect from your mother. So, if this is a gift I can give you, I'll just be happy if you accept it…anyway, I'll just get my phone and call a friend who I'm sure I can stay with."

Maggie picks up her suitcase, stops in front of Livie, hugs her, and whispers in her ear that she loves her. The words are still sitting in Livie's head as she watches Maggie move to the living room and towards her phone, which she left on a chair.

Livie listens as Maggie phones a friend, Rita, and asks if she can stay with her for a few nights. Livie hears enough of the conversation to understand that Rita was expecting the request, as if she was waiting for it. She has a bed ready for Maggie, and dinner is already on the stove.

Maggie is about to hang up when Livie interjects.

"Maggie, let's have dinner here together before you go?"

Maggie smiles, nods, and turns her attention back to her phone as she tells Rita she will be there after dinner. Livie is certain she can hear the surprise in Rita's voice.

Looking to thwart the silence from simply filling the room again, Livie quickly makes her way to the kitchen.

"Let's see what our options are for dinner." Livie opens the fridge door and calls out what she sees. "There's some chicken…and broccoli…eggs…bacon…and…and…tofu?" She grabs the tofu and turns to face her mom, who is still standing in the living room with her phone in her hand.

"You eat tofu now?"

Maggie pauses as she looks at her daughter like she has interrupted a deep thought. She flits a smile that stops before it reaches her eyes and remains standing where she is.

"You might be surprised to hear of some of the changes in my life, Livie."

"Okay...cool. So, what would you like for dinner, then?"

"Well, before you arrived, I made a fish casserole...but it's in the freezer."

"Hmmm...what kind of fish?"

"That would be the trout that I caught."

Livie raises her eyebrows and squints at her mom, as if trying to see something she missed before.

"Did you *kill* the fish you caught?"

"Well, it's not in the casserole alive."

Livie's face lightens into a smile as she lets out a snort and a chuckle.

"So, I guess we'll have the casserole then?"

"It's frozen, Livie. It'll take over an hour to cook."

Livie turns around, back to the fridge. She bends down to pull the handle on the freezer at the bottom and sees the casserole there. She looks at it as if it will jump out into her arms, thinking that it comes with a fish and a hook. The hook being that it would be too late for her mom to leave after they finish dinner. Her back stiffens at the thought.

As Livie kneels in front of the freezer, she feels her mom's presence behind her.

"You should just leave it there, Livie. It'll take too long to cook, and you need some time to yourself."

The tension in Livie's back suddenly releases as her shoulders drop. She turns her head to look back at her mom, allowing her face to convey the pleasant surprise she feels.

"You don't have to look so shocked, Livie. I meant it when I said I'd leave so you could have the place to yourself. I'm not going to allow some fishy casserole to steal that from you."

Livie lets out another snorting laugh before she can contain it, and Maggie puts her hand on Livie's shoulder.

"It's good to hear that laugh of yours and that you can still find humor in my silly comments. So, how about just some good old bacon and eggs for dinner?"

"You don't want tofu?"

"Nah, I only ever put it in my smoothies."

"Smoothies, really? So when do you make those? ...Don't answer that, I'll cook us the bacon and eggs."

Maggie backs away from Livie and moves over to the stove.

"Sounds good. How about I put the kettle on for tea?"

Maggie moves to the living room while Livie cooks their dinner. Livie feels a warmth of satisfaction that she was able to maneuver the conversation so that she is making dinner—she expected her mom to insist on cooking because it is her kitchen. This way, Livie is able to have a conversation with her mom without having to look at her directly.

Livie jumps right in, asking her mom about buying the cabin. Maggie confirms that she bought it with her savings and a small mortgage.

"So, what about your place in Boston?"

"I gave it up, Livie. I held on to it for a while, but then I was finding I was just here most of the time, and every time I left, I just wanted to get back here."

Livie turns to face her mom, her face projecting concern, her voice soft.

"But what about your job with the dentist?"

Maggie works for a dentist, processing bills and insurance claims and taking care of other clerical duties. It's a job she has had for almost ten years—easily the longest she has ever been in a job. It provides her with the security that eluded her life for decades. Or it used to.

"You don't need to worry, I'm not unemployed."

"But you're not working for the dentist anymore?"

Maggie explains that she has largely been working online from home since moving out to the cabin. She had an agreement with the dentist to go into the office for two days every two weeks. But since the internet shutdown, she hasn't been able to work from home, and the dentist wants her at the office full-time again. She is still discussing it with him and hopes she can figure out a way to work from the cabin even without the internet. Meanwhile, she has picked up a part-time job as a cook at a local eatery.

"Okay, but what if he says you have to be at the office or you lose your job?"

"I dunno, Livie. I wasn't enjoying going in every two weeks and was hoping to work here full time. I've wanted to change the current of my life anyway. Maybe this will help."

"The current of your life?"

"Maybe it's more like tearing down the walls of my previous life and building a new one."

Livie flips the eggs and bacon onto plates and butters the toast while Maggie fills her in on the changes in her life and takes a seat at the table.

Maggie starts to speak as if she is telling someone else's story.

"Several years ago, for the first time in my life, I started saving money in a significant way, with no real plan for it. While contemplating what to do with the rest of my life, I spent some time observing others who seemed happy with their lives, wondering what could make me happier. What I saw was all the brokenness in my life. I noticed that happy people usually have solid, deep, and intimate relationships with their families and friends. They have purpose in their lives. They know how to take in the moments and enjoy them. Moments with people they love, or with nature or art, or the joy of completing something they take pride in. I had little of any of that..."

Livie tries to ignore the complicated jumble of feelings teeming inside of her as she listens to her mother's story.

"I lived a life of fear and anxiety. It was...overwhelming at times. I was so angry all the time, I didn't even know why, and then were the long bouts of sadness."

Livie carries a plate of food for each of them and takes a seat across from her mom. Maggie pauses to say thanks and takes a mouthful before continuing.

"I just wanted to be happy, so I decided to focus my attention on that. I went from observing to talking to people, and I discovered that success, as our society defines it anyway, doesn't guarantee happiness. In fact, just striving for success tends to make happiness *more* elusive. A friend told me that she works at her happiness every day. She said that what you do and your surroundings matter, but what matters more is your mindset. 'The mind is its own place, and in itself can make a heaven of hell, or a hell of heaven.' So I decided I had to work harder to be happy. To adopt a work ethic of happiness.

"But I just couldn't get it where I was, Livie. I needed to change my surroundings. I needed to make a real change in my life...I needed to figure out where the intersection was between the broken person I felt I was, and that person I wanted to be."

"And you found it here at Deerfield." Livie states this in a flat tone, as a fact, without the emotion it should contain. Deep down, her mom is making the wall Livie has built crumble, but she still wants to play tough.

Maggie pauses as she looks intently into her daughter's eyes, searching for some acceptance, some understanding.

"It's okay Maggie, you're safe to have good memories here. I do too, actually. I think...well, my last time here was painful, that's all."

Maggie reaches across the table to grab Livie's hand as she looks at her and silently mouths a "thanks".

They sit eating in silence for several minutes, as if the dance of their conversation has hit a bridge without lyrics, which they have to pass over to discover what is on the other side.

Livie, with her plate near empty, pushes out from her seat and gets up.

"I'm going to put on some tea, want some?"

"Sure...though I shouldn't be too late getting to Rita's."

With her back to her mom, Livie finds it easier to shield the emotions she kept tethered down over dinner. She puts the kettle on for the tea and stares at it while continuing the conversation.

"So, when did you move out here then?"

"Last winter, about nine months ago. This is my first summer here."

"I had no idea."

"That's because I didn't want you to know until I had myself more established. I wanted to make the changes in my life first, then show you."

"But I'd already seen the cabin...well, maybe not with the new deck."

"Not the cabin, Livie. I wanted to show you that I have a different life and that I'm a different person. I'm happy here, and I don't have the same anger that's just ready to explode." Maggie pauses and draws her hand to her mouth as she lowers her voice to just above a whisper. "I know I didn't demonstrate that very well to you earlier today."

Livie turns around to see her mom with her face buried in her hands.

"It's okay Mom. If I'm honest about it, I was looking for something to give me a reason to leave. I provoked you."

Maggie looks up as a tear snakes its way down Livie's cheek. The emotion jumps between them, and Maggie's voice cracks as she pushes out her next words.

"I'm so sorry, Livie."

Maggie gets up, and Livie meets her at her seat. They embrace.

The whistling sound of the kettle boiling intrudes into their space. Maggie looks into her daughter's eyes and then makes a move towards the stove.

"I'll get it. Why don't you sit and relax? You made us dinner."

Livie throws the question over her shoulder as she makes her way to the living room couch. "So, I guess you'd really like to see the internet come back, and then maybe you can keep working from here?"

When her mom doesn't immediately respond, Livie fills the silence with the speech she rehearsed and delivered to Hannah about why they need the internet back. How much the medical and banking sectors rely on it, including the whole economical infrastructure. How the loss of the internet will result in deaths and the medical system will no longer be able to respond as quickly—that there has already been an increase in suicides reported.

With two cups of tea in hand, Maggie turns towards Livie and interrupts her mid-sentence.

"I can tell you have a lot to say about this, Livie. I've heard it already, to be honest. You should stick around for the rally in a few days. You could hear Theo speak; I'm sure you will find a kindred spirit in those views."

"Maybe I will...but you say that like they are *not* your views too?"

"Oh, dear...of course I want the internet back. It makes my life much easier and helps with my job for sure. But I do wonder sometimes if it's a better life. Before there was even an internet at all, the world was just simpler, and I think safer. You've only known a world with the internet. I can remember a time when it wasn't so invasive."

"Invasive?" Livie's tone demands an explanation.

"Yes, I think that is a fair word to use. There's a human cost to having the internet in every aspect of our lives."

Livie replays her mom's words in her head. A simpler, safer world. The human costs of the internet...*Hmm, sounds a lot like what I heard from Fairleigh in the coffee shop,* she thinks.

Livie squints and fixes her now fiery eyes on her mom.

"Maggie, our world, as you put it, has been chaotic and extremely unsafe for many because we have lost the internet."

Maggie glances skyward, towards the beams holding the roof up, as if they would shine a light down to end the debate she wishes she didn't start.

"Okay, you know what, I think we should chat about this another time. Before I head over to Rita's, I really would like to hear how you're doing. How's your job going? Are you enjoying living in Washington still? Those kinds of things."

Livie takes a hard look at her mom. She was expecting some sort of woof or dismissive response, particularly as Livie reverted to calling her Maggie. Did she just witness her mom swallowing the response she really wanted to give? Her voice projected sincerity, but was her warm smile forced? Livie could easily interpret her mom's questions as disingenuousness, laced with hurt feelings from the past—ready to pounce on the conversation at any moment. Her mom showing any genuine interest in her life previously came in small morsels, if at all. Livie decides on her usual self-preservation response in an effort to just change the subject.

"I'm fine. The job's good, and Washington's my home."

"Oh Livie. I seriously doubt that. All of us have had our lives shaken with the internet going down. I get that you may not want to talk to me about it. It's just that...well...as I said earlier, I'm making changes in my life, and one of those is that I want you to be in my life more, and I need to start somewhere. If you don't want to share details about your life with me, that's up to you. If that's the case, maybe you can tell me how your friend Hannah is doing?"

"Hannah's fine."

Maggie takes a deep, audible breath.

"Okay, maybe I should just head over to Rita's. Livie, there must have been a reason why you decided to come up to the cabin and spend time with me?"

Livie can see her mom trying to build a bridge between them, but each time she makes some progress, she knows she just starts tearing it down again. *You are not being fair here.* She can hear Hannah's voice in her head. *Why did she come out here?*

"You're right, life has been chaotic, and the uncertainty of it all has caused a lot of anxiety. I guess I came here looking for some peace from it all. Some grounding in a familiar place. So much doesn't feel familiar anymore."

"That's what I found here, Livie. Peace and grounding in a familiar place."

"You mentioned earlier that you wanted to find the intersection between the person you were and the person you want to be. So is this the place that gives you that?"

"It's helped, but that intersection is a mindset and an approach to life as much as anything. This place has given me the peace and perspective to change my outlook on life. I guess that's why I am reluctant to just go back to my previous life...even if it costs me my job."

Maggie goes on to describe her life at the cabin and mentions several new friends she has made, including Theo and Rita.

"Livie, you have structured a life that values your relationships with your friends. I know that because of the way you talk about them. You've been wise and have invested the time and energy to build those relationships. I haven't been." Maggie pulls at the lint on the arm rest of her chair. "I have burnt and walked away from more relationships than I've built."

"Sounds like you are changing that, though?"

"I am, and it has made my life richer. You've inspired me that way."

Maggie goes on to tell Livie about the new activities she has been getting into with her growing new list of friends. She mentions fishing, canning, playing bridge, birdwatching, and canoeing, each with a chuckle and an anecdote.

Livie fills her mom in about the uncertainty of her job and her experience working with Hannah. She holds back telling her about the sudden rift between her and Hannah.

"Oh geez, look at the time. I'd better get going to Rita's."

"I guess it's that time. But Mom, while I'm here, how about we plan some time for you to introduce me to your new friends? And maybe we could go canoeing together?"

Maggie fills her in about some of her friends and tells Livie that Rita is the friend with the canoe. They make plans to take it out the next afternoon. Maggie grabs her suitcase, and they step outside onto the deck, where they lock into an embrace that lingers.

"I love you Livie. And I'm proud of you," Maggie whispers into Livie's ear.

"I know Mom, and I'm proud of the changes you've made in your life."

Livie watches as Maggie gets into her car. A cool breeze hits her cheeks, and she smiles at the refreshing feeling it provides. As the breeze subsides, everything seems to stand still in time for a moment. The moon is at three quarters, its light throwing shadows through the trees. The distinctive hoot of an owl pierces the silence. Livie stands there for several minutes, taking deep breaths as she takes in the beauty around her and feels the warmth of contentment washing through her.

Livie's phone buzzes when she steps back into the cabin. She doesn't recognize the number.

"Hello?"

"Livie? It's Larry."

Her boss. The same guy who told her they didn't have work right now—"maybe never." He left her wondering about the future of the career she had built with hard work and long days. *What does he want now?* The call is an unwanted intrusion into her evening, and Livie doesn't answer right away.

"You there, Livie?"

"Yes, yes. What's up Larry?"

"Look, I realize I basically laid you off when the internet went off, but I am phoning with some exciting news. You in town?"

"Um...no, I'm not. I'm at Deerfield Lake."

"Deerfield Lake? Where's that?"

"It's several hours away. What's the news, Larry?"

"Well, I can't get into it too much on the phone. It's highly secretive and confidential. But I have secured a major government contract and, like, it's a real game changer Livie. I need you back at work."

Livie can hear the delight in his voice as the words come out fast and in one long breath. It hits her cold, though. She has stopped thinking about work and isn't anxious to jump back into whatever this is.

"Well, I'm stuck here for at least a few days as my vehicle is getting worked on, so I don't have transportation."

"Really? What happened to your vehicle?"

"Oh...well...Larry, I'll tell you another time. What's the contract about that's so exciting and urgent?"

"I really can't say much on the phone...I actually shouldn't be talking on the phone about it, in case someone is listening in."

"Listening in? Do you really think..."

Larry cuts her off.

"Yes, I do. It's a risk. People shut down the internet. Accessing cell phone calls isn't a huge leap for the non-interneters."

"Non-interneters?" Livie is familiar with the term, but asks the question as if she is naïve.

"Yeah, you know, the people going to rallies and such, saying they want to keep the internet from coming back on. The government thinks some of them could be behind what or who shut it off in the first place. That's why they contacted us...to do surveillance and to infiltrate them."

Livie knows that Larry loves a good story. She's sure that the thrill of the hunt of an investigation and the surveillance required have him bursting to tell her more about this new government contract. She just needs to tease it out of him.

"Oh...interesting. So the government wants us to watch them and find out what they are up to?"

"Listen, I've said too much already. Any calls should be kept under two minutes, and I'm probably over that now."

"Is that why you called me from a number I didn't recognize? Two minutes on a call, is that part of the contract?" Livie laughs through her nose as her voice dips with sarcasm.

"Oh, there is that sneaky laugh of yours. I miss that too. But listen Livie, there are some unusual...well strict rules around this one. I can fill you in more in person. Can't you get back here tomorrow? I really could use you. We need to sit down and map out a plan. Your ability to analyze things and blend in easily is what I really need here. We haven't had any real work since the internet went down, and this is a huge opportunity."

Livie tells him she would do what she can to try and get back sooner. Larry hangs up with the same urgency he had on the call—as soon as he confirms that he will be calling her again the next day to chat more.

Livie puts her phone down and looks out the window, seeing that a fog has rolled in.

Her conflicting thoughts and emotions gather and pile up against the fog. Her incompatible feelings of hurtful resentment and love towards her mom. Her desperate need for Hannah's friendship and thoughtful advice on what she should do next. The anger she feels from their last exchange, which has created a gully between them that neither are willing to cross. The job that gave her purpose just a month ago, which she has now lost all interest in—until this sudden call. If she takes on the work that Larry described, would it dig a wider chasm between her and Hannah? Would it push aside the time she has committed to with her mom?

She stares out the window as the thoughts circle in her head. The fog has grown deep and penetrating and is making its way onto the porch. She looks down at her phone and dials the number from the last call.

It rings several times, and she is ready to hang up when she suddenly hears Larry's voice.

"Larry, I was thinking, I'm ready to move on with my life now, and I'm not sure..."

"Please leave a message after the beep...*beeeep*."

Livie's shoulders sink at the realization that she just got interrupted by Larry's voicemail—something she has experienced all too often in the past.

She turns her phone off and looks back out the window, straining to see through the fog.

Inhale. Exhale. Carry on.

Chapter 11
Finn's Quest

Finn has only been in the meeting room for fifteen minutes, yet there are so many words, phrases, and arguments on the tip of his tongue—all clamouring to be spoken out loud. But...he sucks them all in, holding his tongue and smiling as if he is one of them.

It isn't that he completely disagrees with what the crowd stands for or what their "cause" is about. It's the hyperboles, the exaggerations, the so-called facts they play loose with that he finds so grating. Statements like "the world is an easier place to live and survive in without the internet." *Well,* he thinks, *some of life is certainly simpler and thus easier, but you can't just order what you want online anymore.* That has made life more difficult, not easier, though maybe less hectic. The loss of the internet has killed a lot of businesses, and the economy has spiralled down with it. Sure, some things are rebounding, and some new businesses have even come out of the ashes, so to speak. But the loss of the internet has brought on a lot of chaos. And with that, a steady current of anxiety that is prevalent on the faces of many.

He finds the mantras they salt their speeches with to be quite grating. Things like: "The world is a friendlier place." It almost uncorks him and begs him to stand up. Sure, some parts are "friendlier", but many things are decidedly less friendly. The simple inability to collaborate with like-minded individuals from around the world has made it less friendly, he believes. He wants to debate these points. Have a real discussion about them. But this isn't the crowd for that, and he doesn't want to come off as an outsider. He needs to earn their trust.

His journey to making his way into this secretive, seemingly exclusive meeting, has put much of what is dear to him in his life at risk. He isn't about to let his skeptical anger hijack that—as his mom would have warned him. His job, ability to get future work in his profession, and many of his friendships could be scorched if he doesn't tread carefully.

He came to be in this room, or rather barn, full of people after surreptitiously skulking behind Hannah for a week to watch her coming and goings. It wasn't even Hannah who led him to this place, but someone he saw her having a clandestine meeting with in a coffee shop. Following that person turned out to require a fair bit more stealth, including a few late nights of hanging out by her apartment, as she would often leave for somewhere in the middle of the night. He dubbed her "Foxhole" in his mind, due to her look and secretive nature. That all brought him here, at 2 a.m. in the morning. To this rather drafty barn. A place he now fears might *be* a foxhole, where he has potentially trapped himself with no real escape route other than the way he came in. Before arriving at this place, he even managed to make himself a button that matches those worn by some of the people he saw "Foxhole" meet with.

Shortly after he arrived, he scanned every face in the room, expecting to find Saba here—but to no avail. Perhaps she wasn't invited to this meeting? Perhaps she isn't part of the Friendly World Network after all? He can still remember when she started referring to it as the "FWN", as if the acronym added sophistication. Coming to the meeting, he was convinced he'd see her here. He could feel his heart racing when he arrived as he braced himself for a potential confrontation with Saba. Still, "catching" her in this setting was the whole purpose of involving himself in this charade. Well, that, and maybe some deep curiosity along with his tendency to toy with mischievousness.

He first started suspecting that Saba, or maybe he should say Chandni, was part of the Friendly World Network when he saw her real name on the magazine in her apartment a few months earlier. He later confirmed her name when he surreptitiously lifted her ID from her purse.

After that, he began to wonder what else she was keeping from him. He didn't see anything else related to the number—322—he saw written on the piece of paper that day in her apartment, but it lingers in his head. What could be the meaning of it? He knows what 322 means when accompanied by a skull and bones but doesn't believe that it can possibly be that.

Contemplating the various reasons why a person would keep a separate identity from their real one, he kept coming back to the thought that she was a spy. As his mind mulled over the possibilities, pieces of a puzzle circling in his head started to click together and form a story. Tiny incongruities formed a pattern. Saba making plans with him and then suddenly being unavailable; strange phone calls she'd exit a room to take; people she would say hi to on the street and in shops that he never met and wasn't introduced to. She led another life apart from him, and somehow he had been oblivious to it. Blinded by his infatuation. In denial to support his fantasies.

He thought about the various rallies and events he joined her at and the people she seemed to know as old friends. The many conversations about the internet and the wealth of information she could draw on about what the world was like before the internet. A world she never lived in. Where would she get such information? As Finn thought about it more, he realized that it was like she came armed with many arguments for an internetless world. He could see the widening of her calculating eyes whenever she was given a counter argument to the internet-free world. As he came closer to concluding that she was a spy, the logic of it all fell into place. A spy for the Friendly World Network. Part of the very people that brought the internet down.

He tried several times to catch her in a moment that would confirm his suspicions, but she was clearly well-versed and skilled at espionage. She had concealed it from him, her lover, and was able to keep it buttoned down even when he was deliberately looking for signs. For clues. For anything that confirmed she was part of the FWN.

Frustrated by his failed efforts to catch her out, he thought of confronting her, but then he'd miss an opportunity, and besides, she might simply deny it. He knew she could easily conjure up some other story for the dual identities, just like she would come up with reasons for being unavailable for periods of time. But if he could catch her at a meeting with the FWN, she would not be able to deny it. He could then unravel the mysteries of the woman that he still cared for very much.

This all brought him to his quest to get inside the FWN and find out what they were really about without having to join their so-called cause—even if he had to give the appearance of drinking some of their Kool-Aid. That is when he sought out Hannah. Hannah was clearly all in on the internetless world, and while he didn't believe she was part of the FWN, he thought she may have connections within the FWN. He was right.

At first, he took a quizzical approach with Hannah about why she thought the world was better without the internet. When she started using phrases like "a friendlier world," "life is simpler," and "relationships fuller"—terms he had heard from Saba—he knew she likely had connections within the FWN. Just like Saba did. Or so he assumed—as doubts are now straying into his thoughts. He really thought he'd see her at this meeting. But he has scanned all the faces he has seen here. Several times he noticed someone from afar and thought it could potentially be her. Then he'd see their face and be disappointed. She clearly isn't here. With the late night and emotional investment he expended to get here, the exhaustion is beginning to catch up with him.

Finn makes his way to the bathroom to collect his thoughts. As he walks there, his thoughts are to find a route to simply slip out of this place. He's already invested enough time in this, and he had nothing to show for it. His mind is made up. After a quick visit to the loo, he'll just walk out the way he came. If anyone asks, he'll say he is stepping out to get some fresh air. He approaches the bathroom door when he hears his name being called out in an inquisitive tone.

"Finn?"

The voice registers with him, but he can't place it. His first thought is to ignore it. Pretend he didn't hear it. He doesn't want to be recognized here, unless it is Saba, and it clearly wasn't her voice. Before he can make his exit to the loo, he hears his name again, this time too loud to pretend not to hear.

"Finn?!"

He feels the movement of people turning around him, curious to see where the voice is coming from, which has now captured the attention of many in the vicinity. Finn turns as his mind registers who the speaker is.

It is the voice of someone he thought might be important for his career in an internetless world. His shoulders sag at the sudden realization that perhaps he has been duped. As he pastes on a smile and turns to greet Nita, he lectures himself for not seeing that she is part of the FWN.

He met Nita through Hannah when they were walking together in the park one day. Nita happened to run into them, and Hannah introduced her as her friend and colleague. Somehow, Finn took that to mean they worked together, and it hit a blind spot in him. He didn't stop to suspect that Nita could be with the FWN, as she almost immediately took a liking to him and quizzed him about his technical knowledge and skills. Later, Nita had him over to her place with some other friends of hers to see if he could hack their computers. She told him that his hacking ability was a valuable commodity, as many people didn't know how to retrieve information from their own computers since the internet went down. When he was able to produce some long-lost files off her computer, she simply responded with "brilliant". She said it with such enthusiasm that he began to wonder if she had a crush on him. She told him she had connections with people in business who could really use his skills. This made her unforgettable to him. As he briefly thinks back to that night now, he scolds himself for not seeing through it, and his excitement for what it could have meant for his future comes crashing down.

Finn turns and immediately acknowledges her, projecting excitement in his voice that belies his feelings.

"Nita! What a pleasure seeing you here."

Nita acknowledges him with a nod and then moves rapidly to close the space between them as she reaches out for his arm. Her voice is quiet and low as she looks him directly in the eyes.

"Come with me, where we can talk more privately. You look quite alarmed to see me here."

They start walking towards one of the back walls, Finn following her lead.

"I *am* surprised to see you here, Nita. I thought I was concealing that, though," Finn whispers.

"Well, I think everyone could see that smile was a mask to hide your real feelings. But don't worry about it, Finn. I'm sorry I couldn't reveal my involvement with this group earlier. I had to be certain you were sincere about your interest. I was actually quite hopeful I might see you at one of these gatherings sometime."

"Really? I don't know how I missed seeing you earlier. I thought I scanned all the faces that are here. I'm sure I would have noticed you."

"You probably did, but I was in a hidden room with some others when you came in. I saw you come into the barn. You were scanning faces? Hoping to see Hannah here?"

"Hannah, no. Um...I mean, sure I thought she might be here."

"Oh, so someone else? Hannah isn't part of the FWN, Finn. She does make it easier for us to keep tabs on a friend of hers who is working for the other side, but that is the extent of her involvement with us right now. She likes to pretend she is part of the FWN, but we're still not certain enough about her to invite her to something like this."

"I wasn't invited, and I got in."

"True. Your invite was rather inexplicit, shall we say. Finn, there's someone I would like you to meet."

Finn is contemplating the fallacy he has been operating under—that no one knew he was seeking out the FWN—when Nita starts leading him towards a tall, slender but broad-shouldered man with piercing blue eyes. Finn stops, abruptly ending Nita's momentum as well.

"I don't believe I ever told you that I was all in on a world without the internet or joining the FWN, but you expected me to be here tonight?"

Nita looks at him and reaches out to straighten a dangling strand of his hair. It's an intimate gesture; something that Saba often does.

"Finn, I know you are now processing much of what's happening here, and that's actually why you're here. Besides your superior technical skills, which could be a great asset to us if deployed properly, your natural skepticism and inquisitive mind fits very well into the culture that we promote here."

"That's great, but I don't think you answered my question, Nita."

"You're right. We didn't know for certain that you would be here tonight. We were hopeful, though. Finn, I believe your true destiny is what brought you here. Now let me introduce you to someone who could change your life."

Finn looks past Nita and sees that the striking gentleman is now just several strides away and making eye contact with him. Finn smiles and nods as if to acknowledge the recognition; his disappointment about not seeing Saba here hitting him. He really didn't come here for any other reason, and now it appears that Nita has other plans.

"Finn, this is Casey Aquilar. I was telling him about your particular skills."

Casey reaches out his hand to shake Finn's. His eyes, piercing and confident, stare into Finn's.

"It's a pleasure to meet you, Finn. Nita tells me that your skills as a hacker are exceptional. She actually says you could be one of the best she has seen."

Finn turns and smiles at Nita to escape Casey's stare.

"Well, thank you for that gracious compliment. I'm sorry, I'm...well, I'm new here and don't know anyone. Who are you?"

Casey immediately relaxes his posture. He is clearly a person who could command a room or charm an individual to follow whatever path he leads them on.

"My bad, and I apologize. I should have done a better job of introducing myself." Casey leans in close to Finn and lowers his voice. "While I don't like to advertise it, I am, along with Nita here, part of the founding leadership of the FWN."

Finn looks over at Nita again and then back to Casey. "Of course. Well, perhaps I should tell you more about myself then?"

"Oh, no need to Finn. I know you work at Georgetown University, and I know you received a package about your life but didn't react to it—or seem overly concerned about it."

If Casey's aim was to make Finn feel vulnerable, he hit the target. Finn's voice is weaker than he intends when he responds.

"Okay...so is there a reason I was invited to this meeting?" Finn surprises himself with the acknowledgement that his presence here has somehow been choreographed without his knowledge.

"Of course there is. If Nita is correct about your skills, we could really use you in this battle."

Finn lets out a serrated chuckle.

"Battle? It seems you won that already with knocking the internet off."

"I know you are a clever man, Finn. While we have very powerful backers and supporters, you know there are forces working to restore the internet. We also have other plans the other side knows nothing about. I'm sure your response is designed to tease more information out of me. That'll come as our trust in you grows. That's if we can trust you? Can we?"

Finn slightly straightens his posture, pushing his shoulders back and chest out. *In for a penny, in for a pound,* he tells himself.

"Absolutely. I'm here to support keeping the internet off."

He surprises himself with the assuredness of his words, but something clicks inside of him, and he knows if this is going to work, he has to at least project the impression that he is all in.

"Alright then. We have a little test for you that will give you the opportunity to demonstrate that trust. We will have to set up a meeting to lay it out for you, but the gist of it is we need you to access someone's computer and tell us what they have been up to without leaving a trace that you were there. Think you could be up for that?"

"Sounds intriguing. It sounds fairly simple. Is this a computer in an office somewhere?"

Casey gives Nita a look as his right eyebrow rises. "I hope this fellow is up for the risks we will need him to take."

Nita looks at Finn and continues, tagging in for Casey.

"The computer is in someone's apartment. Another of our operatives will break in for you at the right time. Your task will be to access the information on the computer. Perhaps you are thinking that doing that and leaving no trace of your presence will be easy enough for someone with your skills. However, the computer belongs to a tech geek like you, and it will likely be equipped with a sophisticated tracking device and a complex password."

Casey looks at Nita and tags in again.

"In addition, your time to do this will be limited. The operative who will break in for you will be watching the door and will tell you when you need to leave, which could happen quickly."

Finn steels himself and in a demonstration of his readiness, he pushes out enthusiasm that he hopes doesn't appear simulated.

"Sounds right up my alley. Working under pressure in secret. What kind of information are you hoping I'll be able to get from the computer?"

Casey looks at Nita and speaks to her directly, as if Finn isn't there.

"I think we need to first set up the initial test we talked about. He's a bit too self-assured about this and needs to understand the risks involved here."

Casey then turns to Finn and leans in closer. His voice is soft but steady.

"You will learn more in due course. Nita here doesn't even know who it is we are targeting. We keep the circle of knowledge tight and on a need-to-know basis."

Nita jumps in before Finn has a chance to respond.

"So, the next thing you need to do is approach your friend Hannah and ask her if she can find out when and where the FWN meets. You are not to tell her anything about this meeting tonight. This is a test for Hannah too, as we expect she will go to meet our operative at a coffee shop—the same person who induced you to come here tonight—to seek the information. We also want to see if she shares it with her friend that we are keeping tabs on. Hannah should come back to you with information that will lead to your assignment."

As Nita is finishing her sentence, Casey talks over her.

"This assignment, Finn, is likely the most important of your life so far. You don't want to let us down. I don't have to tell you how far our reach is if you, in any way, betray the information we will be trusting you with."

Chapter 12
A Spy Amongst Us

The night crawled by, skulking away with hours of sleep that Livie felt her body crave. Yet, at 4:30, as her alarm jolts her awake, she manages to crawl out of bed and push her body down the stairs for some coffee.

When she crawled into bed earlier, her mind wandered to the times she and Twiggy would rise before the sun came up. The rascal that she was, Twiggy would pull the blankets off Livie to force her out of bed, insisting that they get up and not miss the sunrise. Livie would protest and pull the blankets back but would always give in to Twiggy's "we can do this" mantras. They'd head out in a boat on the lake to watch the light come into the sky. Before the sun could make a complete appearance, they would watch the fish jumping (as they only did in such numbers at that time of the day). It was during those times that Livie found the most peace and joy at the lake. Twiggy's persistence leaps into Livie's mind as the alarm sounds and she hears her voice say, "We can do this" and "you need this."

Sipping coffee from her mug and holding a flashlight with the other hand, Livie makes her way down to the lake and sees the rowboat tied to the wharf. The water is a sheet of glass, the nearby trees reflected on its dark surface. The moon is still hanging in the sky and lending just enough of its light for her to climb into the boat, untether it from the dock, and slowly row out towards the middle of the lake.

As she rows, she looks down to see the oars pierce the glassy surface of the water. The sun's light starts bleeding into the sky and is reflecting on the water when it starts to happen. It's a few quiet splashes at first. Livie can feel her cheeks stretch into a smile as she relishes the excitement of anticipation. The splashes become a symphony of sounds, from tiny ripples in the water to hefty explosions, then loud thuds of fish hitting her boat. A fish lands in the boat, and Livie lets out a scream of delight.

The rising sun starts to dominate the sky, and the symphony of sounds in the water starts to die down. Livie lies back in the boat, closes her eyes, and allows the sun's heat to warm her. *This is what I needed,* she tells herself. Some time alone, in a setting where magic can happen and take her back to the times with Twiggy that provided the inspiration for many of the decisions she made in her life. The water is quiet again, and Livie can hear Twiggy's voice telling her to just be courageous and go for it; to not let others dictate the boundaries she has to play or work in. "You are right Mom," she finds herself saying out loud into the blazing sun. "This place does have some great memories." She lets the morning air fill her lungs as images of her mom leaving the cabin last night dance in front of her. She pushes the air out of her lungs and decides that her mom should come back to the cabin. It is time she gave their relationship a chance.

She sits up straight and starts rowing back to shore, allowing the experience of the morning to fill her with delight and joy—knowing she can find those things in her life. How could she hang on to those joyful feelings now? She stops rowing for a moment and watches the water trickle off the oars, creating tiny droplets that fall into the lake. Out of the corner of her eye, she sees movement at the shore's edge and turns her head. The stillness and peace fill her as her eyes scan the shoreline. She sees movement again and spots him.

A red fox, its beautiful coat of silver and red glistening in the morning light. It moves silently, with sleek and graceful steps along the shoreline. Livie takes in the beauty of the creature with its white tail, furry black feet, and elegant body outline—when she sees the object of its desire. A small rodent, *maybe a vole,* she thinks, that the fox is stalking. She looks at the fox again as it leaps through the air towards its prey. Startled, Livie quickly turns away and refocuses on the oar in the water.

Taking a moment to allow her breathing to return to normal, Livie again takes in the drops of water that drip from the oar, forming tiny circles in the lake. She smiles in response to the calmness it brings her.

Livie watches those drops and thinks it's time she acted on what is next for her, instead of thinking about it and waiting for the action to come. She remembers a Japanese word that Twiggy taught her. *Ikigai.* What is her main purpose now, in this world without the internet? Where does her sense of meaning lie, now? Her mind goes back to Twiggy, her words on courage and not being restrained by the boundaries others have set. Why does she have to accept that the internet isn't coming back on? Maybe she can be part of the solution to bring it back? She can put her skills and experience as an investigator to work to help bring it back. Something Hannah said flashes through her mind:

An unlived life isn't worth examining.

She closes her eyes for a moment and gently shakes her head, as if to erase the sudden image of Hannah that pops up in her mind. She picks up the oars again and rows with new purpose, thinking of the things she could do. She determines to map out a plan. A life where she would truly have her independence as she often dreamt of. Her own plan. Her own company. She is determined now to get back and start working on it. Put pen to paper. Brain to action. Abstract to concrete.

The boat glides towards the dock, and soon its tip kisses the dock's edge. As Livie reaches out to pull the boat closer, she sees someone coming towards her in the distance. A tall, lanky man in business attire who is walking with purpose, his image temporarily lost in the trees. Livie remains sitting in the boat as she squints to make out the man in the trees, when she hears her name float through the air.

"Livie...glad I found you."

It's her boss, Larry. *Or former boss,* she tells herself. But here he is, all the way out here. In business attire? Why?

Livie climbs out of the boat and ties it up.

"Hi Larry, what brings you out here, and so early?"

"I actually got in late last night and stayed at a motel, but I couldn't sleep any longer, so I took a chance that I would catch you here early. You said you were staying in Deerfield Lake, so I figured perhaps you'd be out on the lake this morning. Anyway, I have some exciting news."

"You drove all this way after our call yesterday? Why? And," Livie motions with her hand to acknowledge his attire, "what's with the dress-up? Pretty casual setting out here."

"I'll explain everything. And my business look...yeah, I can explain that too. I don't have much time though, and I want to get to why I'm here."

Livie motions for them to walk towards the cabin.

"After we spoke last night, I decided to make my way out here. I have some business close by, which I'll tell you about in a second, so I figured it was best to come meet you in person." Larry speaks with urgency and excitement.

"So, you are probably wondering what my news is?" he prods when Livie doesn't respond.

Livie looks up towards the cabin and thinks of how peaceful the morning was before Larry arrived.

"I'm doing pretty good actually Larry, how are you?"

"Oh...sorry, I guess I just thought I'd jump straight into my reason for being here. I'm good, especially now. You enjoying it here?"

"Yeah, I am actually. This is a good place for me to clear my head and think about my priorities in life."

"Okay...well, I hope that you'll see what I'm going to share with you as the big opportunity I know it is. Though..." Larry scans their surroundings, as if for effect. "It will take you away from here."

The squawk of a crow in a nearby tree intrudes in the moment of silence after Larry speaks. They both look up at it.

Livie lets out a snorting laugh at the sound.

"Well, I'm not a fan of those creatures. 'Damn crows!' That's what my mom used to say when they would dive bomb us by the cabin sometimes." She pauses before adding, "But Larry, I kind of want to be here right now."

"Oh...okay, well, how about we get back to the cabin and sit down and talk about it. I'm sure you'll find that I can convince you otherwise."

Live lets out another snorting laugh, this one filled with disdain. Larry should know her well enough by now to realize she doesn't respond well to people who seem to think they know what's best for her.

She changes the subject as they complete the walk back to the cabin, telling him about her experience out on the lake with the sunrise and the fish jumping. She feels the joy rising in her again as she tells him how much she loves the wonderment and magic of it all—that she wants to get more of that back in her life.

They arrive at the cabin, and Larry, still appearing full of energy, yields to a seat at the table as Livie goes to the kitchen to put the coffee on.

"Livie, I'm wearing what I am today, because when I leave here, I'm going to meet with some government officials. It's in a secret place close to here actually, it's about matters that are highly confidential and potentially world-changing. I want them to know that I'm a professional and they can trust me."

Livie puts on the coffee to percolate as she moves towards the table to join him.

"Okay, so what does that have to do with me?"

"What has it got to do with you?" Larry responds in an incredulous tone. "Livie, I want to bring you in on this. This could be your future."

"Okay, I'm intrigued and do want to hear this, but Larry, I'm going to be the one that decides my future."

"Of course, Livie. I didn't mean it that way. You said you want to have more of that wonderment and magic in your life, well...this. could. be. it."

Livie looks at him and steels her determination not to give in to his.

"Let me get our coffee first."

Livie gets their coffee and brings the cream and sugar, which her mom always has ready, out to the table. Larry pours cream and three heaping spoonsful of sugar into his coffee. Live watches and thinks, *No wonder he's so wired at times.*

"Livie," Larry takes a sip of his coffee and lowers his voice as if the crows outside might be listening, "they want us to help bring the internet back."

"Really? How are we going to help with that?"

Larry stares at her for a moment and turns his head to look at the door, as if someone might suddenly walk through it.

"Are we here by ourselves?"

"Yes...my mom is staying with a friend. Larry, we're practically in the middle of nowhere. No one can hear us."

"There are no devices around that can record us?"

"Like what?"

"Oh come on Livie. You know, a TV, a phone, the fridge. They all have speakers and cameras in them."

"Okay...look, you're being a bit paranoid now. Nothing is recording us, okay? Wow, must be some secretive thing you have to share?"

Larry either misses or ignores the sarcasm in her voice as he leans in closer to her and lowers his voice to a whisper. Livie thinks of Draw doing the same thing when they stood under the mulberry tree near the Washington Monument.

"Livie, like I told you last night, they want us to spy on the anti-interneters, to infiltrate them."

Livie nodded, thinking back to her strange conversation with Larry the night before.

Larry lowers his voice again. "Well, they don't just want us to infiltrate the FWN. They want us to find out who the leaders are. They want us to help capture them and bring the internet back."

"You make it sound so simple, Larry. How would we even begin to do that? I don't think it will be as simply as spotting people with signs and buttons at a rally. I am sure the Friendly World Network wouldn't make their leaders so obvious in public."

"See, you are already thinking like I need you to for this job."

"Larry, have you been talking to Draw?"

"Draw? You mean Draw Nedwons?"

"You know another Draw?"

"Of course not, and no, I haven't heard from him, why?"

Livie watches Larry's expression, looking for any evidence that he may be hiding something. But other than his overall anxiousness, she doesn't pick up anything.

"Never mind. Just thought this is the kind of thing he'd come up with."

"Livie, this isn't some paranoid conspiracy theory. This is real life. The internet is down, and the government want us to help bring it back."

Keeping his voice to a whisper, Larry adds, "Please Livie. Will you come with me to meet with these government officials?"

Livie sees the intensity in Larry's eyes and nervousness in his posture. As he talks, she looks towards the stairs that lead up to the bed she crawled out of so early in the morning.

She nods and whispers, "Let me just grab something from upstairs. I'll meet you down there." She points to the treeline at the edge of the property, then heads into the cabin.

When she gets back outside, Larry is nearing the trees. Livie jogs over to catch up to him.

"I think we will be more comfortable talking about this out here." she says. "Don't get me wrong, there's nothing recording our conversation in there. I'd just rather not whisper, and I need to understand what this is all about. What would be expected of me."

Larry turns to face Livie and places his hands on her shoulders, as if he will need to hold her up when he tells her what they will be doing.

"Livie, the government believes that if they find the perpetrators that shut down the internet and bring them to justice, they can bring us back our internet world. They want us to play a major role in this. They're offering us a contract that would make us both very wealthy."

"So...we're going spy on people that want the internet to stay off and report that to government, and somehow that will..."

"Livie, as you already pointed out, it would not be that simple. This isn't just about watching some people and what they say and do. They want us to infiltrate the Friendly World Network and find out how they did it. How they turned the internet off and are keeping it off. They want us to identify the key players so they can be arrested and interrogated."

Livie is reliving her conversation with Draw and almost mentions his name again, but she stops herself. At this moment, the only person she trusts in these conversations is herself.

"You say *we*. Why are you including me in this? Larry, I figured you basically fired me."

"I didn't fire you…look, I apologize for the words I used at the time. It was a confusing moment, and I thought the ground had collapsed under me. But I need you now. We're a team in this. A man and a woman."

"Ah…so that's it, then. You need a woman to help with this, to *infiltrate* the network as you put it."

Larry stops and stares at her. His eyes are intense and his voice is loaded with new substance as he responds.

"Livie, you don't always need to be so skeptical. That skepticism you are voicing is part of what makes you so good at this work and what will make you good at what we have ahead of us. But right now, this is something you should embrace. This is truly an opportunity of a lifetime that others simply won't get and would die for, like literally die for. I also need to say, that yes you are the right person for the job. And yes, that is in part because of your gender and age. But that shouldn't stop you from jumping at this opportunity."

Livie senses there is more Larry isn't telling her.

"So, you said the government officials are meeting you somewhere close to here? That sounds awfully convenient. We are basically in the middle of nowhere, Larry."

"Look, I'm just going by what they told me. I'm waiting for instructions on the specific location, which I could get any minute now. But I know it's in a town nearby."

"What are you not telling me, Larry?"

"Okay, look, they asked about you specifically. They want you involved in this. I thought that would excite you more. You need to seize this Livie, before it passes you by. If I leave here without you on board, there will not be another chance."

Livie takes in Larry's words and the emotion and passion he delivers it with. She's still not sure he is telling her everything, but it reminds her of when he interviewed her for the job she took to work with him. He described it in a way that excited her and made her want to catch the wave. She can hear Twiggy's voice over Larry's now. Time to be courageous and think outside of the boundaries others have set. Her thoughts suddenly leak out in a whisper to the air.

"Maybe this is my ikigai now."

"Sorry, what's that?"

"Oh, it's okay Larry, I was just thinking out loud."

"Okay...so what is it then? Are you in on this or not?"

Livie smiles and nods her head.

"I'm in."

Larry beams with satisfaction. "Hey, so what did you grab from the cabin before you came back outside?"

"Oh, just my personal protective device and some cash." Livie sees the look on Larry's face at her response. "But hey, it's not because I'm scared of you...you just seemed rather skittish at the table, and I thought maybe you were followed here by someone."

"I see. Well, what we are about to embark on is highly sensitive. I just don't want to take any chances."

"So, you aren't then?"

"Aren't what?"

"Being followed, Larry? You were looking towards the door so many times, I half expected someone to come barging in."

"No. I've been careful and watching out for any suspicious activity around me. It's one of the reasons the government officials are meeting us out here in the country. We are actually going to meet them in a secluded old cabin, I'm told, that is not far from here."

"Really? A minute ago you said a town nearby, now it's a cabin in the country?"

"Livie, I am just being careful about the details. Your suspicious nature makes you good at this work, but my motives here are sincere."

"Okay, well let's hope these people you are talking about have sincere motives too. Did you tell them I'm out here and that is why we are meeting somewhere close by?"

Larry drops his eyes to the ground, which answers the question for Livie.

"Just trying to make this as easy as possible for them, and it is a secluded, quiet setting out here."

Livie looks right at Larry. A wave of his hair has drooped over his right eye. She wants to reach out and move it out of the way. Her pulse spikes at a sudden and real connection she feels with him.

"So, you really have planned this out with me being included."

"Of course Livie. I need you for this. We're a team. We've always had synergy together in our work, and we will get that back with this incredible opportunity. We could change the world. Change it back to what it was."

"You really think we can do this?"

"Don't you?" Larry looks at his watch. "They are expecting us in half an hour. You're coming, right?"

Live reaches out and touches him on the shoulder in an out-of-character gesture. "Of course I am."

Larry's voice cracks with the excitement he feels at her response. "Wonderful. Do you have anything nice to wear?"

"Um...not really. It'll be fine Larry. I just need to phone my mom first and let her know."

"Well, I guess one of us will look like the field staff, anyway. I'm so glad you are on board with me on this Livie. Wouldn't want to do it without you."

They walk back to the cabin, and Larry asks if Livie can think of anyone who may help them infiltrate the Friendly World Network. "We may be asked that by the government officials today," he adds.

Livie's mind has already started to churn with such thoughts, so she responds immediately, "Yeah, a couple I think. I just need to think it through a bit more."

Larry nods. "We can take my vehicle," he says. "I've cleared it of any listening devices."

This reminds Livie that her vehicle is in the shop being repaired, and she briefly fills Larry in on what happened. They agree to use his vehicle until Livie can come back for hers a week or so later.

Livie goes inside to grab some things from the cabin while Larry heads to his vehicle to wait for her.

As she steps onto the porch, Livie's thoughts skip between Draw's words about getting on the inside of the Friendly World Network and becoming "friends with the enemy," as he put it. She wonders how she could use this opportunity to build a bridge between her and Hannah—at least until Hannah eventually discovers she is a spy working against her. That Hannah is her enemy, essentially a double agent working against her friend.

Livie turns the doorknob to open the door when, over her shoulder, the sound of a crow's squawk rings in her ears. She stops and looks up at it, wondering how she can get in touch with the two people she thinks can help her infiltrate the FWN.

She doesn't remember where Draw lives, but maybe Larry has the information in a file that has not been lost with the internet. Before she seeks out Draw though, she thinks she will plan a visit to Green Planet and hopefully run into the first new friend she met after the internet went down.

Chapter 13

Hannah & Finn's Deep Dive into the FWN

Hannah is walking towards the Washington Monument, sipping from her Green Planet coffee mug. When she downed that first sip of caffeine, her senses were alive, on alert. They have been for the last several months whenever she went into Green Planet; her nerves taut from the apprehension of possibly running into Livie.

Yet, her anxiousness wasn't making her run away. Quite the opposite, as she has been frequenting Green Planet almost daily since her altercation with Livie in the park over four months ago. Despite her anxiety, she held on to some semblance of hope, like a skin she couldn't shed, that she would run into Livie. That they would cast aside their differences; bury their disputes and harsh words. That they would resume their friendship as if none of it ever happened.

There is another person that keeps bringing her back to Green Planet. Fairleigh. Hannah can remember the emotion in Livie's voice when she described her conversation with Fairleigh the day after the internet went down. When Hannah met Fairleigh for the first time, a few weeks before that St. Paddy's Day rally, she immediately knew it was the same person Livie had described. The woman in earth tones with brown hair in pigtails, a long thin neck, and an authentic warm smile had been easy to spot.

Hannah didn't know whether she would see Fairleigh at Green Planet today. They have never arranged to meet; she has just come to know when Fairleigh would likely be there. Though many times she had hoped Farleigh would be there, she wasn't.

When Hannah walked into the coffee shop, she was relieved to see the person she considered a mentor sitting in her regular spot, sipping her coffee from that same brown thermos. But this time she came seeking something from Fairleigh. The first time Hannah met Fairleigh, she wasn't sure about her involvement with the Friendly World Network. The second time she met her, she saw the FWN logo on Fairleigh's thermos. Her first thought was that it is Fairleigh's initials, but then something suddenly clicked into place as she thought about it.

When she asked the simple question, "Are you part of the Friendly World Network?" Fairleigh answered with her eyes without saying a word. Today, Hannah went seeking information from Fairleigh about the FWN for a friend. Information she was certain was surrounded by a high degree of secrecy. She didn't know whether Fairleigh would trust her enough to reveal anything.

Fairleigh surprised her with her answer, and now Hannah is heading to the Washington Monument to meet her friend. The hot coffee keeps her hands warm as she holds onto it while walking, and her mind drifts back to Fairleigh.

Oh, how many times has she wished that Livie would waft in like a dream when she and Fairleigh were sitting together. Fairleigh would be the perfect buffer between them. Her inviting, non-presumptive approach would require Livie to sit with them. The conversation would flow, and they would have an inherent mutual interest in what Fairleigh has to say. Livie would challenge her on things, and Hannah would ask passive-aggressive questions that would elicit explanations. Then, when they said goodbye to Fairleigh, they would leave Green Planet together as friends again. From there, Hannah would be free to tell Livie about the many things she has learnt from Fairleigh. How Fairleigh erased any thoughts she had that the world would be a better place if the internet came back on.

Fairleigh helped Hannah appreciate how much more she enjoys her job without the internet. She feels she is doing real social work for the first time, without the interruptions of emails or clients who have looked things up and believe they know better than her. That somehow, without the training she has had, they could do her job.

She is treated more like a true professional in the post-internet world. Her knowledge and experience are respected unlike ever before. Fairleigh teased this out of Hannah as she listened to how her job has changed without the internet. Fairleigh's words, which really resonated with her, still sing in her head. "Sounds like you are now treated like the professional that you are without the interference of so-called experts that are just a click away?"

Then there is just how much simpler her life has become. When Fairleigh asked her how she was sleeping, it was like she knew what the answer was going to be. Once Hannah was over the shock of the loss of the internet and had moved on, her sleep became much better. "Better than before the loss of the internet?" Fairleigh asked, though it was more of a statement. A statement that Hannah confirmed with a simple nod. *Maybe that's Livie's issue,* she thinks. *She has not found a way to move on, yet.*

Hannah initially thought that maybe the change in Annie would have persuaded Livie. If Annie could move on and change her life post-internet, why couldn't that inspire Livie? Hannah's thoughts go to another client that she wishes Livie could meet, Stacey.

Hannah has had Stacey in her life for three years. She has had to rescue Stacey's daughter from her and place the child in foster care. She had to phone the police for Stacey when she claimed she was being cyber bullied and threatened on social media. She has received countless emails from Stacey. Some paranoid, some demanding, some sad, some angry—and many that were just plain incoherent and confusing. Despite all that, she has only actually met Stacey face-to-face once, and that was through a small crack in a door that she couldn't even get her fingers to fit into. Stacey would email her, join her for a virtual call—always with her camera off. Hannah had a picture of Stacey in her electronic file, and that is the only way she knew what she looked like. Stacey was a mystery. A paranoid person who pushed people out of her life and wanted help, but only on her terms. She clearly avoided actually meeting anyone who could help her. Hannah wondered at times if the Stacey she knew from her file really existed or was actually someone else altogether.

That all changed after the internet went down. Stacey needed Hannah, and she couldn't email her. She couldn't stalk her on social media. She was forced out of the shadows that social media and the internet had provided. She had to meet Hannah—face-to-face. The first time was awkward, but instead of the angry person Hannah expected to meet, Stacey was scared. Frightened, actually. Since then, she has seen Stacey open up and become more comfortable in her own skin and in her surroundings. Stacey even told her recently that she hopes the internet doesn't come back on, because she sees that world as "dark and scary." Living in the shadows is so often not living at all.

Maybe Livie could also move on if she were to go back to work and discover a renewed enthusiasm for her profession? Something like the satisfaction Hannah has found in her casework with individuals and families—like Stacey. When Stacey was in the shadows of the internet, she endured a lot of cyber bullying, which was the catalyst for a lot of her anxiety. She couldn't escape. That is what the shadows do: provide the comfort of secrecy and the prison of fear. That was Stacey's life with the internet. That fear she felt would manifest her anxiety and cause her to recede further from normal life. Then, deep in her isolation, Stacey herself would become the bully at the end of some cyber discourse. Stacey revealed all this to Hannah in one tearful night.

"No more cyber bullying," Hannah whispers out loud, wishing the whisper would catch wings and reach Livie's ears. Just thinking about it inserts a pause into Hannah's breathing as she thinks of

Stacey and two other clients who took their own lives as a result of cyber bullying. Would they be alive today if the internet never existed?

Hannah wishes she had some way to start the conversation with Livie about all this. She wishes Livie could witness her at work. To see how she has discovered that she can adjust and change along with peoples' needs, like never before—the opposite of what the latest algorithm in her computer would have told her to do. Clients that used to hide in the shadows now want face-to-face human interaction. Hannah herself is no longer worried about her confidentiality being violated by clients who used to stalk her on the internet. Now she is recognized as a professional. Her experience and skills are given more honor. No longer can anyone just find answers (or perceived answers) to their questions online. No longer can anyone question what she does by searching for some alternative online. Clients are no longer dealing with the constant online scams out there.

Hannah whispers into the void, talking to herself. "Life is better without the internet. I believe it in my soul. Life is simpler, less stressful. I'm not spending time seeing how many liked my last post. My job doesn't follow me after hours like it used to, with emails and demands."

Even before she received that package, she was always on alert about what was being documented about her life. Who knew about the secret things in her life? Turns out many of those secrets were readily available to anyone with enough tech savvy to unearth them. But now that technology has evaporated, along with the internet. She feels more at peace and at ease.

Hannah wishes Livie could see and experience what she has. She also wishes she responded to Livie better that day at the rally. She misses her friend, as much as she is frustrated by her. She can't see a bridge between them, though. The river between them is too high, has too much debris, and neither are willing to sacrifice their positions or be vulnerable enough to try and cross to the other side, even to see the other's point of view. She starts to think that maybe *she* needs to make that move; at least to hear Livie out on her pro-internet views.

Hannah sips her coffee, engrossed in the daydream her mind has taken her on, when she hears her name called.

She sees Finn's figure in the distance as he waves at her, standing tall and thin like a pencil. She yells that she is coming as she thinks about her long-time friend and former lover. Another person that she and Livie have in common. Livie would roll her eyes and scorn her all the more if she knew that Hannah and Finn were now conspiring together. Moving towards Finn, she can feel a grin rip across her face as she thinks of them conspiring to keep the internet off. She pauses to take a glance around and then over her shoulder, almost expecting to see Livie and the start of a low-grade earthquake. Looking ahead, Finn remains planted in place, his straight posture standing out as she makes her way into his shadow. He gives her a warm smile and cuts to the chase.

"Did you get any details on where they're meeting?"

Hannah inclines her head in an apologetic manner and leans towards him conspiratorially.

"No. She wouldn't give me that. But she told me of someone who might...not a name really, but a place and time to meet someone who might."

"Sounds like some cloak and dagger thing. When and where is it?"

"Well, it's not that simple, Finn. First you have to go somewhere to find an envelope that will give you those instructions."

"Oookaaay. You and I are doing this together then?"

"No, just you."

Hannah gives Finn the instructions and directions to an abandoned gold mine. She tells him that he has to be there at 5 p.m. tonight. Finn looks at his watch and quickly calculates how long it will take him to get to the mine. He looks down at the piece of paper Hannah has handed him.

"This doesn't leave me with a lot of time. Is this real Hannah? How do I know that the envelope will be there, that this mysterious person exists?"

Hannah picks up the nervous, almost scared energy coming from Finn. It's a side of Finn she's not used to seeing. She tries to calm him down, keeping her tone even without much inflection. It's a technique she uses with clients when they are anxious.

"I can trust Fairleigh. I know it's real. She phoned the person when I was talking to her. I could hear her making the arrangements, and she wrote down those instructions you're holding."

~~~~~~

Finn almost abandoned this whole idea on the drive up Huckleberry Creek, navigating an old dirt road overgrown with weeds. This felt like some wild goose chase to nowhere, and a little creepy too. But he has arrived, at least according to the map. From here it's just a short walk in the woods to where the mine should be.

He walks northeast as directed by the instructions, and sure enough, like something from another time, he spots a stone monument—the tomb noted on the map. He stops and looks at the tomb's inscription, which relates the death of a twelve-year-old boy who died after "stepping on a rusted nail." The date of the death is October 28, 1928. Finn stares at the tomb for several moments, marvelling at the structure that has stood for over a century and wondering about the story behind it. Following the instructions, he looks behind the monument on the ground, and sure enough, he sees a piece of paper in a plastic bag.
~~~~~~

Finn pulls the folded paper out of the bag and sees a series of jumbled letters: NMV UYL LNVDS NVSYV. He recognizes it immediately as a monoalphabetic substitution code—one made famous by Mary Stuart, who reigned over Scotland after King James died in the 1500s. Finn recalls his history lesson on the code and the story of Mary Queen of Scots as he looks around for evidence of anyone else in the area. He nods his head, as if someone is watching and he needs to acknowledge that he accepts the test that the code offers. Is there some way they would know he could unscramble this?

He pulls out a pen and his notepad from his pack, which he was told to bring, and sets out to decipher the code. He writes it down first:

NMV UYL LNVDS NVSYV.

In the code, each letter of the alphabet is replaced with another letter, according to a key. It doesn't take him long to determine that the two Ys in the code are Es, due to their placement as vowels. They could be Is or As, but he assumes they are Es. V occurs four times, including twice at the end of words, so he deduces that the Vs are Rs. He writes down his progress so far.

_ _ R _E_ _ _ R _ _ _R_ER

With this, he guesses the first word to be OUR. That means the Ns are Os. He fills in the blanks he has solved so far:

OUR _E_ _OR_ _ OR_ER.

He writes down ORDER for the last word, which mean the S is a D. That makes the third word _OR_D so far.

He stares at the third word, and the missing letters appear to float in front of his eyes and fall into place as he writes down WORLD. As that makes the L a W, the second word is now _EW. He lets out a sly grin, looks around as if someone is watching, and nods his head again, recognizing that he has solved the code. He completes the password he knows he will need for his next test.

OUR NEW WORLD ORDER.

He stares at it again, and the words send shivers up his spine. Looking up from his notepad, the sun hits him, bringing colored dots in front of his eyes. He holds up his hand to shield the light and gives his eyes a few seconds to adjust. According to the instructions, the mine is within a few hundred feet of the gravesite. He steps forward, scanning the area, then moves towards a small knoll to his right that sits above a gulley. On top of the knoll, the ground-hugging shrub of a bottlebrush buckeye catches his eye—with its green leaves and dragon-shaped flower buds that haven't yet burst into the snowy white flowers they will become.

Having reached the knoll, he makes his way down the gulley, which is peppered with other low-level shrubs. The serrated, glossy green leaves of the arrowhead viburnum catch his eye. He walks past the arrowhead shrubs, pleased that their bright blue berries are not out yet—as they would likely attract wildlife. On alert, Finn picks up his pace as he moves up the low hillside coming out of the gulley. As he crests the hill, he spots a rusted square entrance framing the mine's opening. The mine rises up like a butte, and the rusted machinery of old mining equipment sits on the flat ledge above the mine.

Finn scans his surroundings again, the hair on the back of his neck intoning that he may have a visitor nearby. He can hear his breath and heartbeat as he stands straight and still, waiting for something to happen.

He feels a breeze rushing through his hair, and then it suddenly stops. Just above the mine, he sees a faded image that looks like a skull with numbers below it. While the last number is broken at the end, he is certain the numbers are 322. The image stops him in his tracks as his heart races. He quells the desire to sprint away from the scene and remains standing, staring at the numbers for several minutes.

He looks around again, and his gaze fixes on the rusted machinery sitting about the mine's opening. He spots a wire that is camouflaged in the same rust color as the machinery. The wire winds from the bottom of the machine into the bottlebrush buckeye that hugs the ground in front of it. He searches the bush, its green leaves light from the sun. The wire reappears in his view, now green and turning to brown as it meshes with the ground. He squints to make it out in the bright sun and spots it snaking on the side of the mine's opening before disappearing into the haunting blackness of the shaft.

"Well, now or never," he whispers, letting the words settle for several seconds, as if some shadow behind the bushes might hear him. "In for a penny, in for pound," he tells himself as he musters his courage.

Finn pulls out the headlamp he brought for this, attaches it to his head, and peers into the mine. His senses on alert, he hears the noise of the wind ruffling the leaves of the bottlebrush buckeye and whistling as it wafts through the mine's opening. Finn's heart is beating in his ears.

He sees the wire, now the color of the dark grey and black of the mine's walls. One last look over his shoulder, and Finn descends into the mine. It is clearly in a dilapidated state, like it has been neglected for many years. He can see the veins of several tunnels in the mine; some are partially blocked by fallen rock. Rock and debris are evident everywhere, and he instinctively reaches up to his head and feels the flashlight, wishing it was a helmet. He stops and moves his head from side to side, allowing his light to scan for an obvious direction to proceed in. He stops as the light catches an area where the tunnel branches off to a section that appears to widen. He jiggles his shoulders and head to shake off the willies he feels and moves towards the area his light is directing him to.

Finn moves to where the subsidiary tunnel widens, the crunch of rock under his feet filling his ears. He looks up at the ceiling of the mine, gauging its stability, and surveys the jagged ceiling with its many shades of black and grey. His breaths are deliberate. In and out. The sound of his heartbeat continues to drum in his ears.

Finally, he spots it—the meticulously camouflaged wire zigzagging further down into the mine. "There you are," he whispers. At least he knows the path to follow now.

Finn is moving more slowly now as the tunnel becomes narrower. His headlamp doesn't reach as far as he wishes it would, and he needs to shine it on his feet occasionally to avoid stepping onto uneven ground and to keep his nerves in check. He looks up to confirm that the wire is still there and spots it on the ceiling. His eyes follow it as it meanders towards the wall and corkscrews down to the floor. He can't see it yet, but his shoulders sag with some relief as he realizes that the computer—where he will need to enter the password—must be close.

When the light from his headlamp hits the computer, which is larger than he expected and eerily dark and quiet, he glances over his shoulder, as if expecting someone to be there. Someone ready to give him further instructions or to make him regret that he has got himself trapped in a dark hole in the middle of nowhere. With a skull and the numbers 322 at its entrance. The thought sends a shiver up his spine.

The computer sits on a bit of a ledge inside a hole in the wall that seems to have been built just for it. In front of it, a keyboard is propped up on its side. Finn kneels and peers at it, looking for any further instructions. He sees none. He reaches up with his hand, wipes the sweat from his brow, grasps for the keyboard, and then plops it down in front of him.

He presses down on the button that sits on top of the computer and watches it come to life. Within a few seconds, which seem like several minutes, the black screen disappears, replaced by a florescent pink background. Then suddenly, in black block letters, his instructions appear: ENTER YOUR PASSWORD, FINN. The cursor blinks below the words, waiting. He glances over his shoulder again and takes a deep breath. He feels the hairs rise on his back, like something is crawling up his spine and making its way across his neck. The cursor continues to blink at him, and he looks at it as if it is threatening him. "Now or never," he whispers into the void, rubbing his sweaty palms together before placing them on the keyboard. He types in OUR NEW WORLD ORDER.

The screen goes blank. Finn stares at it and into the darkness. Words appear on the screen, one at a time.

TURN. OFF. YOUR. LIGHT.

Finn reaches up, feels the sweat dripping from his brow, and turns off his headlamp. The screen emits a bright flash, leaving colored spots floating in front of his face. A few seconds pass, and the picture the computer just took of his face appears on the monitor. Finn's prior sense of confidence comes crashing down.

Finn stares at the reflection of himself on the screen and watches it slowly fade, leaving everything dark again. His heart is thumping, measuring the seconds going by. He counts in his head. One...two...three...four. He gets to twenty-seven. It feels like a hundred. He reaches up to turn his light back on, his gaze transfixed on the dark screen. His light hits the screen, and the bright, florescent pink light on the computer returns. He counts. One...two...three...four...fi—he stops, and his breath catches as the words appear across the screen in bold black letters.

DRAW NEDWONS IS YOUR TARGET.

"My target?" he whispers into the dark, quickly darting a look over his shoulder. His gaze lingers, expecting to see someone there. He looks back at the screen again and sees additional instructions.

GO TO THE BACK ENTRANCE OF THE ART STORE BY THE MONUMENT.

TOMORROW, TWO P.M. WE KNOW YOU ARE ALWAYS ON TIME FINN.

He stares at the screen, waiting for more. The count in his head starts again. One...two...thr—the screen goes blank.

Finn lets a shiver vibrate through his body, as if he can just shake off the heebie-jeebies he's feeling. He puts the keyboard back where he found it; the habit of cleaning up after himself stays with him wherever he goes. He turns and heads back to the exit at a brisk pace, only stopping to take a deep breath once he has both feet back in the bright sunshine of the mine's opening.

He gives the rusted mine equipment a quick glance before turning around to make his way back to his vehicle. Then he hears something by the bottlebrush buckeye that hugs the ground at the mine's entrance.

He turns back around, stares towards the bush, and sees what has his heart racing. A deer. They catch each other's eye at the same time. Deer and man, staring at each other. Asking each other, "Where did you appear from?" The deer stands frozen, inspecting Finn with its black-tipped ears. His fur gives off a purplish brown hue in the sunlight. He brusquely twitches at the shoulder, where a fly is devilling him. The tiny movement startles Finn, as if he's expecting someone and not just a deer, or a small fly, to suddenly appear.

Finally, the deer surrenders the space they occupy, turns, and dashes away. Finn feels spooked and wants to shed the feeling like a husk. Just peel it away and leave it there. He twitches his shoulders like the deer did to shake off the feeling, turns, and heads back towards his vehicle.

He is within a few feet of the old gravesite when an object on the ground by the tomb catches the sun's light and flashes at him. He scans the area around him as the wind flaps his shirt against his body. The object is a picture of a man. He picks it up. A man in a bowler hat with what he'd call a bird's nest of a beard. He flips it over and reads the words on the back.

DRAW NEDWONS

His "target"—as the computer showed him. He looks at the picture again and says the name out loud: "Draw Nedwons. Who are you and what have you got to do with me?" As he finishes the words, the wind whistles in the trees and he scans the area. "Hey, is someone here?!" He stands still, anxious. Wanting to know who left the picture yet hoping no one responds.

He turns and races back to his vehicle, slumps into the seat, locks the doors, and stares out. No movements catch his attention. He turns the vehicle on as his vision becomes blurry from the moisture in his eyes. The kind of tears that are born from relief, even joy.

~~~~~~

It's 1:57, according to Finn's watch. He knows that with the internet off, his phone is no longer perfectly in sync with Greenwich time. So, the time on his watch might be like most devices that don't automatically correct themselves—behind a minute or two. Perhaps he isn't early but just on time as he stands outside the barn, which is the location he was given. The road is dusty, and he sees no other vehicles on site. Perhaps he has the wrong location? His ears are pricked up and picking up sounds he'd otherwise ignore. The swish of the wind passing through the metal weathercock on the barn, metal scraping metal of a train in the distance as it runs over the tracks, his own heart beating like a drum. Then he picks up the faint sound of breathing directly behind him.

"Don't turn around."

Finn stands still, surprised to hear a woman's voice; one with a French accent. He resists the urge to do the opposite.

"I know you don't always follow the rules. You're the kind that colors outside the lines and often looks for angles others would miss. It's one of the reasons we recruited you."

"Recruited me? I..."
~~~~~~

"Yes, I'm sure you sought us out. Following the crumbs we left. Regardless, it doesn't matter. We're giving you an opportunity to show your loyalty by gathering the information we need to stop the enemy's sympathizer."

"Sympathizer?"

"Yes, someone who doesn't work directly for their government but has been feeding them information. He's like you, a computer wizard and a hacker. He's very good, and he broke one of our codes that we thought was unbreakable. We need to find out what he knows and stop him."

"Draw Nedwons?"

"Yes. Did you know about him before you visited our mine?"

"No. Not a name I recognize."

"You didn't hear about him through your friend Livie?"

The mention of Livie's name sends a jolt of anxious current through his body. How much do they know about his life and friends? The question also makes him bristle with resistance.

"No."

"Well, perhaps he used a pseudonym online and you've interacted with him without knowing. You can find that out when you break into his computer."

Finn makes a move to turn around and feels her arm clutch his from behind.

"Don't turn around."

"If I'm to be trusted, shouldn't it be a two-way street? Shouldn't I know who I'm dealing with?"

"I am with the Friendly World Network. That's all you need to know right now."

Finn swallows his sarcastic response—that the Network could use a lesson or two in being friendly. Instead, he refocuses on what they want.

"How am I going to break into a person's computer if there is no internet? Unless you have access to it somehow?"

He knows the answer to his question from what he was told at the Friendly World Network's secret meeting, but he wants to see if this person knows about that conversation.

"No. Of course we don't. The internet is down for everyone. That includes those of us from the Network. To gain access to Draw's computer, you will have to break into his apartment."

This response tells him that the woman doesn't know what he was told, so he gives a bit of a push back.

"Hey, I don't know about breaking and entering."

"Really? So it's okay to do those things online as you so often did? You know, hacking people's cameras and watching them in their private homes or just looking at their pictures and their files? That's not really any different from physically breaking into someone's place, is it really, Finn? But don't worry, we will have someone go with you that will make sure you can get in there to access Draw's computers. That person will break into the apartment for you and stand guard while you work your magic."

"Work my magic?" Finn says with feigned confidence as sweat seeps out of his pores and dampens the edge of his hairline.

"You know what I mean. You get a copy of his files and leave no trace that you were in his system. Now, I'm going to put a piece of paper in your hand. It contains the instructions on where to meet your contact to get into Draw's place and what you need to do when you are there."

"What exactly am I looking for on this guy's computer?"

"Don't worry, I'm sure it will be obvious to you. You can expect his files to be encrypted. But I'm sure you'll figure out a way to access them."

Finn feels the paper crunch into his hand. He immediately raises it in front of him and pries it open, like a present, hoping he will like what he sees. He unfolds a sheet of paper with two stickers in the shape of a navy-blue capital G—the unmistakable symbol of Georgetown University. His employer. He looks at the stickers intently and sees that they will hold data. He knows this technology and thought it was only the domain of a small, elite group of computer scientists. The data he collects from Draw's computer will be transferred to the stickers.

Finn reads the rest of the text on the paper quickly and is contemplating his next question, like why he needs to wear a mask and bring a loaded pistol as stipulated in the instructions. He opens his mouth to voice his objections when, like a light breeze whisking at his back, he feels the sudden absence of whomever was behind him. He swirls around like a top, but he is too slow. She's gone. He looks at the paper again and studies its contents.

When the mysterious Network lady said that he'd have to break into Draw's place, he had a sudden desire to run and escape from this whole thing. But now, his curiosity about what could be in Draw's system has him straining at the leash, ready to bolt to the apartment and break in himself.

Chapter 14

Hacking the FWN

Livie feels the adrenaline coursing through her body, though she knows the energy it brings will deliver a crash later. It was just over an hour ago that she was feeling the calm, peaceful tranquility of her time on the water. She felt her head clearing out the clutter of voices. The disputes and chaos they brought were fading, and a clear plan emerged from the fog.

She'd create a business for herself without the internet. She'd attempt to reconnect with Hannah, even swallowing some pride and hurts to make it happen. She'd do the same for her mom. She'd seek out a real relationship with Maggie. She'd stop permitting the unceasing babble of the past to overtake her dreams. She'd work on filling the craters in her heart.

Then Larry arrived on the lake shore. She was dismissive immediately and just wanted him to leave. He was a disruption she didn't invite. A potential fly in the ointment. But then, as he talked about the opportunity he offered, her resolve weakened. It truly sounded like something that could properly utilize her skills and make a real difference. His excitement was contagious—just as it used to be.

So here she is now, pushing aside the plans she formulated in her mind while out on the lake and embarking on a new adventure with little information as to what it would hold.

She looks out the window of the car and, through the rain, sees the outline of an old cabin nestled in the trees. The moss, wet from the rain, that covers the cabin's roof catches her eye. Smoke is billowing from the chimney, signifying life, though she sees no other vehicle in the vicinity.

"I thought you said we were meeting them in a cabin? Looks more like a rotten, broken-down barn to me. Are these people really that serious?"

"I understand your skepticism Livie, I'm just following the directions I was given. They were probably limited in what they could find on short notice. But I don't see any other vehicles."

"Someone is here."

As if on cue, a towering figure emerges from the cabin and starts walking towards them.

The figure dominates the view with his broad shoulders, reminding Livie of a football player she dated in high school. Strong, tall, handsome, but short on brains and intuition. He could read a play developing on the football field but couldn't pick up the basic hints she'd give him.

Larry stops and winds his window down a fraction as the figure with the icy blue eyes approaches them. The hulk of a man speaks in a husky voice, as if he has swallowed some gravel.

"Move your seat back, leave the car running, and get out. I'll move it to a secure place out of sight. You and your guest can go inside. They're waiting for you there."

Livie's nose flares from the stranger's cologne, which has swirled into the vehicle and is biting her on the face. She becomes acutely aware of her own breathing. She turns to catch the hulking figure's eye, who still has his palm on the partially opened window as he waits for Larry to open the door. She is about to give him the stink eye when a tattoo on the palm of his hand catches her attention. It is a realistic tattoo of haunting eyes, creating the impression that they are looking right at you.

Larry turns to Livie.

"Well, here we go, I guess. Not sure why he wants me to move my seat back though."

"Probably so he can fit in behind the wheel," Live responds as she abruptly opens her door to exit, hoping the fresh air will wash away the stranger's scent. As she gets out, Livie pulls out her umbrella. Larry grabs his satchel from the back seat and moves quickly to join her outside.

As they make their way towards the cabin, Livie intuitively starts surveying the scene. The log cabin, built on a brick base, is in a dilapidated condition. The moss she saw on the roof is also pervasive on the walls of the cabin. The back of the cabin is consumed by tangled vines that have made a home there. She is surprised that the cabin is even functional. She looks past the vines and sees an overgrown dirt road behind the cabin, and a small bridge beyond that. She assumes there is a river there and that that is where the vehicles are being kept. The thought causes her to look back at Larry's car, which is still just idling there. The large man must be waiting for them to get inside, she figures.

Livie pulls the umbrella close as they step inside, and she can feel the heat flush her cheeks. She immediately sees the glow from a woodstove.

"Welcome. Lemme give you a few mins to settle. There are seats for you both at the table here. Would you like something to drink? We have coffee and tea, or if you'd prefer something to take the edge off, there are shot glasses for vodka or rum."

The person addressing them is one of four in the room. He speaks slowly, with his southern accent slipping out at the end of his sentences. He gazes at them with deep-brown eyes and a confident stature that tells Livie he isn't merely there as a gracious host. *Maybe the accent is something he puts on when it suits the message,* Livie thinks. Just like the coal-black peacoat he is wearing. Livie remains standing and glances briefly at Larry to ensure he isn't going to take a seat either.

The next person to catch Livie's eye is the only other woman in the room. Her straight, long black hair flickers in the light the woodstove offers. Livie looks at her expression and sees mild contempt. As the two briefly stare at each other, Livie concludes that it is likely the woman's natural expression. She is holding a beige folder that she clutches defensively to her side. But then she breaks into a wide smile as she introduces herself.

"My name is Jing. You must be Livie."

Livie nods in acknowledgement as she looks at the others' faces. One of them she can't make out, as he is looking out the window and is standing towards the back of the cabin. The wavy black hair that sits on his shoulders look oddly familiar, as does the toned body she imagines is tucked under the hoodie he is wearing. Her gaze is fixated on him for a few seconds when the other person in the room introduces himself.

"And my name is Ervin. You are most welcome, Livie and Larry."

It strikes Livie that her name is said first as she turns to the man who spoke. He looks Hawaiian, with his rich, tawny skin color, or maybe Middle Eastern. He smiles with a warmth that matches his posture and welcoming words. His eyebrows rose as he said Livie's name, and she thinks it's a bit odd to see someone in this setting who appears to wear his emotions on his face so easily. He clearly knows who she is.

"Thank you, Ervin. Larry gave you my name?"

The response comes from the mystery man, who keeps his back to her as he continues to gaze out the window.

"We all know who you are, Livie."

Livie recognizes him from the way he stretches out the word who. She recalls their conversation outside her apartment the day after the internet went down. She saw him a few other times, including the brief interaction they had at the St. Paddy's Day rally. Those exchanges were similar. Always casually probing about her life. She assumed he was merely hitting on her. His occasional presence had him creeping around her dreams at times. She thinks, *Hannah is right, he is beautiful.* While she can't see his face at the moment, his sunken eyes and long eyelashes flash into her mind as if he is in front of her.

"Raf...you are not someone I expected to see here," Livie says with a hint of an accusation.

Raf remains steadily looking out the window as he responds.

"Well, if by that you are asking if my interactions with you over the last several months had a specific purpose...well," Raf turns and locks eyes with her, "you'd be right."

Livie senses she's in a carefully scripted scene and needs to be careful to play her part. She doesn't respond to Raf's comments and breaks the stare, looking past him towards the window he was looking out of.

Larry looks at Livie in confusion. He clearly isn't following the plot that he is suddenly caught in. Larry opens his mouth to speak, but before he can join the conversation, the guy who is clearly the leader of the group jumps in, his southern accent filling the room.

"Okay, perhaps you two should take a breath and get a drink? We can end the larking and get down to business."

Livie turns, leans the umbrella against the table, and reaches for the rum. She looks at Larry and reaches for two glasses. Keeping her voice casual, she projects confidence and control.

"Before we get down to business, how about we complete the introductions? I haven't heard who you are or who the Goliath is that met us outside."

Livie pours rum into two glasses and hands one to Larry. She suppresses a smile that would convey the satisfaction she feels at taking control from Larry in their part of this script.

"Very well. My name is Sutherland. You've been introduced to most of my team here." Sutherland points at each individual as he names them.

"Jing has a degree in computer engineering. Jing will walk you through the details of what our plans are for you." He pauses to allow Jing to smile and fix her gaze on Livie before he motions across the room.

"And Ervin here can lend you his expertise in being a mole and not getting caught."

Sutherland doesn't motion towards Raf but instead looks at Larry.

"You know Raf. He recommended you to us, with the help of your friend Larry here."

Larry looks like he is about to respond when the door opens—bringing with it a waft of cool, wet air and cologne.

Livie's nostrils flare in response as she looks at Sutherland.

"And Goliath? Who's he?"

"Goliath. That's a good name for him. Let's just leave it at that. Unless of course you give us reason to call you David. You should know he carries more than just the toothpick you may have seen."

Livie looks over and sees the knife dangling at Goliath's side. "And you? Is Sutherland your last name or first?"

"You will get to know the people in our group on a need-to-know basis, as trust builds."

Livie looks at him and thinks if the internet was still on, once she got home, she'd have been able to find out who he is in minutes. She bets she'd find that Sutherland isn't his real name and that the accent is fake too, or perhaps a remanent of his past that he is holding on to.

As Sutherland is finishing his sentence, Jing steps forward, lifts a piece of paper from her beige file, and places it upside down on the table. She fills the air with her Chinese-accented voice.

"We have two broad objectives for you, Livie. One is to infiltrate the Friendly World Network. We believe a starting point for you may be your friend from the coffee place—the person you know as Fairleigh. You'll want to work on getting to know her better, including finding out her real name."

Like a tag team, Sutherland jumps in as Jing is finishing her sentence.

"The second big task is for you to bring someone in to join us in this endeavor—to return the internet to the people. It comes with a twist and could be tricky, though I am sure you are up to it. You need to bring that person in to work with us but also keep him at arm's length so that he still feels he is an independent."

"Okay, why would that be important?"

"He doesn't trust governments in general, and we have reason to believe the anti-interneters are tracking him as well." Sutherland reaches for the piece of paper just as he finishes his sentence and flips it over. He looks up and sees the surprise in Livie's eyes as she looks at the black and white photograph. Jing's voice draws Livie's eyes away from the picture.

"Of course, we are aware you're familiar with this person."

Larry, tired of being a bystander, finds his voice.

"As am I. I'm sure we can deliver on what you are asking. I have a large file on him at my office."

Livie watches Larry out of the corner of her eye. She can see the same intensity in his eyes and nervousness in his posture that he exhibited at the Deerfield cabin. He knows full well that this isn't going to be that simple. It's now also clear why she was specifically sought out to be a part of this. She is the connection to this person; Larry only knows him through her. *What else do these people know?* she wonders. Her mind is churning to formulate questions and statements to take some control of the conversation. To tease out what else they may know.

"Larry has a lot of information on him indeed, so we are familiar with his capabilities. But I'm not so sure it's going to be as easy as you might think to bring him into this little party of yours. Keeping him in the dark about what you really have in mind for him would be another matter altogether. He's a very paranoid and suspicious person. You likely know how intelligent he is, but you may not know how quickly he can pick up on cues from people's body language and tone of voice."

"Livie, we can do this. We've kept him in the dark before."

Livie looks up at Larry now and sees the sweat beading on his forehead.

"Draw wasn't in the dark as much as you imagined, Larry." Livie turns her head towards Sutherland. "I'm not saying we can't do this." Livie points at the black and white photo of Draw, which looks like it was taken when she met him in the park recently. "That man is quite volatile and somewhat unpredictable. He latches on to theories quickly and then holds on to them with great tenacity. He's also smarter than *anyone* in this room." She pauses for effect and looks directly at Jing. "Anyone...We may need a backup plan if he becomes overly suspicious that we have him essentially working for the government. He could bail or simply disappear if he feels he's been misled."

As Livie is speaking, Jing moves towards her and flashes a wide, inviting smile in a show of solidarity.

"I think we can all see why we chose you for this assignment. You not only know the target very well, you understand how to read a situation and read people." Jing focusses her gaze on Sutherland, who gives a slow and slight blink of his eyes. Livie catches the nearly indiscernible gesture as permission that she may proceed. *The scene is unfolding as if being carefully choreographed,* she thinks. Jing turns her attention to Livie again.

"We will rely on your skills and expertise on this, Livie. If you believe we need to bring Draw in fully at some point, we will look to you on how best to proceed."

Jing then gives Livie and Larry further instructions on infiltrating the Friendly World Network. Livie is told she should elicit as much information as she can from her friend Hannah. Jing gives further context as to why Hannah may be important. "You already know that Hannah was at a rally where Annie was introduced on stage and gave a speech. They have been at two other rallies together since, and Annie, with Hannah, are clearly becoming more of a feature at these events. We think this may indicate that your friend Hannah is closer to the FWN than we first realized."

"Former friend, that is," Sutherland adds while he remains standing and looking out the window. Livie is staring at Raf, trying to gauge his involvement in this, when she hears the comment. It hits her as she is transported to the shifting sands of her relationship with Hannah. A relationship that she is about to take on a ride that could sever it for good.

As she is thinking about Hannah, she feels Sutherland's sudden gaze on her as he adds, "We hope you can handle things with Hannah and keep your emotions in check."

Larry, seeing himself as the steady diplomat, jumps in in an attempt to calm the sudden tension.

"You don't need to worry about Livie when it comes to Hannah or anyone else. She's a professional who knows how to get the job done."

His comments to not worry has Livie worried. *How much do they know about my life?* she wonders. She takes in Sutherland's gaze and then looks over at Raf.

"And what about him? What role is he playing in this drama?"

Raf is stared down by Jing as he answers with a smile.

"We're going to get to know each other better."

Jing softens her smile towards Livie.

"Livie, I'm sure you can appreciate that this is a delicate and carefully thought-out operation that will require ongoing improvisations. As part of that, we require that you take on Raf as your boyfriend." Jing gives Raf a quick, stern glance. "In public, that is."

"I work best alone."

An abrupt gust of wind hits Livie's cheeks, and she looks towards the door to see that Goliath has left.

"He's retrieving your vehicle."

Livie turns from Jing to Sutherland, who is still staring out the window.

"If Goliath is going to be part of these future parties of yours, can you tell him to lose the man perfume? It gives me a headache and is making me irritable."

Jing is the one that answers.

"Noted. We will talk to Goliath about his cologne, though your interactions with him should be limited. We do intend to give you a fair bit of autonomy in this Livie, but there will be occasions where you need a sidekick…a prop, if you like."

"I don't need a sidekick."

Livie casts a glance at Raf and watches him move across the floor. Like a red fox stalking the rodent, he moves with balletic grace. His beauty and physique strike her in that moment, and she suddenly recalls him telling her that he spent time as a mixed martial-arts fighter. He abruptly stops behind Jing, where she can't miss his presence. Livie looks at him as if he is about to pounce.

"And I'm suddenly some prop?"

Sutherland moves towards the table, giving the impression that he is stepping onto the stage and blocking the exit to the door—framing his authority over the situation.

"Forget the sidekick and prop comments. Livie, you will be the lead on this. Raf will be there to support you and be another set of eyes. He will also provide a buffer for you when dealing with Hannah."

"And if I don't agree to this?"

Jing, picking up a slight gesture from Sutherland, jumps in.

"Livie, you need to trust us on this. You will have a lot of autonomy, and many times you will be working alone. Some things *are* open for negotiations and some things are not. We do need Raf close to you, and the arrangements we have worked out with the two of you are already in place. We're going to try and limit the number of required events or things you go to together. Ervin will prepare you to be a mole, but we don't intend to dictate how you get inside the FWN."

"But with Raf, everything is already in place?"

Ervin, as if ready to play his part in the production, moves towards the window and looks outside as he speaks.

"We have made preparations for Raf to move into your condo and have set up several hints for Hannah that he's in your life. This way, she won't be surprised to find out that you two are dating."

"What kind of hints are you talking about?" Livie's voice carries emotion that she has been keeping in check.

Ervin hands Livie a picture of Hannah. It shows Hannah in front of Livie's building.

"This was taken a week ago. Hannah has been watching you, or at least showing up at your place at random times. We've made sure when she does, there's something there that gives her the impression of Raf's presence. We're sure as you re-engage with Hannah, she won't be surprised to hear that you and Raf are together. It will give you something to talk about."

Livie looks over at Raf, hoping to calm the roiling current of emotions she is keeping tamped down. His long eyelashes flutter as he returns her gaze. Hannah's words as to how attractive he is return to her. She shifts her gaze, now wanting to avoid looking at Raf as she focusses on Sutherland.

"I'm not sleeping with him."

"What you two do in private is none of our business. We know you can talk a cat out of tree, Livie. You just need to look like a couple and from the same station."

"The same station?"

"Ah, you understand the double meaning."

Silence sits in the room; it is clear that Livie is expected to take its place. She looks down at the table as something to focus on as she contemplates her next move. Resistance seems futile and a waste of energy. She doesn't trust these people, but knows if she plays things right, the situation can be used to her advantage. She can play the game as well as them. She lifts her head high, pushing the silence out.

"Okay then. So, what's the story you have on how we became a couple?"

Sutherland stares at Raf as he answers.

"That's up to you. We've told him that you can make up that story and he will have to play along. Part of it has to include that Raf has convinced you to join the non-interneters crowd." Livie opens her mouth as the desire to protest screams within her, but Sutherland looks at her sternly before continuing.

"You should approach it like the adventure it will be. Time to step through the looking glass, Alice."

Not wanting to be lectured more on the subject, Livie ignores the Alice comment and lifts her eyes towards Raf again. His flowing, shoulder-length hair, those long eyelashes with the drooping bedroom eyes, and his strong facial features are distracting. Her heart suddenly thuds in her ears. It takes her to one of her midnight dreams, and a tremor of excitement courses through her. She suspends her normal cautionary approach and relates the gist of her dream to the others.

"I came back after an exhausting day with my mom. It was pouring rain, and I got soaked getting to my place, only to find out I couldn't get in the building due to a police incident out front. Raf was there and offered that I use his place. I showered and warmed up. He gave me something hot to drink and eat. That was the start of it." She skips the part where Raf joined her in the shower.

"Do you know what I find strange?" Ervin asks, still looking out the window.

"You have demonstrated in the past that you can blend in, gain people's trust, and elicit information from unsuspecting individuals while determining their motives. Those are impressive skills. You also have a strong independent streak and don't appreciate others dictating things. Yet, you clearly would have noticed Raf showing up in your life at various times and didn't suspect a thing? Is that truly accurate, or is the physical attraction your kryptonite?"

Livie feels things slowing down as Ervin is talking, and she recalls the recent instances where she just happened to run into Raf.

It is like a thin veil has covered her eyes, obscuring her view as she looks at the wooden floor and sees, for the first time, the grass that has sprouted through the seams. In her mind's eye, she sees Raf standing there through the grass. It's just outside her condo. He's talking, with excitement in his voice, about a handwritten letter he received from his mom, who is overseas. It was like he had never received a personal handwritten note from someone. Livie never stopped to wonder how such a letter managed to reach him in this new world of theirs.

She knows that, on her best days as an investigator, she can see events unfold at a slow pace, almost like time is passing in slow motion. She remembers every moment, every twist and turn of events down to the smallest detail. She smiles, thinking back to her experience on the lake with the fish jumping and the light coming into the sky as the sun made its appearance, seeming to freeze time. Yet somehow, she missed it with Raf. Somehow, she lost that ability in moments of burning desire.

She tilts her head towards Raf, seeing through the fog of the dreamlike veil that appears in front of her eyes. She sees his beauty and sex appeal and understands the burning desire she feels. While the view is still obscured by the veil, she can see through it now with newfound focus. She can see beyond Raf's sex appeal, knowing that alone isn't strong enough to cripple her in such a way.

With the loss of Hannah in her life and the rollercoaster of emotions with her mom, she wants to matter to someone on an emotional level. Raf gives her hope for that with his intense eye contact, attention to detail, and inquisitive questions. He reads her feelings accurately. His attention is like the poison arrow that spiraled through the air and pierced Achilles's ankle. Combined with his distracting attractiveness, it overrides her ability to slow things down and see life from a bird's-eye view.

The guys she was always interested in were those who carried themselves with a self-confidence that wasn't some kind of façade. Raf doesn't have that, and maybe that is why she dismissed him—except when she'd admire his looks or when he'd creep into her dreams. Even though he doesn't have the same aplomb she does, he does have an authentic manner about him. His air of trustworthiness doesn't seem simulated for the occasion, which is the impression she gets from Sutherland. She looks over at him, realizing he is here now, in this damp, stuffy place where her options have narrowed.

She takes back a bit of control. Ignoring Ervin, she looks towards Sutherland again. He has moved towards the corner of the room, where he is conversing with Larry in quiet whispers. She abruptly interrupts them, raising her voice and casting it in their direction.

"Raf hasn't convinced me yet to join the non-interneters, as you put it. The story doesn't fit with the last time Hannah saw me. It needs more texture before we go there."

Sutherland nods at Larry, moves away from him, and looks at Livie.

"Very well, we will leave the two of you to work that out. But the clock is ticking. The non-interneters must be stopped before they gain much more momentum." Sutherland scans the room, looking at each individual to make his point, before focusing on Larry again. "I trust I don't need to remind you what is at stake here and how urgent this operation is."

Until his quiet little meeting in the corner with Sutherland, Larry's presence was no more notable than the cobwebs in the rafters of the cabin. He now takes his cue from Sutherland and steps towards the table, pausing to look at Livie. It's a look she has seen before. A look that says, "this is my part, and you need to play along." She has seen it many times. The one time that sticks out in her mind the most is when they were completing an investigation for what turned out to be a local mafioso. At the meeting where they shared what they found with the client, they were paid in cash, which was odd enough. Larry's look gave her the instructions she needed. The lift of his left eyebrow, the pleading in his suddenly puppylike eyes, and the contrasting sternness in his closed-lip scowl. She was to keep quiet and let it play out. He'd fill her in later.

Larry lifts his satchel and plunks it down on the table. With a slight thud, the satchel hits the surface and sends up a scattering of dust.

"Absolutely, and it's the reason I brought the contract with me for our services, based on the terms we've discussed."

As Larry lays out the contract on the table, the door blasts open. With it comes the push of damp air and an unpleasant scent that greets Livie like a slap in the face, leaving a series of colorful spots in her field of vision. She throws a loaded stare at Sutherland, as an exclamation mark to her earlier statement.

Sutherland turns away from her and towards the looming figure at the door.

"Yens, ostavaysya na meste."

With his words, the cool, damp air from outside enters the room again, and the scent exits.

"So, Yens is Russian, is he?"

Sutherland looks at Livie, too late to mask his surprise at her response. Clearly, he doesn't know everything about her.

"Goliath understands several languages," Sutherland ends the conversation with Livie as he looks at Larry.

"If the terms are as we discussed, including the reporting requirements and deliverables, I'm sure they are fine."

Livie looks down at the document. The pay is a flat day rate. This surprises her, and she plans to convey her disagreement, but her voice wavers as she asks her next question.

"What terms are you referring to?"

"I assume Larry has not had the opportunity to explain all those to you, but in general, you will report to Jing once every seventy-two hours at a minimum, and Larry will report back to me in general on the plans and strategies. Also, Ervin will meet with you in a secret location at various times to give you his advice on infiltrating the FWN."

Livie casts her gaze towards Jing, content that it is her and not Sutherland she will discuss the details of her activities with.

"And the deliverables?"

"Larry can go over them in detail with you, but we expect you to infiltrate the Friendly World Network and report back to us what their plans are and to gather intel on how they shut down the internet."

"So, you don't know how they did it?"

"You can assume we know a great deal of what they did. You're going to help us fill in the pieces of the puzzle we don't have yet. Including what their plans are going forward."

Sutherland moves to the table, picks up a pen, and signs his name next to Larry's on the contract. As he does, Livie takes in the strange scene. She can't recall physically signing a document in years—she has rarely seen it done, other than in movies. All her signatures are electronic. She'd always insist she be sent a paper copy, though. Something instinctive in her that never completely trusted the security of the electronic cloud. She can't stop the sly grin that hits her face as a thought strikes her. *Perhaps not everything the internet brings is so agreeable?*

They conclude their discussion with a plan as to what will happen next. Livie will get back to Washington and arrange a get-together with her friends, including Hannah. This will be the gateway to re-establishing a relationship with Hannah. One with a purpose. A "nefarious one," as Finn would probably say.

As they exit the cabin, the fresh, damp air fills Livie's lungs, and she responds by taking a deep, audible breath. Her steps are languorous as they move towards the car, which is now back from wherever Jens took it. Her mind is still churning, processing what occurred in the cabin. Larry seems to sense this as they slowly walk to the vehicle in silence.

Inside the car, Larry looks over at Livie. When he speaks, his tone is apologetic.

"We didn't really have time to talk about the contract beforehand, but it's a good deal for us, Livie."

Livie keeps her gaze out the window as she responds, "Five thousand a day certainly jumps out. How much of that I am going to get?"

"Thirty percent."

She turns her head towards Larry, reading his expression.

"Seems I'm taking more risks here. Sixty percent."

Larry looks at her with surprise splashed all over his face. Thirty percent would be much higher than Livie has earned before, yet she is asking for more.

"I'll be covering the operating expenses. At thirty percent, you'll likely still end up with close to half of what's left over."

"Fine, fifty percent then." Livie keeps her eyes fixed on Larry. The message is clear: she isn't backing down.

"Livie..."

"Look Larry, I'm clearly putting myself at risk here. Not just my lifelong friendships, but my very life it seems. We can always go back in there and work it out with your guy Sutherland, if that's his real name."

Larry presses the start button on the vehicle, then looks at the view from the backup camera on the screen as he puts the car into reverse.

"Okay, fifty percent it is then. Glad we are a team again, Livie."

"Larry, you essentially fired me when the internet went down." She knows they have covered this already, but she is struggling to let it go.

"It was a difficult time, Livie..." He glances over at her, his eyes pleading as he hits the gas to move forward. "For everyone...we need to move past that for the challenge ahead."

"I'm still processing some of this, Larry. It's been a whirlwind twenty-four hours. That contract you signed wasn't with the government, it had some numbered company name on it. What's up with that? Do we really know who we are doing 'bidness' with?"

Larry lets out an exasperated breath.

"Come on Livie, you know contracts with government are rarely with them directly. They use contractors and other individuals. It gives them a buffer and limits their liability. This is legit, Livie. It's real good money, too. You must agree with that?"

Livie doesn't respond. She looks ahead, watching the wipers clear the rain falling on the windshield.

Larry turns onto the road back towards Deerfield Lake, but after a couple of minutes, he pulls over and parks on the side of the road. He turns his body in his seat towards her.

"Look, you have reason to be upset about what happened, and I can't change that. But we've been a good team in the past, and this is a chance of a lifetime. We're in this together."

Livie closes her eyes as he finishes his sentence. She knows he's right. She needs to let go of her grievances—even if she hasn't had proper time to air them and get her piece of justice. She takes a deep breath, opens her eyes, and looks at him.

"You're right, we do. Let's get back so I can get my stuff and we can plan our next steps, okay?"

Larry nods his head, puts the vehicle back into drive, and accelerates back onto the road.

"Okay then."

Livie knows they need to concentrate on their common enemy and that their conversation needs some traction in that direction.

So, I thought that was a well-crafted piece of theatre back there. I think we played our parts well. You?"

"I picked up the distinct smell of fear."

"Fear? From whom?"

"Them. Sutherland especially. The stakes are high on this, Livie. They're counting on us."

"Of course they are, but I'm still trying to adjust to the idea of basically working for Brant."

"Brant? Why do you say that?"

"Oh come on Larry, Brant built his election campaign on technology, and since the internet went down, he has been grousing that he'd get it back up and running. Now here we are working for the government, or a contractor of the government, to get the internet back. Brant must be behind this, even if he's several steps removed."

"Ah, I guess you're right. But we're working with individuals who don't seem to work directly as government employees, but as contactors—so that at least makes us several steps removed from the government and Brant himself."

"Not sure that brings me much comfort."

"You can see that, Brant aside, working to bring the internet back is a good thing, right?"

"I guess so."

Chapter 15

Finn Finds Draw

Finn has been waiting in the back corner of the bar for several minutes. It's a spot where he can see all the human traffic in front of him, including all those coming and going through the entrance.

As soon as he sees the bowler hat enter the bar, he feels a tinge of nerves rise inside him. Sinking into the booth and forcing his shoulders to relax, he nods at the bowler hat, which nods in turn and takes a seat across from Finn.

Almost in unison, the first words they speak to each other are the same.

"You are Livie's friend."

Silence follows. They awkwardly stare at each other, neither wanting to echo the other again. Neither knowing who should speak first. The pause lingers and finally both nod at each other at the same time, followed by a mutual sigh as they continue mimicking each other.

Finn knows a fair bit about Draw. He knows that he keeps his place meticulously clean, just as Finn does his own place. He knows that everything on his computer is at least triple protected by passwords, firewalls, and complex equations. He also knows that even if he hadn't imbedded a note for Draw in his computer, Draw would have known he, or someone, had been in his system. *What does Draw know about me?* he wonders.

"So..."

"Well, I guess we have established that we have a mutual friend in Livie, who may be the biggest reason we're meeting."

"Certainly not the only reason."

"Hmmm...I got your message on my computer. It must have been risky for you to leave that."

Draw's question, which is really a statement, means he must know Finn was there to gather information for someone else.

"I suppose. Though I'm certain no one picked it up, except you of course."

"Can I assume you accessed everything on my computer, including the hidden files?"

"All your files are hidden. If you are referring to the deeply concealed ones through the backdoor you created, then yes. I know that you have details on the locations of the central computers."

"Not all of them, as you probably know...or could guess. I'm missing one, maybe two. The missing links to turn this whole thing upside down."

"I figured."

"Do you have that information?"

Finn has an idea where the missing central computer is based on information he was able to lift from the FWN. But he'd like confirmation first and isn't ready to pitch what he has found to someone he just met. He needs to know what Draw plans do with it.

"No, I don't."

Their voices harmonize again as they both ask the same question.

"Who are you working with?"

"You go first."

Finn nods at Draw. Draw nods at Finn. Finn decides to break the stalemate.

"I work alone."

"So do I."

"I doubt that."

"Ditto."

Draw is stoic, showing no emotion.

"Why did you leave details on my computer to meet me then?"

Finn studies the character in front of him. His bowler hat, like some sort of calling card, the scraggly beard, the oversized coat that he hasn't taken off. Draw certainly doesn't look like the most technologically intelligent person Finn has ever met.

From his experience at the university and his own pursuits, Finn prides himself on having interacted with many of the most sophisticated, knowledgeable, and intelligent people in his field. His mother often told him, "If you think you are the smartest one in the room, you are in the wrong room." While he often feels he is the smartest person in the room, his mom's words pushed him to learn more by seeking out people with higher intelligence. The words also kept him humble enough to accept that he wasn't always right and could learn more—without being overly intimidated by those with superior knowledge.

Now here he is, in the back corner of a bar with someone he believes would always be the smartest one in room. He's certain there are things on Draw's computer that he missed and likely would never find. The level of sophistication he saw on that computer was unlike anything he ever encountered before. He looks at Draw, trying to analyze him, feeling a hint of intimidation.

"You said you could turn this whole thing upside down. What do you mean by that?"

Draw stares at him without a blink. The silence lingers. Finn holds his tongue, takes a drink of the water on the table, and looks past Draw to the waitress who is moving towards their table.

"Well gentlemen, you here for something to eat, or drinks?"

Finn orders a beer and some chips with salsa. While not hungry, he wants something on the table for a distraction. Draw orders a soda water with lime.

Finn watches the waitress leave as Draw moves to the side of the booth. Draw looks out into the bar now, the change of position giving him a clearer view of everything.

"I'll move too, so we can both see the bar and each other," Finn responds to the movement. He slides his body to the right. Both men can now look at each other and have a clear view of the bar.

"You're certain this place is safe, I assume, and that you were not followed here."

Draw states it as a fact, then continues.

"You asked me what I mean by turning this whole thing upside down. I believe you know the answer to that. We need to bring the internet back on with a new internet. One that doesn't allow governments to steal people's personal information."

Who's this guy working for? Finn wonders. It's the question that keeps rolling in his head. It has been asked and answered. He needs to come at this from another angle.

"Why do think Livie is important in this whole affair?"

"Affair. Interesting choice of words. She's straddling both sides, it seems. When you accessed my computer, I knew they figured out the connection she has to me...and to you."

The rhythm of silence beats on the table as the two look at each other, seemingly studying the other. Each wondering what the other is thinking. The waitress arrives, breaking the hush.

"Your drinks and snacks, gentlemen." She places the drinks on the table with the salsa and chips in the middle. "I'll get you each a small plate for the chips. Would you like anything else?"

"Not for me, thanks. No need for separate plates. The chips were ordered by my friend here."

Finn's eyebrows lift at Draw calling him his friend. Draw picks up on this as the waitress leaves.

"I think it would be wise for us to be friends in this. For our safety, Livie's, and for a better world."

Finn leans back a smidge at Draw's words.

"So you want me to help you?"

"Isn't that why you left that message on my computer?"

Finn reaches over for some chips, dips one in the salsa, and shoves it in his mouth.

As Finn is munching on the chips, Draw turns his focus to the bar and the entrance. Draw came here primarily for the location of the central computers and to find out what else Finn knows. If he can get Finn on his side, with his connections and intelligence, that would be a bonus. Draw has the coordinates for four of the central computers. He knows there are at least two more. He hopes Finn has that information. He needs to get it from him, or this meeting will have been a waste of time.

"If you didn't leave that message on the computer to help me, I have no need to continue this discussion. I would appreciate it if you will tell me what you know about the locations of the central computers."

Finn swallows the last of the chip in his mouth, takes a swig of his beer, and looks out towards the bar.

"I know that you have the locations of three of the central computers."

"But you have the coordinates for more than that. How many do you know about?"

Finn reaches for another chip, dips it in salsa, and pauses just before putting it in his mouth.

"I have information on five of them, which includes your three." Finn shoves the chip in his mouth and crunches down. He knows about one other computer—the one in the mine he has been too. He looks at the bowl of chips and salsa, thinking of that location. It's a chip he intends to hold on to, unless he finds Draw trustworthy and knows their interests are the same.

"Do you have that information with you, to give me?"

Draw takes a drink, looks at Finn stonily and waits for him to finish his chip.

"Have another drink, Draw. I'm just going to use the bathroom."

Draw watches Finn exit the booth, wondering if he is stalling. He needs to know that Finn came here to share something with him, or he won't stay long. He's tempted to leave now, but he needs that information from Finn. He can do a mental calculation to determine how the computers would interact with each other, and if Finn's five locations include all four that Draw knows about, there could be as many as three more computers. If those five locations give him two new ones that he doesn't know about, it could potentially close the loop for him.

Finn needed some time to think away from Draw's piercing stare. He's already told him that he has information about five of the computers, so he should just give it to him as he planned to. But he can't figure out if Draw is truly working on his own or for someone else. *What is his true agenda?* he wonders. Draw's mannerisms - and that stare of his - are also giving Finn a familiar arrogant odor of a know-it-all. It makes him want to resist on principle. He turns the tap on, cups some water, and splashes it on his face. Looking in the mirror, his mind sifts through his feelings.

It doesn't help that he is conflicted about his own interests. He wants to see the internet returned; however, some of the less invasive aspects of the world without the internet resonate with him. He doesn't trust either side in this battle. He is confused about what his role is in this and how he got this deep into it to start with. Part of him wants to just run from all of this; preserve his own safety and sanity. Would the FWN leave him alone if he did? He only gave the FWN information on three of the computers. So, they know Draw is onto them, but hopefully still too far away to be considered an immediate threat.

He reaches for a towel, his thoughts swirling as he dries his face. If he just gave Draw the coordinates for all five computers he knows about, maybe this could all come to an end more quickly? But to what end? Draw's question was valid: why did he leave that message on Draw's computer to meet him? He has always been able to get out of any trouble his curiosity has driven him to before. He exits the bathroom, the question still pulsating in his mind.

Finn grabs his jacket as he returns to the booth with Draw watching him. He reaches into the jacket's pocket and pulls out a sticker. The sticker, clear with black lines on it, is attached to a clear piece of wax. He places it on the table between them.

"A data sticker. Clever way to store information. If you suddenly decide you don't want it shared, essentially all you have to do is destroy the sticker."

Very few would know what a data sticker is or looks like. Even fewer have the means to lift the data from it, let alone be able to create one.

"I assume you wouldn't have trouble lifting the data from it?"

"You've been inside my computer and know enough about my abilities to answer that." Draw pauses and looks directly at the sticker, as if he could lift the information from it with his stare. "I assume the coordinates for the five computers are on there?"

Finn keeps a finger on the sticker to remain in control.

"That's correct."

Draw leans in, looks at Finn, but makes no move to take the sticker.

"So, are you going to give it to me or destroy it?"

"Why would I destroy it?"

"Cause you are trying to decide if you can trust me with it or not. The thing is, you don't have a choice. You know the way out of all this is to bring the internet back. I'm your hope for that. If I leave here without that sticker, you won't see me again."

Finn is looking at Draw directly now. He wants to shout that this threat of his is a bluff. Draw's question of why he left that note on his computer rings in his ears. He has the answer.

Finn pushes the data sticker towards Draw, keeping his finger on it.

"The coordinates for the five central computers are on there for you. I need you to help me find out more about the workings of the FWN, including who is behind all of this."

Draw looks out towards the bar; Finn is just glad he's not staring at him.

"That's where our mutual friend comes in. It would be dangerous. For all of us."

Chapter 16

Back At Green Planet

Livie keeps replaying scenes in her head from their meeting at the cabin in in the woods. Her mind has taken her back there ever day in the three weeks that have passed since. Dissecting it, making sure she didn't miss anything. Subtle things, like Goliath's tattoo, which she has since researched by asking various tattoo artists about it. The meaning she discovered is rather menacing—it's predominately a Russian tattoo that means "I'm watching over you." A set of eyes staring out you. *Creepy,* she thinks.

Since that day, she has been avoiding meeting with Ervin or anyone else that was there, except for Raf, who lives with her now—or at least sort of, as they mandated.

She needed some time to conduct her own investigation into things without any interference. This has annoyed Larry, who tells her their contract requires that they communicate regularly. He says it in a way that suggests she may not get paid if she doesn't fulfill that part of it. She dismisses his concern. She will communicate with them, in her own time and only concerning the information she decides to share. Not getting paid isn't what worries her. The sinister agenda behind all this is what disrupts her sleep. Managing what she communicates is the only way she can maintain some control of the situation. At least for now.

She has made six discoveries so far: the irregular comings and goings of Fairleigh; Finn has also been tracking Fairleigh's movements and appears to be on the Friendly World Network's side; Draw is probing her about the internal workings of the Friendly World Network and knows something about their use of central computers; there is some sort of threat involving satellites, though she doesn't know from which side; someone with knowledge about the satellite issue has an unusual tattoo of a skull and bones and the numbers 322; and, she can't trust Ervin.

In her investigative work, she has often thought that if you were to hide a tree, the place you'd choose is a forest. The Friendly World Network is too big to not stick out, unless they blend in. The rallies they have been organizing are part of their propaganda and serve as a diversion. It's not where she expects to find those inside the Network. So, she decided to spy on Fairleigh, the person she knows who is closest to the Friendly World Network. At least that is what she thought. Now she wonders if that might be Finn, as she spotted him snooping on Fairleigh as well. Then there's his connection to Saba, who may also be part of the Friendly World Network. Livie still shakes her head thinking of those two as a couple.

Watching Fairleigh, she once saw her covertly hand something off to someone on a busy street corner. Following that person led to others, and then others. Five moves later, like watching a game unfold on a chessboard, she was led to a meeting of three people that occurred outside a movie theatre. Using her pocket binoculars, she read their lips from a distance. Well, at least a few words that she managed to pick up, as the three individuals stood close together, like they were three teenagers with secrets to share that they didn't want others to hear. Except these weren't teenagers, and one had a rather menacing tattoo on his forearm. When she adjusted her binoculars and focussed on it, Livie saw a skull and bones with the numbers 322 below it.

The person didn't seem to match the ominous tattoo—an older man with a receding hairline, a sports jacket, and a casual expression that didn't seem to ever leave his face. She also picked up from the lipreading that there was some plan involving satellites, as she saw them mention satellites several times.

At that point, she felt that she had gathered enough intel to see what Fairleigh could confirm. Livie didn't have a complete picture of things yet, but she was close enough to feel the thunder that was coming.

This all brought her to her interactions with Ervin, who asserted himself into the picture a few mornings earlier.

Ervin's words are playing in her head. He assured her that "the target," as he put it, would be at Green Planet this morning. She was to act "blasé" when she saw the target. Again, Ervin's words. That part she gets and resonates with how she would have approached this. She had planned to act relaxed and nonchalant anyway. But his suggestion that she should act like she is short on time and may not have any time to chat, she was less certain about. Particularly with the knowledge she has already gathered. She knows from recent developments that their time may be shorter than she has appreciated. *The sand is running out fast,* she thinks. Time to get the cards on the table, face up.

"I thought time was of the essence," she told Ervin. His soft, assuring voice plays in her head. "We don't have a set time period, though it's true we must move quickly. But this is a delicate situation, and mistakes could set us back. We need you to gather information from her, but your primary goal is to get her to engage you and ultimately have her invite you into their circle."

After the whole scene in the cabin, she told them she didn't need to meet with Ervin for any advice on infiltrating the FWN; that she could handle it. When she didn't receive any response telling her otherwise, she figured she was good to proceed her way, though Larry kept telling her that Sutherland wasn't happy about her lack of communication. Making Sutherland unhappy just added fuel to the rebel inside her.

But then Ervin showed up at her door that morning. Like a carefully choreographed scene, he was there coming out of the elevator just as she was leaving her place. She was going to make her way to Green Planet and had it all planned out. When she saw him, she simply said, "Hi Ervin, strange seeing you here. I know you don't live in my building, so if you came to see me, I don't have time right now." Then she walked past him, intending to ignore him.

He stood outside the elevator as she got in. The doors started to close, and she simply smiled at him when he said, "You won't find her there today." Livie pressed the button to open the doors, glared at him with suspicious eyes, and inserted an agitated edge into her tone. "Find who, where?" He paused long enough that she had to press the button again. She was wondering if he was deliberately trying to agitate her when he let the doors start to close again—before putting his leg in the way to force them open.

"Livie, I can tell you exactly when Fairleigh will be at Green Planet, and it won't be today."

"I thought we were only going to meet in some secret location? Coming to my place like this is hardly that. It's an intrusion."

"You're not the only one that likes to go off-script. You also seem to be avoiding me. I hear you've refused instructions to meet with me."

"Alright, let's plan to get together sometime. For now I need to go. So please, get out of my elevator."

Ervin nodded his head in resignation and moved his leg free from the elevator door, allowing it to close. *That's one for me,* Livie thought as she made her way to Green Planet anyway. She had done her own investigative work and had a lead on when and why Fairleigh would be at Green Planet today. She was certain Fairleigh would be there, in the same spot she always was. As she made her way down the street, Livie rehearsed how she would bring up the topic of the Friendly World Network.

But Fairleigh wasn't there, of course. Ervin had probably made sure of that.

Now here she is, back at her condo. Unsurprisingly, he was outside the elevator, waiting for her. Wanting to show him that she's still in control of the situation, she hands him a coffee from Green Planet and invites him in.

She's ready to jump in with her distinctive brand of resistance, as she expects him to lay out all their plans for her and what she's expected to do. But his first words throw her off her own plot.

"You were right. Fairleigh should have been at Green Planet today. You did exceptional detective work to figure that out. Elite level, actually. Fairleigh's movements are very irregular, yet you somehow, in just a few weeks, figured out she'd be there—with no internet to help you. It would have taken experienced investigators months to figure out." Ervin sips his coffee, looks at her with wonderment in his eyes, and shakes his head as if in disbelief. "How'd you do it?"

Livie turns from him and makes her way to the window, sipping her own coffee. She wonders if this is all part of the script of the play she is in. Is he buttering her up for something, or is he genuine in his praise? She squints as she looks out towards the Washington Monument, taking a few moments to clear her thoughts. She casts her eyes down to below her window and sees bicycles where she previously saw cars.

"Do you think the non-interneters will be able to bring back driverless commuter cars?"

"I don't know that they care, Livie."

Livie turns around and sees that Ervin has taken a seat on the couch. She pivots back towards her view of the monument.

"Oh, believe me, they care. Actually, they have a general plan to re-establish a number of conveniences the internet gave us. Things like restoring easy, cheap telephone communication with video and access to a person's medical files. They want travel to be safe and easy to arrange again. They want the GPS systems to function properly so things like driverless cars can come back. Well, the GPS issue is at least a debate amongst them."

"Hmmm...not sure how they would do all that without the internet. If they truly want to help people, they'll re-establish things like online banking and the ability to pay with a card."

"They won't do that. They want to go back to a cash-based society. That's deliberate on their part."

"Really? So, they want that, but not a horse and carriage society?"

"No, they don't want horses and carriages. They want to reclaim some of the advantages of the internet, but not all of it. They want the old, printed newspapers and," Livie holds up her fingers and mimes air quotes, "They want real journalism." She pauses briefly and moves to the kitchen to dispose of her coffee cup and get a glass of water. Then she moves back to her position by the window and continues.

"They also want the forgotten birthdays, the abandon that comes without thinking everything is being recorded and marketed. They have even talked about the internet again as a new entity where search and social media algorithms only allow for truth and social relevance, and...oh, I think a return to periods of pure boredom. A more authentic world where the voices of common people matter, they say. Pretty altruistic, I'd say."

"So how did you discover all this?"

Livie, water glass in hand, turns back and moves towards Ervin, projecting a curious look to mask the distrust she feels. She thought he might challenge the accuracy of her intel, but the fact that he didn't has her on high alert. She's looking for signs that he may be nervous hearing about her revelations. Are they things he's genuinely surprised to hear, or did he already know about it all? She stops to stare intently into his eyes.

"Before I answer that, tell me how you knew Fairleigh wasn't going to be at Green Planet today. Clearly, she was supposed to be there."

Ervin averts his gaze. His eyes appear to soften with a half-smile as he answers like he anticipated the query.

"She was given a more urgent assignment to complete."

Livie returns the half-smile, turns, and heads back towards the window. She looks out at the monument. Ervin's answer begs for a further question about what the urgent assignment might be. He's likely ready for his answer. But she might already know the answer, and this is a dance with a beat she wants regulate.

She decides to offer a half-truth.

"Okay, my turn then. Raf." She says his name with a deliberate naughty tone. "That was a good idea; was it yours?"

She hears the low chuckle from Ervin, who then catches himself.

"No. I was skeptical you'd go along with it, and it would just become something more to manage." Ervin suddenly looks at her intently. "I guess I was wrong. Sounds like you're friendly with him after all?"

Livie looks out the window and then closes her eyes as she makes a mental note to talk to Raf about keeping certain things confidential. She sees that warm smile of his and feels the confident assurance that it will not be a problem. She turns back towards Ervin. She looks at him and surmises that he somehow has access to some of the Friendly World Network's plans, but not really what they are all about. Like she suspected, they are focused on the high-level plans of the Network and what they will do next. They seem to miss the undercurrent of values and desires that are driving those plans. She wonders: *Is Ervin as sly as a fox, like Raf, or is he really just good at bullshitting and covering up what he doesn't know?*

"Okay then, what next? When can I expect to see Fairleigh at Green Planet?" Livie asks.

"Before we get to that, we need to talk about what your approach is going to be when you meet her."

"Haven't I demonstrated that I can figure that out on my own?" His response has her leaning towards good old-fashioned bullshitting to make up for what he doesn't know. Why doesn't he just tell her?

Ervin's voice softens, as if he wants to slow the dance down suddenly.

"Livie, I'm not here to tell you what to do. Clearly, you can figure out a lot on your own. But two heads are better than one, and maybe you don't see it yet, but I have insight that could help you here."

Livie looks at him with a skepticism bordering on scorn. Ervin rises from the couch and moves towards the window, joining Livie as they both turn to take in the view towards the Washington Monument. He looks up.

"Is that one of those magnifying blinds that can give you a better view of the monument?"

Livie looks up at it. "It is. Got it from my realtor." She looks back out the window. "I prefer the more authentic view that has not been enhanced. Something that doesn't shut out all that one may see to just focus on one thing."

Ervin turns to her.

"Let me share with you some of the things I can see with the Friendly World Network. Then you can choose which deserve your attention and which don't."

Ervin goes on to give her his insight into the Friendly World Network, including that Fairleigh is a computer geek of sorts, something Livie already knows. He says she was called to an urgent meeting about something to do with plans for the new world order, as they call it.

Livie's mind is calling bullshit. Ervin doesn't seem to know that much, which is why he is talking in generalities. She thought he might mention the satellites, but he makes no mention of any concern brewing over "man's artificial stars," as Raf put it. He could be hiding something from her, and she isn't ready to dismiss that idea entirely yet. Knowledge is power in this game. She has information he doesn't have. What *does* he have?

Ervin also opens up to Livie about his personal life. He tells her about his son, Darius. He speaks with raw emotion in his voice as he tells her how worried he is for him. Darius, he says, has become more and more isolated since the loss of the internet and has stopped communicating with his father. He's worried that Darius has lost his way in this world. Livie finds it curious how someone so skillful at gathering secretive information about the lives of others could so easily wear his emotions on his face.

She still isn't sure what to make of Ervin. Is he entirely genuine, or is this all part of his schtick to win her over? When he expresses concern about Sutherland and others' volatile ways of working to bring the internet back, she begins to wonder whose side he is on. Are his comments about Sutherland a warning of sorts?

But she can't deny his strong spirit, and she comes to realize that it would be to her advantage to treat him like an ally instead of resisting him. At least she should give him that impression.

"Ervin, I'm sorry I've been so difficult. I see now that it would be better for us to work together," she says, smiling at him fully for the first time.

He seems pleased by her change of attitude, proceeding to give her further insight into the Friendly World Network, including details about their "code of ethics," as he calls it. A code that includes a required solidarity to their cause, a "buddy system," and a series of rituals they do to "look out for each other." Ervin, like Livie, can see how the code could be their Achilles' heel. He gives her details she wasn't aware of, and she starts processing what and how to share these with Raf—to confirm what she is hearing.

Livie's visit to Green Planet the next day would change the course of her approach once again.

~~~~~~

As Livie stands in line for her coffee, she looks over and sees Fairleigh. They smile at each other. Something's wrong in Fairleigh's smile. Livie picks up on it immediately, like it was a signal to her. Fairleigh's stressed. Livie can see it in the forced nature of the smile, the crinkle in her forehead, and the stiffness evident in her shoulders.

Livie looks at her phone and sees that she has an unexpected text from Raf.

"So, is it busy at Green Planet today?"

Odd, she thinks. He must just be checking in with her. She types "Y" and grabs her coffee.

With her coffee in hand, Livie makes her way to the seat beside Fairleigh, which appears to have been reserved for her.

"Nice seeing you! It's been a while," Fairleigh says.

Livie nods in response. Better to let Fairleigh take the lead in the conversation. She senses she may want to talk.

"How've you been?"

"I'm good. Like everyone else, adjusting to this new normal."

Fairleigh nods. "I'm concerned that society isn't adjusting so well. Like the pandemic of 2020, many are bracing for what might be next."

Livie looks intently into her eyes. Fairleigh wasn't just musing about possibilities. This was a statement. She can see it in her eyes. Livie decides to take a more direct approach.

"Hey, can you tell me more about the satellites?"

The surprise on Fairleigh's face gives Livie a partial answer. Something is up, and she senses Fairleigh needs to tell someone.

"Why do you ask?"

Classic deflection question, Livie thinks.
~~~~~~

“I dunno, just wondering what role they may play in this new world of ours.”

Fairleigh looks away and towards the window. Even from the side, Livie can see the fear growing in her expression. She hasn’t seen this side of Fairleigh before. Something has her anxious and on edge.

“Well, if the satellites become compromised, it could plunge the world back to the 1960s.”

Livie pauses. She waits for Fairleigh to say more or to look back in her direction.

A few long seconds pass, and Fairleigh turns her head back towards Livie, catches her gaze, and looks down at her coffee. Livie joins her in watching the steam rise from Fairleigh’s coffee mug.

What was conjecture is now as real as the steam coming from the coffee. For several seconds, the only sounds that fill the air are the background chatter of others in the café and the barista grinding coffee beans.

Livie sees the deep contemplation in Fairleigh’s suddenly tightly closed lips. The fear hasn’t left her face, though she tries to hide it by keeping her eyes on her coffee mug. Livie thinks of the initials she knows are embossed on the bottom of that mug and decides to break the silence. Time to place some of her cards face up.

“Do you think Fort Meade could be compromised by plans to alter the satellites?”

Livie knows Fort Meade, the nation’s center of intelligence, information, and cyber operations was likely already compromised, but she is fishing to see what Fairleigh knows and if the question would get any reaction. National security has to be a concern, even for those wanting a so-called simpler life.

Fairleigh intensifies her downward stare, avoiding eye contact. Her voice is just above a whisper.

“I think you know that Fort Meade is already vulnerable.”

Livie concentrates on Fairleigh's body language and sees her shoulders slump and her arms move close to her body, as if she is cocooning. Like she is protecting her body from something. Something has her scared. Livie decides to be direct.

"Does the Friendly World Network want to take the satellites out of commission?"

Fairleigh looks up at the question and directly into Livie's eyes.

"No. Certainty not. A new world order is the objective, not war."

Livie looks at her face. She takes in the passion in her statement; the fear in the small creases by her mouth.

"Who wants war then?"

Fairleigh grabs her coffee mug and starts to stand up.

"I've said more than I should. I need to go."

Livie reaches out and grabs her elbow.

"Wait. Can we plan to meet again sometime?"

Fairleigh looks over at Livie and scans her body as she processes the request. They have never "planned" to meet before. This is a request that breaks through the hard sediment of this being just a casual friendship. The dance is moving beyond a carefully choreographed waltz.

"Why do you insist on referring to it as the Friendly World Network and not just the FWN, like everyone else?"

"I just think when you use acronyms for an organization, people forget who they are or what they stand for. Just like the so-called "Friendly World Virus," Livie mimes air quotes, "they are the Friendly World Network."

"Alright then."

"So, can we plan to meet?"

"Yes. Two days from now, at 1:30 p.m. There is a mulberry tree close to the monument."

"I'll be there."

"Okay. Make sure you're alone and that no one knows you're with me. I'll do the same."

As Livie watches Fairleigh exit Green Planet, she feels a sudden wave of fear for her friend. She sees Fairleigh as someone who truly believes in a non-internet world. It's why she joined the Friendly World Network and became a champion for them. But does she know their true agenda or the desire for world domination that lurks behind it? Has she figured that out or does she just suspect it? Is she just one of their puppets in this?

Livie reflects on the expression that crossed Fairleigh's face at the mention of the satellites. She looked like someone who was spinning too many plates.

Livie's thoughts then circle to Finn. She knows from watching Fairleigh's movements that Finn has been watching her too. Why? He must have a reason for trying to get closer to the Friendly World Network. He has Saba; why wouldn't he use her instead?

Livie closes her eyes and thinks of what she knowns about Finn. His tech skills. His propensity for getting himself involved in conflict—like a moth to the flame of danger. She opens her eyes. Maybe he's trying to find out how they did it too, so he can bring the internet back?

She needs to find out what he knows. She can't ask Saba. She doesn't trust her. Her mind ricochets from Saba, to Finn, to Hannah, to her mom, to Ervin, to Raf. There are so many people in her life that she can't trust, rely on, or go to.

Time to have a real chat with Raf and find out what he truly knows.

Chapter 17

Who Can You Trust?

Livie opens the door to her condo, bracing herself for the report she is expecting to give Ervin. Her mind is also on Raf, as she is clear in her head about how she is going to approach him. They've made a good connection, been friendly towards each other, but there are things she needs to know. *The time for playing house is over,* she thinks.

Raf is in the kitchen as she comes in, and as soon as their eyes meet, it is clear on his face that he knows something is up.

"Raf, I have some direct questions for you, and I'm not interested in vague, purposeless responses."

Raf immediately makes his way to her and surprises her with an embrace, which he uses to whisper in her ear.

"Not here. I'll make a move to leave abruptly. Meet me on the walk towards Malcom X."

Her eyes immediately scan around her place as if someone might be listening to them. It makes her want to scream, as the pent-up anger of the situation is boiling in her. She walks over to the window to look out at the monument and blow off steam, while Raf grabs his jacket and leaves the apartment. As she works to regulate her breathing, Livie's mind goes to Ervin. Why wasn't he here when she returned? She was certain he'd be waiting for a full report from her on her interactions with Fairleigh. What does Raf know about Ervin?

Livie turns and grabs her jacket. She was going to wait several more minutes, but the urgency for answers that is pulsating through her propels her towards the door.

~~~~~~

Raf turns when he hears her behind him.

"Oh, thank God it's you. I felt someone coming up behind me."

"Did you think it could be someone else? And if so, who?"

Livie is beside him now and has slowed her pace to match his. They are walking on the sidewalk on Florida avenue. They can see the brown stone wall of Malcolm X Park in the distance in front of them. There is a bench nearby that Livie points to—thinking it will be easier to talk while sitting. She wants to be able to read Raf's facial expressions as he reacts to her questions. Raf nods in response and moves towards the empty bench to sit.

As Livie sits down beside him on the bench, she launches into the questions that have been circling in her head.

"So, back there you seemed relieved that it was me behind you. Who else do you think could have been following you?"

He turns to look at her directly, his long eyelashes picking up the sun's light and showing off their softness. He appears to study her face for a few seconds before responding. *Gawd, why does he have to be so beautiful?* she thinks.

"It's not what you're thinking. I don't know that anyone would follow me, I'm just not sure who I can trust right now."

"What's making you feel that way?"

Raf looks away and towards the street, speaking in a quiet voice that disappears on the wind.

"Do you know that Ervin spells his name with an E? It's E. R. V. I. N."

"Actually no, I didn't know that. Why does that matter?

"Maybe it's nothing, but I knew an Ervin with an E from school years ago and he was Iranian. Perhaps this Ervin is also Iranian. He looks like he could be."
~~~~~~

"Hmmm, okay. Not sure why that's relevant. Is that a concern for you because of your Jewish background?"

Raf quickly turns his head to look directly into her eyes—as a direct and emphatic no to her question. He pauses and then looks out towards the street again.

"Did you know that Ervin was following you today?"

Livie can't hide the surprise on her face as Raf looks at her. Sitting together to read facial expressions cuts both ways. Playing in her head is the image of the dark silhouette she saw in the shadows as she entered Green Planet.

"I'm pretty sure I saw Finn in the distance when I went into Green Planet, but not Ervin. You have information that I was followed?"

Livie thinks back to how odd it was that Ervin was not waiting for her at her apartment earlier. Raf must know something.

"I watched you leave for Green Planet today, and within a minute or so, I saw Ervin on the street moving in the same direction."

"You sure? I mean, could it have been someone else?"

"It was him. No question. I pulled out your binoculars to confirm. I watched him following you until he was out of sight. I considered following him, but then figured the normal thing would be for me to stay put."

"So is that why you are not sure who you can trust? Because he was following me, and he may be Iranian?"

"Why would they have an Iranian involved in this to bring the internet back?"

Livie looks at Raf, who is still staring into the street. What is churning in his mind? She has become accustomed to Raf's ability to swiftly analyse deeper meanings behind seemingly small facts, but she isn't sure what he is getting at. She decides to try and fish it out of him.

"Brant's group seems to have recruited people from various nationalities in this. Jing is Chinese."

"Brant's group?"

"Sure, I could say the government, but really, isn't Brant behind this quest to bring the internet back." Livie states this as a fact rather than a question to see how he responds.

"That was my initial understanding of the situation. It just seems like there is a more sinister agenda behind this than I realized."

"Raf, what happened today that caused all this doubt?"

Raf looks at her briefly, faces back towards the street, and stares off into the distance with a contemplative expression.

"As you were getting ready to leave, I received a text from Jing. I've never received a text from Jing before. I almost thought it might be a hoax. The text said that Ervin was not going to come by today as he was being diverted to another assignment. It was from her text that I discovered he spells his name with an E. Why was she texting me this? I responded asking her that, and her response was simply to remain where I was and wait for further instructions. I was looking out at the street when I got that text from her, and that's when I saw Ervin."

Livie is looking at Raf, trying to read his expression from the side as she processes what he is saying and what it could mean.

"Is that why you think my place is bugged?"

Raf turns his head and looks at her again.

"I don't know that, Livie. It's just that you and I were talking about Ervin this morning, saying that he was likely to show up. Then I get a text from someone who hasn't texted me before saying he isn't coming. Maybe I'm just a bit paranoid. But there is something else I haven't told you yet."

Raf looks away towards the street again, and Livie responds more loudly than she intends to, unable to contain her excitement. "What?!"

"Livie, Ervin was packing a gun. I was sure I saw an outline of one in his pocket, and when I zoomed in with the binoculars, I confirmed it. I thought of calling you, but then got paranoid that someone might be listening in."

"That's why you texted me?"

Raf nods in response.

"I can see why you were part of the Mossad in the past."

She knows Raf will understand the meaning behind her reference to the Mossad. Her statement is a reminder to him that he has his own secrets that she knows about. Sutherland and his friends know nothing about his history as a spy for Israel's foreign intelligence agency, the Mossad—at least as far as he knows. She knows he needs to keep it that way, and she needs him to tell her everything he knows. She hasn't even gotten to the other questions that have been swirling in her head.

"We must trust each other, Livie, for this to work. Ervin, Jing, and Sutherland believe we're working together for them and may even have become lovers. Regardless of this, I'll keep feeding them information about you that has just enough truth in it to keep them at bay. And I know you understand the importance of keeping my secrets under lock and key, so to speak."

They are now looking at each other intensely, and Livie is trying to discern if his statement is genuine or meant to protect himself. It offers a window of opportunity that she doesn't plan to miss.

"I agree Raf. And with that, I have some questions, and I need straight answers."

Raf reaches over and touches her hand.

"For sure. I will answer any questions you have, and then maybe you can fill me in on your visit with Fairleigh?"

"Absolutely, but let's first talk about Ervin. I didn't have any interactions with him, even if he was following me, but you said he had a gun. Was that for protection you think, or some aggressive action of sorts?"

"Given that you didn't hear from him, I think we should assume it was for protection. That of course begs the question, protection from what or whom?"

"You have a theory?"

"Ervin must feel some vulnerability to carry a gun. Either it's from internal sources or from someone within the FWN. He has a reputation for being a double agent of sorts, so it could be either. Jing's text left me thinking that maybe Ervin got offside with Sutherland or someone."

"You know I was avoiding getting together with Ervin until yesterday, when I couldn't avoid him. What's *your* relationship with Ervin been like?"

"Well, after I was recruited by Sutherland and his group, Ervin seemed to go out of his way to befriend me."

Livie hears Sutherland's name and just thinks "Brant", as she is sure he's behind this. The thought that she is essentially working for Brant continues to grate her.

"So, like what? What did he do?"

"He really just started chatting me up about personal stuff, and now that I think of it, he went out of his way to tell me about his life growing up in Florida and being an American."

"What do you mean by 'now that you think of it?'"

"I just didn't clue in before that he's Iranian. It seems odd and makes me wonder about his true upbringing. Maybe I am biased, but I had a girlfriend who was Iranian, and she didn't trust Iranian men."

"We don't know for sure that he is Iranian, right?"

Raf gives a nod that has skepticism written all over it.

"Okay, so how *did* you get recruited by them anyway?"

Raf sneaks a quick glance behind him, as if he's about to share something quite sensitive, and he lowers his voice.

"The events this morning have me thinking about that as well. At the time it seemed to be rather random. I should have suspected something else from the beginning."

Between thoughtful pauses, Raf quietly tells Livie how he met Jing at a theatre play in the park and they struck up what he figured was a random discussion. They talked about political matters and the importance of technology in our lives. Then, a few days later, the day after the internet went down, he ran into her at a bank. She told him that she had already been contacted by a government group to bring the internet back.

Livie was listening intently, wondering how and when she came into play in this matter.

"So, that first day when I was walking home and ran into you, was that just a coincidence or was it planned?"

Raf lets out a sigh.

"I had no idea at the time what I was doing in bringing you into this, honestly."

Livie's mind goes back to that first day, remembering Raf's chattiness. Like dusting off an old memory, what rises to the surface is his mention of Brant saying the internet would be coming back on, and then something about possibly scoring some cash. The context for it all has now changed.

"Okay, tell me more."

Raf explains how Jing told him that they were actively working on recruiting tech-savvy individuals and people with strong investigative skills. When Raf mentioned Livie, Jing jumped on the suggestion like it was fresh air in a stuffy room. She then coached Raf to first work on befriending Livie more and finding out where she stood on the internet debate before acting on anything. Later he received instructions to leave it to them to do the actual recruitment.

"The plan sort of just unfolded from there. At the time, the whole thing gave me some purpose in a confusing world, and they provided me with cash. But today's events have me questioning everything." Raf pauses before adding, "Livie, I think perhaps you were the real target for recruitment all along."

"Really? Yet somehow *you* end up in that cabin with them and right in the middle of this plan to move in with me. You seemed to be going along with it like it was your idea."

"It wasn't. Honestly, you have to believe me. They're paying me very well, and when they suggested the plan that included me getting closer to you, it just seemed like a win-win for me."

"Oh, come on Raf, you're much more sophisticated than that. You had to think there was a reason they wanted you so close to me."

"Of course I did. But I didn't know what that was exactly, and I just figured I would find out along the way."

"So, have you found out?"

"Not a hundred percent for sure, but I wonder now if you were truly the one being indirectly recruited through me."

"Why?!"

"I don't know exactly. I think it must be because of someone you know or can get close to in your investigative work. I'm not sure it's about getting you inside the FWN. That may be a ruse of sorts."

Livie looks at Raf and surmises that he is being sincere.

"Well, we should work together to find out who that someone is."

Livie looks around to ensure she doesn't see anyone she recognizes. Realizing they have been sitting there for a while, she suggests they get moving and head back to the condo.

"Let's head back together and see if we can find out where Ervin and his gun got to. Time to start asking direct questions."

As they stand, Raf turns to her and smiles in a clear effort to lighten the mood.

"You still have to tell me about your visit with our mutual friend today?"

Livie returns his smile and starts walking as she talks.

"I saw a different Fairleigh today, Raf. Until today, I've only known her as this calm, down-to-earth, practical person. Today she showed a vulnerability I've never seen from her. She appeared anxious and maybe even frightened."

Livie moves a bit closer to him to ensure no one can overhear them as she tells him about her conversation with Fairleigh about the satellites.

"I wonder if there is a plan to manipulate or even take out some satellites? If so, who would be behind that?"

Raf simply states, "That would require a high level of sophistication, not to mention access to information and weaponry. Someone very powerful and connected to a government would have to be behind it."

"Like the Russians, maybe?" Livie muses.

Livie then tells him about the meeting she set up with Fairleigh, and they talk about how best to approach it.

"I think it's time for us to change the music in this dance and be direct with our questions. I think Fairleigh might be ready for that," she says.

"Makes sense, but doesn't that run contrary to their stated desire for you to infiltrate the Friendly World Network? I mean, Fairleigh might just recoil and share nothing if she sees you're not just a curious outsider?"

"Raf, you must know by now that I'm not just going to follow the script crafted by Sutherland or Brant or whomever."

"Fair enough. When's your meeting with Fairleigh, or perhaps I should say Jody?"

Livie, while still walking, motions towards the Washington Monument with her chin.

"In two days, in the park by the Washington Monument."

"I think you need to be extra careful with this meeting. There could be danger lurking where you may not see it."

They are within half a block of her place and close to turning the corner towards the entrance of her building. She slows her pace and looks at Raf. Something else must be on his mind.

"Is there a particular reason why you're concerned about that?""

Raf moves so that he is walking close beside her. She almost expects him to reach out and touch her. Then he stops and takes out his phone.

"I have something else I need to ask you about."

Livie looks directly into his eyes. She has always found when someone has something specific to say, their eyes and body language can tell you as much as their words. Raf looks dead serious.

"Really? What's that?"

Raf passes his phone to Livie, which displays a picture. Livie looks at with interest. It's a blurry photo of a tattoo on someone's chest. The tattoo looks like a skull and bones. There are numbers embossed below the chin of the skull. She can't quite make it out, but it looks like a three and two twos. She keeps her expression neutral as she hands the phone back to him.

"Okay, so a tattoo on someone's chest. Not sure how you got that blurry picture, but what's your question?"

"Have you seen that tattoo somewhere before?"

Livie looks more closely at the tattoo and her nostrils flare in response, as if she smells something ominous.

"I don't think so. Looks kind of creepy to me, but must have some specific meaning?"

"I'm wondering the same, and I haven't found out yet. When I was watching Finn the other day, I saw someone with him, and they seemed to have some disagreement. So, I followed that person afterwards to where he lives. The next day, I followed him again." Raf pauses as if what he is about to say needs careful thought. He starts walking again, Livie beside him, following his lead now.

"I didn't tell you this earlier as I have been processing it myself. That picture I showed you is of a tattoo on the person who had the disagreement with Finn."

"Really? How did you get a picture of his chest?"

"I took it from a distance. He was on the ground, shirt open and dead."

As Raf says this, they both see the entrance of her building. Jing is standing there, seemingly waiting for them.

Jing makes eye contact with them and appears impatient and tense as they approach. Livie attempts to keep things light.

"Jing, certainly didn't expect to see you here. Hope you are well? You just in the neighborhood or is this a visit about something specific?"

Jing seems to bristle at the question.

"Let's just get up to your place and talk about what we need you to do."

The trip in the elevator up to Livie's condo is a silent one, with Jing standing by the elevator panel as if her presence there will make it go more quickly. Livie looks at her with curiosity and a sense of rising annoyance. What right does Jing think she has to come here and just demand things?

Reaching the thirteenth floor seems to take longer than usual, and it is with a sense of relief that they exit the confined space of the elevator. As Livie punches in the security code and opens the door to her condo, she voices the first words spoken since they left the street.

"I'll get some coffee on for us."

"I didn't come here for coffee," Jing says, her tone still clipped and businesslike as they all enter the condo.

Livie quickly proceeds to the kitchen to grind some beans regardless of Jing's words. The grating sound of beans being ground fills the room and prevents Jing from saying anything else. As the sound comes to a halt, Livie turns to speak before Jing gets a chance.

"So, what did you come here for then Jing? And before you answer that, you should keep in mind that you are a guest here. This is my place."

Jing moves towards the window as she speaks, so Livie can't see any of her facial expressions. Her voice is terse.

"I need to know exactly what you found out today from your contact at the coffee shop, and then I have some directions to give you."

Livie looks over at Raf.

"You want some coffee, Raf?" Raf nods in response. Livie puts two cups down in front of the coffee maker and pushes a button to release the drip of coffee.

Jing is still looking out the window, clearly waiting for Livie's response. Livie decides she isn't going to relinquish control of this conversation like that.

"Before we get into any of that, why are you here and not Ervin? I thought we might see Ervin back here."

Jing doesn't move and answers in an even, emotionless tone.

"Ervin is no longer with us."

Livie moves closer to Jing. "What does that mean? Was he fired? Did he disappear?" Her tone now has an edge to it.

When Jing doesn't respond, Livie elevates her voice and growls, "Look at me and answer me Jing. Where is Ervin?"

Jing turns to face her and reveals no expression as she repeats, "He is no longer with us." Her eyebrows dip a bit.

Livie picks up on the small movement.

"No longer with us? Does that mean he's dead?"

Jing is clearly trying to hide any emotion she feels, but Livie's keen eye notices the slight flare in her nostrils and the further tightening of her closed mouth.

"Livie, I'm not here to talk about Ervin. I need to know what came out of your meeting today with your coffee friend."

Livie looks at Jing, thinking that clearly, she didn't get the memo that Livie doesn't respond well to ultimatums.

"I'll be giving my report to Larry."

Jing looks intently at Livie. "Forget Larry, and don't worry, you will get paid. Just give me the information."

Livie moves past Jing towards the window herself and looks out at the monument as she contemplates her response. Jing fills the silence.

"Stop playing games Livie. You don't want to mess with these people, trust me. Just give me the information."

With her back now to Jing, Livie tries to keep her anger tamped down.

"You know on the day the internet went down, the driverless cars crashed. That's what woke me up and how I discovered the world had changed. I don't think it's going to just change back as quickly. Real change usually comes with patience."

Livie wants to push the gas pedal to the floor on this and slam on the brakes at the same time. Should she laugh or scream at Jing? One thing is certain, she doesn't want to be in her presence any longer.

She turns to face Jing now. "I will give my report to Larry. I'm going to ask you once, politely, to leave my home. Now."

Jing pushes her shoulders back as if getting ready for a standoff. "This is not a good strategy on your part Livie. You don't want to make enemies of these people."

"These people? Doesn't that include yourself?"

"Believe me, I will be the least of your problems if you don't cooperate."

Livie walks past Jing and picks up her phone from the kitchen counter. "As I have said, I will give my report to Larry. Now, you are an unwanted visitor here and as such are trespassing. You need to leave, or I will phone the police."

Jing looks at Raf for support. Raf just stands quietly and looks back at her, his expression one of hopelessness. Jing gives Livie one last look, turns, and leaves.

As the door closes behind her, Raf opens his mouth to say something, but Livie interrupts him.

"I think we should take a shower."

Livie is in the bathroom first. She turns on the shower and then turns to Raf, who is now standing by the door he just closed behind him.

"I don't know if there are any bugs in here, but in case there are, this is the best way I could think of to drown out our voices. I hope you don't mind?"

Raf moves closer so she can hear him over the sound of the water.

"Why didn't you just give something—anything—to Jing?"

"I don't know what she knows already or what she is seeking specifically. Not sure I would have satisfied her with what I was prepared to tell her. Raf, there's something up with the satellites, and I want to see what I can find out before I say anything to Jing or that group."

Raf looks up at the steam coming from the shower, as if the cloud it is forming can provide answers.

"It might have been safer to give her something. What are you going to share with Larry?"

"I don't know yet. Probably that Fairleigh's real name is Jody and that I'm making progress in getting a meeting with the Friendly World Network."

"Are you?"

"I don't think so. I have to talk to Finn and Hannah. But first, tell me about the dead guy with the tattoo."

Raf tells her how he was following this guy who he saw with Finn. The guy was carrying a case with him that looked like it could contain a firearm. When the man climbed a hill and went into the woods, Raf kept his distance and would have lost him, except he saw him go down from a gunshot. He moved closer and saw someone hovering over the man and then rip open his shirt, revealing the tattoo. That's when he took the picture before he high-tailed it out of there. In the steam, Raf looks distraught just retelling the story.

"I didn't sign up for violence. I escaped a previous life with violence and don't want to be involved in that again. And now Ervin is missing."

"He's dead, Raf. The question is who killed him? Same question for the person you saw, though we don't know who he is. Maybe they are related, one killed from each side—like a gang war of sorts."

"Jing didn't say that Ervin is dead."

"Yes, she did. It was in her face." Livie reaches up to massage her forehead, the thought of talking to Ervin's death weighing on her. She talked to him less than twenty-four hours earlier, now he was dead. She continues to massage her head, eyes closed, seeking relief from the tension in her. Her impulses are shading into emotions she is trying to project elsewhere. She can feel the heat of the steam from the shower behind her and Raf's eyes on her. She opens her eyes and goes through the list that is building in her mind.

"I need to think about what to do next. Who is it that I know that has me involved in all this? We should go by the house of the dead man with the tattoo to find out who he is. I really need to talk to Finn. And meet with Draw. And Hannah and Fairleigh. And come up with something for Larry to keep a lid on things for now." Livie lets out a breath and looks at Raf, his beautiful face and toned body right in front of her. A little smile cracks her mouth, and her eyes fill with sudden mischief.

Raf opens his mouth to speak, but Livie puts her index finger to her mouth to indicate silence.

"Right now, I really do need a shower." She reaches down to pull her top over her head.

~~~~~~

Hannah is scanning old texts she sent to Livie, hoping for some insight or inspiration on what to do next. Her fingers rapidly scroll through the texts. She stops at one she sent Livie before all this started.

"The unlived life is not worth examining."

She snickers as her mouth expands into a warm smile, and she hears Livie's voice as she reads her response to the text.

> "I don't think unlived is actually a real word...thanks, my friend. Thanks for the chat last night. I get what you're saying, I need to stop contemplating what I'm doing with my future and get moving. I'm just not sure I can break free from Larry so easily to venture out on my own. It's a scary proposition. But you have inspired me—as you often do. I know I can always count on you. You're always there for me, and I don't know if I could navigate this life without you Hannah."

Hannah wipes her face with the back of her hand and takes a breath as she hits the button on her phone to call Livie. It rings twice, then stops. She hears someone breathing. The breathing is deliberate and contemplative in nature; she can sense it. She thinks she might hear a second person breathing as well. Just when she expects the line to go dead, she hears the voice of her old friend instead.

"Hi Hannah. Sorry, just got out of the shower. I was thinking of you and that we should plan to meet. I'll be in touch, okay?"
~~~~~~

Chapter 18

Baby-blue Heeled Shoes

Having left the park after her clandestine visit with Draw, Livie is on her way to Green Planet again.

Thoughts of what Draw is asking her to do are circling in her head. Brant's group—as she refers to Sutherland, Ervin, Goliath, and Jing in her head—probably doesn't realize how much Draw has figured out. The conversation with Draw seemed surreal and at times fragmented. Yet it had an intensity to it that created its own force. Draw really believes in her, almost too much, with too much intensity. That somehow, she is the one, like the only one, who can get inside the Friendly World Network and find the central computer or computers for him to bring the internet back. But she kept asking herself, who is he working for? Is he truly on his own in this? Asking him about the satellites was on the tip of her tongue many times. But she held back because she isn't certain what is driving him in this quest. When she asked him who else is helping him with this, he looked away before saying he works by himself. It was the only time in their conversation that his body language didn't match his words.

But now she needs to focus on her next task—thoughts of which are making her heart thud in her ears, in sync with her heels hitting the pavement. Her pace is brisk, and she rubs her hands together, feeling the sweat between her fingers. She wants to stop, jump up and down, and shake out her nerves. But it wouldn't be practical, considering where she is and the heels she is wearing. She starts to lecture herself to keep her emotions in check. She is determined to project an air of certainty and self-confidence, without coming across arrogant or indifferent.

With that in mind, she lifts her head up straight, keeps her posture at its tallest, and picks up her pace. The clicking of her heels hitting the pavement with each step now chimes in her ears. Her eyes catch the tips of the baby-blue shoes as they hit her vision in front of her. She can feel the sly grin appearing at the thought of the tiny zipper on the back of the shoes. She whispers quietly to herself, "Zip it up, Livie."

With Green Planet now in view, she scans the various parked cars nearby but doesn't spot Hannah's. Her shoulders sink in relief as she picks up her pace. She was hoping to arrive before Hannah but is a tad late after the longer-than-expected visit with Draw. The pleasant thought of getting settled first has just hit her when she sees the figure in the doorway of Green Planet waving at her. She quickly swallows the sour expression that must have hit her face in response and moves swiftly towards the door.

"You beat me here."

"Well...you're late, actually. I almost wondered if you were...um. Glad you made it."

They stand looking at each other for a few seconds that seems to pass at a snail's pace. The customary hug that was always part of their greetings when they got together is absent. Hannah breaks the awkward silence and reaches out to affectionally touch Livie on the shoulder.

"Hey, I like those shoes of yours."

Livie finally reaches over and gives her a hug. She steps back and motions towards the inside of the coffee shop with her chin.

"Well, instead of sitting in there with all the background noise, how about a walk?"

"Those shoes must be comfy, despite the heels, if you are suggesting a walk in them?"

"Of course they are. After all, someone who knows me well picked them out for me."

The air between them seems to be warming. They both smile at each other with a natural ease that, at least temporarily, pushes aside the disagreements that have boiled under the surface of their relationship since the internet disappeared.

"So, what do you have mind? Maybe a walk around the park by the monument?"

"I'm there a lot. How about the other direction from here to Malcom X?" Livie knows that Meridian Hill Park, or what is also known as Malcolm X Park, is a safer location for Raf to pick her up later, and there would be a risk of running into Draw near the monument. But it would be a short drive to get there.

"Oh...okay, shall I drive us there then?"

"If you don't mind. If you have your car here?"

Hannah points to a silver electric vehicle nearby. "It's not mine, but a friend's. We are...kind of sharing a vehicle these days."

"Really, anyone I know?"

Hannah looks at Livie with a curious expression.

"I guess we both have a fair bit of catching up to do. How about we get in the car first?"

~~~~~~

Draw left Livie with a spring in his steps. The excitement is coursing through his veins. She believes in everything he told her. He told her about the codes that he has been able to unlock and that he knows almost everything about how they shut down the internet. He isn't quite as close as he led on, but he really believes he can solve the missing link if he gets access to the right computer. He can bring the internet back but doesn't think he can do without her, and now she is ready to help. Finn remains another possibility if she can't come through. If Finn isn't sure about trusting him, perhaps he will trust
~~~~~~

Livie to feed her the necessary information. *Better to have a couple of irons in the fire,* he thinks.

He is still navigating who to trust on his side in this quest. Regardless of that, he tells himself, he believes Livie will come through for him. She has the chutzpah to do it and to aid him in realizing his ultimate dream. To bring true order to the world.

~~~~~~

During the short car ride over to Malcolm X Park, the two women casually chat about the weather and the traffic. The tone is light, and the air filled with apprehension. As they exit the car to walk around the park, Livie knows that she will have to open up the conversation to get what she needs from Hannah. She decides to start by asking questions about things she knows, to test how honest Hannah will be with her.

"So, how's Annie doing?"

Hannah walks towards the trail ahead and briefly looks over at Livie with a curious stare.

"Look Hannah, I'm seriously interested. Yes, I wasn't pleased to see her there with you at that rally, but I was also glad to see that she seemed to have grown in her confidence and even found a voice. She seemed to be able to move on with her life. Is that the case still?"

Hannah picks up her pace slightly, forcing Livie to match it. It's like the conversation is fueling her energy, or perhaps she is using it to create pauses, allowing her to process.

Livie catches up and is walking beside her when Hannah answers.

"She's doing well. Finally getting some stability in her life. She owes a great thanks to you for setting up that housing arrangement with Hugo."

Livie knows all this from Hugo of course, but she masks any knowledge.
~~~~~~

"I'm happy to hear that. Hugo's a good guy, so I'm glad it's still working out." Livie decides to probe more about what she learnt from Jing and Sutherland about Hannah and Annie.

"Annie go to any more rallies with you?"

Hannah picks up her pace yet again, and Livie rushes to catch up. Hannah answers as Livie gets within a couple of steps of her.

"Yeah, a few. I think she enjoys them. It gives her interactions with other people."

No mention of Annie speaking at any of the rallies, as Livie was told in the cabin. Hannah is being guarded what she shares, it seems. Livie decides to leave it for now and pivots the conversation to something else.

"So, you kind of hinted that you might be involved with someone. Care to share?"

Hannah stops and faces Livie. "So, is this how it's going to be? We're not going to talk about all the ill feelings and the rift between us? We're just jumping into what's going on in each other's lives?"

A crow caws in a tree nearby and startles them both, causing a timely pause as both of them turn to look at the creature. Livie watches the bird fly away and feels Hannah's eyes back on her as she answers.

"If you want to talk about the things that have driven us apart, I'm certainly more than prepared to do that." She turns and looks at Hannah. "I just thought it might help if we first caught up on each other's lives a bit."

"Okay then. Yes I *am* in a new relationship. His name is Grant, if you must know."

"That's nice Hannah, I'm happy for you. What's he like?"

"What's he like? Well, let's see. He's attentive, inquisitive, very articulate. He freely expresses his emotions. And he is very handsome with strong features. He's smart and artistic. In fact, he is a musician."

Livie carefully swallows any emotions she feels as Hannah tells her more about Grant. Hannah tells her that he's a professor at a university and then finally reveals that he's older than her. She pauses to see Livie's reaction. Livie keeps her feelings from reflecting in her eyes, though her jaw drops a bit, opening her mouth slightly. She tried to hold in the reflex, but she never pictured Hannah with someone older. Hannah seems to have changed in ways Livie didn't realize or expect.

Hannah continues to talk about her love interest, including how they met by chance at a bar one afternoon after she attended a rally. He initiated the conversation when he saw her sign from the rally, came up and introduced himself. She talks freely and openly about Grant. It sounds like they are planning a life together. She smiles as she relays parts of his personality.

"He is quite opinionated on things, but respectful in listening to others' views. Sometimes, our interactions remind me of us, where he will challenge something I say in a direct or sarcastic way, then allow me to move the conversation to something else without harboring ill feelings—even if I know I didn't change his mind. Though I have to say he has changed my way of thinking more often than not."

As Hannah talks, Livie's mind starts churning. She and Hannah always used to talk about their romantic interests in great detail. How far she is into this new relationship is just further testament to how disconnected they have become. Then, as Hannah mentions they met following a rally, something clicks in Livie's mind. There is something Hannah isn't saying in this story.

"Wait, do I know this Grant from somewhere? What's his last name?"

"I'm not sure, why would you think that? His last name is Solbey, but..."

"Solbey? Is he the guy who spoke at the rally we were at?"

Livie is now suspicious of every relationship, it seems. Hannah says she met Grant at a rally, but if it was the rally he spoke at, clearly she would have recognized him when he supposedly approached her? *Was it truly a chance encounter?* she wonders. Hannah's evasive response just adds fuel to her suspicion.

"He may have. He has spoken at some rallies. Livie, he's just a very genuine guy who has really helped me process a lot of things in my life, both from the past and going forward."

Livie suddenly interrupts Hannah as she probes further.

"Hannah, have you talked to him about me?"

"About you? Why would that matter?"

"Oh, I don't know, just curious, I guess."

"Well, of course we have talked about you. You have been such an important part of much of my life. You and I haven't spoken for months until now, and yes, Grant has helped me process a lot of things related to that. He knows you are a pro-internet sympathizer."

Livie turns the term "pro-internet sympathizer" over in her mind as they continue their brisk pace. She hasn't been called that before. She takes some solace in the fact that the term doesn't give away how involved she is. But she needs to know more about this Grant's interests. Catching her breath, she slows down a bit, and Hannah slows down too to match her pace.

"So, Grant is part of the Friendly World Network then?" Livie intends it as more of a statement than a question—to see what response she gets.

Hannah lets out one of her snorting laughs that Livie has heard so many times before. She smiles at the familiarity of it.

"Livie, not everyone that wants to keep the internet off is part of the FWN. You have to know that? Grant, like me, just wants the internet to stay off. He's actually more passionate about it than I am. That doesn't make him part of the FWN. There are a growing number of us that just wish that whatever fight there is going on to bring the internet back would stop. Normal, smart rational people who have their lives together. People like Grant and Finn."

"Finn?"

"I thought that might get a rise out of you, but you shouldn't look so surprised. Finn may be a computer geek, but you know how smart he is, and *he* wants to see the internet stay off."

Livie almost snorts hearing that. She may not have gotten along with Finn over the years, but she always appreciated his skeptical perspective on things and principled approach to life. She knows he has been working for someone related to the non-interneters, but she's also fairly certain he hasn't wholeheartedly embraced their philosophy. She is actually quite concerned for Finn and that he could be navigating dangerous territory without understanding all the risks. She decides to dig a bit deeper and makes a bold, dangerous statement.

"You know Finn is with Saba. It seems to fit that they have been involved directly with the Friendly Work Network." Livie watches for Hannah's response, but the comment seems to bounce off her as idle chatter.

"Hey, enough about me and my life. Who's the girl in those baby-blue shoes seeing?"

Livie smirks at the clever way Hannah has avoided looking straight at her and avoided the topic of Finn altogether, instead moving the focus to Livie's shoes. Hannah bloody well knows who she is seeing, and Livie anticipated this question long before they started their walk together. *Time to test how forthcoming Hannah will be,* she thinks.

"Well, you remember that attractive younger guy from Israel that lives close to me?" Hannah gives her a quizzical look.

"His name is Rafael. You called him beautiful when you met him."

"Livie, I've called lots of people beautiful. What's he like?"

"So, you seriously don't remember him?"

"Well, maybe if you describe him and tell me more, I will." Livie wondered if Hannah would play coy. She didn't expect her to admit that she had seen them together, but she didn't expect her to act this dumb—as if she doesn't know who Raf is.

Livie decides to join her in the dance of deception and withholding information. She describes their relationship as a new one and mentions nothing about them living together. Instead, she talks about them often going over to his place, as if they have separate apartments. Livie knows that Hannah knows this is a lie. It's a tit-for-tat response.

"So does Raf want the internet back on like you?"

This is the opening Livie was waiting for. The opportunity to get Hannah to truly open up to her as to what she knows and maybe what Grant has been feeding her.

"Raf is on the fence on that, and to be honest, he's dragging me there too."

The comment stops Hannah in her tracks. She can't hide the surprise on her face. Livie knows instantly it's a comment that Hannah will dine out on for a while. This is the bridge, more than the shoes, that could bring their friendship back. Well, that is as long as she can conceal the truth from Hannah.

"So...you're no longer entirely sure we should get the internet back on?"

"Well, let's just say that I'm not as convinced as I was before. My mom is enjoying life much better without the internet, and I know a few other people are too. It has me rethinking things a bit."

Livie tells Hannah about her experience at Deerfield Lake with her mom and that her mom has bought the cabin. She mentions the water bottle she left there—the one that Hannah gave her.

This leads to a nostalgic trip down memory lane for them both. Hannah made many trips out to Deerfield with Livie and knows the memories well—the good and the bad. Hannah was also there for Livie through many discussions about her mom, including the heartache and frustration she brought to her life. Somehow this topic leads to rehashing old memories from their university days: Hannah's relationship with Finn and Livie's series of dating partners at the time. It's like old times—trading stories, feasting on the same exaggerated versions of some, and the renewal of old jokes. The conversation ebbs and flows with laughter and excited voices, often followed by tears and hugs.

One round of laughter is just petering out when they both look up and see Hannah's, or rather Grant's car. They have walked the entire park circuit and are now within a couple hundred feet of her vehicle.

"Well, we're back. You have any other plans? You could come over to my place for something to eat, if you like?"

Livie is tempted by the offer but also isn't sure it would be wise at this stage. She'd like to meet with Finn and Fairleigh first and see what information she can gather from that. But then, if she goes, she might meet Grant, a connection she might find useful.

"I'm not sure if I can make today work. Would I meet Grant?"

"I don't think so. I could contact him, though oddly he hasn't been in touch with me for the last day or..."

"Really? Have you tried to contact him?"

"Of course, and it's a bit strange, but he does get busy with work and stuff. I'm sure I'll hear from him soon." Hannah motions towards the car. "I have his car after all," she says as she lets out a nervous laugh.

"Well, I'd like to meet him sometime. I don't think today is going to work for me anyway, sorry."

Hannah's face shows a sincere measure of disappointment.

"For sure. What's your schedule like this next week?"

"Can I get back to you on that?"

Silence suddenly falls between them as they make the final steps towards Hannah's car. Hannah pulls out her keys and presses a button on the fob to unlock her vehicle. Livie stops and faces her.

"Hey, I'm so glad we did this. This has been good for me, and I know we'll get together soon. I think I'm going to walk home from here, so can I phone you later?"

Hannah reaches over and gives Livie a strong, extended hug.

"For sure. Livie...you need to know that it just about crushed me thinking our friendship may have been destroyed."

"Me too. How about we focus on the future now?"

"Let's do that."

Livie turns and makes her way towards the path in the direction of her home as she hears Hannah's voice shout out at her.

"Hey, how about we get the gang together again soon? You know, with Finn, Preet and Bo, and maybe Saba too?"

"Let's do that for sure, at my place. Just like we did the night of the election."

The last comment has Livie suddenly thinking about Finn and formulating a plan to get in touch with him. As thoughts of Finn and Hannah are prowling her mind, she catches a familiar, hulky figure in her peripheral vision. She doesn't think he has spotted her, and she quickly makes her way to the nearby forested area, where she disappears into the trees.

She can now get a clear view of him. His oversized frame and bulbous nose stick out as she imagines his icy eyes. Her nostrils flare just looking at him from a distance. The way he is looking around, like he is looking for someone, tells her that him being here is no coincidence. She watches him pausing frequently as he looks around. She wonders whether he followed her or Hannah here. *Must be me,* she figures as the image of those eye tattoos flash across her mind.

Oddly, he appears to be alone. Finally, he seems to give up and leaves the park. Livie moves slowly out of the trees, crouching low, keeping her eyes on the direction he disappeared in. Slowly she emerges from the trees, like the picture of the old apes evolving into man, gradually coming out of her crouching stance to an upright position.

She phones Raf and asks him to pick her up near the Lutheran church, thinking that would be as safe a place as any.

~~~~~~

On the ride back to her condo, Raf is clearly anxious to tell her about something he discovered about the satellites. Livie is about to tell him everything about her visit with Hannah when the mention of the satellites stops her in her tracks.

"What did you find out and from *whom*?" She emphasises the end of the question, thinking that information could be just as important.

"I reached out to an old friend I know who previously worked for the government and—" Raf pauses as he turns the corner up 16th Street. His pause lingers, and Livie can't take it anymore.

"And what Raf?"

"Perhaps we should pull over to chat about this more?"

"No...well not here anyway. I think I was followed in the park. Let's find a quiet place where we have a good view."

Raf suggests the Hampton Courts area and starts heading in that direction. Livie is too anxious to wait before they get there.

"So why not spill the tea now? What did you find out about the satellites?"

"Okay, just don't freak out or stare at me trying to read me somehow, alright?"

"Agreed. What do you know?"

"Apparently there is a detailed plan and strategy to take out all the satellites. Kind of like a space war."

"All of them?"
~~~~~~

"Every last one, I'm told."

"Wow!" Livie sits contemplating the implications and who might be behind it as she waits for Raf to get them to a quiet spot by Hampton Courts.

No wonder Fairleigh had that fear in her eyes. She must know something about this but isn't pleased about it. Is it coming from the Friendly World Network, and why? Fairleigh told her that they wanted a world with less intrusion into people's personal lives, but one that always uses advances in technology. She even talked about a new version of the internet that would be "friendlier". This plan would clearly go in the opposite direction. Is she second-guessing what the Friendly World Network is doing, or is someone else behind this? Livie gets her answer as Raf finishes backing his vehicle into the corner of a parking lot where they can see anything coming towards them.

"My old friend told me that the information is very sensitive, confidential, and dangerous. He told me about it because he's hoping someone will do something to stop it, but he was naturally afraid to tell me."

"Did he tell you who's behind this?"

"He said he isn't sure but wonders if it's Brant and his people."

"Brant? How does that make sense? Brant's trying to get the internet back on."

Raf looks at Livie as she processes what she just heard.

"I know your mind is churning now with what this means, and I have been trying to figure it out myself. I think it might be that, if Brant can wipe out the satellites and then bring the internet back, they can control the message better."

"Who's your friend?"

"Livie, his name needs to be kept under lock and key."

"Understood. Who is he?"

"I always knew him as Forrest Momoa when he worked as an agent for the FBI. He goes by Keanu now."

"Hmmm. A former FBI agent. Haven't heard of him. Did he give you any clue as to how we might stop this from happening?"

"He didn't. Just that if we can get our hands on the details of the plan and get it into the right hands, maybe we can stop it."

"This all sounds kind of crazy. Anyway, meanwhile, did you find out anything about the dead guy with the skull and bones tattoo?"

"Not yet. Didn't have much time, and when I went by his place, there were a lot of people milling about."

"Okay. Time for me to arrange to meet with Finn, I think. Maybe he knows something about the satellites, and he may be in deeper danger than he realizes. I was followed to the park today. I'll tell you more on the drive back."

Chapter 19

The Ghost of the Internet Looms

When Finn got the rather insistent message from Livie that they needed to meet to chat about their "mutual friend," he was more than a little curious. They quickly made arrangements, with Livie directing the where and when.

Finn parks on 16th Street. As he approaches the cascade fountain at Malcolm X Park, he feels restless; the questions are drumming in his head. *What exactly is this about? Why has she set up this meeting now? Is there a significance to meeting in this park?* Livie was specific that they had to meet behind the thirteen-basin cascading fountain. He considered parking on W street to approach the fountain from the back, but he feels more secure in the open space at the front, where there are more people.

He stops to stand still and scans the fountain, including the thirteen large, tiered, semi-circle basins the water is cascading down. The area is large, and he is on high alert for any unusual movements in the crowd. The area is full of people—including several that are walking on the steps next to the fountain and others just watching the fountain and taking pictures. As he makes his way to the treed area at the back of the fountain, he looks around for Livie or anyone else he might recognize—conscious that someone could be following him. He turns at the eastern corner at the back of the fountain and stops just as he gets to the front of the treed area, where he stands still.

The tumult of noise at the front of the fountain has all but disappeared at the back. He's in the exact spot Livie described for them to meet, and he looks at his watch. 12:58. Two minutes early and no sign of Livie. He has always known Livie to be prompt. On time. He didn't expect to arrive before her, and his nerves are pulsating. Voices coming from the fountain murmur around him and thud in his ears. A bird chirps and a branch snaps in the trees. He hears the sounds as if they are all magnified.

Finn begins to think about what has brought him to this place. Did Livie contact him because of Draw or Hannah? A lot has transpired after his meeting with Draw, including additional information he secured. The nature of the information and sources have spooked him. He has lost his nerve. The rush of excitement he felt being involved in things has evaporated within him. He longs for the simple, mundane existence of his work at the university. He isn't sure he can escape to that if he shares everything with Draw. His options are to either do nothing with the information or get it into Livie's hands. Neither of those paths guarantee an escape, but he has to do something.

Then there's Hannah. If Livie has contacted him because Hannah told her that he's a supporter of the non-interneters, she might be seeking more information about the inside workings of the Friendly World Network. He knows Livie would suspect he hasn't bought into everything they are selling anyway. He may have found their relationship crusty over the years, but he has always admired, even feared, her abilities to read a situation and perceive what a person's true motives are. It's the reason why he decided to come. He's counting on her in this.

He has made it inside the Friendly World Network. They trust him. Hannah believes he is a supporter, and though things are rocky with Saba, he believes she does too. He has been working out a plan to walk away from it all, but it's a delicate strategy. He wonders how much Livie knows. Could she blow his cover on this whole thing? That old fear of what she may have figured out is why he is now standing in this park. He needs her to understand what is happening, but he wants to be the one to share it.

He looks at his watch again. 1:06. Where is she? Being tardy or unreliable is not her style. Ever. He hears the crunch of a twig in the trees nearby, and then another. He focusses his attention on the vicinity of the noise. There's someone there, but in the shadows. He can only make out a silhouette, when suddenly he feels a hand on his arm. He jumps in response.

"Geeesus Livie!"

"Sheeesh...I'm sorry, didn't mean to startle you. I just want to make sure I haven't been followed here. You see anyone suspicious?"

Finn takes a moment to look back in the direction Livie appeared from.

"I haven't, but there are a lot of people here. You're late, and I was beginning to wonder if you were coming."

"I was here, but just waiting for the right moment and making sure I wasn't followed."

"Why do you think you'd be followed here?"

"Finn, cut the bullshit. We both know that we are traversing in dangerous company these days. Let's move away from here. Walk this way with me." Livie points towards a path that makes its way into the treed area.

Part of Finn wants to push back and refuse to go with her. Her abrupt comment means she likely knows at least some of the things he's been up to. But how much? That old fear of what she knows but isn't saying yet creeps into his mind. It is a cocktail of that fear, curiosity, and the need for her help that propels him to follow her into the woods. The fact is, he has something for her. But only if the conversation offers enough comfort that he can trust her with it.

~~~~~~
~~~~~~

Livie moves them to an isolated spot away from the crowd, where their conversation will be muffled by the trees. Finn has been on her mind a lot lately. Still not sure whether he'll be an ally or foe, Livie regrets her harsh words at the back of the fountain. She decides to take a friendlier approach, but without giving up ground on what she knows about Finn that he likely doesn't realize.

"Look, I know you and I have often been at odds with each other. I do thank you for meeting me here."

"For sure. Your message was something to do with Hannah?" Finn figures it's best to guess that Hannah is the mutual friend Livie referred to. If he says Draw and he's wrong, it could cause the discussion to traverse waters he isn't sure he's prepared for. "What's this all about?"

Livie buys time before she responds, looking around to ensure no one is listening nearby. Finn is playing coy. He knows this isn't really about Hannah, but about him. She decides to play along.

"Hannah appears to be closer to the Friendly World Network than I realized. There are some dangerous people involved, Finn...I'm concerned. What do you know?"

Finn now looks around for anyone listening in, clearly stalling for time as he thinks how to respond.

"I think Hannah will be fine. She isn't that deep into the FWN. But who's pushing the bullshit now? You're not meeting me here about Hannah. This is about me. I suspect you know what I've been up to and are fishing for more. Before you answer that, you should know that if I'm going to share anything, I expect you to reciprocate."

Like a cat, Livie pounces with a question she knows will be at least partially answered by Finn's body language and the speed of his response.

"Okay. So, tell me, whose side are you on?"

Finn pauses as he looks past Livie's shoulder and then directly at her. Softness and admiration flicker in his eyes as he looks over her shoulder again—as if someone in the distance needs to hear what he has to say.

"You don't come at things sideways. Always straight on."

Finn lets out a breath and looks at her to see if she will fill the silence. Livie doesn't take the bait and instead grants him a simple, closed-mouthed smile of acknowledgement.

"I've turned that question you asked over and over in my mind during the last several months."

"Yet, are you not on the non-interneters' side?"

"You see anyone behind me?"

"No."

"Thought I heard someone, but maybe it's just my nerves. I've been working with the FWN."

Classic avoidance, she thinks, *doesn't answer the question.* Mindful that he's going to ask her to reciprocate with information, she decides to answer her question for him.

"So in other words, the Friendly World Network thinks you are one of them—a non-interneter. But you're not. You're working with them to gather intel. The question is for what purpose?"

"I think I've answered your question, so now it's your turn. Who are you working with to gather intel about the FWN?"

Livie closes her eyes as she pauses to absorb the exchange. She opens her eyes and focusses her stare on Finn, a simple smile making its way across her face again.

"Well, let's just get all our cards on the table, face up, shall we?" Livie gives Finn a moment to see if he will take the bait and watches his eyes flutter—giving her the confirmation she is looking for—before she continues.

"I've been hired by some people I don't really trust to get inside the Friendly World Network to find out how they turned the internet off."

Livie sees the surprise in Finn's eyes, which he's trying to conceal by maintaining eye contact with her. This time, she jumps into the silence.

"If you're thinking that you didn't expect me to reveal so much, particularly given your closeness with Hannah, you have to realize that I know things about your activities in this chess game. Things Hannah doesn't know."

"Okay, so is this what you expect now...that we will trade secrets?"

"Finn, the deeper I get into this, the more I'm finding both sides have their own version of evil motives. How about you? What are you discovering on your side?"

Finn looks away, staring into the distance over Livie's shoulder. He whispers, as if to himself.

"It's not my side."

Finn now takes the lead, suggesting that they walk as they talk. As he makes his way deeper into the trees, Livie follows.

"If they're not your side, why are you making them believe you are one of them?" she asks as casually as she can muster.

The crunch of branches under Finn's feet hits their ears as if it is echoing in the forests. They both stop to look around briefly. Finn takes a deep breath, then lets the air out of his lungs slowly.

"Livie, I'm discovering that there's a lot more sinister going on here than people realize. There are people within the FWN who are sincere about a life without the intrusive nature of the internet...but there are others within the network who have another agenda—world domination."

"So is Hannah one of those in the FWN who is sincere, though naïve?"

Finn looks directly at Livie.

"You must know that Hannah is not part of the FWN. She follows them and knows a few people, but she isn't really part of the network. Though her new boyfriend is a concern."

Livie parks the new boyfriend comment in her head.

"But you're part of them. You have a coffee mug or something with the FWN stamped on the bottom?"

Finn lets out a sly smile that shows in his eyes and turns to walk further down the path.

"I have the coffee mug, yes."

Livie wants to know more about the sinister parts of the FWN and their plans for world domination, as Finn put it, but she knows he is unlikely to share too much, unless she opens up about what she knows. She knows how to get his attention.

"The Friendly World Network isn't the only side that is plotting something sinister. I have reason to believe those wanting the internet back have murderous intentions, and then there are the Russians. They seem to be up to something."

Finn reaches to move a tree branch out of the way as he glances back at Livie, a nervous edge in his eyes.

"The *Russians*? Like what?"

Livie picks up on the sharp tone in his voice as he says "Russians" and figures he must know something.

"Well, I'm not sure entirely, but you look quite concerned. What do you know about the Russians?"

"Not as much as you might think. Just that with the internet, they were often using cyber warfare of various types to interfere with governments around the world. I've often thought they're more sophisticated and dangerous than the average person realizes. I have found them to be more advanced in their knowledge and methods than the Americans. They also seem suspiciously absent in the FWN, and..." Finn looks around and lowers his voice.

Livie notices his reference to the Americans as some third party, like he isn't one himself. She files that away in her mind as she prods him to finish his sentence.

"And what?"

"Well, I can't be certain, but I thought I saw a Russian following a bit too close to me the other day."

The statement startles Livie and she tries to suppress her surprise, but it is apparent in her falsetto tone as she responds.

"Really? Where was that?"

"Coming out of the coffee shop. Maybe it's nothing. What do you know about the Russians?"

"Not much really. Tell me, do you know anything about a skull and bones tattoo with the numbers 322 below it?"

Livie's question stops Finn in his tracks. He stops and stares directly at Livie. Sweat from his brow is snaking down his cheek. He caught her question like a heavy ball thrown at him and held on tight. Not sure what to do with it, he just stares at her.

"Finn, what does it mean?"

His voice is a fading whisper that is lost to the air.

"Brotherhood of Death."

Livie moves closer to him.

"What did you say?"

Finn bites the inside of his bottom lip, grimacing with anxiety. He looks into Livie's eyes, but his stare seems elsewhere.

"I'm questioning why I'm here."

Livie looks at Finn intensely as she is suddenly hit by compassion for him.

"Finn, you must know that there is great danger in this dance you're being drawn into."

He nods a response. She grabs his arm to emphasise her statement. For some reason, she thinks of Ervin and the man with the skull and bones tattoo.

"Lives will be lost in this battle, Finn. I'm certain of it. I'm worried for you."

Her words cause him to look down, hiding his expression.

"I fear..." His voice is cracking despite his efforts to keep it in check. "...I don't know the music or the steps of this dance you mention. At least not well enough. Maybe..."

Livie waits for the moment to pass for Finn to finish his sentence. He finally looks up and past Livie.

"I should go."

Livie reaches out to touch his arm again.

"You might think you can straddle both sides of every argument and position. You can't do that here. Not with this. It's too dangerous. You'll make enemies on both sides. Ruthless enemies, Finn."

Finding his voice, Finn is quick in his response.

"You don't know me as well as you think or what my motives are. Besides, doesn't all that apply to you too?"

His voice grows soft with his last question as he looks away. Livie catches his gaze and follows it.

"I know lots about you Finn."

He avoids her stare by moving his head, but she follows it with her own, and he catches her eye out of the corner of his, even as he works to school his face. Livie continues before he can.

"And I say this because of my deep concern for you."

He looks away again, his voice a whisper.

"I know. I've put my hope into that." Finn looks directly at her as he speaks.

Livie moves closer to him. Their noses are now a few inches apart, and their eyes, both soft, are focused on each other. Livie tilts her head slightly when a crack hits their ears—a branch breaking.

Livie catches her breath, hard. She looks past Finn's shoulder as Finn looks at her for a signal. She sees a figure moving sideways in their direction. She pulls Finn in closer, kisses him on the lips, and whispers into his ear.

"We should exit in opposite directions. I'll go to my left, towards the 16th-Street entrance, and you go to the right, the 15th-Street entrance. I'll call two minutes after I've left the park."

Livie starts to pull away, but Finn holds on and whispers back.

"Wait. You asked me—but whose side are *you* on?" Livie looks him in the eyes and sees anxiety coming down in a sweat trickling from his brow. What Livie doesn't see is that Finn used the opportunity to attach a sticker to the back of her shirt, just under her collarbone.

"I'm in the same situation as you Finn, just working for the opposite side."

"Livie, the ghost of the internet is looming with evil intent behind it, and someone needs to stop it." Finn glances over her shoulder as he finishes his sentence.

Livie pulls away abruptly and briskly sets off towards the nearest parking lot. She phones Raf, her breathing heavy.

"Hey, I'm just existing the park. Are you here?"

"A block away. Which parking lot are you heading to?"

"Turn around. Don't come. I'm being followed, and I don't need whomever it is to see us together. I'll make my way home on foot and meet you there."

Still breathing heavily, Livie reaches the edge of the parking lot. She sees an empty vehicle and makes her way towards it. Better for the person following her to think she came by car. Then, as she steps into the parking lot, the thought hits her that if the person followed her here, they'd know she didn't arrive by vehicle. How would they know she is here then?

Even as those thoughts strike her, she decides to stand beside the door of a grey compact, as if it belongs to her, regardless. She turns around and scans the area for a sign of the figure she saw by the fountain. She's good at this. It's something that has helped her with her investigative work. She can pick people out of a crowd. There are a lot of people in the park. Some sitting on blankets in the grass, a group playing catch with a football, a musician playing a guitar and seeking donations, others walking dogs.

But no one that matches the silhouette the saw by the trees. No one suspicious, looking for her. Could she really have lost him that easily?

She scans the area quickly again. She also sees no sign of Finn, though she suspects he's at the parking lot on the other side of the park. She looks at her phone, searches for Finn's number, and hits the call button. The ringing sounds loud in her ear as she continues to scan the area. After the fourth ring, his voicemail kicks in, and she presses the button to hang up.

"Geez Finn, where are you?" she says to herself as she replays the last part of her conversation with Finn in her head. She told him to head towards the 15th-Street entrance—but would he? What if his car is parked at the W Street entrance, or even off Euclid? She starts lecturing herself for not asking him where he parked his car. He could be anywhere in the park. Then his words ring in her head: "You don't know me as well as you think or what my motives are." Could she have misjudged him?

She hits his number again on her phone and gets the same four rings and voicemail. This time, she leaves a message.

"Finn...." She hangs up abruptly as the thought that someone else might hear the message strikes her. She phones again and leaves another message, keeping her voice light.

"Finn, I hope you're well. I'm just calling to see if you want to get together with our mutual friend. Call me back when you get a chance."

She looks out again, her head moving from left to right, scanning the area like a predator looking for its prey. She might be the prey, but something skips inside her—pushing her to go on the offensive.

She hits a button on her phone and puts it to her ear as she starts a brisk walk towards the 15th-Street parking lot.

"Raf, are you still in your car?"

"I'm back in the condo, why? Do you need me to come back?"

"Yes, but can you meet me at the 15th-Street entrance?"

"Sure, which one?"

The question stops Livie in her tracks. Why didn't she give Finn more specific instructions?

She's now standing on a slight rise in the ground. She plants her feet slightly apart and scans the area around her, like a lioness on her perch, looking for anything out of the ordinary—anyone with eyes on her. Then, like a jolt of caffeine in the morning, things suddenly become clear. She didn't ask Finn because she was trying to get away.

But she isn't the prey. Finn is.

Chapter 20

Finn's Inquisition

Even with the sack over his head, Finn immediately knows where they are headed as soon as the tires hit the dirt road. He can picture the green leaves and dragon-shaped flowers of the bottlebrush buckeye. *Maybe their snowy white flowers are out?* he wonders in a daze. He can imagine the scene—those white flowers and the glossy green leaves of the arrowhead viburnum. The place would be quiet, as if mandated by nature. Add in a deer like the one he saw, and the place would give off a scent of peacefulness.

He's allowing his mind to be distracted as it's a bit delusional. Is this really happening to him? He was just spying to gain access to a secret meeting, hoping to find out what his girlfriend was truly up to. How did it all lead to this? Perhaps he stepped too close to the edge on this one?

As the car rumbles up the dirt road, he wishes he never left that message for Draw. Wishes he never met him. Wishes he never lifted that information about the satellites from Saba's computer. Among all his suspicions, he never pegged Saba to be working for Brant. He now wishes he never met her.

~~~~~~

Finn's eyes are still adjusting to the dim light, but he can see three blurry figures in the cave with him. The chair he's strapped into is oddly comfortable, with arm rests and a soft back of some kind. His feet and arms are fastened to the chair, and there is a strap across his chest. His forearms are free, and with them, he can stretch the
~~~~~~

restraints a bit as he pushes his back into the chair. The movement helps with his vision as his eyes adjust, and he is starting to get a clearer picture of what's in front of him. He can't make out their faces, but he recognizes the lanky, bald figure as the same silhouette he saw in the shadows in the park. The bald head moves closer to him, and he feels a drop of spittle hit his face as the raspy voice addressed him.

"You know why you are here, Finn?"

Oddly, on the drive in, he was expecting such a question. He plays dumb, as planned.

"To solve some mystery code you have?"

The smallest of the three figures steps out of the shadows. Her voice has a stern edge to it.

"I think you've solved all the codes we need you to. We're not here for any more games, and you have information that we need. Information that you will give us. How long we're here and how much pain it causes you," she pauses for effect as the third and easily largest figure steps out from the shadows to stand beside her, "is really up to you."

She puts her hand on the chest of the giant beside her as if her hand is a stop sign. "Let's make this easy, okay Finn?" Seeing the two of them before him makes him think of *Beauty and the Beast,* though the woman also reminds him of the character Cersei Lannister from *Game of Thrones.*

Since they grabbed him at the park and shoved him into the vehicle, he has become more and more resolute that he isn't going to tell them anything. He has already played a card in this game they don't know about. At least, he is fairly certain they don't. The image of the data strip he left on Livie comes to his mind. As long as they don't know about it and Livie gets it into the right hands, he can survive this.

The bald one speaks again, his raspy voice not quite as close to Finn's face this time.

"Let's start with something easy, shall we? Where is Draw?"

Finn coughs at the question as he holds back a chuckle. That's a question he doesn't know the answer to. He knows that Draw disappeared shortly after he met with Livie, but he doesn't know where he went. He doubts Draw would tell anyone. He coughs again before answering.

"If he's not at his place, I don't know."

The woman he has dubbed Cersei steps forward. Her voice has the same stern edge to it.

"You know he's not at his place. He's disappeared. We know you met with him in secret. Where did he go?"

The news that they saw him with Draw bites him like a vicious snap that seems to numb his ears as the sounds around him fade into the background. *What else do they know?* he now wonders. He hopes the reaction he feels inside doesn't show on his face, as he focusses on the Cersei figure. He hopes she sees the blankness in his stare.

"I don't have any idea where he is." He stops himself from adding "honestly", recognizing that he will likely be answering their other questions in the same way. Questions he may know the answers to.

Cersei immediately responds with a hand gesture to the beast figure, who quickly moves towards Finn. He has tie-downs in his hand that Finn didn't notice previously. As Finn is processing what he is seeing, the beast blocks out the light in front of him. In an instant, he feels the pain of his wrists being grabbed, stretched, and tied down to the arm rests of the chair.

The bald inquisitor steps into Finn's field of vision. He has a hammer in his hand with a small round head. Finn focusses on the hammer head when someone behind him grabs his ears and pulls back his head. He can feel the breathing of the beast behind him as a strap is slipped across his neck, securing his head to the back of the chair. His mind goes into a dreamlike state—an escapism that ignores his present situation.

His mind drifts back to something he was thinking of when traveling in the vehicle with the sack over his head. It's something Saba said to him. He can hear her words as if she is the one in front of him now, speaking in that lecturing tone.

"Finn, you're stuck in facts. You organize things by facts that you know. That's where you're getting stumped. What is happening with these changes are not just based on some facts or a series of facts you're trying to put together. It's a personality, a force. Stop focusing on facts. Facts are dead. The internet was full of dead facts. We're talking about an idea here that grips us and makes us alive. A personality. Batman to the Joker. Superman to Lex Luther. Sherlock Holmes to Moriarty. It's Abel to Cain. Christ to Satan."

Finn hears Saba's words in his head and is reaching for them in his mind, searching for their meaning, their purpose.

Cersei's harsh voice breaks through his thoughts.

"Finn...Finn! Are you not listening? Where is Draw? Time is running out for you to start answering our questions. Let me explain how this is going to work. I'm going to be asking you a series of questions. You answer them. I may...*may* choose to repeat the question if you don't answer. But if you choose not to answer or you just remain silent, that'll be seen as a deliberate aggressive action on your part, and it will get an aggressive response. Now, where is Draw?"

Finn doesn't answer. He's no longer able to see everything around him, and he just looks at her with a blank stare. She shakes her head at him and motions with her chin to someone close to his side. Finn can just make out the bald head beside him and is processing what is happening when he is jarred out of his trance by a sudden pain in his right index finger.

He lets out a scream that echoes down into the mine. Even as the pain threatens to overtake his thoughts, he knows no one will hear him from outside this place. He's been here. He knows how secluded it is. He wants to move his head as the pain rises, but he can't. His breathing is heavy.

He knew when they were driving up here that this was coming. Are they deliberately focusing on his hands? So that he can't type on a keyboard? He expected he'd experience some pain, and now he is lecturing himself to focus on something else. Something other than the pain. Saba's words are still drifting in his mind.

His breathing slows down as he sees Cersei's lips moving in front of him. He focuses on her words.

"Finn. We need you to concentrate now. This isn't going to end until you give us what we need. It's going to get worse. A whole lot worse. What's going to happen is I'm going to ask you direct questions. Questions we know you know the answers to and have information on. Information that you. will. give. us." She pauses after each deliberate word, as if waiting for his acknowledgement. He blinks slowly in response.

"Good. While we still need to know where Draw is, what we also need to know is what other information you got from him that you have not already shared. To be specific—information regarding the location of the central computers. Now is not the time to play games here, Finn. Your gathering information from Draw and not passing it on is seen as an act of war."

Finn slowly blinks again. He doesn't show any emotion. *An act of war? What are they talking about? Do they think I'm working for someone that wants war? That may be Livie, but it's not me. I've been a lone ranger in all this.*

"Which central computers does Draw know about?"

Finn looks at her, trying to think through the pain. What do they already know? He gave them information about a central computer Draw knows about in a remote location near Austin, Texas. It was the easiest one to give, as it's located in the US. He hasn't said anything about the one located in this cave, the one near Glasgow, the one near Bryon Bay, Australia, the one near Toamasina, Madagascar, or the one near Drarga, Morocco—all of which Draw knows about. Do they know that Draw is also aware that there are others he hasn't discovered yet? He knows they exist, just not where they are. He figures if he finds the location of one of them, he will find the rest. The missing links, as he has referred to them. Finn can hear Draw's words in reference to the ones he hasn't discovered: "The card that if pulled will make all their plans collapse." Finn knows where they are though. *And now, so does Livie,* he thinks as he answers the question.

"It's in a remote location near Austin."

Cersei's response is stern and abrupt.

"I told you that now is not the time to play games. You know more than that. I'll ask you one more time. What does Draw know about the central computers?"

Finn looks at her; her stare is intimidating. It compels him to say something, not just remain silent.

"He doesn't know about the one that's here. In this cave."

Cersei nods at the bald head beside Finn. Bracing for the pain, Finn bristles, as much as his body will let him in his strapped-down position. He screams as he feels the pain shooting up his hand to his arm from the middle finger of his right hand.

Finn is breathing heavily as Cersei moves closer, her face now within a foot of his.

"You have a moment to catch your breath, and then I want to hear what central computers he knows about. In detail. Specific locations."

Cersei steps back and Bald Head passes in front of Finn, the hammer swinging by his side.

Finn watches him as he disappears into the shadows of the cave. Cersei's stern stare is on him when Bald Head reappears in his view. In his hand is a shorter hammer with a large head on it. The sight of it makes Finn think of the hammer of Thor.

The bald head disappears to his side. Cersei speaks in a matter-of-fact, emotionless voice.

"Now is the time to answer. Finn."

Finn slowly blinks at her. His mind is racing through the risks of telling them everything that he knows. The risks to Draw. The risks to their world. Saba's words come back to him. He's caught in a conflict that has fiercely zealous beliefs driving it, almost like a religion. *As it has often been with world conflicts,* he thinks. But it's not his conflict, so why doesn't he just let it go? He stares at Cersei and sees the bald head in his peripheral vision. He sees evil in those eyes. He decides to resist.

"I've given you what I know."

The pain as his left hand is crushed by the hammer is immediate—it sends his body into a reflexive heave as it attempts to escape the chair he is strapped into. The chair barely moves as he realizes that it too is being held down. He feels the breath of the beast on the back of his neck.

Cersei and Bald Head disappear into the shadows, and Finn is left to scream and cry in his pain.

He is left alone with his pain for what seems like hours, but in reality is probably more likely thirty minutes or so, he figures. His sense of time is eluding him. The coolness of the air in the cave hits his drenched face. He looks out and can see nothing but the profile of the beast in the darkness of the cave.

Finn tries to focus on other things in his life and sees their faces before him. His mom. His friends. Hannah. Livie. Agrafena. His guy friends and colleagues at the university. He sees Draw.

His mom's face appears before him, and everything else fades into a blur in the background. He feels her love and encouraging words. Encouraging words that were always specific as to what was happening in his life. What would she tell him to do now? Should he give up? Let this be someone else's battle? He can hear her words too. "Always do the right, pure thing that is in keeping with your values." But what are the values he's protecting here? His mom often told him, "Put on *your* oxygen mask first." He can't help others unless he first helps himself. Can he protect those he loves if he's in this cave?

He's in a trance, the pain pulsating through him as he decides that he will give up what he knows about Draw. He has to get out of this place and figure out a plan to protect the people he loves. The image of his mom's face remains clear in front of him. Her soft eyes and smile. He's confident it is the right decision.

Cersei's cunning emerald-green eyes suddenly appear where his mom's were a second before. His mom's smile lingers in his mind for a fraction of a second before it's replaced by Cersei's stern, closed mouth below those striking eyes. He sees Bald Head beside him as he works to avoid her eyes. His mind goes to the image of Thor's hammer when the beast appears in front of Cersei. He's carrying stacks of lumber that he places in front of the chair before he disappears back into the shadows. Silence and Cersei's foreboding face are in front of him now, waiting for something to happen.

Finn hears the sloshing of water as the beast comes back into view, carrying a large trough-sized bucket of water. The beast stops in front of him, blocking out the rest of the light, and puts the bucket of water on top of the stack of lumber at his feet. Finn feels a splash of water hit his knees as the giant leaves it there and disappears somewhere behind him.

"Okay Finn. We're done playing games here, and I have questions for you now that we have no tolerance for anything but direct answers."

Finn's ready to tell them what he knows about Draw. He's just going over it in his head when Cersei's voice breaks through his thoughts. She has moved closer to him, standing over the bucket. He can't avoid her glare.

"Tell us what you know about a plan with the satellites."

The question startles Finn, cutting through his pain and thoughts. He can't stop his body from quivering. *Is this what this is really about? They don't know about the plan with the satellites?*

Finn knows the plan. He had the data on where all the satellites are located and how to connect them all, in detail that only an expert could fully understand. He put that data on a data strip and deleted all other copies, including anything on his computer. It's the data strip that he stuck onto Livie's jacket in the park. If they came after him and not Livie, they must not know that he passed it on to her. *What do they know?* As the thoughts circle in his mind, he's paralyzed, not knowing how to respond.

He feels the chair lifting from behind him and the breath of the beast on his neck as his body is lifted and tilted forward. His view is now of murky water in a bucket. Cersei's voice fills his ears.

"The satellites, Finn. What do you know?"

Finn doesn't answer. He can't. Fear and confusion course through him. He feels suspended in his thoughts, just like his body is suspended over the water.

"One last time, Finn. The satellites."

Seconds pass by that seem like minutes as Finn watches sweat trickling down from his head and making tiny splashes in the water.

Suddenly and quickly his body is moved upward as his head is plunged into the water. He can now feel a hand on his head, holding it down.

He holds his breath, counting in his head. He figures he should be able to hold his breath for at least two minutes. He hits 150 in his head. He's feeling dizzy. 151...152...153...154... He opens his mouth, and it fills with gritty, dirty water.

In an instant, his head is no longer being held down. Finn's pulled up and back sitting in the chair, now wet. Bald Head is in front of him, looking him over. His hands and shirt are wet as he checks the straps holding Finn's hands down and cinches them even tighter. Finn feels the same tightness administered to the strap from behind him as the beast's breathing hits the hairs on the back of his neck.

His hands, chest, and head hurt. He's breathing heavily, taking in gulps of air as large as his lungs will allow.

Bald Head has moved to his side again, and Cersei is in front of him, a step back from before, appearing to avoid the dirty water.

"Finn, if you want to be able to leave this place, you need to focus. Satellites. What are the plans and what do you know?

Still catching his breath, Finn's mind is racing. What would be the impact of telling them? Destruction and war? Or maybe the outcome would be better?

His mind is in a fog, and with the uncertainty of the outcome, his instinct to not make a decision is overriding everything else. Information is power, and right now he still holds that power. He stares back at his inquisitor and blinks slowly—his only response. She nods to the beast behind him, and he feels his body lifting again.

With his body suspended over the water, Finn takes a large gulp of air as he accepts his fate. Just as the air fills his cheeks, his head is plunged into the murky water again. He closes his eyes as he feels the hand on his head holding it down. He begins the count in his head. Concentrating to release the air in his cheeks to his lungs as slowly as possible, he starts to feel the slip of consciousness as he hits 172 in his head. 173...174... He stops counting and sees his mom's face in front of him again. She's smiling, and he decides if they lift him out of this before he loses consciousness, he will tell them everything he knows.

Seeing the approval in his mom's eyes, he opens his mouth and lets it fill with the gritty water. Keeping his eyes closed, he's ready to say goodbye to his mom when his head is forcefully lifted.

He's quickly lifted into the chair and slammed back down on the ground. He opens his eyes. His lungs take in the air with desperation. Breathing heavily, he is consumed by relief that he's still alive. He's ready to give up. This is someone else's fight, not his. Time to let it go. Time to step away from the edge and tell them everything he knows.

Seconds…maybe minutes tick by as Finn's breathing slows. Cersei is standing in front of him. He can't see Bald Head, but he can hear the beast breathing behind him. Cersei takes a step back and her voice cuts through the air.

"We will give you a few more seconds here to catch your breath. I trust you are thinking about everything that you are going to tell us. You should start with the satellites. What you know about them and the plans for them. In detail."

He blinks at her as an acknowledgment and then heaves more air into his lungs. He hopes she understands that he just needs some more time to catch his breath before he speaks. *The satellite information must be what they are most after here. How do they even know I have information about the satellites? I didn't get it from Draw. Is that what they're thinking? They know something, but what? The safest thing is to just tell them all of it. Why do I care what they know at this stage? I will tell them everything except where I got the information from. If they insist, I will say Draw. They don't know where Draw is, and when I get out of this place, I can get to him before they do. If I say I got it from Draw though, I will have cast my chips with a side I don't trust. But who can I trust anymore in this anyway?*

Finn's thoughts are swimming in all these questions, but as his breathing starts returning to normal, his mind is made up. He will tell them everything he knows about the satellites. How many there are, their locations, and how to communicate with them all. He looks directly at Cersei and blinks slowly to indicate he is ready. Ready to end the pain and drama. Ready to get back to rebuilding his life without taking any sides in all this.

"Seems you are ready to talk," Cersei says, motioning with her hand to someone on the side that he can't see.

A figure steps in front of him. At first, Finn thinks it's someone new, as he has no shirt on, and Finn's breathing spikes briefly in response. Strangely, he feels relieved when he sees the familiar bald head as the man looks him in the eyes and checks his restraints. Now that Bald Head is shirtless, Finn notices a tattoo on his right chest. He sees a skull in the tattoo, but it's too close for him to see the rest. His breathing is almost back to normal, and he's ready now. Time to get this over with.

After pulling the restraints even tighter, Bald Head steps back, a smirk on his face as he takes a moment to admire his handiwork. It's in that moment that Finn sees it. The full tattoo of the skull and bones with the numbers 322 below it. The same tattoo Livie mentioned in the park. The same image he remembers from studying secret societies when he was in university. It stood out to him for some reason. Maybe it was because of their connection to the Illuminati and their influence and manipulation of world events. *The Skull and Bones. The Brotherhood of Death, as they are known. Of course. I should have figured this out earlier.*

Cersei breaks through his thoughts.

"Okay Finn. It's time now. We will take that bucket of water away as soon as you tell us everything you know about the satellites."

Seeing the tattoo on Bald Head has taken him to another place. Another place that is full of fear and death. A place that also reminds him of his values. Like looking at a scene through a camera that suddenly comes into focus, revealing images in a different light, Finn can see it all now. He now sees who the Joker to Batman and the Lex Luther to Superman is.

When he gave that data strip to Livie, he hoped that she would get it in the right hands or maybe destroy it. That she would figure out the best course of action; be the hero in this. Now he just hopes she can get it to Draw or someone who can change the course of things.

The part he has played in this drama is all in focus now. He sees the role he and others have played. Draw, Nita, Grant Solbey, Hannah, Fairleigh, and most of all Livie. He can see why they consider Livie a valuable pawn in their game. As the thoughts swirl in his head, there is one thing Finn is certain of. Regardless of the outcome or the cost, he will do anything to protect his friends.

No matter what they ask him or what they do, he will remain silent.

Chapter 21

Livie's Decision

It's been three days since Livie turned her back and left Finn by the fountain in Malcolm X Park. Three long, largely sleepless days that have focused her attention on the people that are important in her life. It has also paralyzed her—she can't decide what to do next. Livie prides herself on being a person of action, but in the last three days, she has been analyzing things in an exhausting loop that leaves her more confused each time. It has left her wearied, with every option penetrating the depths of her vulnerability.

After leaving Finn in the park, the ripples of which would haunt her for years, she briskly walked back to her apartment, her mind pinballing from what happened to Finn to what to do next. The intensity of the day and walk had her sweating. She unzipped the jacket she was wearing and took it off. That's when she spotted the data sticker that Finn had stuck on the shoulder. She stopped and peeled it off to study it. At first, she wasn't certain what it was. Then she focused her eagle eyes on its details and could see the ridged black lines imbedded in the sticker that seemed to contain some sort of data. She knew it was something Finn had left her. Something he may have risked his life to give her. But how was she going to access the information on it? She didn't have anything to read data off a sticker like that.

On her walk back, she decided to withhold the knowledge of the data sticker from Raf, even though he could likely help her access the data. She had to find another way and keep the information to herself until she knows what it is. Immediately she thought of Draw as someone who could help her. If not Draw, she reasoned, maybe she could break into Finn's apartment. He was likely to have a scanner that could read the data sticker somewhere. The thought of Finn brought Hannah to the surface of her thoughts. *Hannah,* she thought, *might still have the code to get into Finn's place.*

Before entering her condo, she phoned Draw. The phone just rang and rang. The tune sounded familiar—but she couldn't place it. She found it excruciatingly agitating but let it ring a dozen times before she hung up. Draw never had voicemail before, so why did she let herself get frustrated this time? Her nerves were on edge.

She had rehearsed the outline of what she would tell Raf about Finn, but all those thoughts were dispersed by the news Raf shared when she returned to the condo. Raf didn't even ask her about Finn before he launched into his news.

"So, I was able to find out the name of the guy murdered in the woods. The guy with the skull and bones tattoo. It wasn't easy. I had to snoop around his apartment building and really couldn't get inside with so many people around. I gave up for a bit and returned later when there was a fire in the building. People were standing outside while the fire crew was there putting it out. I chatted with one of the residents there and got a name that I'm certain is him. It sounds like it was his place that caught fire. That can't be a coincidence."

Livie, already fretful from the events of the day, was a bit impatient with Raf, as she really didn't need to hear another story.

"Good story Raf. What's the name?"

"Dr. Grant Solbey."

Livie must have looked stunned at his revelation. She felt suddenly numb as the image of Hannah with Solbey flashed before her. It was an image she had constructed in her mind, as she had not seen them together.

"You sure that's the name?"

"Positive. You look a bit...surprised. You know him?"

Livie left Raf standing there as she retreated to her bedroom, where she frantically called Hannah. The phone rang four times, and Livie's anxiety rose with each ring. She was relieved when Hannah finally answered. She could sense the edginess in Hannah's tone from the first words.

"Livie. I'm so glad you called. I haven't heard from Grant in four days now, and I'm getting worried. I'm just heading over to his apartment now to see if he's there. I'm kicking myself for not doing that sooner. I've been just too damn busy and caught up in my own shit."

"Hannah, before you go there, we need to get together. I have something to tell you."

"Tell me? About Grant?"

Livie couldn't imagine sharing the news over the phone with her friend.

"No...no, it's about Finn, and it's urgent. I'm leaving now, where can we meet?"

Livie gets choked up thinking back to what followed when she and Hannah met at Green Planet. She found it hard to look into her friend's eyes at that moment without letting her own emotions narrate what she had to tell her, so they went for a walk. The movement of the exercise gave her the space to get her emotions out. She glanced over at Hannah and could see the dread in her eyes as she told her that Finn had gone missing. She didn't tell her anything about meeting him in the park, just that she had seen him and had tried contacting him since, without success. Hannah offered several explanations, including that maybe he met someone new or had gone away somewhere. Hannah's voice had a desperation to it. A desperation to find a plausible answer.

Livie tried to give her friend as many moments as she could on their walk to process the information about Finn, but time was running out, and she had to tell her about Grant. They stopped at a bench. When Livie told her what she knew about Grant, Hannah's emotions erupted. She dissolved into Livie's embrace, unable to control her loud cries of anguish.

They sat there in their joint sorrow, Livie looking around for anyone that might be watching them. As Hannah started to collect herself, she caught Livie looking around, and fear gripped her.

"Are we in danger too?"

What followed after that felt like a whirlwind of activity that Livie was caught up in.

Hannah went to the cabin at Deerfield Lake—a safe haven. Livie filled Raf in on details about Finn and had him actively looking for who may have taken him. The next day, she went to the park to meet Fairleigh as planned. But Fairleigh wasn't there, and after waiting almost two fretful hours, always on alert and scanning the area, she finally left. Had Fairleigh disappeared too now? She felt frozen, uncertain what to do.

Now here she is, in her condo, looking out at the monument as the events of the last three days are drumming in her head. She's waiting for Raf to come back, hoping he will have news about Finn's whereabouts. She's glad that Raf had her place scanned for any listening devices and that it came up empty. She needs to feel safe here.

She still hasn't figured out how to access the data sticker. Several calls to Draw resulted in more annoying, endless ringing. She can hear it droning on in her head each time before she tries Draw again. It doesn't help that she finally remembered the tune—it's from a song by the Crash Test Dummies.

Where is he? she wonders. She squints towards the monument. "Where are you?" she whispers. Her thoughts drift from Draw and the help she needs with the data sticker to the faces of Finn and Fairleigh. Looking out the window, her mind sees the two of them standing in front of the monument. She closes her eyes and tries to shake the image from her mind.

Needing to refocus, she phones Hannah. They have plans to get together tomorrow, and now she has an idea.

"Hey, how are things at the lake?"

"Good. Your mom has been so accommodating and lovely. Insists on cooking for me. It's so peaceful here too. Feels safe."

Livie can picture Hannah there and wishes she was with her.

"Wish I could join you. I'm working on trying to locate Finn. We still good to get together tomorrow?"

Livie doesn't want to tell anyone about the data sticker but needs a way to access it. She knows Finn must have a data scanner in his place, and Hannah might have code she needs to get in. She floats the idea to Hannah, telling her that maybe if they searched his place, they could find some clue as to Finn's whereabouts.

"Okay. I have a code, but I haven't used it in a long time. You sure it's a good idea to break into his place? What if we get caught?"

"Hannah, we are both worried about him and out of other options, unless you can think of something else?"

"Okay then. Do you just want to meet at his place at two tomorrow?"

"How about we meet at Green Planet first? We could grab a coffee and then go together?"

"Yes, let's do that."

Livie is about to ask her more about her mom when she is interrupted by the doorbell.

"Rafael has arrived," it intones.

Live calls out "unzip!" and confirms 2 p.m. at Green Planet with Hannah.

Raf quickly fills her in on how he tried to find out what happened to Finn. He tells her that he went by Finn's place, as they had before. This time he asked around, but no one has seen him in several days. Same story at the university. He also looked into what he could find out about the Skull and Bones 322 or the "Brotherhood of Death." He tells her that he found a reference in a book at the library about a secret society known as the "Order of Skull and Bones" that apparently is credited for the creation of the atomic bomb. The article also states that they seek to bring a new world order, but there was no mention of a symbol for the society. He doesn't know if they are connected.

The term "new world order" catches Livie's attention, but she doesn't let on. She's not surprised that Raf didn't find Finn.

"So basically, you've come up empty?"

"I guess you could say that, except that Finn has not been seen near his place or at the uni since his disappearance."

A sense of sadness strikes Livie as Raf's words reinforce that Finn's missing and may not be alive.

"Well, at least that should help me with Hannah tomorrow."

"With Hannah tomorrow?"

Livie let the words slip out before she could catch them. She didn't want Raf to know about her and Hannah's plans to go to Finn's place. Now she has let the cat out of the bag, so to speak.

"Hannah and I just made plans to try Finn's place tomorrow. Hannah thinks she may have the alarm code to get in. I'm not optimistic, but if we can get in, we could see if there are any clues in his place. Knowing he hasn't been there is quite helpful, so thanks Raf."

"Well, I think you're wasting your time. I tried to find a way in, but the system appears to be protected by a facial-recognition device. The only way to unlock it is if the right person standing in front of it. I would assume that only Finn's face can open the door."

The news arrives as another discouragement, though not a surprising one, for Livie. If she can't get into Finn's place, how is she going to find something to read the data sticker? She decides to change the subject.

"Okay, let's review where we are at and what we know. Ervin was killed when you say he was out following me. We don't know by whom, or rather, by which side. Maybe we've had it wrong thinking it's the Friendly World Network. Perhaps it's our side? Or the side we've been working for, Brant's? Solbey was killed by someone with a skull and bones tattoo. We know Solbey was part of the Friendly World Network, as he spoke passionately at their rallies." Livie pauses as she walks towards the window to look out at the monument, and Raf fills the gap.

"Solbey had a skull and bones tattoo."

"Right." Livie knows this, but somehow in the flurry of activity, it seeped out of the storyline she was piecing together in her head. Her heart skips a beat at she thinks of Hannah.

"You said Solbey spoke at *their* rallies?"

"Oh come on Raf, we are not still debating that, are we? They organized those rallies to make them look like community events. Classic propaganda."

"Alright, I just think as they carried on, they had a more organic feel to them. At least more people were joining them from the streets so to speak, maybe even organizing them."

"Well, regardless, why are we talking about this? Let's move on." Livie has her back to Raf as she speaks. She is still looking out the window as Raf responds.

"Okay, just thinking, what if there's another force out there...another side that could be involved?"

Livie turns around to look at Raf, gauging the seriousness of his comment.

"Let's park that for now and look at what else we know."

"I think Ervin was killed by our side, as you put it."

"Why do you say that?"

"I'm not sure. I have a bad feeling. And we can't trust everyone we've been dealing with. Jing showing up like she did...she knew Ervin wasn't coming back.'

"Good observation. Fits with what I'm thinking. Then Solbey was killed by his side?"

"I'm not sure about that one. Something about him doesn't sit right in all this."

"I was thinking pretty much the same...Alright, then we have Fairleigh who's missing. I can't see her just blowing off the meeting she set with me. Where'd she go? Is she still alive?"

"She was involved with the FWN. If she is in trouble, it's likely because she did something or knows something that they are unhappy about."

"That pretty much mirrors my thoughts on that too. But then who took Finn? I've been thinking he was taken by Brant's people. Maybe they have been following him and figured he knew something."

"You know what the connection to Finn is, right?"

Livie tilts her head, staring at Raf with the question "who?" in her eyes.

"You are, Livie. You're the connection."

Livie is careful not to react, keeping her expression neutral.

"Well, there's also Draw. We know Finn met with Draw."

"True. And who is the connection to Draw? Maybe I could ask the same question about Fairleigh?"

Livie turns to look out the window again before Raf can answer his own question.

"Have you stopped to think that maybe you were recruited into all this because of your connection to Draw and maybe Finn as well?"

Livie ignores his question.

"I think maybe we're making this more complicated than it is. The Friendly World Network is about bringing in a new world order. The Russians must be behind it, and maybe the Chinese too. Fairleigh said something about starting a war if something happens to the satellites. It all makes sense if you think about it. The plan has a certain simplicity to it. Take the internet down, causing all kinds of chaos. Get our government on its knees. Then send out sensitive personal information to blackmail people, scaring them into supporting the internetless world. Then stoke the propaganda machine with newspapers, orchestrated rallies, and operatives out there doing your bidding—like Fairleigh. Don't get me wrong, Raf, Fairleigh may not have known she was supporting some sinister plot. That's part of the genius of this plan. It draws in all kinds of innocent people who are desperate for a simpler life. All these people we know that are dead or missing either had information the other side, our side I guess, wants, or they were a problem for the overall agenda of the Friendly World Network."

"Alright then. So, at this point, besides making sure we don't get killed, what role are we playing here? I'm sure Jing will be back on our doorstep shortly looking for something from us."

"I was thinking about that too. Besides trying to find out what has happened to Finn, I think we need to get information about the satellites and find out why they have become the focus here."

"What's next then?"

"Well, Hannah and I are going to try and get into Finn's apartment and see what we can find out there. Could you find out more about who Solbey was? This skull and bones thing must be something. I'll keep trying to reach Draw, but perhaps you could go by his place and see if there is any trace of him?"

"Sure. You'll have to tell me where he lives."

Looking at her reflection in the window, Livie shakes her head at herself. Of course, whenever she met with Draw it was always at some other location—never his home. If she had his address at all, which she now doubts, it would be in a file somewhere with Larry.

"Come to think of it, I don't know where he lives. We need to find out."

"I could ask Jing? They wanted you to reach out to Draw; you'd think they know where he lives."

Livie closes her eyes, contemplating the idea. It would show Jing that they are working on their mission and cooperating, even if they're not. But then they might also surmise that she can't reach Draw and that he might be missing.

"Yes, do that, but make it sound like we want to follow him or something, not that we can't reach him."

"That could be tricky. I'll try."

"Good. Then, if you have time and can find out more about Fairleigh, that would be helpful too."

Livie moves towards the kitchen as if it is time to put things into action.

"Alright. You know if I start poking around about people that are dead or missing, someone may notice. We're taking a lot of risk," Raf says.

Livie looks up at Raf, who is still standing in the living room. She sees the sincerity in his serious expression and his slumped shoulders. A sign of resignation rather than cooperation.

"Raf, you can disengage right now if you want. Let me go to Finn's apartment and see what we find out, then I'll go from there?"

Raf moves towards her.

She thinks he might be looking for affection, which she is not in the mood for. Not with everything that is marauding through her mind. She knows she has been rather aloof with Raf since Finn disappeared, and she feels a trifle bad about it. But her interaction with Finn in the park that day, followed by his disappearance, has changed things in her.

Raf stops a few inches away from her.

"You don't sound very convincing. The reality is you need help with this, and I can do it. I'll be fine and extra careful. Old-fashioned investigative work, as you would say. Though I think you might need a sophisticated tech expert to get into Finn's place."

Raf's words give her an idea. Something she should have thought of before. She reaches out and hugs him affectionally.

"Thank you Raf. I'm going to head to my bedroom and phone my mom."

Livie steps into the bedroom as she hears the front door close. Raf must have decided to go for a walk or something. She phones her mom.

Livie's mom is chatty, telling her how much she enjoys having Hannah there. Livie is waiting for her mom to ask why she called. When Maggie asks her when she might be coming to the lake, Livie seizes the opportunity.

"I was thinking of that myself. I need some help on a computer matter, basically how to lift the information off a data strip I have. Do you, or maybe Theo, know anyone?"

"I don't sweetie. Theo might; let me check with him and get back to you."

That's what Livie needed to feel better about things. A backup plan. She falls into her bed backwards, and her body welcomes the relaxation it brings.

~~~~~~

About half a block from Green Planet, Livie sees Hannah parking. Just as a spot is vacated in front of the coffee shop, Hannah accelerates towards it and pulls in.

They agreed earlier to take Hannah's car, so Livie walks towards her friend. As she approaches the car, which she knows was Grant's,
~~~~~~

she wonders if Hannah has been to Grant's apartment, and if so, what did she see?

"You still good taking your vehicle?"

"For sure, hop in."

Hannah turns the vehicle back on and backs out of the parking space as Livie immediately voices the questions on her mind.

"Hey, I know this was Grant's car. How are you doing?"

"Oh, I miss him, and maybe driving his car doesn't help. I'm still processing things I guess. Struggling to move on."

"I think that's natural, Hannah. Don't beat yourself up about it. Did you go by his apartment?"

There is a long pause before Hannah tells Livie that she did. She found the apartment had been mostly reduced to ashes from a fire that also took two apartments next to it in the building. She wasn't allowed to look inside, but she didn't see anything reminding her of Grant anyway. The whole experience left her feeling hollow, as the loss became that much more real.

"Well, I don't think we'll see anything like that at Finn's. What do you think we'll find there?"

As she asks the question, Livie is holding down her fear that they won't be able to get in.

"He's a very neat and tidy person, so the place will be clean and organized. And...oh, Livie, I forgot, he has a cat. If he hasn't been there, who's been looking after Turing?"

Livie can't help but smile at the question. It's an emotional smile. *Typical of Finn,* she thinks. Naming his cat after the World War Two computer scientist.

"Cats are pretty independent as long as they can find enough food."

"Turing isn't very friendly, except with Finn. He never seemed to like visitors."

They talk about their concern for the cat as a substitute to talking about Finn.

Livie suspects that Hannah is avoiding the same feeling she has—that his place will look like no one has been there for close to a week. If Finn hasn't been back to his place, is he alive?

Not wanting the thought to consume her, Livie turns the conversation back to the cat.

"So, this cat of his. It's purely an indoors cat?"

"Yeah, I think so. Why?"

"Well then, we probably don't run the risk of it bolting out the door when we arrive. What does it look like?"

"It's grey and black." Hannah points down the street at a set of duplexes. "There's his place now."

Silence fills the car as Hannah parks on the street in front of the duplexes and they both get out.

"It's this one." Hannah points at the one on the right. Livie knows which one is Finn's immediately.

On the door, above a traditional lock, is a device with a screen. It is clearly used to open the door. Hannah looks confused.

"This is new...I don't see a keypad for me to enter the code."

Livie points to the screen. "I think it opens with this. Maybe facial recognition?"

Hannah clutches her purse and starts to unzip it. "I have a picture of Finn in here."

Livie reaches over, touches Hannah's hand, and stops her.

"I don't think a picture will work. How about you try your face?"

"Okay." Hannah stands in front of the screen and looks directly at it. Nothing happens. She adjusts her position slightly. Nothing. She moves again. Still nothing.

"It's not working. How are we going to get in?"

Livie starts knocking on the door.

"Finn?! Finn?!"

Hannah joins her.

"Finn?! Finn?!"

They both hear something move inside and look at each other. They knock again.

"Finn?! Finn?! Finn?!"

They pause and again hear something moving inside.

They are both ready to knock and start up their chorus for Finn again, when they hear the meow of a cat.

In unison, both of them relax their shoulders.

"Well, we know the cat's alive." Livie regrets the implication in her statement as soon as she says it. She immediately seeks a distraction and scans the area to the left and the other half of the duplex. "There has to be another way in here...maybe the neighbors?"

Hannah lets out a deep breath. "I was hoping we wouldn't need to try breaking in. Before we do that, how about you try your face?" Hannah points at the screen.

"It won't work. I've only been to Finn's a couple of times, and it was before he constructed that thing." Livie moves to the left, looking for an entry point between the two units. Seeing nothing obvious, she looks up to see if the roof would offer any hope.

"Well, why not try it anyway?"

"Alright then." Livie moves to stand in front of the device and looks right into it.

The click of the door unlocking rings in their ears.

They look at each other with surprise, relief, and even a sense of joy. Livie turns the handle to open the door slowly, still thinking of the cat.

They were not prepared for what floods their eyes as soon as the door is open.

Eerily quiet, except for the sound of the cat now meowing at their feet, the place looks like a storm swept through it, leaving a mess in its wake. A couch is turned over, papers are scattered on the floor, a chair lies sideways, and drawers are open, exposing the clutter inside them. The cabinets in the kitchen, bedroom, and bathroom are also wide open, as if someone tossed the place in a hurry. Livie sees what looks like the remnants of a computer station, with wires and cords dangling—but no computers.

Livie and Hannah look at the mess in stunned silence for several minutes. Hannah picks up the cat and lets her voice into the room.

"Holy shit!"

"Geez, I wasn't expecting this."

Hannah looks at the cat as if it may have the answers.

"How'd they get in here?"

Livie is thinking the same thing, but only after she wonders who "they" are. She scans the room for any clues, and her eyes focus on where the computers should be.

"Well, let's get started and see if we can find out the answer to that question and who may have done this. You want to find something to feed Turing, and I'll start looking around?"

At the sound of its name, the cat stirs and looks at Livie.

Livie heads towards the computer desk while Hannah makes tracks to the fridge.

In amongst the scattered papers, cords, and wires, Livie spots something that she hopes is what she needs. In the bottom drawer, under some papers, is a grey device that looks like a small electric razor. She puts her hand on it, and before taking it out, looks over towards the kitchen. She sees Hannah petting Turing, who is eating something out of a bowl.

"Found something for him to eat, did you?"

"Not much in the fridge." Hannah opens the fridge as if she needs to check again. "Nothing edible anyway. Found a can of tuna though. Turing is chowing it down quickly."

"He must be starving."

"Must be. The food left for him probably ran out days ago. Find anything over there of interest?"

"Not yet. Lots of loose paper and pens."

"Alright...I'll go check out the bedroom and see what I can find."

Livie removes her hand from the drawer and searches the drawer on the other side of the desk as Hannah disappears into the bedroom. Turing, seemingly finished with the tuna, follows her.

Seeing that her friend is now out of sight, Livie reaches back into the first drawer for the small device she spotted and pulls it out. It really does look like a razor, and if she didn't suspect otherwise, she would have assumed that's what it is. She takes it in her hand and presses the button under her finger. A light zips diagonally from the head of the object to where her finger rests on the button. The movement of the light surprises her, and she almost drops the device in response. She turns it over. There is a screen where the light came from, and at the base of the button, where her finger was, she sees a slit of an opening. It doesn't take her much to see a microchip inside the slit. Below the slit, the letter "L" is written in felt pen.

Livie looks towards the bedroom, where she sees Hannah's shadow moving in the room.

"Hey, any luck in there?"

Hannah comes to the doorway of the bedroom to look out at Livie.

"Not yet. I've been through the drawers and the ensuite here. Going to check the pockets of his clothing in the closet next. You?"

"Nothing of significance."

Hannah retreats back to the bedroom.

Livie watches her figure disappear, reaches into her jacket pocket, and pulls out the data sticker. She places the sticker on the desk, holds the device above it, and presses the button. A light appears again, but instead of zipping across diagonally as before, it moves gradually and intentionally. She watches as the light appears to read what is on the data sticker.

Livie looks at the device again and whispers, "I found it, Finn." She stuffs the scanner and the data sticker into the pocket of her jacket. Just as she's removing her hand from her jacket, she is startled by Hannah's voice.

"Hey, I may have found something."

Before Livie can respond, Hannah's moving towards her, Turing following close behind.

"Well, whatever you found, you seem to have also made a new friend." Livie nods towards the cat.

"Yeah, he's friendly with me today. I guess the trick is to starve him for a few days and then feed him a whole can of tuna. Anyway, take a look at this."

Hannah hands Livie a crumpled-up piece of paper.

"I found it in the pocket of one of Finn's pants."

Livie looks at the handwriting on the paper, trying to make sense of the words. There are several random scribbles on the paper, a list of grocery items in the center, and written in the right corner is:

Saba – Brant

Give L the information to deliver it

"What do you think it means Liv?"

"Well, it looks like Finn drinks bourbon."

"Ha ha, very funny. You know I'm not talking about the grocery list, or whatever that is, but the other things in the corner about Saba and Brant and someone referred to as L...wait, could that L be you?"

"Oh, I don't know about that. What information could he possibly be referring to?" Livie thinks of the data sticker in her jacket as she asks the question.

"I don't know. Just a thought. The other note though. Is Saba really a Brant supporter?"

The question hangs between them for several seconds before they decide to complete their search, but they find no other clues of Finn's whereabouts or who ransacked his place.

~~~~~~

On the drive back to Green Planet, they are both clearly tired from the day's activities, as silence fills the car. Turing is resting quietly in Livie's lap. Livie agreed to take the cat, as Hannah said she couldn't have it in her place, and leaving it there was not an option either of them could live with.

Hannah pulls up beside Livie's car to let her out.

"So girly, what's the plan now?"

"I think you should go back to the cabin at Deerfield. I'll plan to join you in a couple of days. If I find out anything else, I'll let you know of course. You okay with that?"

Hannah nods her head in agreement, they hug, and Livie exits the vehicle. Before Hannah can drive away, she lingers by the car door.

"Hey, thanks for today."

"Same to you. Livie, you're my best friend and I love you girl."

"Same for me Hannah."

Hannah's vehicle is just leaving her sight when Livie hears a voice behind her. It's the barista from Green Planet.

"You're Livie, right?"

"Yes, why?"

"This was left for you." The woman hands her a piece of paper.

Livie unfolds the piece of paper and stares at the words:
~~~~~~

Meet me off Independence Av, across from the southeast corner of the National History Museum. 6:15 p.m. tomorrow, Oct 30th.

- F

Chapter 22

The Satellites

After receiving the note at Green Planet, Livie returns to her condo with Turing in her arms. She's anxious to share the note with Raf to get his reaction, but instead is presented with another note, this one left on the kitchen counter.

> *Didn't discover much today. I will continue tomorrow. I won't be here tonight.*
>
> *Raf*

She shrugs internally. She's tired, and although she's wondering what's up with Raf, she has more pressing matters to attend to. First—find out what's on Finn's data sticker. Over the last several days she has speculated endlessly about what could be on there, and now she finally has the scanner that will allow her to read it.

She takes the scanner out of her jacket, pops the microchip out of the slot in the back, and is standing in front of her computer, ready to put it in, when the exhaustion from the day—from the last several days—descends on her like a cloud. She puts the microchip into her laptop even as her body is clearly opposing what her mind wants, telling her she needs to rest. Feeling a shiver making its way through her bones, she sits down as if in a trance, like she needs to do something, and turns the laptop on. Within seconds it comes alive, the cursor blinking, asking for the password. She enters "twinkie2019", and a photo of her and Twinkie at Deerfield Lake fills the screen. The image disappears as the computer reads the data from the microchip and another screen takes its place. It shows three numbered files. She clicks on the first one.

The screen fills with a list of coordinates. She stares at the top one:

39.784° 56' 54.3732" N, 87.092° 39'19.2024" W

The numbers start to blur in front of her, so she closes the laptop and heads to bed.

A tempestuous dream prowls through her sleep.

> She has just left Finn standing behind the fountain. A cold breeze wafts against her face, causing her to turn away. The turn brings a figure into her peripheral vision. Someone with a gun—heading straight in the direction where she left Finn.
>
> Livie turns to see Finn still standing there. She breaks into a run towards him, coming at him from his side. She wants to call out his name but doesn't want to draw attention to herself. Out of the corner of her eye, she can see the figure to the side of her. They have either not seen her yet or just haven't reacted.
>
> She's within a couple hundred feet of him when Finn turns to move in the opposite direction. She slows her pace to a brisk walk as she catches her breath.
>
> Finn, hearing her breathing, turns and sees her. His face is plastered with fear. She takes the final steps, embraces him in a hug, and whispers in his ear.
>
> "Someone is coming for you. We need to get out of here."

Still embracing him, she sees the figure over Finn's shoulder, now moving faster, heading straight towards them. She looks Finn in the eyes and kisses him.

"Let's go!"

She takes his hand and leads him towards the edge of the park at a vigorous pace. She sees a group of people congregating by a vehicle and decides being amongst a crowd of people, even a small one, would provide them with safety. But just as she is moving towards the group, a large man in a trench coat steps out from their left and makes a beeline for them.

"We need to run." Livie points to their right. "This way."

They are running towards another park exit, but it is blocked by a cast-iron fence. Still holding Finn's hand, Livie veers to the right, heading for an unobstructed exit further up.

As they approach the exit another figure appears, watching them with piercing eyes. Livie abruptly turns them around. Finn squeezes her hand, stops, and lets go.

"Stop! We're in an exhausting loop here...we need to think."

He's right. Catching her breath, she hears the sound of a train in the distance. Livie grabs Finn's hand again.

"The train! Come, let's get there!"

They break into a sprint towards the far exit and towards the train.

Not stopping to see who is behind them, they exit the park. They can see the train in motion in front of them. They pause briefly and let go of each other's hands.

"There!" Livie points to an open car on the train and starts to run, Finn beside her.

The train is moving moderately fast. Livie matches its pace and runs alongside an open car. She can feel Finn running beside her when she leaps and rolls into the it. Lying on the dusty wooden floor of the train, she looks out and sees Finn still standing on the ground, growing smaller as the train speeds past him. His sad eyes are on Livie as the man with the gun comes up behind him.

Livie awakes to a movement on her bed, frightening her for a second, until she hears Turing's meow. She looks over at the cat. The sight of it dispels the willies from the dream and shakes her back to where she is.

She can feel the sweaty nightgown sticking to her back as she slowly moves out of the bed. Turing quickly moves to her feet.

"Hannah said you weren't very social, so what gives? Guess you're hungry?"

Moving to the kitchen, Livie looks over to the desk where she left her laptop closed, thinking of what awaits her there. She looks down at Turing, who's still circling her feet.

"I need to get some coffee first, and you something to eat."

She slowly moves to the espresso maker and pushes the button. Standing there, she can smell the coffee seeping into her pores as the beans grind, willing her to come out of her slumber. The scent of coffee continues to intensify as she completes the task of pressing the beans and watches the espresso drip into her mug.

Turing gives out a loud meow as he looks up at her.

"Alright, I'll get you something to eat." Livie opens the fridge to see what she has. Her eyes fall on some left-over salmon. She looks back down at the furry creature making noise in her kitchen.

"Looks like I have a real treat for you, but first, I'm getting myself some coffee."

She reaches back over to the espresso maker and turns a knob to pour the water in for the final touch on her Americano.

A couple sips of coffee packs the punch she needs to feel her day can start. She pulls a dish out of the cupboard, opens the fridge, and deposits the salmon into it. Taking another sip of her liquid awakener, she places the dish on the floor and watches Turing bury his head in it.

With Turing happily purring while he eats, she takes a couple more sips, walks over to the laptop, and opens it up.

The figures that she vaguely recalls seeing the night before fill the screen again. Taking another sip of coffee, she sees what her clouded mind couldn't register in her exhausted state. It's a list of coordinates. As she did the night before, she looks at the first one to see if she can make sense of it.

39.784° 56' 54.3732" N, 87.092° 39'19.2024" W

"Sure would be helpful to have the internet for this." She looks down the list and counts the coordinates. Eight. Eight different sets of longitude and latitude. Does Finn think she was sailor in a past life?

Turing is back at her feet again. She looks down at him as he rests between her legs.

"Well Turing, how am I supposed to decipher this?"

She looks back up at the computer screen and moves to open the next file when her phone lights up with a text message. She picks up the phone and reads the message.

I'll come by later tonight.
Raf

"Whatever," she says into the air as she flips her phone face down and goes back to the laptop. The cursor is sitting over the second file. She clicks the mouse to open it.

A long spreadsheet pops up. At the top, in bold block letters, it reads:

WORLD'S SATELITTES

She takes a sip of her coffee as she scans the spreadsheet. The first column is a list of sequential numbers, starting from one. The second column contains names. Her eyes move down the spreadsheet, reciting the names in her head as she sees them.

Ariel Navestar 72. Napryazhenie. Themis. Odin (Canadian). Aerocube 144. Luca. Sortie. China 19. Echo, Glory. Rosat. Odin (Swedish). Swift. Odin (French). Akari. Zootopia. Shinsei. Omidi. Cosmos. China 4. Bolt. Gamma-Ray Encanto. Red-Eye 5.

She stops at Red-eye and takes another sip of coffee before moving the cursor to the column headings. She moves it from one heading to the next, stopping at each one.

NUMBER. NAME. ORIGIN.

Under ORIGIN she sees countries listed. USA. Russia. Japan. Canada. Australia. China.

Back to the headings, she moves the cursor further across.

ECEF. GNSS.

She sees numbers and formulas below the columns.

X-BAND.

Single-digit numbers below the heading.

HIGH/MEDIUM/LOW ORBIT.

Almost all the entries are described as LOW, with a few MEDIUMs. She assumes if she scrolls further down, she will see some HIGHs. Instead, she continues moving the cursor across the headings.

SPEED (kms/second).

Many numbers are triple digits. The highest she spots on the current worksheet is 163. She looks down at Turing.

"163 kilometers per second, Turing. That's a little fast for my liking."

Turing perks up when he hears his name and rubs his chin against her leg.

She turns back to the screen and moves the cursor to the next heading.

DISTANCE TO EARTH (Minutes).

What she sees below this heading are a lot of double-digit numbers, but also some with up to four digits.

She hovers the cursor over one of the numbers and it shows a complex formula, like some kind of algorithm. She moves her cursor up to the next heading.

CLOSEST TARGET.

Below this she sees several entries that simply read Moon. Others list what appears to be the name of other satellites. Still others appear to be what she recognizes as planets or other moons, like Ganymede and Callisto.

She lets out a breath, trying to make sense of all this. She sees other headings, including: CORRDINATES, AGE, PURPOSE.

She stops at purpose and looks below it. Listed are: Military, Communications, Weather, GPS...

She looks down at the bottom of the worksheet, moves the cursor to the bar on the side, and shifts it to the bottom. The last entry is number 8132. The number of satellites listed. She scrolls back up to the first entry.

Livie rubs her face and rakes her fingers through her hair. She looks down at Turing, who is resting at her feet with his eyes closed, looking content.

"You're looking peaceful down there. This stuff doesn't disturb you?"

Turing stirs and looks up at her, as if acknowledging that she is talking to him. Livie reaches down and scratches him around the ears—he immediately starts to purr.

"So, what do you think this all means, and why would Finn go to such effort to hand this to me?"

At the mention of Finn's name, Turing looks up at her and stretches out his paws.

"I know, I miss him too."

Livie looks back at the screen, her cursor now hovering over the third file. She looks back down at the cat, then clicks on the third file.

"Password Required" pops up on the screen. The cursor blinks below the words expectantly. She glances down at the cat and enters "Turing". Below Password Required it now reads, "Incorrect password. Attempt 1 of 4."

She looks at the screen, stretches out her arms, feels the dry sweat on her back from the night before, and looks back down at the cat.

"Well, time for a shower before I see what more confusion I can find here—*if* I can get behind door number three."

Turing follows her to the bathroom.

Livie turns on the shower and lets it get steaming hot before she gets in. She likes a hot shower. While undressing, she guesses password possibilities out loud to the room.

"Hannah." That's too easy.

"Livie." Could be, but also too easy.

"Brant." Finn is often ironic. It's possible.

Thinking of their other connections, she lists more possibilities.

"Saba, Preet, Bo." Maybe it's not a person, but a place or thing. More ideas percolate up.

"GW. Monument." Maybe it's one of the esoteric words he uses a lot.

"Penumbra. Parsimonious." She lets out a breath. What other words?

"Esoteric." Maybe it's that simple?

"Finn."

The mention of Finn gets Turing's attention, and he starts to paw at Livie's legs.

"Ouch! Not on my bare legs Turing." Livie reaches down and pushes him off her. Seeing his sad eyes, she scratches him under the chin.

"It's okay. I need to get into the shower anyway. Then I'll need more coffee. Now scoot." She nudges the cat towards the door.

The steam from the shower releases into the room as soon as she opens the glass door. She quickly jumps in, closing the door behind her. The water hits her skin with a force and heat that she has to endure for a few moments as her body acclimatizes. The different characters and numbers from the files Finn left her are swirling around in her mind, as if floating within the steam right in front of her.

How can she make sense of it all? What do those eight different coordinates represent? Locations, but of what? Wouldn't you need a geologist or a rocket scientist to make sense of all that data?

She lathers up, cleaning her body, seeing numbers within the soap. Numbers that don't make sense. *The numbers,* she thinks, *like a soup, must stir up into some sort of plan*. A plan involving the satellites. What is Finn hoping she will do with this information?

She turns off the shower and lets her body drip-dry for a few seconds as the steam dissipates. Closing her eyes, she hopes that her meeting tonight will clear things up.

Stepping out of the shower, she grabs a towel, her mind now back on the password to access the third file. As she wraps the towel around her body, Turing comes back into the bathroom, as if to greet her.

"Well, hello there. You came in unannounced." As soon as she says the words, her eyes open wide. She reaches down and picks Turing up.

"Come, let's go. I think I just discovered that damn password."

Tucking the end of the towel under her, she sits down in front of the laptop and opens it again. The same screen appears.

"Password Required."

The cursor is blinking above the words, "Incorrect password. Attempt 1 of 4."

She places her fingers on the keyboard and types in "unzip".

The screen goes blank, and then a document appears in front of her. It's a letter. Addressed to her.

Livie,

I've trusted you with the locations of the eight central computers that could bring the internet back.

I've also given you the stolen information on the satellites. There is some "new world order" plan that goes with this information. I don't know what it is.

You must get this information into the right hands to change the course of history.

I have not made any copies.

I am getting out.

Finn

The words "I am getting out" crack open in front of her.

"I am getting out," she whispers into the room. She looks down at Turing, who is weaving between her legs.

"You're hungry again already? Did I not feed you enough? It's okay, I'm hungry too. I just need to figure this out first. 'I am getting out.' Was that his plan going to the park? To give me this information and then disengage from everything, maybe disappear?"

Turing responds with a loud, "Meow!"

"Alright, let's get something to eat. I don't think tonight's meeting was in the plans before all this, so hopefully it provides the answers to these mysteries."

~~~~~~

The night sky is clear, and the sun is setting, presenting Livie with a view worthy of a postcard. The orange and yellow hues shoot light through the trees as she walks between them on the path down Independence Avenue, towards the museum. She looks up and sees the near-full moon has made its entry into the night.

With her hands stuffed into her pockets to keep them warm in the crisp temperature, Livie fingers the data stick that she transferred the information to. The museum closed nearly an hour ago; it's a Thursday evening, the night before Halloween. It's quiet out. At any other time, she would enjoy this walk with peace and contentment. A couple, holding hands, are walking towards her. She fingers the
~~~~~~

flashlight in her other pocket. Darkness has already begun to descend on the night.

The stage is set, she thinks, *for whatever this clandestine meeting I'm walking into will hold.*

She walks past the couple, exchanging greetings of "evening". Rounding the southwest corner across from the museum, her senses are on high alert, watching for any movement. She picks up her pace and checks her watch. 6:13 p.m. She has timed this just right. She sees a figure coming from the east, stopping by a thicket of elm trees. She isn't close enough to see more than a dark profile, and the person has now moved deeper into the shadows of the trees.

Livie slows her pace, keeping her eyes on the area ahead. She doesn't see anyone in the dim light, and she wonders if her mind was playing tricks on her. Then she hears the cracking of feet on dry twigs among the trees. She stops. Whoever is out there has stopped as well.

"It's Livie. Who's there?"

There's no response. She stands there, seeing the vague outline of a dark figure hidden in the shade of the trees. *It's like a standoff of some sort,* she thinks.

"Okay, I'm coming in."

Livie takes a few steps forward when she hears a voice she recognizes immediately.

"You alone?"

"Of course."

"I'll wait for you here."

Wanting to take back some control, Livie stops and stands still, as if holding her ground.

"There is no one else out here. It's better to talk in the moonlight. We can always jump into the trees at a moment's notice if need be."

She leans slightly forward, listening for the voice, but hears nothing but the whistling of a faint breeze. She stonily speaks into the air.

"Look, I'm not coming in there. You need to come to me." Livie scans the area briefly. "It's safe. No one is here."

She keeps her focus on the treed area when shafts of moonlight hit the figure as they come out onto the pathway. They lock eyes.

"I'm glad to see you here. Why didn't you show for our meeting last week?"

As the person steps closer, Livie can see her face for the first time. It is filled with anxiety.

"It wasn't safe."

"For whom?"

"For me...or you, Livie."

"Why wasn't it safe? What changed?"

She sees fear plastered on Fairleigh's face, a stark contrast to the person she met at Green Planet nearly a year ago. Her voice wobbles as she pushes out her next words.

"I came across some information I wasn't supposed to...I think they found out...I fear I'm a target."

"What information? The satellites?"

Livie feels the adrenaline of getting another piece to fill her bingo card as she watches Fairleigh's eyebrows rise and her shoulders sink.

"So, you know it's about the satellites. What *do* you know?"

"That's not how this is going to go. You sent me the note to meet you here. You go first. Who's 'they' that found out, and what do you know about the satellites?"

Fairleigh looks past Livie and around her. The silence lingers.

"There's no one here but us. What do you know about the satellites?"

Fairleigh's gaze seems to focus on Livie's mouth, then her eyes, but her stare is looking through her.

"There is a plan...a plan that will take out all communication." Fairleigh's voice is even, as if these are words she has rehearsed and just needs to push out. "Communication that tells us what the weather will be and when storms will come. Communication that gives us navigation, GPS...that allows us to communicate with each other from a great distance. Communication that navigates our planes and gives our military security. It's a plan that will change our world, plunging us into darkness. A plan that will likely cause a world war."

As Livie takes in Fairleigh's words, the figures from Finn's spreadsheet float in front of her. She stuffs her hands deep into her pockets, feeling the data stick.

"What is that plan?"

Fairleigh's eyes show a sudden focus as she looks directly into Livie's eyes and then looks away.

"It's something that will cause so much debris in space that satellites won't be able to function. It could impact our climate and environment too. Livie, it involves eight thousand satellites."

"Eight thousand one hundred and thirty-two...to be exact."

Fairleigh looks directly at her, alarm on her face. A light suddenly sneaks up on the side of Fairleigh's face. Livie follows it up to the sky.

"What's that?"

Fairleigh turns to look behind her. They watch a string of lights fly across the sky in unison, from west to east. Livie thinks of aliens from a movie she watched, ready to invade earth. Within seconds, they see another string of lights coming from the other direction. These seem to be slightly larger.

Livie and Fairleigh stand silently next to each other, fixated on the lights. They both gasp as the two strings come together, causing an explosion, like fireworks in the sky. Just as they are catching their breath, they see another explosion in front of, or maybe on, the moon.

Fairleigh abruptly turns to Livie.

"It's happening. It wasn't supposed to be for at least another week. There was still time!" Fairleigh stops and places her hands on Livie's shoulders. "There was still time, Livie!" Fairleigh turns around again to watch the scene in the sky.

"Now it's too late...I need to go."

Livie reaches out, tries to stop her.

"Wait! Where are you going?"

Fairleigh turns back to face her.

"To prepare my life to live in this new world or ours. You should do the same, Livie. I don't think anyone will be chasing either of us down now."

With that, like a dissipating vapor, Fairleigh runs and disappears into the night.

Chapter 23

Life in the Post-Internet World

Three years later, November 15, 2036.

Livie looks out of her window towards the monument. She briefly glances up at the magnifying blind—a blind she has still never used. *Maybe it's time to get rid of it,* she ponders. *Time to accept some things the way they are.*

It has been nine days since the election, and just like four years earlier, she had a group of friends over to cheer on the candidate running against Brant. And just like four years earlier, Brant won. But this time round, the emotions amongst her group of friends had a very different vibe to it.

Hannah was there. So was Preet and Bo. But no Finn. No Saba either, though even if they knew where she was, she most likely wouldn't have been invited. A couple of new friends joined the gathering, including Hannah's new boyfriend, Vyas. Raf also came by, which surprised Livie. After the satellites went down, he just disappeared, leaving only a note. When he showed up at Livie's place a day before the election, her first instinct was to reject him. But then his beautiful face and compelling story dissolved her hostility. Her mom recently told her that she had learned to let go of grudges and seek out forgotten friends. To forgive. If her mom could do that, so could Livie. So, she invited Raf to the election-night gathering.

The two election nights, four years apart, could not have been any more different. The atmosphere on this election night had none of the excitement for a different outcome like they had hoped for four years earlier. They all came expecting a Brant victory, so it really was just a group of friends getting together to catch up—using the election night as an excuse.

No sudden event followed this election. The internet had been lost for four years, and other than a few fanatical believers still bearing placards declaring the pending return of the internet, people had accepted, even embraced, a world without it. This time, there was no broadcast from the Friendly World Network, although Livie believes they still work behind the scenes to ensure the internet remains a relic of history.

She moves away from the window to her kitchen, her thoughts now on the evening ahead. She has them all coming over again tonight: Raf, Hannah and Vyas, Preet and Bo. Her mom and Theo are coming too. They would add a different element to the crowd, but Maggie is in town, and Livie couldn't say no when she asked to come. Her mom promised that Theo would keep his passionate pro-internet and pro-Brant comments in check.

Livie stands in the kitchen, contemplating what to do first to prepare for the night ahead, as she works up the energy to tackle things. Turing purrs at her feet, having just finished off the tuna in his bowl.

The daily newspaper sits on the counter. A headline on the front page catches her eye. *How Brant got re-elected without bringing the internet back...page three.*

Livie turns the page of the tabloid-style newspaper to page three and reads the piece written by columnist Abelina Balogun.

> Brant won on a promise of the advancement of technology and to make "America Dominate Again." When the internet went off, he made daily promises to bring it back, even declaring several times that it would be back within hours or days. That was in 2032.

The internet never came back, and with its loss, technological advances have been set back, not forward. While that last point might be debated by some, the reality is that Brant has not been able to deliver on the technological advancements he promised in 2032. That is because the internet was lost hours after his election.

Yet, despite that, here we are in 2036, and Brant has been re-elected as president in a race that was never really in doubt. How did he pull it off?

To answer that question, let's step back to the situation prior to the 2032 election. In the years leading up to that election, China and Russia had taken over as the dominant countries in terms of science, commerce, and technology. Russia's advancements in technology were clearly in the lead. Even in terms of military, America's position at the top was in doubt. The ascendence of China and Russia to these thrones as the new world powers allowed them to set much of the world's agenda. As Americans, we did not admit this at the time. We simply ignored the cracks in the foundation of our so-called supremacy when we hung out our flags.

Against this backdrop, Brant entered. His slogan, "Make America Dominate Again," resonated with many. Many Americans wanted to return to a time when they felt secure in the knowledge (real or not) that they lived in the dominant culture of the world. That they lived where everyone else wanted to be.

Brant promised to make this happen, and the use of technology was a cornerstone of this promise. He was unabashed in saying that he'd advance America's agenda in the world using technology and by "being on the cutting edge of all technological advances in every field." His campaign, which included sending text messages en masse to all Americans, except those that deliberately opted out of them (which just showed him who his opposition was), was meant as a harbinger of things to come. His government would dominate technology and all the propaganda they could leverage with it.

But then the internet went off. Why didn't Brant's plans crumble with it?

The loss of the internet was a fulcrum that could have upset everything in Brant's agenda, and initially it did just that. He clearly understood this early on with his loud proclamations that it was coming back on. He had people on the job, don't worry. He was going to get it fixed. In the next seventy-two hours. Then the next seventy-two hours. Then the announcements of it coming back on stopped. The fix he promised didn't happen.

When the satellites went down, some even began to wonder if he orchestrated it—like some mad scientist at the helm. The evidence we have (or have been fed) point to the satellite attack having come from elsewhere, and while Brant wasn't making any more proclamations about the internet coming back on, he still had his team feverishly working to bring it back. Reports of dead Russians found in parks and in apartments testified to that.

The attack that took out the satellites changed everything. Can you believe that was three years ago now?

Once the satellites were gone, it was clear that the internet was not coming back soon, if ever. From that point on, we saw Brant pivot his message and agenda. Instead of the loss of the internet being the catalyst of his demise, it became the open door to his rising popularity. He was still using the slogan, "Make America Dominate Again," but now in the context of a post-internet world.

His new slogan could be "What is old, is new." He has made statements like, "We are passing the torch to a new generation of Americans," and "We are focused on those things that unite us, instead of belaboring those issues that divide us." Both statements were lifted from John Kennedy's words from a different era.

Perhaps nothing emphasized this more than when Brant brought the Summer Olympics to Los Angeles in 2034. The Summer Olympics were set to be in Beijing in 2032. The loss of the internet led to the event being cancelled, and when Brant declared that America was ready to host the Games in LA in 2034, many thought it was a delusion. China was furious, but when athletes from around the world declared that they wouldn't go to China, Brant won the debate. He then rolled out the government treasury to ensure our athletes would dominate the podium, which they did. We talk about that Olympics with pride, and Brant often referred to it in his recent campaign. The fact that the Russians and Chinese boycotted the Games isn't something we mention—after all, it is irrelevant if America is back on top where it belongs.

Now, here we are in 2036, and as our society has settled into the post-internet world, with a greater emphasis on the local rather than the global, it is like we have been transported to a version of the 1960s—just like Brant's borrowed slogans. A time when America replaced Great Britain in the leadership role as the dominant (there's that word again) voice. We are even back to a version of the Cold War with Russia, the 2030s edition, with China as a major player. Both sides are building nuclear arsenals again. Embargoes are a popular tool being used in propaganda campaigns. Brant has acknowledged this, even reveled in it, as a war with China and Russia. He plays on the America psyche to believe in itself—conveniently overlooking unfavorable elements of history. "We've never lost a war," he has said.

It's astounding that we haven't seen the rebirth of satellites as each side takes credit for scuttling the others' launches. The space debris still present from the destruction of the satellites is clearly an issue as well. Meanwhile, the arms race is upon us again.

The formally iconic *Mad Magazine*, with Alfred E. Neuman on its cover, is back, a familiar sight on coffee tables across the nation.

Even sports seem to have lined up to support the "what was old, is new again" concept. The Yankees won the World Series, the Celtics the NBA championship, and the Green Bay Packers the NFL. To keep the west in the party, the Seattle Kraken won the NHL's Stanley Cup.

We've returned to movie theatres en mass. People are coalescing around community events, which have become places of gossip and networking. Meanwhile, "virtual" meetings and gatherings have all but disappeared, except for those who use their mobile data and a series of repeaters, with their annoying delays.

So here we have Brant again. Is it the same version? His first term was spawned by a fear of America losing its footing in the world. Then, in his first year with the internet lost, America seemed to be slipping further. Now it seems his references to sixties-style living, accompanied by quotes reminiscent of Kennedy, sired a second term. A second term that seemed unimaginable three years ago.

Leading up to this election, Brant's opponent posed a simple question: "What will it be America, the old or the new?" In Brant, many felt they got both.

Whether it is reality or not, many feel that America is truly the dominant force in the world again. With that, Brant fulfilled his promise from his first term. If you think that is all just propaganda, welcome to the recycling of what was old into something new.

Livie flips the paper back to the front page, expressing her thoughts out loud to the empty room.

"Pivot. What bullshit. More like duped a lot of people. Just wait for the protests when he starts a real war somewhere. Well, at least I'm not working for him anymore."

Turing meows as she speaks, as if in solidarity with her thoughts. She bends down and scratches him below the chin.

"Glad you agree. I'm sure Finn would have too."

Even as Livie vocalizes her feelings, she tells herself to stop before she takes a deep dive backwards to what it was like three years ago when things were spiraling out of control. A journey she frequents in her mind.

When Finn disappeared, she felt her life was in danger, yet he left her with a data strip that could have changed things. Whomever he intended her to get it to, she didn't make it in time before the satellites started crashing down, and her life with them. The ghost of the internet has truly haunted her because of what happened during those intense few days. The disappearance of Finn and Draw roam in her thoughts and haunt her frequently. Raf disappeared too, but at least he left a note.

She can't prevent the last image she has in her head of Finn appearing before her. His anxious expression as the wind ruffled his hair before she left him standing there in the park. She has replayed the scene in her head like a movie many times over the last few years. Why didn't she realize the shadowy figure lurking in the woods was after him and not her? It's a question she has asked herself many times as she replays alternate endings in her head.

She forces herself to refocus and casts her eyes towards the framed picture hanging beside her doorway. It's a photo her mom gave her of the view from the cabin, looking out towards Deerfield Lake. The peaceful image shakes her out of her dreamlike trance and puts a warm smile on her face.

After the satellites went down, she retreated to the cabin, where she spent several days taking in the peace and quiet of the place. That is where she formulated her plans for her own private investigative firm. Hannah was there too, along with her mom. They encouraged and supported Livie. They laughed and cried as they spitballed so many ideas for her new "PI Firm," as Hannah put it.

She put so much of that into action too. The post-internet world has given her work more meaning. She doesn't have the ability to search for clients as she did with the internet, but then, neither do others. Her work is more in "the field," as she puts it, than in an office, staring at a screen, as it was before. Without the internet, she doesn't have the anxiety of clients checking everything she comes up with and second-guessing her. She feels more respected in the work she does. She has done so well that she has hired a couple of associates.

She walks over to the picture to look more closely at it. Her mom gave it to her, in the frame, after she left the cabin with her business plans and renewed energy. The peace the picture radiates truly reflects much of what she has discovered in her life. Like most, she suspects, she has her moments when she still mourns the loss of the internet—though those moments are fading as time goes by. But in general, her life feels more calm, peaceful, and fulfilling. Her relationships with her friends are stronger than ever, and she talks to her mom regularly—and actually looks forward to it. *Well, mostly,* she thinks with a chuckle.

While her mom can still grate her from time to time, Maggie truly has changed her approach to life. Her mom's words as she was leaving the cabin that day still resonate with her.

"Livie, there are things I have discovered that have changed my life. I have sought to mend old quarrels and seek out forgotten friends. To let go of grudges and to spend more time listening. To forgive. To appreciate. To find the time. To show gratitude and to take pleasure in the beauty around me."

She's glad she took the time to listen to her mom that day.

She shakes her head now, thinking how she fought so hard to get the internet back and was even willing to work for Brant and his group to make it happen. Now she couldn't imagine being part of such a cause. She has no desire to disrupt the life she has created for herself, post-internet.

She lets out some air from her lungs to release all the heavy thoughts and looks at her watch. Time to get ready for the tribe.

"Hannah has arrived."

Since the internet went down, Livie's doorbell only recognizes faces that she has programed into it, but she feels safer that way. She looks at the camera and sees Hannah's face staring at her with a look that says, "Are you going to let me in?"

"Unzip!"

Hannah opens the door and walks in, her smile drawing light from the room.

"So glad you are the first to arrive. You're early too. But where's Vyas?"

"He's coming later." Hannah hands Livie a bottle of wine as she reaches down to take off her shoes. "I wanted to come early so we could have some alone time, just the two of us."

Livie holds up the bottle of wine. "And a bottle of wine. Shall I pour us some?"

Hannah gives her the "of course" look with her eyes as she bends down to pet Turing, who has come to the door to greet her as well.

"So, this cat sure isn't anything like the anti-social creature I remember with Finn."

Livie moves to the kitchen, takes out two wine glasses, places them on the counter, and pours some red wine into them.

"Maybe, like me, he felt he should learn to appreciate the people around him more after Finn went missing," Livie states.

"I miss Finn too."

Livie didn't mean to make Finn the topic of their discussion and would rather not. She changes the subject.

"So, at the election night party, the discussion amongst our tribe was a lot about what changes we've all gone through in the last three years. What do you think tonight will be like?"

"I dunno. Your mom and her guy are coming too?"

"Yes. That's right, my mom and Theo. I'm not sure she'd refer to him as her guy though. She tells me they're friends."

"Ya, sure. Whatever. You think it will be a different dynamic with them coming?"

"No, not really, and they're coming a little later anyway. I'm interested in hearing more about how Preet's business is going. The other night she talked about it a bit, but we didn't get into any deeper details."

"For sure. But hey, I have a question I want to ask you."

Hannah's expression has changed, and she suddenly looks serious.

"Hey, I know that look. You didn't come early just for some girl chat. Something's on your mind. What's up?'

"We haven't had a real discussion about Finn, since...well since his disappearance."

Livie looks down at Turing, as if he might help with this. "Oh okay...what do you want to talk about?"

"Well, how you are feeling about it? And you've never told me what actually happened in the park that day."

Livie takes a drink of her wine and holds the glass by the stem as she moves towards the window and looks out.

"How do I feel about it? Honestly Hannah, I miss him and am..."

Hannah moves to the window, stands beside her friend, and reaches for her hand.

"I miss him too. What's troubling you about it?"

Livie turns and looks into Hannah's eyes as moisture gathers in her own. Whatever held her back from expressing her emotions before breaks open, and she blurts it out.

"I am haunted by the possibility that I had a hand in his disappearance."

"Why would you say that?"

Livie explains why she met Finn in the park that day. How she texted him and asked to meet him at a specific location there. She tricked him to meet her, saying it was regarding, "our mutual friend." Livie bends her fingers into air quotes as she says this and looks back out the window.

"That's you, Hannah. The mutual friend."

"Okay, but he would have met with you regardless, and you weren't meeting about me anyway."

"True."

Livie continues telling Hannah what happened and how she sought to meet with Finn because she found out he was working with the Friendly World Network, but she suspected his motives were not pure. She needed intel on the FWN and figured he could help. But after spying on him for a while, she became concerned that he was also getting in over his head. Then someone with the pro-interneters—Brant's people—was murdered. Someone she was working with and knew well.

"Hannah, he was murdered when he left my place to follow me." Livie's voice squeaks in a way she did not intend. Hannah moves closer to her and takes her hand again.

"Anyway, he was murdered by this guy who had some skull and bones tattoo with the numbers 322 on it. I thought Finn might know something about that, so I planned to ask him."

"Did you?"

"I did. I'll get to that."

Livie continues talking about how she knew that Finn was working closely with the Friendly World Network, but she also discovered that Saba was actually a Brant supporter.

"Saba?" Hannah interrupts her. "Whatever happened to her?"

"I don't know...I don't care."

Livie resumes as if the interruption hadn't occurred. "I needed information from Finn, but I was also unearthing a sinister plot that he seemed to be in the middle of—something to do with the satellites. I was scared that he was getting too involved with very dangerous people, and that he had no idea how dangerous they could be."

Her voice is getting lower, just above a whisper, as she talks. She has relived much of this in her mind many times but has not vocalized it. When she met Finn in the park, she had a plan. She needed information from him, and then she was going to map out a plan for him to get out of everything. She even had a safe house of sorts set up for him to go. But the plan unraveled when she saw that she was being followed in the park. Well, she thought she was being followed because she had noticed being tailed in the days leading up to that meeting. For some reason, despite her fears for Finn, she just didn't clue in that he could have been the one who was being followed.

Livie pauses to keep her emotions tamped down. Hannah uses the moment to reach out and hug her friend.

"It's okay girl. There's no way you could have known. He was likely being followed anyway."

Livie looks at Hannah briefly before turning to cast her eyes towards the monument again.

"I'm not so sure of that. My presence there may have attracted them. I never did get to ask Finn all the questions I had, but I did ask him about the skull and bones and the numbers 322. The question seemed to send a shiver through his body, and he whispered, 'the Brotherhood of Death.' After everything that happened, in the days that followed, I never found out what that means."

"That sounds ominous. Who do you think took him?"

Livie thinks for a minute to formulate a response. At first, she thought it was someone from Brant's group, as she had been followed before and figured this new tail was for her. But it was for Finn. Livie hasn't told anyone about the data strip Finn left on her.

She thought it was too dangerous. After the satellites went down, that danger seemed to dissipate, and she has kept the data sticker in a locked drawer since. She has wondered if it might come in use at some point or help to find Finn. She did some of her own digging to try and locate him, but there was so much confusion and chaos at the time that she just hit walls in her efforts. Once she looked at the data strip, she figured Brant's group or the Russians probably took Finn. He was walking a dangerous line between the two. She figured Draw might know, and she even reached out to him without success. Draw had disappeared too.

She decides on her answer. "It could have been either side, as Finn was involved in activities with both."

"Why would they take him though? Did he have information they wanted?"

Livie can tell that Hannah is just trying to figure out what happened and why. Like Livie, over the last three years, she has probably been trapped in the theatre of her imagination with these questions a few times. They've avoided talking about it before. Or maybe it was just Livie avoiding it. She just couldn't get the words to spring out of her thoughts. Now Hannah is probing, and she can't avoid it.

"Whoever it was, I think they believed he had information about either the satellites or how the Friendly World Network took down the internet, or maybe even both."

"So, what did he tell you about the satellites?"

"I didn't get the chance to ask him, but—" Livie is interrupted by the sound of the doorbell.

"Preet has arrived."

"Shit! I guess time was just flying by there. Let's continue this after the tribe leaves later?"

Livie nods in response. "Say, I could use a few minutes in the bathroom to freshen up. Could you let Preet and Bo in and greet them for me?"

"You bet. I got you girl."

Hannah watches Livie disappear into the bathroom and then calls out, "Unzip!"

Chapter 24

The Tribe Together Again

Livie stands in front of the mirror in her bathroom. Prowling her mind afresh are the possibilities of what may have happened to Finn and what he may have gone through. Her emotions seep out, and she works to keep the sound of her sobs from escaping the bathroom walls.

She washes her face and then decides to take a shower, knowing that anyone else who arrives will assume that she is just getting ready for them.

Meanwhile, Hannah gets the snacks ready, sets out the glasses for drinks, and lets the visitors in as they arrive.

Livie takes longer than she expected, but she doesn't want to step out to greet her friends with wet hair, so she takes the time to dry it. Feeling fresh and ready, she exits the washroom and sees the whole tribe there. Hannah, Vyas, Bo, Preet, and Raf. Her mom and Theo haven't arrived yet.

Preet is the first to spot her.

"Livie! We were just discussing how we all grew up as these digital natives. That when growing up, if someone talked about a life before the internet, you thought they came from some other planet. But now, how are our kids going to react when we tell them about this thing called the internet that was such a large part of our culture growing up?"

"Sounds like a lively discussion. So, are we all assuming the internet is lost forever then?"

Vyas, who has fit in seamlessly with their tribe and is never shy to pipe up, is the first to answer her question.

"I don't think so. It's just that we've all adjusted to a world without the internet. There's a comfort in that. And it's kind of fun to play the what-if game. Image the internet doesn't come back, and we are all explaining it to our kids someday?"

Bo lets out a laugh at the suggestion and adds his voice.

"I don't know if I will talk about it as something I miss. I can still watch *The Simpsons* at twice the regular speed, with all the laughs in half the time."

Bo's comments bring another round of laughter. The laughter and smiles that fill the room allow Livie to park the heavy discussion with Hannah in the recesses of her mind.

The conversations that follow are framed by each of their experiences growing up and how different the world has become. The stories flow like a well-conducted orchestra with uproarious laughter, lots of teasing, and wide smiles. All accompanied by regular pours of wine and spirits.

Vyas tells them about growing up in Fiji and how he joined a kids' club called Castaway Island. A story about how he was snorkeling with the kids from the club and caught the fin of a stingray causes Hannah to gibe, "I bet that story gets better every time you tell it."

Each member of the tribe has multiple stories to tell, and there is a happy hum vibrating throughout the place. Livie smiles, thinking how happy they all are together.

Hannah gets up and starts making mojitos as Raf is describing how, as a kid in Israel, he caught a turtle that was bigger than him. He tried to pick it up as he talked to it. They all laughed as they imagined this little kid at the beach trying to carry this massive turtle.

As the laughter subsides, Preet turns to Livie.

"Hey, your turn Livie. You must have some adventurous stories from growing up?"

Livie doesn't usually talk about her years as a kid and starts to think of one that would be safe and funny to tell, when she is interrupted by the doorbell.

"Maggie Romée has arrived."

"Unzip!" Hannah yells without hesitation.

As soon as Maggie and Theo are in the door and have hung up their jackets, Preet brings them into the conversation.

"So, Ms. Romée, we were just telling stories from our childhoods, and it's now Livie's turn. Any interesting, funny stories you can tell us about her?"

Hannah catches Livie's eye to see if she sees any worry in them. Livie acknowledges her with a smile and a slow blink, indicating that it's okay.

"First, call me Maggie, please. I know Theo and I are easily the oldest in this group, but we don't need that reminder. And...actually, I have a story for you about Livie and the bright-green frog." Maggie pauses and looks at Livie, who gives a very slight nod of permission.

As Hannah is pouring some wine for Maggie and Theo, Maggie starts a story about how Livie tried to catch a bright-green frog at Deerfield Lake when she was a kid.

"Livie spotted this bright-colored frog early one morning, but soon discovered it was too fast for her little hands. For several days, Livie would rise early—before anyone else was up—in a quest to catch the frog. One morning, she came back drenched as we were all just starting breakfast. I guess she tried to follow the frog underwater."

The crowd lets out a collective laugh as Livie just smiles while shaking her head in response to the fun.

Maggie then continues to tell them how Livie took one of her uncle's fishing nets one day and cut it up. She then made herself a smaller net, using the branch of a tree. Before Maggie can continue, Preet interrupts her.

"Wait, how old was she?"

"Oh, I'd say about six."

Preet then looks at Livie. "Do you remember this?"

Livie nods as Maggie continues. "I followed Livie down to the lake the next morning, as I was concerned that she might go for a 'swim' again. I knew I wouldn't be able to dissuade Livie from making the trek down to the lake in the morning. I watched her make a failed attempt to catch the frog in the net. I kept my eye on Livie as the frog swam away, and she followed it. Knee-deep in the water, Livie followed it until it rested on a rock in a little cove nearby. There were other frogs there too. I saw Livie put the net down and just watch the frogs until she heard her uncle calling her for breakfast. So, there you have it. At a very young age, Livie showed that inquisitive nature and investigative techniques that we all see her use today."

Preet chimes in.

"Very true, Ms....Maggie. I'm curious though, didn't you think it was strange that she put down the net she constructed and just watched the frogs?"

"Not really. Livie was always a deep thinker, but she also valued noticing and observing things over thinking about them. She has always had an appreciation for nature too." Maggie looks over at Livie with admiration in her eyes before she continues. "I think seeing that frog in a different setting with other frogs kind of ended the hunt for her as she took in the peace the moment offered."

Livie listens to her mom finish and then jumps in.

"Okay, that all sounds way too deep. I was just six, after all. Thanks for not sharing how upset Uncle Dean was when he saw that I destroyed his net."

Maggie's telling of the story instantly makes her part of the group. Hannah even declares her and Theo as part of their "tribe".

Preet looks at Maggie with some wonderment in her eyes.

"It seems you appreciate this non-internet world more—the step back into the past, as some would say. You must remember the world before the internet?"

Maggie gives Preet a warm smile, clearly contemplating her answer as the sudden pause hangs in the air. Then she breaks it, speaking in a soft tone.

"I do, and let me tell you that while I much prefer this world that we are in now, there are many things from the past that we certainly don't want to bring back. It may be easy for a white person, for example, to romanticize a past generation. That is most certainly not the case for many other ethnic groups, particularly Black people and indigenous groups, though there are others too. The racism in our country crippled, traumatized, and in some case outright murdered people because of the color of their skin. We must never forget that. It has taken us several generations to get to where we are as a more inclusive society, and we have a way to go still."

Maggie pauses to look at each one of them to emphasize her point. "It's up to all of us to make sure we don't slide back in that regard and hold our leaders to account when they act differently."

"When they act differently?" Bo asks.

"Yes, unfortunately I think that is the case. Power and greed are powerful forces."

Livie looks at her mom with pride, amazement, and some shame. Oh, how she wishes she didn't waste so many years being angry at her mom. Hannah looks at Livie, and sensing the feelings coursing through her, reaches out to touch her hand.

Maggie witnesses the exchanges and decides to break through the quiet contemplative mood she has breathed into the room.

"Look, before you all think that deep, contemplative sympathy is something I always kept in my wardrobe, let me tell you another story about Livie when I didn't act so favorably. It's a story about the time Livie got herself stuck in a pigpen and lost my new dress shoes when we pulled her out."

Maggie then goes on to tell a tale about a time they visited a friend's farm. Livie headed outside wearing her mom's new dress shoes because her own shoes were "too dirty." Later, in some game she was playing with her friends, Livie ended up stuck in the pigpen, her feet sinking deeper and deeper. She started crying for help. When they pulled her out, Livie's feet were bare.

"I couldn't do anything but watch, helpless, as the muck oozed over my shoes," Maggie said. "I lost my cool, and while my friends were laughing at the whole episode, I wouldn't let Livie forget it for years. Whenever there was a family gathering, I'd find a way to weave the story into the discussion."

Livie nods, smiling widely at the story. "True, you were a bit unkind to me about that, but you have to admit, it is a family story for the ages."

"Indeed, it is." Maggie nods in agreement as she reaches out to touch her daughter's arm.

The tribe continues telling stories from their childhoods, even Maggie and Theo. When it starts getting late, Livie calls cabs for Preet and Bo and for her mom and Theo, who are staying in a hotel. Raf is taking the train, and Hannah plans to stay a bit longer.

With that, the evening is winding down when Preet makes a comment to Livie about her mom.

"Your mom is fun to be around and seems really grounded, Livie."

Maggie hears the comment and looks at Livie.

"Thanks for that kind observation Preet, but let me assure you that I have been far from the person I am today. I used to hate life. Despised it, actually. I had my own pain to deal with, inflicted on me from various sources, and I was pretty bitter to be truthful. Livie could tell you how most of my life was one big protest after another about how I felt I was hard done by or mistreated." Maggie pauses as she looks over at Livie.

"But then I discovered there was no goodness in acting that way and that it only produced more suffering and heartache. There are endless reasons in the world to despair and become restless and bitter. I came to realize that the cost of those demons of rage and bitterness left me with broken relationships and a largely unlived life. I decided not to pay those dues anymore. I decided to live life with hope, love, and appreciation for the people and things around me. I decided to forgive—especially myself. In that, I chose to live." Maggie scans the faces of all those there.

"And I want to thank all of you for inviting me and Theo to such an enjoyable evening. This tribe, as you call it, is a lot of fun."

Livie reaches out immediately and hugs her mom.

As everyone is putting their jackets on, Livie moves to the kitchen to fetch the unconsumed alcohol to return it to her guests. Her phone is sitting on the counter, and she sees a new text notification. She gives it a quick glance.

"Can we meet? D." She grabs the phone and quickly types, "Who is this?" A second passes as an R is added to the D. *Doctor who?* she thinks. Hannah sees her and comes towards her, and Livie places her phone face down on the counter.

"Everything okay?"

Livie rubs her forehead with her fingers.

"Of course."

"Okay, it's just that you looked a little startled." Hannah finishes her sentence with a glance towards Livie's phone.

Livie turns to hug everyone goodbye, and Hannah joins her as everyone exists the condo, leaving the two of them standing there. Livie moves back towards the kitchen, speaking to Hannah over her shoulder.

"I do have a text I have to attend to. Do you want some more wine?"

Hannah declines and moves to sit on the couch.

Livie picks up her phone and turns it over. The name jumps out at her, like it lifts itself from the text. Draw.

Livie turns so Hannah can't see her expression as she types.

"Is this really you Draw?"

She taps her phone, waiting for a response. Seconds tick by, and she calls out to Hannah.

"Would you like some water?"

"Yes, please." Hannah starts to get up from the couch as she answers.

"It's okay, you stay there, I'll bring it to you."

Livie pours them both a glass of ice water from her fridge and brings them over to Hannah. She hands Hannah her glass and then raises hers in a toast.

"To a great night."

Hannah clinks her glass against Livie's as Livie turns back to the kitchen.

"I'll be just another minute," she states over her shoulder.

She picks up her phone and sees the text that would change the night.

"Yes, it's me. You're probably surprised to hear from me. I'll be by the mulberry tree in the park in an hour. Meet me there. I can't respond after this message. I'm destroying this phone."

~~~~~~

Hannah was a bit mystified when Livie left her hanging, telling her that they'd have to continue their chat about Finn another time. But after the phone call, Livie's focus was squarely on Draw.

After three years and no news, she figured he was dead. If he's alive, could Finn be too? What has Draw been up to? She knows
~~~~~~

he's not one to just lie low. What does he want with her? Her imagination is running wild as she stands in the dark, wearing a hoodie, out of reach of the streetlights and with a view of the mulberry tree in the park. She needs to see Draw arrive first, thus the hoodie—something she is unlikely to be identified in, especially from a distance. She needs to be certain that it is him. She fingers the data stick in her pocket. The data stick she transferred the information from the data sticker to. The data sticker that Finn gave her three years ago.

She scans the area around the mulberry tree. The moonlight filtering through the branches of the trees look like light beams raining down on the wooded area. In the shadows, she sees the outline of a familiar bowler hat. Still cautious, she focuses her eyes on the darkness to get a better view of the figure. She sees no beard, and the figure's attire certainly doesn't include the baggy pants she would expect to see. Instead, the person appears to be in jeans, and their posture is straight and confident. Fearful she could be walking into some trap, she fingers the data stick in her pocket, regretting bringing it.

As she gets within a couple hundred feet, she watches the person walking around the area. While not slouched over, she recognizes the distinctive duck walk. Seeing it relaxes her and moves her forward, whispering ever so slightly.

"Draw?"

He looks her way, and she catches that piercing stare. She walks up to him and stands with him under one of the tree's large branches. They are in the dark, except for a sliver of moonlight that is reflecting off the ground in front of them.

She's still startled and relieved to actually see him standing there, like some ghost that has come back to life. She resists the urge to hug him as she moves in closer and whispers.

"I was shocked to hear from you, I thought you were dead. Where have you been the last three years?"

"Yes, sorry I haven't been in contact and if that caused you grief. I had to disappear for a while and regroup."

"Okay, but what have you been up to and where have you been?"

"Livie, I've been working for the same side I always have."

Livie gets the familiar feeling of frustration she always had with Draw when he spoke in riddles and didn't answer her questions directly.

"Alright, look Draw, I'm not sure why you have contacted me now. What *is it* that you want?"

Draw looks at her with his disturbingly piercing eyes. Even in the darkness, she feels the power of his stare.

"I'm here to inform you of something, so that you can prepare yourself. I also need your help with something."

Livie doesn't like the sound of this, nor the leadup to another riddle she expects is coming.

"Okay, but before you tell me any of that, you need to know that I went looking for you. So, answer my question as plainly and directly as you can. Where have you been the last three years?"

Draw moves to her side, as if he must change positions to share a secret. In the movement, Livie catches a glimpse of a tattoo on his forearm. It's a set of eyes that eerily matches his piercing stare. She's certain he didn't have that before.

"Before I answer that, you must swear to me that you will not tell anyone. You can't tell anyone that you even saw me here tonight."

"Sure, of course Draw. I don't know who'd I'd tell anyway. So, spit it out, where have you been?"

"Russia."

Livie can't reconcile what she just heard with what she knows, so she asks again.

"Where?"

"Russia, Livie. I've been in Russia working on a plan that we are close to executing—now that Brant has won a second term."

Livie has always known Draw to be a bit elusive and mysterious, but she has never found him to be untruthful.

"Why Russia? What were you doing there?"

"I have been working to expose Brant and his corrupt government. It's Brant who threw our world into chaos to fulfill his agenda—to manipulate people into thinking America controls the world. We were just waiting for him to win his second term. When we start launching satellites en mass, there will be war. But, when we get the internet back up, everyone will know that it was Brant and his cronies that shut it down to begin with and then took out the satellites."

Livie looks at him, startled, processing what he's saying.

"That's crazy Draw. Brant shut down the internet? I am pretty certain it was the Russ—"

Draw interrupts her abruptly.

"Livie, the American people couldn't accept that the Russians and the Chinese had advanced in leaps and bounds ahead of the US in technology. Brant knew his statements about leading the way in technology was all fairy tales and propaganda to get elected. So they devised a scorched-earth plan to destroy the internet and technological advances with it. All as part of their plan to wrestle back the upper hand for the US of A."

Draw speaks with a passion Livie remembers well. The determined, no-debate-needed, passion. She reaches into her pocket to feel the comforting shape of the data stick as she processes what she has just heard.

"So, you're telling me that you are working for the Russians to bring the internet back?"

"It's the same people you were working for to spy on the FWN."

The words hit Livie like a tidal wave coming at her that she can't get out of the way of. She feels herself staggering, swaying where she stands. She steps a few feet back from Draw to regain her footing.

Draw watches her with his piercing eyes, his face expressionless.

Livie whispers into the air.

"He didn't pivot. It was part of his master plan all along."

"You're talking about Brant, I assume? Do you know that he's part of the Skull and Bones secret society, like other past American presidents? We're going to make him pay Livie. You might be able to help us here."

The mention of the Skull and Bones sends a quiver up Livie's spine.

"Help you? How am I going to do that?"

"We had an inkling that part of their plan was to shut down the internet, as unbelievable as it seemed at the time. We tried to stop it. We couldn't. I was trying, with your help and Finn's, to get the internet back up before they executed a plan to take out the satellites, which we suspected might come. But I couldn't locate all their central computers. I believe Finn may have though. Did Finn share that information with you?"

Livie hugs her body with her arms as if to keep herself warm while she feels the data stick in her pocket.

"Why would Finn share that with me?"

As soon as she asks the question, she's doubting herself. Will Draw pick up that she's being elusive? She wishes she had more time to process everything. To measure the risks.

"Finn was your friend. The FWN recruited him because of his abilities and relationship to you. It would only make sense that he'd share what he found with you."

Livie grips the data stick tightly inside her pocket. She decides to turn the question on Draw.

"Last time I saw Finn he was scared and anxious. We were being followed. Even if he had something to share with me, there was no time. Then he disappeared. Do you know what happened to Finn?"

"If I knew where Finn was, I would ask him directly."

Livie feels exasperated with Draw, like she has felt many times before. She came here with curiosity and for some answers.

"Draw, did you say the internet is coming back on?"

"That's part of our plan. If I can get the information on the missing central computers, it could happen fairly soon. You need to know that a new internet would be one that doesn't allow the US government to steal everyone's personal data."

Livie wants to add, or any government, but she holds her tongue as she continues to grip the data stick in her pocket.

"Who else is behind this Draw? Besides the Russians, who else?"

"There are several forces working on this, Livie. You must know that the plan to take out over eight thousand satellites wasn't put together overnight or even in months. It would have taken years. The people who planned it had to devise a strategy to prevent new ones from going up. We must employ the same level of sophistication to combat that."

Livie feels a shiver at the word "we", as if she is part of this. She lets go of the data stick inside her pocket.

"Well, I don't think I can help you then."

Draw nods and turns to walk away. Livie reaches out and stops him.

"Wait..."

Draw turns and looks at her, those piercing eyes boring into her, waiting for her to say something.

"How can I get hold of you?"

"You can't. I'm going back to Russia."

As he's walking away, Livie calls out to him.

"Wait, Draw."

Draw turns to look at her while he continues to move forward.

"Do you know if Finn is alive?"

Draw stops and looks at Livie. His usually blank expression suddenly softens and comes to life.

"I told you; I don't know where he is. I need to go Livie. You take care."

He turns and picks up his pace, disappearing from her view within seconds.

POSTSCRIPT

While this is a work of fiction, the Skull and Bones 322 is real. It is a secret society that dates back to 1832. The reference to 322 is a matter of some debate. It is believed to be a reference to a Greek goddess from 322 BC. However, the 322 reference has been reported to mean different things, including a reference to March 22nd—the first day of Aries.

Members of the Skull and Bones 322 are reported to include past American presidents, including William Taft and George Bush, influential political leaders including John Kerry, supreme court justices, wealthy players in business and commerce, as well as famous actors.

It has been reported that one of the objectives of the Skull and Bones 322 is to establish a new world order in which a small group of wealthy, prominent families are in control of everything.

It is said that the society has influenced and/or orchestrated several significant events in history. These include the handpicking of US presidents, Watergate, the creation of the atomic bomb, and the Kennedy assassination. They have also been accused of providing financial support to Hitler, planning the Bay of Pigs invasion, and using ionospheric research to cause tsunamis and earthquakes, like the one in South Asia in 2004 and a devastating earthquake in Sichuan, China in 2008. It is also said that they have control over the media and the CIA.

It is believed they are an offshoot of the Illuminati. They have been referred to as the International Mafia, Brotherhood of Death, and Order of the Skull and Bones.

All references to the Skull and Bones 322 and the Brotherhood of Death in this novel are purely fictional.

FINAL THOTS AND ACKNOWLEDGEMENTS

Yeah, I know I misspelled "thoughts". In a world where our spelling and grammar are corrected for us and devoid of human intuition, I feel a tremble of triumph when I exercise just a small amount of artistic licence. Besides, using the phonetic "thots' seems more authentic and in keeping with the theme of this book.

Whether you prefer your world with the internet or not, or whether you agree with Livie and her friends' choices, I hope the story causes you to at least pause and contemplate what a friendlier world might look like.

Many are caught in a world of siloed living and the trappings of a tunnel of ignorance that it can bring. We have lost the ability to disagree, it seems. To authentically see the other side and listen. To seek out such interactions and permit ourselves to be changed by them. A sense of community and caring for each other have been sacrificed and too often replaced with a series of likes and algorithms that tell us what to buy, who and what to like, and how to feel.

I write this as AI is dominating more and more of our interactions with the internet, friends, music, lights, appliances, etc. I am not suggesting some luddite approach as the book may intimate with the loss of the internet. AI offers many positives that make our lives more pleasant in ways our ancestors couldn't have imagined. I *am* advocating that we find news ways to slow things down, to recapture a sense of community and caring for each other.

Writing a novel is very much an activity spent in solitude. Hours alone crafting characters and plot lines. Deleting phrases or paragraphs that don't work. Sometimes deleting whole chapters that are best left for a different story or for the basket beside the desk.

How do I come up with the characters? That's a common question for which there is no single answer. While the characters, with their various personalities, strengths, and weaknesses are fabricated in my mind, they are often a collection of individuals I've come into contact with. A character like Fairleigh comes from small exchanges with a couple of strangers, the personality of a deceased former colleague, and a character from another book I read. The person in the book is a tapestry of all of that. Added into that mix is the writing itself, where the character evolves as I write—usually in ways I had not anticipated or planned beforehand. This is where the solitary nature of writing opens up and taps into the various relationships and interactions I enjoy outside of the writing process. Without those, these pages of fiction and thots would not exist.

With that, I owe a heartfelt thanks to many people for making this book possible. The first person I want to acknowledge is the person I dedicate this novel to—my mom. She passed in September 2022 and left me with many memories, experiences, and inspirations on how to approach life. Her spirit is very much alive in me today. A spirit of determination, stick-to-itiveness, openness, forgiveness, and love. At age sixty-five, she retired and decided, with great determination, to change her life. She lost a hundred pounds and developed friendships with a large group of seniors in her community that she had no knowledge of before her retirement. When she passed at age seventy-seven, many of those seniors came out to pay their respects. They expressed the different ways that she inspired each of them. I had completed the first draft of this book when she passed. She was a true cheerleader of this work.

Many have made this work possible by reading drafts, helping me untangle plotlines that gave me writer's block, and offering words of encouragement. Ron Sharp read one of my first drafts while he was on vacation, and many of his suggestions are in these pages. Others who read some of those early drafts and contributed valuable insights and critiques are Emilie Anderson, Gabby Akoury, Liisa Hammer, and my mom, Diane Anderson.

My editor, Susan Gaigher, helped make much of what you've read here more readable and enjoyable. She is very skilled and a pleasure to work with. I owe her my sincere thanks.

Thank you MethodMike and Fiverr for the great book-cover design. MethodMike designed the cover of my first book, *Momentum's Force*, and it was an easy choice to go back to him for this one.

"There are endless reasons in the world to despair and become restless and bitter. I came to realize that the cost of those demons of rage and bitterness left me with broken relationships and a largely unlived life. I decided not to pay those dues anymore. I decided to live life with hope, love, and appreciation for the people and things around me. I decided to forgive—especially myself. In that, I chose to live." – Maggie Romée (Livie's mom)

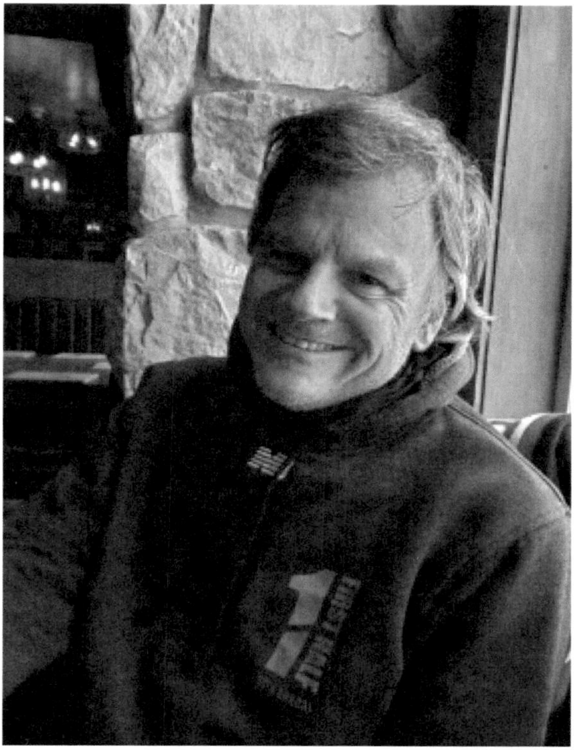

ABOUT THE AUTHOR

FRANK ANDERSON lives in Kelowna. British Columbia. This is his second novel. Momentum's Force, his first novel, is a family drama/mystery based in British Columbia in the 1970s and 1980s.

Frank has worked as a park ranger, forensic forest investigator and union negotiator. He enjoys hiking, running, kayaking, reading and writing. He has five adult children. He enjoys many activities with his children and being a father has brought him many of his greatest joys in life.